KISSES BY CLOCKWORK

Also edited by LIZ GRZYB

Scary Kisses
More Scary Kisses
*The Year's Best Australian Fantasy & Horror 2010 (with
  Talie Helene)*
*The Year's Best Australian Fantasy & Horror 2011 (with
  Talie Helene)*
*The Year's Best Australian Fantasy & Horror 2012 (with
  Talie Helene)*
* *The Year's Best Australian Fantasy & Horror 2013 (with
  Talie Helene)*
Damnation and Dames (with Amanda Pillar)
Dreaming of Djinn

* *forthcoming*

KISSES BY CLOCKWORK

EDITED BY LIZ GRZYB

T≋
p≋ Ticonderoga
publications

for Angela Challis and Shane Jiraiya Cummings

Kisses by Clockwork edited by Liz Grzyb

Published by Ticonderoga Publications

Copyright © Liz Grzyb 2014

Designed and edited by Russell B. Farr
Typeset in Sabon and Campanile

A Cataloging-in-Publications entry for this title is available from The National Library of Australia.

ISBN   978-1-921857-89-8 (trade paperback)
            978-1-921857-57-7 (ebook)

Ticonderoga Publications
PO Box 29 Greenwood
Western Australia 6924

www.ticonderogapublications.com

#47

10 9 8 7 6 5 4 3 2 1

ACKNOWLEDGEMENTS

Many thanks to Marilag Angway, Cherith Baldry, Gio Clairval, M.L.D. Curelas, Ray Dean, Stephanie Gunn, Richard Harland, Rebecca Harwell, Faith Mudge, Nicole Murphy, Katrina Nicholson, Anthony Panegyres, Amanda Pillar, Angela Rega, Carol Ryles, D.C. White, Russell B. Farr, Kate Dunbar-Smith, Kate Williams, Andrew Williams, Deb Wilson, Jacinta Rosielle, Angela Challis, Shane Cummings, Ambre Hillier, Michael Hillier, Tasmar Dixon, Mel Donald, Phil Ward, Lina Piscitelli, Ruza Foster, Nikki Irwin, Andrea Orlowsky, Hilary Donraadt, Frankie Nathan, Kim Astle, Giules Valuri, Jacintha Bell, Helen Grzyb, and the English Department

CONTENTS

THE KISS OF REBA MAUL

RICHARD HARLAND

There had been a time when Verrol Stark would have reacted instantly to the sensation of a knife pressed against his throat, but for one fraction of a second now he was simply surprised. The cold edge remained motionless, more of a threat than a strike. His mind registered the steadiness of the blade and the way the arm angled up over his shoulder from behind. Someone a good deal shorter than himself, obviously, and a professional. Only a professional could have stalked him so soundlessly in the smog.

"What do you want?" he asked.

The silence that followed was a bad sign. No words meant no negotiations. He considered his options: backwards double elbow, crouch and throw, or spin and block. Something about the absolute steadiness of the blade made him suspect that none of the usual moves would work.

The answer came finally in a cool, quiet voice. "You."

"You want me?"

"Yes; you, Verrol Stark."

Worse and worse. The name of Stark belonged to his criminal past. In his new world, he'd revealed his real family name to no one except Astor.

"I call myself just Verrol nowadays," he said, consciously keeping his muscles relaxed. *Don't stop talking,* he told himself. "My stage name. I play with a band."

"Yes, but you're still a killer. You can't leave that behind. It's in your blood."

There was no longer any doubt that the voice belonged to a young woman, maybe even a girl. How could a *girl* hold him helpless like this?

"Don't," she warned, as though she'd read the message his mind was about to transmit to his nerves.

She uttered a sudden loud whistle that pierced the night air and made his eardrums ring. Still, her concentration never wavered, the knife's edge never shifted from his Adam's apple. He had the impression that it was a thin, fine sort of blade like a stiletto. A woman's weapon . . . or an assassin's . . .

There was a sound of approaching hooves and wheels, and a carriage appeared out of the smog. It was a standard London carriage-for-hire with no identifying insignia. The coachman on top was so heavily muffled in coat, cloak and hood that he seemed scarcely human.

"Open the door and climb in," Verrol's unseen assailant ordered.

He obeyed. Even now, she gave him no chance to counter-attack. As he hoisted himself up inside the carriage, she tripped him from behind so that he fell onto his knees on the floor between the seats. Then she stood over him, straddling his legs, and gave another piercing whistle. The carriage lurched forward, Verrol swayed, and she swayed with him. Not for one second did the knife leave his throat.

He felt the touch of her other hand on the nape of his neck. She was feeling for the chain on which his locket hung.

"That belongs to me," he said stupidly.

"Stay still."

"I mean, it's not worth anything. Silver-plate jewellery from a market stall. Only personal, sentimental value."

"Which is why I want it." She drew the locket out from his shirt and lifted it up over his head. "This is what people wear for their beloved, isn't it? With a little picture inside."

"It means nothing to you."

"But it does to you. If you love your beloved, you'll have to get it back."

The idea seemed to amuse her, and she put a wealth of sarcasm into the words 'love' and 'beloved'. Verrol thought of Astor's picture inside the locket and gritted his teeth.

The carriage was travelling faster all the time, jolting its passengers back and forth. "Now we can sit," she announced.

Apparently she believed she had acquired power over him by acquiring the locket. Perhaps she was right. He would have to recover it one way or another.

She changed position to sit facing forward on one of the leather-upholstered seats. She gestured with the knife, and he took his place sitting opposite. The carriage continued to accelerate, now rattling along at breakneck speed.

The glow of passing gaslights cast a flickering illumination into the interior, but it was impossible to form a clear image of the young woman's face, which jumped in and out of existence from moment to moment. Verrol had the impression of a wide forehead, pointy chin, intense black eyes and very white teeth. Her hair was probably black too, though covered with a grey headscarf. If she was beautiful, it was a strange sort of beauty, features dominating over face. She was certainly young, eighteen at the most.

She popped the catch of the locket and the lid opened up to reveal the picture of Astor. "Oh, shame," she said. "No words inside. No 'sweetheart' or 'darling' or 'turtle dove'. Just her. Is *this* what you like these days?"

"You know nothing about her."

"No, and I don't wish to." She snapped the lid shut, raised the chain and looped it round her own neck. "Who do you think *I* am? You still haven't asked."

Verrol shrugged. "You'll tell me when you're ready, I suppose."

"I'm Reba Maul."

Maul? Her first name meant nothing, but her family name meant everything. His whole childhood and adolescence had been ruled by the feud between the Starks and the Mauls.

Her teeth flashed in a brief, humourless smile. "You thought you killed us all off?"

"I never heard of a Reba Maul."

"Because my father kept me out of the fighting. He said I was too young and hid me away. I was eleven years old at the time of the Eden Street Massacre."

Verrol refrained from saying that he had only been twelve when he became part of the Starks' assassination team.

"*And* being a girl," she continued. "Even though I trained as hard as any of the boys. I could've been better than the best of them. I've never stopped training."

Verrol could believe it. "Who *was* your father, then?" he asked.

"Towey Maul."

He willed his pulse to stop racing, kept his face expressionless, wiped all thoughts of guilt from his mind. The killing of Towey Maul had been the ultimate success of the Starks' assassination team. There had been eight of them in the plot, luring Towey away from his henchman, arranging the hidden pistol, guarding the exits and entrances. But it had been he, Verrol Stark, who had fired the fatal shot. If she knew, he was as good as dead already. But did she know? Did the Mauls ever find out who pulled the trigger?

He confronted the danger head-on. "So you're my greatest enemy?"

"Are you mine?"

"No. It's all in the past for me. I left that life behind."

"You're still a Stark, though. The most dangerous of them all. You were in every one of my nightmares when I grew up. I couldn't stop dreaming about you. Hiding in the shadows, looming around corners, inescapable and murderous. Yet not even a full-grown man, only a few years older than me. You killed my uncle Lannock and my cousin Seth, and more besides. You never heard of me, but I heard all the stories about you."

Still she hadn't mentioned her father. Surely she would have named Towey before Lannock and Seth if she knew? He began to breathe a little easier. "I wasn't the only one," he said.

"You were the worst."

The way she said 'worst' didn't sound like simple condemnation, and when the light from a passing lamp caught her face, her frown seemed to express interest rather than hatred. Her next words confirmed it. "But the best for my purposes."

He waited for further explanation.

"I've selected you to help me pull off the crime of the century. Perform well, and you can have your beloved back." She flicked at the locket that hung over the front of her blouse.

"Crime of the century." Verrol turned the melodramatic phrase over in his mouth.

"Yes. And a test for your talents." She sniffed. "I must say, your performance hasn't been very impressive so far. I expected better. Out of training, are you?"

He made no answer. Perhaps the situation would come clearer, but right now he didn't understand at all.

"And I always thought you were so quick and deadly," she sneered.

Verrol stared out the carriage window. They had travelled far and fast; now they were in an area of warehouses, storeyards and factories. They must have passed beyond the residential suburbs to the docklands south of the Thames. The night grew steadily darker, with fewer and fewer lights along the streets . . .

"Stay alert!" she snapped and stabbed out suddenly at his face. He jerked aside just in time to avoid the cut of the blade.

"Are you mad?"

"You're no use to me if you're slow. I want you back the way you were." She cocked her head. "Listen. We're nearly there."

Verrol listened and heard a distant sound like the stutter of gunfire. It continued for two or three minutes, then stopped.

"That's Brunel's Trans-Thames Mail Transport," she announced with satisfaction.

"But . . . that's not possible. My band's playing at the opening ceremony tomorrow at noon. It's too early."

"Ever heard of a test run? They're trialling it tonight with ballast instead of mail. Do you think they'd launch it in public without checking everything first? Brunel himself is on board."

On the last word, she stabbed out again with her knife—and again he dodged. "Better," she said, and her teeth shone in the dim light.

Five minutes later, the carriage came to a halt. A high wall topped with spikes cut off the view on Verrol's side.

"Out," said Reba Maul.

When they emerged from the carriage, the smog was lighter than before, as was often the case near the river. Verrol couldn't see the river, but he knew where he was from the great arc of iron and steel soaring over their heads. The longest, loftiest span ever constructed, impossibly fine and delicate! It rose from the other side of the spike-topped wall, curved up and up like a ribbon of lace, took one final leap from a cable-stressed pylon and vanished into the murky sky. The Flyover Arc for Brunel's Trans-Thames Mail Transport!

"Yes." Reba followed the line of his gaze. "The Skysplitter has crossed over the Arc to the south. Now they're re-loading the shots for its return journey north. We have to move fast. They'll be firing off again in another ten minutes."

They moved along in the shadow of the wall, continued round a corner and came by and by to a massive, studded gate. The wings of the gate stood open, but an armed sentry kept guard over the entrance.

"I'll distract him," Reba whispered. "Kill him if he sees you."

"Kill him?"

"Strangle him, break his neck, you know the ways." She snapped her fingers impatiently. "You haven't forgotten *that?*"

Verrol would have liked to forget. He had left his murderous past behind, transformed into a very different person. He was prepared to bind and gag the sentry, but not to kill him in cold blood.

As it turned out, he didn't need to do anything. Hidden in the shadows, Reba made soft mewing sounds, convincingly cat-like, and the sentry walked towards them, clicking his tongue and calling, "Kitty-kitty-kitty!" Obviously he anticipated no danger and didn't much worry about his guarding duties. Verrol slipped in through the gates, and Reba joined him a few moments later.

She took the lead now and hurried on, hugging the inner face of the wall. They could see the start of the Arc where the rails levelled out at the bottom of the curve and ran on into an enormous barn-like shed. Lights and voices came from the shed, but the surrounding yard was deserted.

Reba sped along on the balls of her feet, her movements lithe and efficient and absolutely silent. Verrol was amazed at her skill. When he thought how she'd been training herself ever since the Mauls and the Starks destroyed one another, he was even more amazed at her self-discipline.

Of course, she was no longer controlling him with the knife, no longer even keeping a watch on him. He could have easily broken away except for the locket. If he wanted the locket, he would have to overpower her first . . . he might even have to kill her. He studied her scarf-swathed head bobbing in front of him. No! He'd done more than enough to the Mauls already. If he helped Reba now, perhaps he could put an end to the feud forever. She seemed to be giving him the opportunity.

The shed was wide open at one end, the end where the rails emerged. Canvas tarpaulins hung in folds on either side like the drawn-back curtains of some vast stage. Reba darted in behind the folds, worked her way forward and peeped out across the interior. Verrol surveyed the same scene over her shoulder.

The vehicle called the Skysplitter stood before them on the rails, bullet-nosed and silvery. It was twenty feet long, with eight wheels and a single window at the front. At the back were massive gun-barrels mounted in concentric circles, at least fifty or sixty of them. Verrol had read about the Skysplitter and seen diagrams in the newspapers, but the reality was even more extraordinary. Brunel's latest marvel seemed to belong to another century entirely.

Reba had entered the shed in the best possible place, on the opposite side to all the lights and activity. Men in overalls wheeled up trolleys laden with cylinders, other men hoisted the cylinders up into the vehicle's underbelly through a hatch at the back. The unmistakable smell of gunpowder drifted in the air.

"Do you understand what's happening?" Reba whispered.

"They're reloading the guns?"

"Yes. Blank charges for the recoil. The explosive force will send the Skysplitter shooting along the rails up over the river."

Verrol had fired enough pistol shots to know all about recoil. The great engineer Brunel had declared his new system of propulsion 'Humanity's First Step beyond the Steam Age'. His aim was to take a short cut over the Thames so that mail could be delivered to the rest of England without having to crawl through the crowded streets of London. He had built the Flyover Arc high enough to clear the tallest mast of any ship entering the estuary now or in the future. Opponents had cast doubt on the scheme's practical value, but no one doubted Brunel's enterprise and audacity.

"Is he really on board?" Verrol asked.

"Brunel? Of course. Always the first to try out his own constructions."

Verrol nodded. It fitted with what he'd heard of the man.

"And very, very rich. Do you know how much he was paid for this venture?"

"No."

"Fifty thousand pounds sterling. Think of it!"

"Is this what—"

A loud clang interrupted Verrol's question. The hatch under the Skysplitter had slammed shut, and workers were hurrying away in all directions.

"Get ready," Reba hissed. "We're going to catch a ride."

There was a flash and a bang from one of the backward-pointing guns at the rear of the vehicle. The onlookers gave a cheer as the wheels began to turn and the Skysplitter rolled forward. They had started firing the blank charges. The next bang made the wheels turn faster, and the shed was filled with gunpowder smoke and echoing noise. Reba grabbed Verrol's hand and ran for the accelerating vehicle.

Another bang, then another. Reba and Verrol sprinted flat out as the Skysplitter picked up speed over the rails. They managed to catch it in the moment it burst from the open end of the shed. Whether the onlookers had spotted them, Verrol had no time to consider. Reba half-directed, half-flung him towards the undercarriage between the two front wheels.

He sprang up just before the wheels could run over him. His feet found footholds on the axle housing, his hands clung to the smooth underside of the bullet-shaped nose. He crouched there motionless, feeling the wind whip through his clothes, hearing the wheels thunder over the rails.

Bang! *Bang*! *Bang*! The acceleration was a great fist pressing him back and back. Then it took on a sudden new angle. When he looked down, the rails were lifting them up, curving away from the ground. They were heading for the sky!

"Whoooo-ooo-ooo!" Reba's cry was audible even above the rush of the wind and the thrum of metal on metal. Verrol glanced across and saw how she stood facing forward, legs braced, without hand holds, pinned in place by acceleration alone. She reached out a hand towards him.

He swung to match her position. She was on the left of the axle housing, he was on the right. He took her hand, and they balanced together against the rounded underside of the bullet-nose.

Faster and faster, steeper and steeper, the Skysplitter soared above the surrounding walls. Every explosion from the rear-mounted guns imparted another jolt of speed. It was terrifying . . . death-defying . . . exhilarating.

"Drink the wind!" yelled Reba, with her mouth wide open. Verrol opened his mouth and drank the wind too.

Up and up and up. The iron frame of the Arc creaked, the steel rails swayed. Already they were beyond the last pylon on the south bank. Verrol could hardly see for the wind beating on his eyeballs, but he blinked away tears and caught a glimpse of the River Thames far below—a mere glimpse of oily, reflective water through the smog.

In no time at all, the gun barrels finished discharging their shots. The Skysplitter continued to climb, but more smoothly now, gliding on its own momentum. The engineering calculations must be very exact, just enough velocity to carry them over the top of the Arc.

Verrol's nerves sang with the thrill of it. He didn't want it to end. Nothing existed but the here and now; sheer intoxicating speed had wiped all other thoughts from his mind.

He turned to grin at Reba and was startled by the intensity of her eyes boring into his. No hint of a grin on her face, but a hungry, burning look. He couldn't be mistaken. It was a look of desire—and it was for him!

How can she? he thought. Where could such passion come from? Was it because he'd been in her dreams for so many years? But . . . those weren't dreams, they were nightmares!

She released his hand and swung away. "Next stage!" she cried.

She unknotted her headscarf and pulled it free. Masses of luxuriant, jet black hair spilled forth and fell around her shoulders. Verrol caught his breath at the beauty of it. He wanted to see her face in the frame of her hair, but already she had turned to lean out on her side of the undercarriage, dangling the scarf from her hand. When he moved to stand behind her, he saw she was feeding the scarf into the axle of the front left wheel.

It wrapped around the spinning shaft, tighter and tighter. When she released the end, it was instantly swallowed up inside the axle housing. So much fabric twisting and twining and clogging the bearings . . . inevitably the wheel slowed in its rotations. Verrol nodded to himself. Given the planning she'd put into everything so far, he had no doubt that Reba's calculations were as exact as any engineer's. The loss in momentum would bring the Skysplitter to a halt before it could reach the summit of the Arc.

"What happens then?" he asked over her shoulder.

"You don't need to know. Just be ready for it. Are you back to the way you used to be?"

Verrol shrugged. It was true; the adrenaline was in his bloodstream now.

"That's how I want you. Living on your reactions, living on the knife's edge. That's what makes you the perfect killer. Like me. Fast and sure, cool and instant."

Approaching the summit of the Arc, the rails levelled out to a very shallow incline, almost horizontal. But the scarf had done its work, and the front left wheel was wholly immobilised. The Skysplitter decelerated over another ten yards, then stopped.

Reba bent at the knees, reached into the top of her boot and drew out her stiletto. She must have hidden it there for safekeeping. Next she reached into the top of her other boot and drew out a second, identical blade. "This is for you," she said.

Verrol might have been surprised at the contrast if he'd thought back to her earlier behaviour. But he was in a very different mood himself by now. When she added, "Kill anyone who gets in your way," he hardly remembered his earlier qualms.

"Trust me," he said.

"That's what I'm doing," she answered, and passed the knife across to him, handle first. "Be quick and deadly. No hesitation. Just like you were when you killed my father."

For a moment everything seemed to come to a stop. She *knew*! And she'd known all along! Verrol's mind spun round and round, but remained baffled by the implications. He was unable to see her face because she'd turned away to look out to the left again. What did it mean? How could she say it so flatly and unemotionally? Didn't she care?

A metallic scrape cut short his thoughts. Someone was sliding back a door in the side of the bullet-nose, someone was looking down and inspecting. Reba and Verrol were hidden under the bulge of the nose—but not for much longer.

"Something got caught in the axle, looks like," a bass male voice called out.

"What?" The second voice sounded more distant, still inside the cabin.

"Dunno. I'll go take a—" The first man broke off with a yelp of surprise.

Verrol didn't need to see to understand what was going on. The first man had just caught sight of Reba standing beside the front left wheel. With lightning speed, she reached up and seized hold of his foot or ankle. She pulled as he pulled, and there was a flurry of shouting and cursing. But the man couldn't draw his foot back in. Reba swung herself upwards, vanishing from view.

Verrol went after her. The man's legs, clad in blue overalls, still hung out over the sill, and he had lost a boot in the struggle. Reba had already dived in through the door. She must have scrambled up over his back, using him like a human ladder.

The man drew up his legs in a hurry, but Verrol didn't need them. Much taller than Reba, he vaulted from the front left wheel, hooked his elbows over the sill and propelled himself upward and forward into the cabin of the vehicle. He reached out with one hand and pinned the man in blue overalls to the floor before he could retreat further away.

The cabin inside smelled of lead paint, lubricating oil and gunpowder. It was a forest of pipes and levers, sprouting a profusion of dials, knobs, wheels and handles. At the front was a wide, slot-like window, but most of the light came from four yellow lamps on the ceiling.

Verrol absorbed every detail at a glance—and also the short man who stood in the middle of it all, staring and frowning at Reba's knife. A short man with a handsome face and side-whiskers, wearing his characteristic stovepipe hat: Isambard Kingdom Brunel. Photographs of the legendary engineer had appeared many times in the London newspapers over recent weeks. In spite of the threat of the knife, he showed no sign of fear.

"What do you think you're doing?" he demanded.

"Robbing you, Mr Brunel," said Reba. "We want your money."

The great engineer hardly seemed to hear. "You've sabotaged my test run. You'll wreck everything."

"Your money," Reba repeated.

"Money?" Brunel stamped his foot. "This is more important than money. This is progress. This is the future."

"Then you'll have no objection to handing over the fifty thousand pounds."

"What fifty thousand pounds?"

"Your payment for constructing the Trans-Thames Mail Transport."

"Oh, that money. It's in my bank account, I suppose. You don't think I carry such sums around with me?"

"But you carry your cheque book, don't you?"

"Of course. You want a *cheque*?"

"Write it out for fifty thousand pounds. Make it out to 'bearer'."

Brunel grimaced. Obviously he didn't see the sense of it; he could cancel a cheque before Reba ever had a chance to present it to his bank. Verrol didn't see the sense either, but he held his tongue. The financial side of the robbery didn't concern him.

The great engineer brought out a bulging leather pocket-book from his coat pocket, then a new-fangled fountain-pen from his waistcoat. He stepped across and rested the pocket-book on a small metal ledge under the window, one of the few flat surfaces among the pipes and levers. Reba followed him with her knife, but he needed no prompting. He wrote out the cheque, signed it with a grandiose flourish, tore out the slip of paper and handed it to her. "It won't do you any good," he said.

"We'll see." She flicked a grin in Verrol's direction. "The crime of the century."

At that moment, an interior door at the back of the cabin swung open, and a tousle-haired young man stepped forward. "Dodds is loading the reserve charges," he announced. "Should we—what's going on?"

"Everything under control," said Brunel calmly.

"Who are these two?"

"Thieves and saboteurs." Brunel put away his pen and pocket-book. "They disabled one of our wheels. Tell Dodds not to fire any more charges until we've fixed the damage. A new thrust would only send us off the rails."

The young man stared at Reba and Verrol for a second, then made to scurry back through the door. But he was nowhere near quick enough. Verrol sprang across, grabbed him by the collar and rammed him hard against the side of the door.

"Better if you wait here," he said.

The young man was white and trembling with fear. He seemed almost hypnotised as Verrol raised the point of his knife before his eyes. "No, don't," he whispered.

"Don't what?"

"Anything. Please."

"*Watch out!*" yelled Reba.

Verrol dodged and ducked as a bullet ricocheted from the metal near his head and went zinging away on a new trajectory. It was the man in blue overalls, now holding a big navy pistol in his hand. The weapon must have been stowed in the cabin for emergency use, and the man had taken his chance to wriggle across and collect it. Luckily he was a poor shot.

As he prepared to take fresh aim, Reba danced across and kicked him viciously under the jaw. His head rocked back, his teeth clicked, and the pistol went skidding across the floor. Brunel bent to pick it up as it came to a stop near his feet.

"Leave him!" Reba cried to Verrol. "We're finished here!"

She raced for the door at the back. Verrol swung the tousle-haired young man aside, followed her through and slammed the door after him. The lock in the door lacked a key, but Verrol knew a trick from his criminal past. He hardly needed to think about it; he drove his knife into the keyhole, twisted the thin blade sideways into the wards of the lock and left it there. Most times that would block the mechanism . . .

The light was dimmer in the vehicle's rear compartment, and the smell of gunpowder was overpowering. Reba held her knife to the throat of a burly, bearded man who knelt on the floor with his arms over his head. Verrol assumed he was Dodds, the man who'd been loading reserve charges into the propulsion system.

Inside the Skysplitter, the propulsion system looked very different to the way it had looked from outside: the breeches rather than the barrels of the guns. Filling the entire rear wall, the breeches appeared as brass-rimmed circular holes packed tight as honeycomb. The steel caps over the holes hung mostly open, but a dozen or more were closed.

"Hatch," said Reba, and pointed without turning round.

She meant the hatch in the floor that had been used to load the Skysplitter on the ground. Their escape-route? Verrol knelt and slid back the bolts that kept the hatch sealed. His pulse was racing, yet he was ice-cool and composed.

The handle of the interior door rattled furiously but in vain. Then an explosive report rang out, the sound of a pistol. Brunel must be trying to shoot through the lock to release the mechanism. Still the door stayed shut.

Meanwhile, Verrol worked free the last of the bolts, and the hatch fell open. One end of it was on hinges, the other supported by cables, hanging down inches above the struts between the rails.

"Go!" shouted Reba.

Verrol slid down the hatch on his back, then swung forward and sprang away. But Reba didn't follow him, not immediately. He stayed balancing on all fours, looking down at the Thames three hundred feet below.

The air was damp and fresh on his face, and a faint stirring of breeze teased his hair. There were several patches of drifting smog, but less overall cover than earlier in the night. Looking upriver, he could see the international docks and steamships, and the myriad lights of the East End casting their yellow glow. The dizzying height quickened his senses and made him feel more wide awake than ever.

Finally Reba came sliding down the hatch. She jumped off and crouched beside him.

"What kept you?" he asked, but didn't wait for a reply. It was time to make their escape before Brunel and his assistants broke through the door. Yet Reba grabbed his hand and held him back.

"Come *on*!" he urged, as another explosion shattered the night. Then he realised his mistake. This new explosion wasn't the sound of the pistol shooting into the lock, but a different, louder, open-air sound: the bang of one of the Skysplitter's recoil-propelling guns. So *that* was the reason for Reba's delay!

The vehicle's wheels were starting to turn, the silvery underbelly was sliding away over their heads. They looked up as the undercarriage went past and the battery of rear-mounted guns came into view. Another barrel spat fire . . . and another, and another. The recoil drove the Skysplitter forward in spite of its one disabled wheel. Once more it was heading towards the summit of the Arc.

"We did it," said Reba. "The crime of the century."

"You're mad."

"Utterly insane. Like you. That's why we can do what other people can't."

Her eyes were fixed on him, while he continued to watch the Skysplitter. It was scarcely accelerating, but there was no doubt it would reach the summit, less than twenty yards away. Between the bangs of the guns, they could hear the metal screech of the disabled wheel skidding over the rail.

Reba stared into Verrol's eyes as if tracking the progress of the Skysplitter there. He remembered Brunel's words to the tousle-haired young man and frowned.

"But they'll come off the rails."

Reba only smiled. "Of course. That's why I did it."

The vehicle arrived at the summit of the Arc, went over the top and began to accelerate down the other side. Its nose angled earthwards, more and more steeply as the incline increased. Though the guns had finished firing, there was no stopping it now. Sparks flew from the front left wheel, and the shriek of metal was earsplitting.

Soon the whole vehicle was wobbling from side to side, transmitting its shudders through the frame of the Arc. The struts on which Verrol and Reba stood also shuddered, yet Reba defied the vibrations and rose to her feet. Keeping a hold on Verrol's hand, she hauled him upright too. She was trembling, but not from cold or fear. Very definitely not from fear.

The shriek became a scream, the sparks flew higher and higher—until the disabled wheel jumped clean away from the rail. The rest of the Skysplitter followed, half on and half off the tracks. The right-side wheels bucked up and down on the struts; then the vehicle tilted all the way over and dived off the Arc. For just one moment, it seemed to hang suspended in the air before plummeting nose-first towards the Thames.

"So *that* was your plan," Verrol murmured.

"Didn't want him cancelling the cheque, did I?"

Verrol shook his head. Surely it couldn't work . . . surely the bank would ask questions . . . surely she would never be able to explain such a huge bequest. And in the meanwhile, four innocent human beings went to their deaths . . .

"A part of my plan," Reba added. "There's more."

Three hundred feet below, the Skysplitter struck the surface of the river with a splash and a brief plume of steam. Then the heavy metal body sank and the waters closed over the top. Only slow-spreading ripples remained to mark the spot.

"Four deaths," said Verrol. "Including the greatest engineer who ever lived."

"So?"

"You don't feel bad about it?"

"Why should I care? Do you?"

Verrol knew what he should say, yet somehow the words wouldn't come.

"Don't pretend to be moral," she sneered. "Don't try to feel feelings you don't really feel. You don't care about those people."

"I've got too many deaths on my conscience already."

"And my father was one of them. What's a few more to a killer like you?"

What do I really feel? he wondered. Suddenly the deaths of Brunel and his assistants seemed irrelevant and faraway. He cared, of course he cared, yet he could step aside from the caring, like another person watching indifferently from a distance. In some curious way, the killing of four innocent people really didn't matter to him at all.

She grabbed his other hand and swung him towards her. There was a strange urgency and ferocity in her movements.

"You're the same as me, Verrol Stark. You're back the way you were, and you're enjoying it. Anything can happen, and you're ready for it."

She pressed against him, hip to hip. Her eyes were so large and luminous they seemed to jump right out of her face.

It's true, he realised. *I'm ready.* He felt supremely alive, keyed up and concentrated, every sense kindled.

"Yes," she breathed. "You love it. You love living inside the moment. No before or after, no ahead or behind. Only this, only here, only me. I win, Verrol Stark. And I *want* you. Now."

She raised an arm, gripped the back of his neck and dragged him down towards her. Her lips met his, voracious and engulfing, and her body moved against him everywhere. It was a kiss like no other, as though she could never get enough of him, as though she'd been starving for this for a very long time. And her savagery was contagious. He gave back kiss for kiss, urge for urge, tongue for tongue. He was both totally sure of himself and totally out of control.

Dimly he sensed that she was tearing at his shirt, bursting the buttons, ripping the fabric apart. Her hand was burning hot against his skin. And cold, something cold . . .

Perhaps she whispered it, perhaps he only imagined it. *"This is for my father."*

The cold was the metal blade of her knife. A long thin shaft of cold that entered deep inside his body and penetrated the organs below his heart. There was pain too, but oddly remote, as if it was happening to someone else's body.

He couldn't stop pressing against her, as she continued to press against him. Yet his mind registered the fact that she was killing him. He even understood the exact course of the thrust, which would become fatal when she twisted the blade upwards into his heart.

He would never have had time to escape the final twist . . . except for the long gasp of erotic pleasure that escaped her lips. For one second she held back—and in that second he pushed her away. She staggered backwards a step, and the blade slid out of his body as smoothly as it had slid in.

He went after her before she could recover her balance. As she tried to retreat a further step, she missed her footing and slipped down between the tracks. She flung up an arm just in time to catch hold of a strut and arrest her fall. Verrol clamped a hand over the wound in his chest and made ready for her next move. Three hundred feet above the Thames, she hung there dangling.

She shook her head as if clearing her mind, as if coming out of a trance. Then she freed her knife-hand by gripping the blade between her teeth, swung herself back and forth, and hooked her legs up over another strut. But Verrol was too quick for her. He reached down with a foot between the tracks and kicked her legs away. She tried again—and again he prevented her.

"Drop the knife," he said.

She could hardly speak with the knife between her teeth, yet she managed a scornful snarl. "You think that'll stop me?"

"An end to the feud," he offered. "I forget you tried to kill me and let you live. Then we go our separate ways."

"Never."

He hardly expected any other response. Obviously she'd been planning her revenge for a very long time. She'd never needed his help for her crime of the century, she'd been fixated on killing him right from the start. Kissing only to kill. And yet . . .

He stared down into her face, seeking an explanation. There were so many things about her behaviour that made no sense. She returned his stare, drawing her lips back around the knife in a grim travesty of a smile.

The sight of the chain encircling her neck reminded him that she still had his locket. With a small pang of guilt, he realised he hadn't given Astor a single thought since the Skysplitter shot up into the sky.

"Drop your knife," he repeated. "I want my locket back too."

"Your locket! Your beloved!" She spoke more clearly, regardless of the knife-edge cutting into the corners of her mouth. "Don't make me laugh! What has she got to do with anything?"

"The woman I love. You wouldn't understand."

"Phah! You don't understand yourself, Verrol Stark. You're the same as me. A killer not a lover."

He could feel the heat of her emotion beating up into his face. It was hate and desire, it was kill and kiss, it was every driving passion all at once. In an insane sort of way, it did make sense. When she had said "I *want* you", she had truly meant it with every possible meaning.

He reached down suddenly between the struts and knocked the knife from between her teeth. She let out a cry of utter rage as she watched it fall twinkling into the void.

"You're helpless now," he told her. "Let me have the locket."

He stretched and fumbled for the chain around her neck. She turned her face up to him, and there was blood trickling from the corners of her mouth. Lines of bright red spread over her skin and made her lips appear grotesque and hideous.

He never caught her final words as she deliberately unhooked her fingers, let go of the strut and dropped.

Her face stayed in view all the way down. Smaller and smaller, yet she continued to stare up at him, and the expression on her mouth made him shiver. It might have been a mocking smile, it might have been a curse, it might have been an exaggerated kiss. It was still in his mind as she hit the water, three hundred feet below, and vanished with barely a splash.

Of course, she had taken the locket down with her.

For a long time he stayed watching, though there was nothing to see. No, it *didn't* make sense, none of it made any sense. He didn't want her insanity in his mind. He only wished he could obliterate the last half hour, which had nothing to do with the rest of his life. His present life was with Astor and the band, and playing their new kind of music. He was no longer the person that Reba Maul imagined.

He rose at last to his feet. His shivers were purely physical now, as his body reacted to the chill night air and the wound in his chest. The adrenaline effect that had cocooned him from pain was rapidly wearing off. He had no idea what internal organs Reba's knife had pierced.

He gave the wound only a cursory examination. From the outside, there was nothing to see apart from a narrow slit oozing blood. He pulled his shirt back over his chest and tucked it in with one hand, while pressing hard on the spot with the other. He hoped to reach a hospital in time, though it would be a very long climb down.

The breeze had stiffened, blowing away the smog and causing the Arc to sway a little. With endless empty night all around, he had never felt so exposed and vulnerable. Fearing dizziness, he focused on the rails and struts directly ahead of him. His route lay over the top of the Arc across to the north bank of the Thames. All of the big hospitals were on that side of London.

He shrugged off the weariness that threatened to overwhelm him, and began his journey. One foot in front of the other, one foot in front of the other. All he wanted was to return to ordinary life and normality.

A thought nagged constantly at the back of his mind: what excuse could he ever make up to explain the loss of his locket to Astor?

DESCENSION

FAITH MUDGE

We of the Mesiorn bloodline did not win an empire by being easy to kill.

But we did become complacent. Half a century of peace lulled us into a delusion of safety. We numbered more than two hundred when the sun rose today; by the time it set, there were four of us left alive, fugitives marked by blood and smoke. Nightfall finds me crouched in a reeking alley while rebel militia search the streets, a guardsman's bayonet gripped between my hands. Its blade is already crusted darkly, but this time I don't have to use it. The sound of tramping boots passes us by and I edge along the wall to the alley mouth to risk a glance up and down the street.

It is strewn with scraps of red, parade banners shredded for the wind, and shattered glass; there are more broken windows than whole ones in this part of the city tonight. I wonder how many of the rioters were raging against the betrayal dealt on the docks, and how many more were just rampant with revolution.

When I'm sure there are no soldiers in sight, I swing the awkward weight of the gun over one shoulder and gesture to the others. The dirigible docks, the river landings, the canals—all these places will be guarded. The rebels mean turn the city into a trap, closing in from every direction until we are crushed, but we are Mesiorn.

We don't mean to *escape*.

From above, the city of Ombelique was a disconcertingly paradoxical sight. A profusion of bronze and sandstone towers spearing through a mist of ground-dwelling cloud, encircled by azure blue—it was, Carmeline had often thought, like coming upon a piece of broken sky shattered across the river plain. As a child, it had always made her eyes turn instinctively upward, to look for the hole that must be left behind.

All that, of course, was illusion. The white cloud was steam from Ombelique's many mills and foundries, the exhaust of its trams and vehiculars; the intense blue was reflected sky in the labyrinth of canals that wove through the streets of the city like the arteries of a human heart, keeping the seat of the Empire in constant contact with its provinces near and far.

Carmeline was no longer a child. She knew what really mattered lay below.

At the prow of the imperial dirigible, she braced herself against the wind, letting it buffet against her immovability, while behind her crewmen and women in red livery swarmed the deck with preparations for descent. As the dirigible lowered, Carmeline leaned forward to scan the palace docks through the mist of steam. Somewhere down there were her daughters, who had arrived the day before with the other children to be drilled for their role in the Empress's parade. At thirteen Lenire was old enough to resent the demand on her time, and young enough to worry that everyone would be looking at her. Her sister Monya was five and easier to please. She was excited at the promise of throwing things during a formal occasion, even if they were only petals.

Carmeline had never considered herself a maternal person before Lenire came along, and had made full use of her imperial privilege in the first months by having a nanny permanently on hand, but as time went on the servant had had less and less to do. Children, Carmeline had discovered, were interesting. They had full as much personality as herself and even less inhibition, though there were those in the family who would have considered that impossible.

And she loved them. Carmeline, who did not believe in a heart's infinity of space, was unnerved by how much she loved her girls. They had only been apart for two days and she could not wait to see them again.

—34—

The landing itself was smooth, exhibiting the practiced professionalism that the Empress expected from all her employees, and from her family as well, as Carmeline had good cause to know. The Empress was her grandmother's sister and the iron matriarch of a sprawling, restless brood who had been drawn in from all corners of the world at her command. The Empire was celebrating its fiftieth year of peace, and it was well known that at the end of the month's Restoration festivities, the Empress would at last announce the name of her successor.

Everyone was coming. Everyone, however much they might deny it, had hope.

The liveried crew formed two rows on either side of the long gangplank, bowing formally as Carmeline swept between them with as much speed as dignity allowed. Her arrival drew inevitable attention from the workers on the docks below, heads turning as she passed. To her, they were mostly indistinguishable at first glance: all factory hands in identical grimy overalls, the only differentiation being the colours of their skin and hair. Most were as dark as Carmeline herself, or the sand brown of the western provinces. A very few were as pale as if they had been bleached in the sun. These were foreigners come looking for a better life in the empire of opportunity, or perhaps descendants of northern slaves, from before the Empress Isrelde's treaties ended the flesh trade. Such divisions, no longer defended by law, remained invisible and omnipresent. The recollection of those days—simpler times, easier times—was one of the many contentions that kept the rich in a state of righteous resentment, while the same memories simmered in the minds of their subordinates.

There seemed to be more hands on the docks than usual, busy with the transferral of crates and barrels. Equipment from the south, perhaps, imported machinery or specialised tools— Carmeline didn't really care. She barely registered the drab gangs of workers, searching instead for the brighter colours that would mean family. The hands scattered respectfully from her single-minded path.

Ahead, a flight of brick steps led down to a broad lamp-lined street. Waiting there was a gleaming red imperial vehicular, and beside it, two girls, one tall and gesturing animatedly, the other hoisted high in the arms of a laughing man. His eyes caught

Carmeline's. *She felt her mouth open to frame his name, more astonished exhalation than actual sound.* Matthian. *She'd not had occasion to say it in too long.*

"Mama!" Monya struggled in Matthian's arms, running towards the stairs as soon as he put her down. Her hands and dress were smeared with the dirt that she was mysteriously, magnetically attracted to; she transferred prints of it to Carmeline by seizing fistfuls of her skirt. Carmeline stooped to drop crimson-lipped kisses across her daughter's chaotic hair.

Lenire was less demonstrative. She waited beside Matthian, hovering slightly behind him, which implied a guilty conscience. Carmeline promised herself she would prod it until she found out why. Matthian knew already, she was sure, but it would be no good asking him—he was forever on the girls' side, no matter what they had done.

"You fiend!" she exclaimed, striding across the pavement. She caught him by the lapels and shook him twice with mock infuriation before turning the remonstrance into a hug. He felt thinner than she remembered underneath his formal coat. Carmeline drew back a little in his arms to study him for other changes and he gazed unhurriedly back, smiling, waiting for her verdict.

"Four months with no word and you still reach Ombelique before me. Confess!" she commanded. "You have wings."

He laughed, allowing his arms to drop from her waist. "You out all my secrets!"

"You have no secrets," she scoffed. "You were born under a water moon, the word written under your skin can only be clarity. What about you, my love?" She turned to Lenire, pulling her into a hug as well. "How go the preparations?"

"Very well," Lenire said, with a smile so bright it had to be dishonest. "Come and see. Aunt Selense sent the vehicular to collect you."

"How sweet of her," Carmeline purred. She liked travelling in the boxy carriages with their high wheels, horseless automation and possibilities for reckless speed.

The driver jumped down to open the door and the four of them climbed in, Carmeline pulling Monya onto her lap as the vehicular puffed into motion. Streets of warehouses bearing the crest of the Empress above their doors rolled past on either side, giving way abruptly to a whirlpool of city traffic as the vehicular left the docks behind and drove across a busy intersection, where long strings of crimson bunting looped between the lamp posts, fluttering above the drably-hatted heads of passersby. Drivers shouted and swore, wheels rattled, whistles and horns rang out from the nearby canals. Even through the cushioned frame of the vehicular, the noise was tremendous.

Carmeline's heart leapt. No doubt there were kinder places, cleaner places, better places than Ombelique. This city was the heart of the Empire, and the trade that was its blood pumped with merciless speed. But its danger, its power, its energy, was what made it beautiful.

It was good to be home.

"Carmeline." The sound of my name brings me around sharply, heart pounding, but it is only Matthian. He is kneeling on the filthy pavement, trying to coax my sister from her foetal huddle; as I turn, he rises. Behind him Lenire sways where she stands with a dazed look that is worse that tears. Matthian pauses with a hand to her shoulder, steadying her with a few quiet words as he passes. He draws me aside so she won't hear what he has to say.

"They can't go much further," he murmurs. "And I can only carry one."

He does not say, *we must stop, we must rest.* He does not acknowledge the exhaustion written into his own face or the limp that has dogged him across the city. This is the way an advisor speaks to the Empress, presenting the facts she needs to make her decision and managing lesser difficulties himself. The realisation makes me want to drop into his arms, beat my fists against his chest and howl until the beast of grief and rage gnawing its way up my throat will let me breathe again—but I don't think I could yet, not if I tried. Because he is right. I am the Empress, and this strength is all we have.

"We are almost there," I tell him, and point. We are only a street's width from Xalibur Bridge; its spikes stand sharply against the sky like the ridged spine of some alien behemoth. Rising above the stark architecture of the bridge are the four snowy domes of the cathedral on the far bank, each topped by its own sabre steeple.

At any other time this crossing would be thick with traffic, even at this hour of the night, but the aftermath of revolution has driven the people of Olembique in hiding. Tonight the streets belong to rioters and militiamen.

"The cathedral? You mean to claim sanctuary?" Matthian tries not to sound incredulous, but he's not good at hiding his thoughts. "The rebels won't honour it. As soon as they learn we're there . . . "

I look at him and remember the first time I noticed him, really noticed him. He had always been there, of course, somewhere on the edges, one of the family's most minor players—the cousin with the strange sandy hair and ebony eyes who was always sliding off to quiz the dirigible staff—but he had nothing to do with me. Then, when I was fifteen, a group of us cousins were sent away to an island province to train in combat. It was, I knew, one of the Empress's ways of identifying possible heirs, so I gritted my teeth against the indignity and made an effort. I was *good* at it. By the end of our training, he was the only boy who still spoke to me. He was not afraid of strength.

My heart clenches. I reach out to grip his arms. "We have to reach the cathedral," I tell him fiercely. "I don't have time to explain. Do you trust me?"

"With my life," he says without hesitation, and smiles tiredly. "Which is fortunate, all things considered."

"How was your journey?" Matthian asked.

"Brief," Carmeline said. "How was yours?"

"Long." Matthian grinned. "How have you enjoyed Samareke?"

"The society there is insular, overstimulated and full of its own importance. I loved it, of course. As the girls have doubtless already told you, though, the Empress has been asking for us to return to the capital permanently, and I think perhaps it's time." Carmeline cocked her head. "Has she made any such insinuations yet in your direction?"

"I don't think she's quite that desperate for family contact."

"Oh, tosh. She loves a good story as much as anyone and you tell the best."

"Have you read my latest book?"

"I wasn't thinking of your books," Carmeline said drily. "I read your study into the world's judiciary systems from cover to cover, as it happens. Could I convince you to choose a cheerier subject for the next? Not that a comparison between the gallows and the axe isn't fascinating in its own way, but . . . "

"That wasn't my point!" Matthian protested. "Execution is the relic of a barbaric past that has no place in the modern world. My book was meant to show alternative systems of punishment— imprisonment, public labours—"

"I already agreed, Matthian," Carmeline interrupted. "And you know the Empress never will. She believes changing one's mind is for lesser people. Wait for her successor to be announced and plead your case with them instead."

Matthian laughed. "I believe I will."

Carmeline leaned towards the window. They were within sight of the palace gates, and in a matter of minutes had rumbled through, wheels crunching on the looping gravel avenue. When they arrived at an exterior courtyard, the driver opened the door again for them to emerge. Matthian waved him aside, climbing out first and helping the girls himself. He offered Carmeline his hand last. As she stepped down, he bent his head close to hers.

"When," he murmured, "should I start pleading?"

She twisted her hand to grip his wrist hard. "Go on ahead, girls," she said brightly. "Tell your aunt Selense that I've arrived; everyone else will soon know."

"What about Uncle Matthian?" Lenire asked, frowning.

"He has an inquisition to answer," Carmeline said. "Go on. I promise I won't hurt him. And see that your sister washes her hands!"

It was a good distraction to choose. Lenire was instantly outraged. "Why is that my responsibility?" she cried mutinously. "I don't care if she's dirty!"

She stalked after Monya, who was already almost out of sight. Instead of following them up the grand steps and through the long colonnade that spanned this side of the palace, Carmeline and Matthian entered by a side door underneath, stepping into a gallery of long windows and curtained alcoves. These were intended for performers to change costumes in and given that no entertainment was arranged at the palace today, all were empty.

Carmeline found a dim, cramped corner that smelled of orange blossom perfume and sweat, and pushed Matthian inside.

"You know!" she hissed. "How did you know? Who told you?"

"No one had to tell me. I breathed in a lungful of rumour as soon as I arrived and tasted your name among the others. If I gambled, it would always be on you." He grinned. "And I was right, I see."

Carmeline made a hissing sound of exasperation, but she couldn't help smiling. She would never have been able to keep this from him for long, whatever the Empress said; she was glad he had worked it out for himself.

"She told me weeks ago. I can't share the news with anyone until it's formally announced. You are talking to the heir of the Empire, Matthian, how does it feel?"

"She looks oddly familiar, very much like a distant cousin of mine. I haven't seen her in so long. I do hope she's not usurping anyone's throne."

Carmeline slapped his arm lightly. "Sourpuss!"

"Never me," he said, sobering, though a smile still lingered around his mouth. "I've known all my life I'd never rule. I'm only a son, after all. Great-aunt Isrelde would rather crown her pet monkey than have a man on the throne, after the mess her father made of the Empire. But you, Carmeline, you have the heart for it. You always have. You'll be magnificent."

From anyone else she would have suspected those to be empty words, a mask for jealousy, but Matthian never told her anything but the truth. Sometimes, too much of it. She, in her turn, saved truth for the people she loved best.

"I will never be a ruler like Isrelde," she said. They both considered their great aunt, an old battle-axe who, at the age of seventy, was taller than most of her grandsons and had a white puckered scar where her left eye should have been. She wore a ceremonial sword at all times and gods help any servant who woke her unexpectedly, for a dagger was rarely far from her hand. She had come to the throne in the Empire's darkest hour and had pulled it together, it seemed, through sheer bloody-minded force of will.

If she had had a favourite among her restless brood, it had never been Carmeline. Her great niece was a city sophisticate with unerringly expensive taste and a string of inappropriate lovers scattered in her wake. At the age of thirty four Carmeline was at the height of her particular variety of sultry, voluptuous beauty, and was only too happy to use it if that meant getting her own way. Her daughters had been born to different fathers, neither of whom remained in their lives. Other members of the family were forever criticising Carmeline's abilities as a mother, possibly all the louder because she didn't listen to a word they said.

Yet the Empress had chosen her, recognising a different but equally potent form of stubbornness that could be shaped into a will of imperial steel. Carmeline had always secretly worshipped her great aunt, placing her on a pedestal of childhood awe and adult amazement. She didn't have the words to describe how she felt to have been chosen, but Matthian didn't need them.

His fingers laced through hers. She was suddenly very aware of how close they stood, and the clean scent of his skin underneath the orange blossom.

"Matthian," she said, more to see his eyes lift in response than because she had something specific to say. "Matthian," she said again, breathing his name against his lips, and the word became a kiss. His hands lifted to her waist, pulling her close, murmuring her own name between kisses.

"I missed you," he said at last, inadequately.

"No one made you go anywhere," she said, a touch waspishly. He sighed.

"Was I to wait until the Empress's hints became an order? She likes knowing that I'm out there, a presence in her territories, even if she doesn't care what it is I'm doing. And if I'd stayed . . . " She saw him duck his head, studying their interlaced hands. "As you said yourself, Carmeline, I'm clarity. I'm not good at hiding what I think. What I feel. And I love you."

Carmeline's breath snagged in her throat. He said it so mildly, as if it were a simple matter of one heart in exchange for another, as if considerations like politics and imperial pride did not come into it. It was not fair, she thought, that she could have so many lovers and it meant nothing apart from a little snide gossip to the family, but with him things were so different. Loving him was a political act, and she knew he wasn't fool enough to forget it.

She kissed him again, harder this time.

"Once I'm formally declared heir," she said, "we can do this in front of the world."

"Well, we can keep some things to ourselves." His hands slid down her back, the skin of his palms sighing over the raised embroideries of her jacket. "We wouldn't want to embarrass anyone."

"Speaking of which," Carmeline straightened. "Shall I go now to greet Selense, or come up with an excuse to explain why the girls arrived so long before we did?"

I am not yet used to the idea that my city belongs to the enemy, and that the enemy could be anyone. In the shadows on the far side of Xalibur Bridge, this almost gets us killed; it is only the smell of tobacco that warns us in time.

Where the bridge meets the road, a group of militiamen stand in a loose circle beneath a gas lamp. Its light is red; all lamps in the city are red, for they were put in by the Empress, and red is her colour. It bathes the men's faces in a bloody glow, turning their eyes infernal, their foul-smelling fug of smoke thickening with each drag of a cigarette. Their chatter is too low for me to overhear. Once again we're forced to wait, barely daring to breathe in case some inadvertent sound advertises our existence.

Selense has both hands pressed over her mouth, rocking back and forth where she stands. I'm braced for a whimper to slip between her fingers, but it isn't her who breaks the silence. It's Lenire. She makes a choking sound, staring up at the bridge, and that small mistake is enough. Heads turn under the lamp, cigarettes drop, weapons are drawn. There are five of them, and only two of us ready to fight.

There is only one thing to do: I have to even our chances.

Catching up a stray stone from the pavement, I throw hard and fast. The lamp shatters, leaving us all in darkness. The soldiers are blinded by the sudden change in light, and showered with glass to boot—I hear swearing, and hope I've done serious harm to at least one. Then I plunge from the alley, bayonet in hand, and I do more than hope.

Carmeline had timed her arrival with precision. The first of the month's ceremonies were to begin that evening with a parade to welcome the Empress home; the docks were cleared hours before she was expected and made unrecognisable by the labours of the palace staff. Lengths of white carpet were laid in a path from the docking point to the place where the imperial vehicular and its attendant armed riders waited to transport her. The route was lined by brass urns, bursting with bouquets in the imperial colours, and an honour guard of the assembled family. Closest to where the dirigible was expected to dock were the children, all in the Empress's favourite crimson, with baskets of flowers to throw in her path. That, Carmeline had to admit, was a strike of genius on her sister Selense's part. The Empress might be a fearsome, cantankerous old warrior with a political instinct as finely honed as a carving knife, but she loved children.

Carmeline herself had been positioned towards the end of the procession, without the distinction of actually being last. Clearly Selense had either not forgiven her yet for the incident with the stolen earrings when she was eighteen, or she'd heard the rumours too. Where she had decided to place Matthian, Carmeline didn't know.

"Mama!" Lenire came flying along the carpeted path, almost falling flat on her face when her toe caught a wrinkle. Servants came sliding out from nowhere to straighten it while Carmeline caught her daughter by the shoulders.

"What are you doing here? The Empress will be arriving any minute!" Even as she spoke, horns rang a salute. The shadow of the Empress's dirigible fell across the waiting crowd, exciting a wave of whispers and exclamations.

Lenire was in tears. "My dress broke! Tallemah pulled me!"

Carmeline snatched a brooch off her own dress. It ruined the line of jewellery she had arranged, but that couldn't be helped. Pulling the strap into place, she fixed it with a golden peacock. Lenire turned to run back into place.

"No! It's too late for that." Carmeline pulled her back. "Wait here with me. You're too old to stand with the children anyway."

Lenire's face lit up and Carmeline realised with a start that she had, unknowingly, said the exact thing her daughter most wanted to hear.

From this end of the crowd, they could not see the Empress land. All they could hear were the cheers, the calls of welcome from the assembled family. Carmeline was still staring at her daughter, wondering how she had missed the point when she had stopped being a child, when the blast knocked them both to the ground.

The blade goes deep into the first silhouette. I jerk it free, let him fall, and slash an awkward diagonal down the chest and rib cage of my next assailant. The darkness works in my favour; I have adjusted to the night, they have not. Behind me I hear the rattle of dying breath and twist quickly—a third rebel slumps to the ground as Matthian pulls a dagger from under his ear. I have never seen Matthian's face so empty. When the last militiaman opens his mouth to yell, Matthian's elbow hooks around his throat before he can make a sound and I run the boy through without thinking.

Five. There were *five* of them. I spin in time to see a shadow round the corner, running for his life, and swear savagely.

"Couldn't you have stopped him?" I demand of Lenire, and hate myself at once. When I go to her, she flinches away from my bloody hand. I ignore that and the shard of pain it sends through my chest, pulling her from her inertia. It won't be long before that man comes back with reinforcements. We need to run.

Selense moans. I turn to her, biting down whiplike words, and see that her eyes are turned upward, like Lenire's were. Following her gaze, I stagger with a wave of nausea. Stabbed through the last two spikes of the bridge, like grotesque guardians, is a pair of severed heads. Even under the caked blood, I know their faces. A nephew, who once got drunk and fell off a ceremonial barge. A cousin who dyed her red hair black to look more like me. Someone found their bodies on the docks, and hacked off their heads, and impaled them on the bridge like criminals.

Nausea ignites into white-hot rage. *I will make the traitors pay.*

Matthian seizes my wrist and I force myself to run, even as the tears burn tracks down my face and Selense's sobbing saws at my sanity. The steel spikes of the bridge have given way to rows of bare-branched jacarandas and a pair of gates triple my height, chained ceremonially open. I think briefly of somehow unchaining them, making a barrier between us and pursuit, but there is no time for that either. We must depend on the cathedral itself. It wavers ghostly white against the darkness, a mirage conjured out of desperation. But the stone of the steps is solid under my feet, and the doors swing open under my touch. It is evil luck to lock a house of the gods. I send up a prayer for forgiveness as I push my bayonet between the elaborate handles. Lenire silently drags over a chair to wedge underneath.

"It won't hold," Matthian gasps. He has collapsed into a second chair, clutching at his injured leg. Blood oozes between his fingers. I kneel quickly beside him, unknotting my sash and winding it tightly around his calf to stem the bleeding.

I remember the great hall of the cathedral by day as awash with light from the vast arching window that stands behind the dais, the stone bright white, a pattern of doves woven into the seemingly endless expanse of azure carpet. By night it is cavernous. Around us, in niches that encircle the entire room, angels of brass and silver gleam dimly. They have the bodies of humans but the heads of wild cats—lions, leopards, tigers, lynxes—and golden eyes turned downwards, so that they seem to gaze impassively upon our plight.

"I cannot run," Matthian says, very quietly, very matter-of-fact. "If you leave me, we may all stand a better chance at survival. You must get the others to safety, Carmeline. Rally whoever remains loyal—"

"Matthian." I interrupt him gently, rising to my feet. "That's why we're here. This cathedral was built by the Empress. What's the use of *promising* of sanctuary, if it cannot be upheld?"

For the first time since we fled the docks, Selense's eyes focus on me properly. A smile twists my mouth, bitter and loving.

"They called her the Fist of the Gods. She made sure that was true."

And I stride forward, across the carpets and the flightless doves, up the steps to the dais, where unconsecrated feet are never meant to tread. I hear Lenire's appalled inhalation behind me, but Selense and Matthian are silent, watching intently. There is no carpet on the dais—instead, a mural, a thousand tesserae painstakingly shaped into the head of a roaring lioness. I kneel before her, place my hand against her crimson tongue, and push with all the strength I have. There is a soft, definitive click.

In the niches around me, a host of angels wake for war.

Carmeline's mind could not process what had happened. The cheers had turned to screams; a boot struck her in the ribs and another trod on her hand as people ran in both directions. She rolled to her knees and found Lenire beside her doing the same thing, more or less unhurt. Carmeline stood, and saw why everyone was running.

Where the edge of the docking platform should have been was a vast raw-edged crescent, as if a beast of unimaginable proportions had risen to take a savage bite. Still tethered there were fragments of the dirigible. They were on fire.

For a moment, Carmeline felt her heart stop beating.

Then she turned, seizing Lenire by the shoulders. "Stay here,"
she ordered. "Stay here and stay down. I will come back for you."

"Mama, what's—what about Moyna? Mama!"

"Stay here," *Carmeline snarled. She hauled up her skirts and ran, leaping through the rubble towards the wreckage. Chunks of stone lay strewn across the docks, familiar bodies trapped beneath them, but she couldn't stop to help them, not until she was sure -*

Someone was there, at the edge of the platform, someone alive. Carmeline cried out and the kneeling woman turned her head. It was her sister, Selense; Selense, one half of her face mangled by shrapnel, bleeding red tears. Her elaborate white dress was so covered in blood that Carmeline could not see where the injuries even were.

"The children," Selense choked. "The children. Gone."

Carmeline came as close to the edge as she could, heedless of the shifting, unstable stones beneath her feet. At the foot of the docking tower was a mass of shattered, blackened stone and the flaming wreckage of the dirigible.

A scream of grief and rage tore free of Carmeline's throat, leaving it raw. She turned on Selense, feeling as if she herself were on fire, her hands clenching so hard she felt her nails cut crescents into her palms.

"Who did this?" she hissed.

Selense rocked back and forth, sobbing incoherently. Carmeline knew she should do something, find some words of comfort, but her hands were trembling with barely controlled violence. If she touched anyone now, it would be to shake the life out of them. She stepped back from the edge, turning to scan the scene behind her. It was shrouded in smoke and steam—for as far as she could see there were only bodies and debris. She strode forward to start searching for survivors.

"Matthian!" she called, shrilly. She stopped to check a fallen woman's pulse; it was her aunt Zecrecia, who had taken Moyna on an elephant ride in the mountains last year. When Carmeline touched her, she realised her aunt's neck had been broken. She was suddenly nauseous, unable to force herself back to her feet. Tears came into her eyes and burned there instead of falling. "Matthian!" she screamed.

A familiar silhouette emerged from the fog. Carmeline was on her feet in an instant, hurling herself towards him; Matthian's arms closed around her. "Lenire," he was saying. "Moyna—Carmeline, where are the girls?"

"Lenire is safe." She managed to choke the words out. "Moyna . . . Moyna . . . "

Matthian inhaled sharply, as if at a punch to the rib cage. His arms tightened around her, and she could feel him shaking.

"What happened?" he whispered. "I couldn't see. How did the fire start?"

Carmeline pulled away from him then, relief washed away by a flood of returning rage. "This was no accident. Someone did this to us."

She saw horror in Matthian's eyes, but not surprise. He had been thinking the same thing. Everyone in the city had known the day the Empress was due to arrive; there had been hands everywhere earlier in the day. Sabotage would have been difficult, but not impossible, not if you knew the right people . . .

"Traitors," Carmeline hissed.

Matthian's eyes lifted over her shoulder. "Selense," he murmured. It was only as he limped towards Carmeline's sister that she realised he was hurt, the fabric encasing his left leg matted with blood. She watched him stoop awkwardly and Selense clung to him like she was drowning. They had always disliked each other. The scene was surreal, an opium haze of impossible things.

Shots rang out in the smoke. Someone screamed, a woman's shrill terror, before another shot cut her off.

"Lenire," Carmeline breathed, and ran. She refused to register the carnage strewn around her, leaping over the familiar bodies to reach where she had left her daughter. Her eye caught crimson and her heart lodged in her throat. Lenire lay sprawled on the ground, unmoving.

Carmeline couldn't breathe.

"Mama?" Lenire rolled over, her face streaked with blood and tears, but alive. "I heard shots . . . I didn't want them to see me—"

"Clever girl," Carmeline whispered. Movement caught her eye and she spun, snatching a bayonet from a guard's cooling fingers, but it was only Matthian, leading Selense. His whole body slumped with relief at the sight of Lenire.

"They've come to finish the job," Carmeline told him grimly, keeping her voice low. "We have to get away."

"The others—" Selense whispered. "Some may still live—"

"If we stay," Carmeline told her, brutally, "we won't."

The angels emerge. They move stiffly, the whirring of intricate clockwork audible with every movement, echoing throughout the cathedral. Lenire backs up against Matthian instinctively, but Selense looks on with a dreamy smile as the shining army gathers, as if this truly is an act of celestial mercy.

I hurry down from the dais, counting my troops. No more than twenty; it will not be enough, but they will win us some time. Their golden eyes swivel to follow me as I go.

"How is it possible?" Matthian asks, wonderingly. He rises and staggers, steadied by Lenire's hands on his arm. "How do they move, how do they know you?"

"The cathedral is one great mechanism. I am the heir—it obeys me as it would the Empress. But not you." I hurry to Selense and pull her, unresisting, towards the nearest door. "The mechanism is unprogrammed; it will act on default. The angels are meant to defend me, but they don't know you are not my enemies. We must reach its core so that I can give it proper orders."

Matthian stirs himself. Together he and Lenire follow me into a dark corridor, just as something slams heavily against the double doors. We all start, jerking around to stare. A second impact jolts the chair out of place and the bayonet bends. The militia have arrived.

I pull the inner door shut behind us. Red lamps bloom in the dark.

"They shouldn't do that," Lenire whispers. Those are her first words since the docks. "Lamps can't light themselves, it's impossible."

"More impossible than avenging angels?" I put a light arm around her shoulders and this time she doesn't shake me off. For a moment her face relaxes into curiosity. Then a scream tears out behind us and all her colour drains away. The fighting has begun.

"Down," I say quickly. "We need to find a stairway to take us down."

There are no openings in this corridor and only one door, at its end, delivering us into a round room that must be the base of one of the towers. I pause, my arm still around Lenire's shoulders, trying to gain my bearings. Each tower is different. I don't know if the Empress taught me all their secrets, or whether I remember them right, but there's no *time*. Gunshots are ringing out behind us, men screaming, dying, fighting back. Now that they know where we are, the full force of the rebellion will be gathering, and twenty angels will not be enough to hold back the mob.

"Here," Matthian calls. He stands by an open archway, built low and narrow. Beyond is blackness. I square my shoulders, taking the lead, feeling my way down the steps. More lamps come to life at my approach, but not many. The dim reddish glow is not reassuring, but then, it's not intended to be.

We are walking into the lioness's mouth, and she is hungry tonight.

"Do you know what Hell looks like?"

"No, Aunt."

"Hell is a war you know you can't win. The Empire had begun to crumble before I was born, but here in Olembique we all felt so safe. I was not much older than your Lenire when I learned how wrong we were. Their boats choked the rivers with black sails; their soldiers filled the streets with death. I stood on this very balcony, Carmeline, and I watched the old cathedral burn. There was no reason for them to do that. It was where the women and children had taken shelter—there were no soldiers, no weapons,

only the sanctity of the gods to protect them. And the warlords' men razed it to the ground, because this was the Emperor's city, and those were the Emperor's people, and they must all burn.

You must thank them now, Carmeline, because without that night I would never have had the strength to win the war. Because of them, I wrought Hell."

I feel the push before the shot. Matthian's hand slams between my shoulder blades; I fall down the final stairs and land hard on unforgiving stone. The breath is knocked from my body. Dazed, I try to lift myself, and I see the gunman on the stairs above me, above us all. He's very young, like the boy I ran through under the lamp. His face is pale and scared, but he's holding a pistol, and he wears the bright crimson of imperial livery.

"For the revolution!" he shouts, levelling the gun at me.

He never fires the shot. Selense gets there first with a dagger, stabbing him again and again, screaming, "You killed them! You killed them!"

When Matthian pulls her away, the traitor slides down the wall, the dagger embedded in his chest, and Selense collapses. That's when I see the impact of his first bullet, a hideous rose blooming across her stomach.

Matthian and Lenire cradle her between them there on the stairs. I roll painfully onto my knees and crawl to them, a terrible numbness flooding through me. Selense's lips move. I bow my head swiftly, but all that escapes her is air. Her last breath is tasteless in my lungs.

Lenire retches emptily. Matthian pats Selense's face frantically, desperate for a reaction, but we all know that she's not there.

I kiss her brow very gently, and I stand up.

The chamber, deep within the crypts, is an echo of the great hall above, vast and vaulted, its walls pockmarked with a thousand niches for the ashes of my family. In the centre of the floor, surrounded by red lamps, is a massive tomb on a broad stone dais. This, we were all told, is where Isrelde's father was laid to rest. This, like everything else about the cathedral, is a lie.

I cross to the tomb, each footstep marked in thick dust, and push aside the heavy stone lid as though it weighs nothing. Underneath is not a body, but a machine—a panel of brass levers that are warm beneath my fingers, the gleaming face of the cathedral's vast engines. When I move my hands, I leave smears of red behind. I don't even know whose blood it is any more.

"Stop!"

I turn slowly. Another soldier, another man in traitor's livery, scrambles down the stairs. He has a rifle to Matthian's head. Lenire lies facedown at his feet, unmoving. I register his existence with a calm that consumes me.

"Those monsters," the man says, his voice shaking, "they're your doing. You can make them stop."

"I can," I say. "I won't."

He thrusts the muzzle of the rifle against Matthian's skull. "They're slaughtering us!" he shouts hoarsely. "You bastards of the Empress, you destroy everything you touch, but not today! Today it's *your* turn to face justice. So make the angels stop, and maybe he lives!"

Matthian looks at me steadily. He's not afraid. My Matthian, he never is.

Lenire's legs scissor, sweeping the soldier's feet from underneath him. He is sent tumbling down as I was onto the stone floor, the rifle clattering from his grip. I smile radiantly at my daughter, my brave clever daughter, and twist every lever on the panel as far down as it will go. The floor begins to shudder. I jump off the dais just in time, for it has cracked in half and a glow like the fires of hell washes outward across us all.

"Slaughter?" I speak softly, but my words echo. "You know nothing of slaughter."

Winged shapes soar from the pit, the whirring of their motion drowning out the rebel soldier's screams for help. Oh, his people will find him, but too late. Far too late. Clockwork demons, clawed and fanged in black iron, their leather wings razor-tipped, are whirling outwards like a living storm. They know their duty.

And the soldier is the first living thing in their path.

I sit on the roof of the cathedral and watch the city burn. Demons swarm across the sky. Even I don't know how many there are—to the rebels on the streets below, they must seem infinite. Perhaps they would rather die than serve the mistress of Hell. Perhaps those screams are the sounds of surrender.

I don't much care which.

Lenire has fallen asleep in my lap. Matthian's shoulder is pressed to mine, his injured leg freshly bound and stretched out at his side. All around us is chaos, but on the roof there is only silence.

"Aren't you going to tell me," I say at last, "that I have to stop?"

I feel Matthian turn his head and turn mine to face him. His eyes are bloodshot from crying, his face etched with pain and exhaustion.

"You are the Empress," he tells me. "No one can do that."

"You could. You could try."

He lifts one hand and gently, so very gently, tucks a bloody strand of hair behind my ear. "When I said I trusted you," he says quietly, "I meant it. You and Lenire are all I have left, Carmeline. Whatever happens tonight, whatever you decide, I will forgive you. I will forgive you anything as long as you survive it."

His hand on my cheek is all that keeps my head upright. I want to fall, and never stop falling, until oblivion swallows me. I will never know who betrayed us. Every face I see for the rest of my life will be a suspect, a potential rebel. I could sit here beneath the sky, above the house of the gods, and let them all burn.

I lift Lenire from my lap. I have no strength, but somehow I stand, and the shadow of a smile on Matthian's mouth holds me up. This is the Empress's city. These are the Empress's people. *My* people.

If I have to live, so must they.

SIRI AND THE CHAOS-MAKER

CAROL RYLES

Siri first saw him standing in gaslight on the Bridge of Divine Harmony. He was staring into the canal, looking out at the crooked balconies jutting from the tenements on either side. Siri knew at once he was a chaos-maker, not so much from the string of obsidian fangs dangling from his left ear, but from the way his eyes narrowed at her approach.

Keeping her face impassive, she looked beyond his shoulder, determined to not let him see that his presence unsettled her.

He held out his hand, palm upwards. "I've heard about you. You're one of a kind." A tiny flame flickered against his thumb, like candlelight.

Siri's step almost faltered. If not for the novelty of the flame, she would have ignored him. "Is that the best you can say? For a chaos-maker, your words lack a certain . . . "

"Chaos?" He snapped his fingers.

The flame leapt through the air and settled on Siri's cheek. She paused as it slid to her chin and danced along her jawline, cold and tickling. Puzzled, she eyed the chaos-maker.

His face was pale and pleasing, as most chaos-makers' were. He wore a grey, velvet frock coat over pin-striped trousers, and a black top hat trimmed with silk. Curious, as to why he wore ornate brass filigree around his left eye, Siri met his gaze. Tiny cogs turned smoothly when he blinked.

Usually, Siri did not care for the melding of mechanicals to flesh, but when she realised that his sea-glass eyes were also constructions, she caught her breath. How could it be? Chaos-makers despised the predictability of clockwork. Their single purpose was to destroy it.

The flame still flickered on her cheek, but Siri did not want to encourage the chaos-maker by allowing him to see her blush. Matching his smile, she glanced at his straight, black hair, then focussed her gaze on a steam dredge in the canal beyond him.

"Did you know that the flame mirrors the essence of its wearer's heart?" the chaos-maker asked.

Still not looking at him, Siri brushed the flame away. It fell slowly in a glittering spiral, then shattered on the walkway, tinkling like glass.

With a barely discernible whirr, the chaos-maker's green irises widened. "Ah, it seems you have a heart worth loving. I could indulge it, if you allowed me."

"I will not . . . " She paused, thinking that he would see her argument as a sign of stupidity, her jingling bangles and coloured beads as worthless. She supposed he thought her inexperienced. But this, she knew, would be her best strategy. Let him think she was no one. Let him believe he was safe.

Glaring, she took stock of his potential for chaos. His magic did not seem particularly strong, but its nuances felt complex, opaque and resistant. If he decided to use it against the city's machinery, he may well succeed in ruining it.

"Sing for me," he demanded.

Siri arched her eyebrows, knowing he was meaning to tempt her. Not with the flame, but with his eyes, as green as a churning sea . . .

"I want to hear you," he said. "A brief song won't hurt me. I want to know if you're the one."

Siri took a step backwards. To protect the city, her melodies must remain secret, unpredictable. If she revealed them too soon, she risked defeat.

Part of Siri dismissed him as a trickster. Part of her revelled beneath his gaze. "Fight me with your chaos. And perhaps I will sing."

She did not wait for him to answer. Squaring her shoulders, she walked away.

Summer blanketed the city in a pall of languor, warming the canals. Moss receded from terracotta rooftops, baking beneath azure skies. Overhead walkways warped. Cobbled streets raised blisters beneath unshod feet. Artisans worked through the night, shutting down their factories at sunrise.

For weeks, even chaos seemed to cower. No one asked Siri to sing to their clockwork. The wooden casings of automatons did not swell. Their inner workings did not rust. Clocks kept perfect time. Engines ran quiet and smooth.

The other singers kept to themselves, even the strongest. Dala and Lydna could not speak without squabbling. Galie remained at home, too distressed to face the long walks to the academy. Lyreth and Fessna whispered about the chaos-maker, their cheeks flushed.

Unwilling to be daunted, Siri returned to the academy daily. She refused to discard her corset and wore her ruched skirts long and layered, displaying her medals of rank proudly on the buckles at her hips. Alone, she practised in the auditorium, not quite calling to the chaos-maker, but not quite dismissing him either. She tried out a new polishing song and watched an old rusted spring turn supple. She composed a banishing tune and imagined the chaos-maker's feet turning to ice as he fled.

Remembering the nuances of his magic, she composed songs that would weaken him, their melodies tuned to make his chaos wither. These songs she kept to herself.

Later, her apprentice, Yaff, joined her. The boy's voice was raw, but held great promise. "Has the chaos-maker asked you to sing? He's asked the others, but he hasn't asked me." He pouted, his blue eyes too anxious and too knowing for his mere seven years.

Siri ruffled his dusty blond hair, making it stand up in spikes. "Think yourself lucky. That fellow is out to wreak more than just chaos."

On her way home, she saw a gathering of workers following a strange, canopied phaeton that rolled silently over the cobbles. No horse pulled it, not a hint of smoke or steam hissed through its brass funnels. Its sides were fashioned from dark, carved wood. White chintz curtains fluttered from its canopy, obscuring the driver.

Siri waited beneath her parasol, watching it approach. She tried to sense the nature of its clockwork, but felt nothing. As it pulled up at the kerb in front of her, the chaos-maker's pale, manicured hand pulled back the curtain. "What do you think of my new invention?" he asked.

"What trickery is this?" Siri snapped.

He threw back his head, his laughter smooth and deprecating. Passers-by backed away.

Despite her misgivings, Siri ran her hand over the phaeton's wooden frame, tracing her fingers over its brass carvings of lions and sheep, hawks and sparrows. She listened for chaos, but heard not a hint.

"How does it move?" she asked.

"You of all people should know that. What do you sense?"

She listened again and heard a faint dissonance of magic, but nothing she recognised. "There's a disturbance, but I cannot feel its source, nor its essence."

He raised his eyebrows. "Do you hear chaos?"

"No."

The chaos-maker's lips curved into a self-indulgent smile.

Determined to find a flaw, Siri peered past the curtains at the studded, velvet seats and caught a hint of sandalwood. "Your carriage is lovely, but I do not trust it."

The chaos-maker offered his hand. "I do not expect you to."

"Then what do you want?"

"Ride with me and see for yourself. I assure you my magic will be to your liking."

Siri paused. She contemplated the carvings on the frame above the chaos-maker's head. Eagles and lambs, hounds and pheasants, moths and flames. "Why sir!" Siri said, affronted. "I do not even know your name."

"Will you sing if I tell you?"

At that moment she longed to, but refused to risk her single weapon against him. She raised her chin. "Maybe."

His clockwork eyelids grew still, his sea-glass irises determined. "My name is Mecklan." He threw her a grin, both disarming and taunting.

Siri felt herself blush at the pure audacity of him. She tried to sense a weakness in his magic—something so small and so hidden that its nature would be revealed. But as the phaeton rolled forward, she sensed only the turn of wheels over cobbles and her own heart beating a treacherous and captivated rhythm.

Evening closed around the city, restless and expectant. Siri practised with Fessna and Dala in the academy, then walked young Yaff home.

"You must eat," Yaff's mother told her. She took Siri up the narrow stairs that spanned the four levels of the tenement—one cramped room for each level and an open scullery at the top. They sat on stools on the crooked balcony, overlooking the canals, bridges and overhead walkways that cobwebbed the city.

Siri sweated beneath the layers of her skirt. "This newest chaos-maker is the strongest one yet. Yaff should stay at home until I've banished him."

"You mean you'll face him alone?" Yaff's mother shook her head, her pale hair gleaming in gaslight. "When I used to sing, the destruction of chaos depended on—"

"Numbers," Siri finished. "For this chaos-maker there can only be one singer. For his kind of chaos, only one song . . . " Her voice trailed away.

"Then tell me, why is he seeking out the other singers?"

"All of us?"

"So I'm told. Don't let the others tell you it's the heat that's making them late for practice. It's him."

Siri frowned. "He thinks he's too clever for us. He wants us to believe we do not have a chance."

Yaff's mother looked at her long and hard. "Remember this, Siri. It is not you who must banish his chaos. It is your voice."

At practice, Dala and Fessna would not sing. Lydna and Lyreth walked out in a huff. "There is no point in wasting our voices," Fessna said. "If Mecklan is a chaos-maker, then where is his chaos?"

"I've heard he's a greedy one," Dala said. "He keeps his chaos to himself."

Siri let out an impatient snort. "Why do you suppose that is?

Because he cares for us? Or because he's waiting to destroy us, all at once?"

Lyreth glared. "Maybe he's changed. Maybe he's tired of chaos."

Disheartened, Siri practised alone in the safety of the basement, singing until her throat ached. That evening, she locked up and strolled along the overhead walkways, following the misty waters of the Blue Wren Canal.

Despite the heat, the city smelled fresh and clean. Steam carriages and barges passed below, their fumes carried high on the breeze. In the artisan factories beyond, automatons clicked and whirred with clockwork precision. Stars gleamed in an unclouded sky.

At the Piper's Inn, Siri found Mecklan looking down at her from an overhead balcony.

"Would you grant me the pleasure of sharing a meal?" he called out.

Ignoring him, she continued on her way. Moments later, he caught up with her.

"What do you want from me?" she asked.

He shrugged and tossed his straight, black hair over his shoulder. The obsidian fangs at his ear gleamed in gaslight. He turned to her, his green eyes piercing. "What do *you* want from *me?*"

At that moment, the air shuddered with the crack of wood splintering. Siri looked up to see a balcony two stories above crumble. It plummeted, an avalanche of timbers, barely missing Siri's walkway before plunging into the canal below.

A child screamed. Siri watched at once helpless and transfixed as a flash of arms, legs and fluttering skirts sped past her in the balcony's wake.

Mecklan shrugged out of his jacket and leapt. He hit the canal in a perfect dive, his body catlike and elegant. For several long heartbeats he remained submersed as the oil-dark waters churned in a welter of froth and wooden railings.

"Mecklan!" Siri called. The water grew still, silent.

Heart pounding, Siri hurried to the walkway's end. She descended the stairs two at a time and arrived at the canal to see Mecklan break the surface, bringing the little girl with him. When he reached the lip of the pavement, Siri knelt down and pulled the spluttering and coughing girl to shore.

A crowd had gathered. "Thank you," a woman in blue overalls said stiffly.

Mecklan drew himself to his feet and gave a twisted smile. He took Siri's elbow and led her away. "Now, what was I saying before? Oh yes, I remember. What do you want from me?"

Siri held his jacket over her arm, but could not remember picking it up. "Right now, I'd like to see you dry again."

His eyes gleamed. "You could sing me dry."

"Your drenching is the wrong kind of chaos."

Mecklan blinked and graced her with a disarming grin. The cogs and wheels at his eyelids whirred.

"At least it's summer," he said, reaching for her hand. "May I?"

"May you what?"

"Walk you home."

Lost for words, Siri handed his jacket to him. As far as she could tell the balcony had fallen naturally, a product of poor workmanship. She could not feel a hint of chaos in its rubble. Carefully, she slid her fingers around his. "Thank you."

They walked hand in hand. Mecklan did not torment her and nor did he insist that she sing. Instead he said, "Creativity nurtures the soul much more thoroughly than destruction can. I'm building my new home outside the city."

At the door to her tenement, his clockwork gaze fixed on her, tentative and silent. "When my villa is ready, you must see it."

He bade her a polite good night. She stood in the shadows, watching the walkway long after he'd left.

News of how Mecklan had saved the child spread through the city. People said that the lack of chaos since his arrival was his doing. The other singers refused to practice. Yaff's mother stopped sending him to the academy. Within days Siri wondered if she, too, had grown tired of singing.

"It's a wicked waste," Mecklan said as they strolled along the Canal of Heavenly Spring. "I've heard you're one of a kind. You should not remain unheard."

"My voice is meant for destroying chaos," Siri insisted. "I'll not waste it on anything else."

The weeks passed and Siri spent her days looking forward to meeting Mecklan at dusk. They'd walk along the canals, dine at Siri's favourite inns, laugh and avoid all discussion of singing. Each night, when they parted, he would touch her cheek and leave a gentle flame in his finger's wake.

Unwilling to trust him, Siri would let the flame fall and shatter.

On the night Mecklan kissed her, Siri's heart hammered in her chest, betraying her true feelings not only to herself, but also to him. "My villa's finished," he told her. "Tomorrow, I'm leaving." He drew away from her, tipped his hat. "You'll find it on the main road heading east, four miles past Birdthistle Ford."

"Maybe," she whispered to his retreating back. "Just maybe."

The days stretched out, vacant and lonely without him. Without chaos to distract her, she could think of little else.

Siri could see the villa even before the carriage began to slow. She could also see Mecklan at the gate, pacing back and forth as if he were waiting for her. When at last she could alight, she barely noticed his clockwork. Even her disdain for chaos-makers did not stop her from hugging him.

"I've watched that carriage pass every day," he said. "Hoping it would be the one." Then he kissed her, slowly and softly, until her heart began to trust him.

He showed her through his villa with all the pride of an artisan displaying a carefully composed work of art. Each room celebrated beauty, each one furnished with tapestries and silks. Automatons played flutes, harps and violins, while in the sculleries, servitors prepared meals with the simulated pride of master chefs.

The days bled into each other, delightful, peaceful, content.

Fruit trees bent low with unpicked fruit. Siri and Mecklan walked beside the river that ran from the foothills and past the orchards. Towards the city, it split into two tributaries, one torrential and impatient, the other serene and deep. Mecklan threaded his fingers around Siri's and led her to the second river, beneath willows with branches that hung like the frills of parasols.

He squeezed her hand. "We're opposites, like the rivers. But, like them, we have the potential to belong."

On their way back to the villa, they skirted the orchards and passed a stone cottage with soaring, arched windows and a steeply pitched roof. "It's to be my workshop," Mecklan said. "When it's complete, I'll show it to you."

"I can sense magic inside," Siri said. "It's simple and harmless, like the magic in your phaeton."

Mecklan grinned. "That's because it *is* the phaeton. It's undergoing repairs."

"May I see it?" Siri asked.

"Yes, of course. But not today. It's getting late."

Hurrying, he led her through a meadow where Siri saw one of his scullery automatons remove a hare from a trap. She winced as it snapped the hare's neck with precise calm. At once, she felt a faint shiver as the hare's soul left its body.

Mecklan caught his breath, his face ashen.

"You felt that?" Siri asked.

He nodded. "It's worse than chaos."

She took his hand, puzzled to find it cold and trembling. If chaos-makers were supposed to revel in death, then why didn't he?

That night, Siri allowed him into her canopied bed. He stroked her cheek with his pale hand, unbuttoned her nightdress, drew it above her head and tossed it aside. Kneeling beside her, he kissed the length of her body, planting candle flames as fine as gossamer in the wake of his lips. These flames, Siri could not shatter. Nor did she want to.

Winter hit in a flurry of rain and wind. As the servants drew the villa's shutters closed, Siri sensed chaos—not the destructive kind, but something odd and intriguing. Reassuring her, Mecklan bought her gowns and trinkets. He kept his automatons fully wound, sending them to soothe her with melodies. At night, he calmed her with his flames.

But soon, the sense of chaos grew darker, its beauty marred by a taint.

"It's nothing," Mecklan told her, sullenly. "Perhaps it's your doing. All that song you have. Never letting it out. It can't be good for anyone."

"Nothing?" Her voice rose. "How can 'nothing' keep me awake at night? How can 'nothing' make me afraid to close my eyes? If you know what it is, please tell me. If it's something that threatens you, I promise I can help."

His sea-green eyes narrowed until only his pupils looked back at her, black and inscrutable. Abruptly he turned away.

Heart hammering, she took herself to the orchards and looked out at the twin rivers. If the two were to ever join completely, what would they become? Would the torrent have energy enough to lose itself in ocean? Or would the dark-water channel sink to never see light?

On the rare clear day when Siri could go out alone, she began to sense a strange magic calling to her from beyond the meadow. She followed its scent and found its source at Mecklan's cottage workshop. When she touched its door, her hand burned from the taint of the chaos beyond it.

The lock was unfastened. Carefully, she stepped inside.

The workshop was as sumptuously furnished as the villa. Siri crossed the cold, marble floor past a brocaded couch and a multitude of gold-stemmed lamps. In a far corner, she found a table arrayed with wooden figurines, each one as tall as her outstretched hand. Some were human-shaped, their faces distorted in parodies of ecstasy, anger and despair. Others were animal-shaped: a cat poised to leap, a deer running, a dog simpering; while others were a grotesque mixture of both.

Their chaos reeked of malevolence. Against her better judgement, Siri found herself seized by a need to sing.

At first she hummed an atonal, visceral sound that rose and fell in time with her breathing. Soon, she began to sense chaos brushing her skin, begging her to release it. Her voice strengthening, she let her song find its own melody.

Music poured out of her, a mournful refrain spiralling in dense ripples. The figurines shuddered. Their arms, legs and wings sprang to life in a discord of clockwork whirring. Their heads nodded and their eyes blinked. Their feet carried them forward, clattering against the table-top.

As one, they came towards her, a waddling, skittering, jittering procession. When they reached the table's edge, they toppled over it, smashing onto the marble floor. Siri felt the unmistakable shivers of souls leaving their bodies. Yet these were wooden things, clockwork toys.

The last one fell. Siri's voice grew silent. Exhausted, she picked up the remains of a tiger and cradled it in her hands. Through a hole in its side she could see tiny brass cogs, ratchets and gears gleaming like fragments of bone. Its body did not feel like a dead thing, merely like something that had never possessed life.

Like the phaeton, she realised. The smokeless, engineless phaeton.

The door creaked open from behind. Startled, she swung around to see Mecklan stride towards her. His eyes gleamed, not at all kindly. "Your song is beautiful," he said. "But your voice wasn't aimed at me. Now I've heard it, I understand what it says."

Siri looked at him, swallowing against anger. "You planned it this way?"

His mouth twitched into the hint of a smile. "I planned it for you."

Siri's blood ran cold. She dropped the figurine, biting her lip as it shattered at her feet. "The souls," she said at last. "How did you put them there?"

He shook his head ruefully. "You really are one of a kind. The others sang for me without hesitation. They could have killed me with their voices, if they chose. Instead, they sought only to please me. You alone refused." He stepped towards her, swaggering, triumphant. "Until now."

"What have you done to them? Where are they?"

Mecklan pointed to the ruined figurines at her feet. "I needed souls to give life to the clockwork." He shrugged. "Singer's souls. Now you've ruined them. Their souls are lost."

"You took all of the city's singers? Dala? Fessna? Lyreth? All of them?"

Mecklan's lip curled. "Every last one, including some from cities so distant, you could not imagine them. Now I must turn to the artisans."

"To put them in the figurines? Mecklan! Why?"

"Why not?" He turned on his heel, strode away.

For a moment, Siri could only stare, her breath hitching in her throat. How could she have believed she could love him?

She caught up with him in the next room. He gestured to a wooden automaton. "This one's for you," he said. "The other's voices were weak, barely enough to give life to a trinket. But you—you're one of a kind—strong enough to animate a fleet of phaetons. But your beauty would be wasted on that."

The automaton smelled of richly, polished wood, its surface pale and unblemished like stone. Its body was the same build as Siri's, its corseted, ruched gown carved into it.

A chill ran up Siri's spine at the realisation that its face was an exact replica of her own. Its wooden eyes, although unmoving, watched her as she approached.

"Sing if you want to," Mecklan said. "It will do you little good."

Siri opened her mouth, but it was not song than burst from her. It was a high, glassy scream.

Mecklan inched forward, his hands outstretched. Flames leapt from his fingers.

Drawing on all her melodies—all her lilts and refrains—Siri hurled her voice towards him.

Mecklan stood unwavering, grinning, his clockwork eyes mocking her.

Frantically, Siri reached into her memory, drew out compositions she had yet to sing. Her voice reverberated, a chorus of destruction, demanding that Mecklan's chaos wither, his wooden statue crumble and his feet turn to ice.

Mecklan's flames leapt again, piercing Siri's chest, coiling inside her. Her voice cut short, Siri reeled backwards. Her soul pulled away, burning. For a moment, she felt suspended between two bodies, her flesh pulling one way and her wood pulling the other.

The world turned dark, cold. She forced her eyelids open to see her own flesh body crumpled on the floor at her feet. Wooden feet.

She wanted to kneel, hold it in her arms and smooth its terrified eyes closed. But her cogs and wheels remained motionless. Her wooden arms hung at her sides.

"Once set in motion, your wheels will never stop turning," Mecklan said. "Your soul gives them movement, but it cannot control them. Only I can do that."

He stroked her cheek and left a searing flame at her jaw. Siri wanted to brush it away, but her arms remained stiff. A wisp of smoke trailed from Mecklan's fingers, coiled about Siri's chest. At once, she could sense the dreadful nature of the chaos that created it. Where her heart should have quickened, a wheel turned inside her chest like a wet, mossy stone.

Mecklan's eyes became fierce and green. "Go to your city. Show them what has become of you. Return to me by nightfall, so I can send you back. Your clockwork will guide you." He smiled, his eyelids whirring. "It's what you wanted, isn't it? Orderliness? Predictability? Now it's yours, there'll be no turning back."

The flame on Siri's cheek died. Her cogs and gears clicked and whirred.

Every day Siri trudged to and from the city. In her wooden body, the journey pleased her because her gears smoothed the way. They took her through fields where women with bent backs scythed wheat and watched her pass.

Without singers to protect the city, machinery fell into chaos. Automatons ground to a jarring, squeaking halt, clocks ran erratically, the artisan's factories closed. Unable to work, people retreated into shadows, clutching their children.

Sometimes Mecklan would walk next to Siri. He liked to brag about the number of figurines he'd carved, the number of souls he'd taken to fill them. When they reached the city, he would look over its ruin. "Chaos," he would say.

Siri could not cry or sing or rail. Nor could she escape. His magic curled like a stench in her nostrils, drawing her to the city, back to the villa, to the city and back. How could she have not sensed it when she was living? How could she have not understood?

"You're still one of a kind," he'd tell her. "And still beautiful. Wood ages slower than flesh. You should be grateful."

Seasons passed. Siri walked, thinking about Mecklan—how her songs could no longer hurt him because now he could predict their melodies. But what if she created something different? How could she force her wheels and cogs to follow her tune instead of Mecklan's? She tried to console herself with the knowledge that in years to come, new singers might be born, but what good would that do? How could she teach them?

Her jaw, where the flame had burned, ached. Her feet creaked, where before their gears had whirred softly.

When Mecklan next saw her, he scowled. He stroked her jaw. "Your wood must have been green when I carved you. It's swelling. "He squatted and examined her feet. "These, too, are green. You won't outlive me after all." Standing, he brushed his hands against his sides and turned away.

Now, he left her to wander between the villa and the city alone. On the rare days they crossed paths, he'd look away. Siri supposed he could not bear her loss of beauty. Although the thought did nothing to affect the heavy wheel where her heart had once been, it pleased her to know that at last she had foiled him. Her new solitude brought comfort. Songs unfolded inside her, each one in tune with Mecklan's chaos.

She promised herself that with time, she would learn how to sing them.

Months passed. Siri crossed fields where farmers would shout at her, blaming her for crop failures or unseasonable rain. Children followed her, taunting, imploring her to stray from her path. As always, she ignored them, knowing they would tire and leave her alone. Except for one—a skinny and bandy-legged boy, dressed in rags. His dusty blond hair stood out in spikes about his ears. Maybe, Siri wondered, if someone could bathe him, she'd remember who he was.

"Can't you talk?" the boy asked. "Can't you even stop walking if you want to?"

Siri remained silent while her cogs creaked and the songs in her chest grew stronger.

"I know why you won't sing," the boy said. "You deserted us with the other singers to play wicked games with the chaos-maker. Then you all lost."

He threw stones at her, tried to topple her, but her gears kept her upright. She longed to lie down, to press herself into the Earth and become part of it.

"I bet you could sing if you knew how," the boy said. "My ma says that the chaos-maker put your soul in wood because he was scared of you. Why'd you let him?"

He ran circles around her, pulled faces, stuck out his tongue. He shuffled backwards in front of her, inspecting her limbs.

"Holy water! Look at those legs," he said. "The wood's peeling away and they're all swelled up like wetted sticks. You got bits of dirt in your feet. You could grow cabbages in there if you wanted."

Sometimes the boy seemed familiar. Siri supposed she had known him once when he was smaller and his face not quite so thin. Then he told her his name was Yaff and she remembered him singing to her at the academy. How sweet his voice had been. How perfect to fight chaos. She supposed there was no one left to teach him. Or perhaps he was afraid to sing.

Some days, when she reached the city gates, she wished she could pass through them and find her way home. People would see her pause and they would turn their backs, accusing her of abandoning them. Sometimes, Yaff would take hold of her arms, urging her to follow him, but her cogs and gears would force her out of his grip, returning her to Mecklan. On these days, Siri's throat would swell with banishing songs, but her voice remained locked, silent.

Her feet grew soggy. Yaff pulled an apple core from his pocket and pressed it into a crack in her foot. He picked up an assortment of flowers from the undergrowth. Scuttling backwards as Siri walked, he squeezed each one into the finer cracks between her toes, scrunching up their petals until they fit.

"There," he said. "Come spring, they'll be pretty again."

Winter passed. Yaff grew thinner and no longer visited her. If not for the seeds burrowing in her feet, Siri would have forgotten him. At first, their pointed husks hurt like pebbles, but when she grew used to them, green tendrils sprouted, boring beneath her wooden shell, tunnelling up to her knees. Gradually, her wood felt supple. Her clockwork no longer creaked.

Then, at last, she met Yaff again. He stared at her feet. "If they swell up any more, they'll burst.

Siri wanted to laugh. She almost did because the roots that spread up from her legs tickled her throat. The tendrils encircling her ankles halted her mid-stride. The stone wheel in her chest thudded damply against a cushion of leaves and moss.

"Sing," Yaff said. He tugged at a blossom growing in the crook of Siri's elbow. "Look at you! Full of life again. Forget about walking. Sing."

Siri lifted her chin. Yaff was right. She could barely feel her clockwork. Instead, something akin to a heart-beat thudded inside her. She opened her mouth, surprised at how the air rang with her laughter.

"Your voice," Yaff said. "You've found it."

Siri laughed again. The melodies that had churned inside her for years rose up. One by one, she set them free.

Chortling, Yaff danced around her. "Your voice is beautiful. You should let Mecklan hear it."

Siri's voice rippled. "For you, I will."

Siri let herself into Mecklan's workshop to find it dark and silent. She crossed the cold marble floor, then froze when its gold-stemmed lamps lit up. Ahead of her, Mecklan reclined on the brocaded couch, surrounded by an army of figurines, their souls shuddering like netted birds inside their clockwork.

At Siri's approach, Mecklan's glass eyes darkened with disapproval. His lips twisted into a complacent snarl. Siri wondered how she had ever loved him. What kind of chaos had he worked on her to blind her to what he was?

"So," he said smoothly. "You think you can defeat me?"

"Maybe."

Mecklan laughed. "You're wasting your time."

Holding his gaze, Siri lifted her voice. Her song rose like a breeze.

"Is that the best you can do?" Mecklan taunted.

"Watch me," Siri said.

She sang again, remembering the years of walking in silence, composing the songs she'd believed she'd never sing. She wove melodies within melodies, each one filled with the agony of entrapment—each one laced with a yearning to be set free.

The figurines whirred into life, their feet clicking against the marble floor. Eyes widening, Mecklan sprang up, lifted a hand. A flame swelled at his fingertip, white and flickering. For a moment, Siri thought he would hurl it at the figurines, but then his lip curled.

"So, this is why you're here. To destroy my creations, release their souls." The flame at his fingertip flared. "You've insulted me long enough."

The flame leapt.

It hit Siri squarely in the chest, reverberating like the fall of an axe. The stench of burning wood stung her nostrils. Despite the pain spreading through her—she refused to let her voice falter. Melodies poured out of her in a torrent of unfettered rage.

The figurines clicked and whirred a frenzied drumbeat of anger.

"*If the chaos-maker dies,*" Siri sang to them. "*Your souls will be freed.*"

At once, the figurines converged on Mecklan. Miniature lions, leopards and cats leapt to his shoulders, tearing through his frock coat, drawing blood. Parodies of men and women scaled his legs, their clockwork shrieking. Birds battered his face. Serpents tightened around his throat.

Mecklan clutched his neck as the figurines clambered over him fighting for purchase. His eyes gleamed like captured jewels, pleading from their prison of wood.

Siri had loved those eyes once. Now she could not bear to look at them.

Lowering herself to the floor, she turned her face away. The air above her shivered, shuddered, cracked, then at last grew still. Certain that every soul had freed itself, Siri let her voice fade.

The final remnants of Mecklan's magic shot towards her, bursting into a chaos of hot, throbbing flames. She beat at them with her hands, her chest burning. Gathering her strength, she hurled her final song.

At once, the flames shattered, fell. Siri sank to her knees as the mossy wheel in her chest, slowed.

The world faded, turned black.

Siri opened her eyes to the puzzling smell of rain and a man's voice urging her to wake up. A shaft of light slanted down from somewhere above, bringing with it a swirl of motes and a spiralling, falling leaf. From where she lay partially on her side, Siri could see Mecklan's brocaded couch, ruined and rotting, piled high with dirt and leaves.

"See," a man's voice said gleefully. "I knew you'd beat him. I'm only sorry it took me so long to find you."

Siri turned her head to see a young man. A stranger. Beyond him, she saw Mecklan.

He was sprawled out on the floor, still dressed in his frock coat and pinstripes. In sunlight, his fleshless skull shone creamy white. His shirtsleeves proffered bleached, bony hands. Around him, amid a pile of shattered wood, the inner workings of figurines glittered like gems.

Siri pulled herself upright, her limbs creaking. Above her, foliage and light spilled through a hole in the workshop roof. The ceiling around it sagged beneath the weight of a fallen tree.

A leaf tickled her face, making her wood tingle. Siri brushed it away, then paused, startled. Glossy green leaves sprouted from her knees. She ran her hand over her carved wooden hair. Her fingers curled through feathery fronds topping her head.

"Do you remember me?" the man asked."

Siri looked at his blue-eyed, bearded face. Spiky, sandy hair fell about his ears. As recognition dawned, the wheel in Siri's chest quickened, squelching against her wooden ribs. "Yaff, you've grown!"

Yaff smiled. "I didn't forget you. I tried to find you, but couldn't see the workshop until after last week's storm. After the tree fell on it."

"Thank you," Siri said at last. "Perhaps some leftover taint of chaos kept the workshop hidden. Perhaps the storm banished it." She flexed her limbs, loosened them up. She ran her hands over her calves and felt the beginnings of nodules and soft shoots pressing out from them.

"I have to go home to my family," Yaff said.

Siri looked down at herself, at the moss and foliage clothing her. "Leave me be." She sighed. "I need time to remember who I am."

Night brought a shower of rain, soothing her charred chest. A layer of fine roots circled her throat and shoulders. Stroking them, she hummed a melody, its cadences comforting her like a sough through leaves. By morning, she knew exactly what to do.

On her way to the city, her limbs moved stiffly, her sense of direction confused. She rested by the rusted carcass of a steam carriage, revelling at the way her feet sank into the wet earth, almost taking root. Reluctantly, she tore them away. "Not yet. Not here."

She reached the city at sunset to find the streets deserted and hints of chaos clinging to the shadows. The artisan factories stood still and silent, as did the rusted bodies of automatons littered around them.

She hummed a banishing song until the chaos and rust retreated.

At the park, the trees stood thin and yellowed. People huddled beneath makeshift shelters, their eyes wary. Beyond them, the city's rooftops and steeples rose crookedly in the air's biting chill.

Siri let her toes sink into the earth. She closed her eyes, smiling as her feet took root and her clockwork turned. Around her, the trees grew green and healthy. The artisan's factories stirred.

Content at last, Siri allowed her cogs and wheels to turn with the flow of her sap, slowing with each passing season. Star-shaped leaves concealed her swelling limbs in a halo of green. Sometimes, Yaff would visit with his boisterous children. Siri held them gently and firmly when they climbed her branches, supporting them so they would not fall.

"Siri," Yaff said. "My daughter's voice is as pure as yours used to be. She'll make a fine singer."

Humming softly, Siri stroked their faces with her wispy fronds.

The seasons blurred and the city hummed with the soft tinkering of workers and artisans. Its trees grew orderly and green. One day, a chaos-maker strutted the perimeter of Siri's outstretched limbs, bragging about the strength of his chaos. Siri sighed, dismissing him with an impatient rustle, showering him with a flurry of leaves. She barely saw him retreat, barely heard Yaff's daughter banish his chaos with melodies as fresh as leaf litter and as sweet as clockwork.

Siri's cogs and wheels slowed, grew still. Her branches stretched upwards, towards sunlight—towards order—and peace.

A CLOCKWORK HEART

AMANDA PILLAR

"Miss, do you need a hackney?"

Mary turned to look at the speaker. Her canvas bags were piled at his feet, their floral pattern faded and worn against the wet cobbles. People flowed around them, heading away from the airship. The air was cold and still, a shroud of coal smoke hovering above the town.

"Will there be one available?" she asked, tugging her red gloves higher on her forearms. The airship dock was crowded, as it was Mercury's only port.

"I could see if there is a hackney ready for you, miss." The man—a lad really—gave her a tight smile and straightened his white gloves before heading away. His red uniform and little black cap merged into the crowd of people and he was gone.

Taking a step closer to her bags, she surveyed the area. Two hundred people milled about her, some chatting, others silently carrying their luggage in gloved hands towards the queue of hackneys.

The lad returned. "Miss, if you come over to the line, I reckon I can get you a ride quick smart."

Mary looked at the attendant and smiled. "Then we shall head over." Reaching down, she grabbed two of her bags and looked pointedly at the lad until he picked up the other two. They were the heavier, but he didn't complain. Then again, with her uncle as his employer, he wasn't likely to. As they walked to the queue, she frowned as she was bumped from all sides.

If they knew who my uncle was . . .

No, she thought; she wasn't that woman anymore. That woman made stupid choices; choices that meant she'd been exiled to this mountain town alone, hauling her own bags across sodden cobbles, waiting for a hackney. Her red-gloves meant she wasn't designed to live in damp climes on mountain tops; that was for the whites, blues and browns—the airs, waters and earths. But then, she wasn't meant to have been ruined, either.

Ruined.

She let the word roll around in her mind. It was ridiculous, the concept of ruination. Her brother tupped maids, got drunk and regularly committed acts of unparalleled stupidity. Her uncle just laughed. Pearson was her uncle's heir, after all. The only thing he'd ever done wrong was don a set of green gloves. And that wasn't really his fault. So what, that the rest of the household were reds? Abilities were abilities, and that was that. But was Mary even allowed to be caught *once* doing something wrong?

No.

Being found in the arms of her lover was apparently a *very* different matter to her brother sleeping with every servant he could find. The terms 'whore' and 'slut' had been bandied about, until she'd pointed out that whores got paid, and sluts had to have more than one lover. And on the topic of sluts, why wasn't Pearson subject to this lecture, too?

Then she was just called stupid.

She hadn't argued that point. Mary had thought she'd been engaged. It'd been too bad her fiancé had already been married.

"Miss?"

Mary started and stared at the attendant. From the look on his face, it was apparent this wasn't the first time he'd tried to get her attention.

"Sorry. Yes?"

"This fella can take you," the lad said, pointing at a cab driver whose hat concealed most of his face. He wore yellow gloves, which signified his affinity for animals. It made sense, although she wouldn't have expected to find too many yellows up here in this town of stone and coal. In contrast to his shadowed appearance, the hackney was a bright green and the chestnut horse appeared healthy, giving its tail a jaunty flick. Maybe this wouldn't be so bad.

Low murmurs began to ripple around her. Mary turned.

"I've been waiting for thirty minutes and she can jump the queue?" A man shoved his way to stand over the attendant, where he then pointed a brown-gloved finger at her. The other men and women surrounding him swelled towards her as well.

The lad tugged on his black cap. "Sorry sir, but this lady gets priority."

"Priority!"

"She's Lord Hargraves' niece, sir."

Mary winced. The man's eyes flicked down to her brightly gloved hands clasping her luggage. He paled and stepped back. It was as if the attendant had announced her uncle was the King. Although, everyone knew who Lord Hargraves was: the man who had destroyed a rebellious city with nothing more than the flick of a red-gloved hand.

"Thank you," Mary said to the lad. She should have waited in the queue, but she was tired and queasy and cold. *Best to brazen this out.* Tucking her bags into the hackney, she ignored the murmurs of the crowd and waited for the lad to load her luggage. Then she climbed inside, folded her hands in her lap, and let out a deep sigh.

Maybe this would all work out.

And maybe she'd wake up tomorrow wearing dark blue gloves.

The hackney slowed over damp cobbles as they approached Mary's destination. Rows of tall stone houses stretched towards the dark, cloud-scudded sky. As the wheels clattered against the pavement, Mary peered out the cab's window at the rows of townhouses glistening in the evening light. She shivered. How could she live in such a place?

The hackney came to a stop. Mary stared at the grey stone house that soared three stories, with gargoyles frowning and growling down at the street below. The driver stepped down from the hackney and stood by the carriage, waiting for her to disembark. He didn't offer her his hand, and her back stiffened at the slight. Once her feet were on the wet stone pavement, the driver reached past her, and plucked out the two heavy bags. Again, she took the lighter two.

Swallowing to ease a suddenly dry throat, Mary strode up the wide steps to the double doors. She hesitated before setting one of her bags down on the dry stoop. Squaring her shoulders, she reached out a trembling hand and picked up the large, brass knocker. Its centre was a snarling gargoyle. *You can do this*, she told herself and rapped the knocker down sharply three times.

The driver put the rest of her luggage down behind her and cleared his throat.

The door hadn't opened.

"In a moment," she said over her shoulder. Should she knock again?

"Ma'am?" the driver enquired.

Mary realised he wanted to be paid. She didn't have any money. She'd never *needed* money before; merchants and creditors used to just contact her uncle's solicitors, or so she had assumed.

Gripping the knocker again, she banged it again, louder. If the door wasn't answered soon, she'd take her glove off and melt the snarling gargoyle into a pathetic puddle of bronze. He wouldn't be so fearsome then, would he?

She heard the driver shuffle forward; "Ma—"

The man who opened the door did not look like a butler. He was tall, towering over Mary, looking down his long aristocratic nose at her and the hackney driver on the stoop.

"Can I help you?" he asked. His voice was deep, smooth, with an accent she was beginning to associate with this mountain town—although she had only heard two locals speak.

Mary went to reply, but she realised he was looking over her shoulder. He hadn't even acknowledged her. Narrowing her eyes, she picked up the discarded bags. "If you don't mind, I would like to come inside. This man needs to be paid."

Without waiting for a reply, she strode forward, sweeping through the foyer and into the hall beyond, seeking the warmth of a fire. She couldn't believe he had just ignored her. The hallway was long and narrow, with tables and niches lining the walls. Using the sense that was as much a part of her as her eyes and nose, she walked towards a flame, not knowing where she was going. Turning down a second corridor, her eyes caught on a metallic gleam. Her anger temporarily forgotten, she approached the glimmer, its appeal almost as strong as that of firelight. Coming to a stop, she stared at a little bird perched on a wire branch. It appeared to have metal filigree wings, wire legs and a clockwork heart. Which ticked.

How . . . odd.

Turning her eyes back down the hall, she realised most of the niches and tables she had passed hosted small metalwork pieces, crafted along the lines of the little sparrow. *Who decorates a house with mechanisms?* It didn't matter. She eventually found a fire, emanating out of what appeared to be a small parlour on the first floor. Let him deal with the hackney driver. *She* was going to get warm.

Quinton, Lord Smitherson, stared at the back of the woman who had just swept by him and into his house. The light from the hall illuminated flickers of red in her dark hair, which had been coiled around the back of her head. She was even prettier than he remembered.

A trembling voice emerged from the doorway. "Milord?"

Quinton turned to the hackney driver. Of course, he needed to be paid. Reaching into his pocket, he withdrew a gold piece and handed it over. The man's eyes bulged under his grey cap. "This is too much, milord." He held the coin out, as if it was burning.

"It is yours," Quinton said. "I have nothing smaller." He reached out, grabbed the two remaining floral bags and stepped back into the foyer of his home. Putting one bag on the ground, he flicked a hand. The doors swung shut on the stunned hackney driver. Shaking his head, Quinton grabbed the bag and headed down the hall. He assumed Mary would have headed towards the parlour, where he'd set up a fire in anticipation of her arrival. He probably should have gone to collect her from the airship dock, but she wouldn't have known who to look for and he may have missed her.

No, he had done the right thing.

Entering the parlour, he saw her standing in front of the flames, hands outstretched, her gloves discarded on the chair behind her. The blaze was higher than it had been before, higher than the fuel could sustain. But then, it wasn't being fed by wood. It was being nurtured by the woman before it.

"Mary?" Quinton asked when she didn't turn around. The warm light cast by the blaze lit the red highlights in her dark hair until it shone like a ruby. He wanted to touch those strands, capture their warmth, the luxury of their softness.

He heard her sigh. "Yes?"

"I'm Lord Smitherson."

"Nice to meet you. I'm your fiancé." Her voice was bitter, and she hadn't turned around. Hadn't even curtsied.

"Is something wrong?" he asked, then cursed himself for an idiot. *Of course there is something wrong; she's* here.

She didn't respond.

"If you don't want to marry me, I will understand." He hoped that wasn't the problem, but she had only met the man she'd been traded for once and that was years ago. She'd never have thought to be married to him then. Maybe she'd caught a look at him as she swept past into the hall and decided that no, she couldn't do this, no matter what her uncle said. Or she'd seen the dank, smoke-smothered city that was Mercury and decided she needed the vistas of the forest and sea that had previously surrounded her.

"It's not that," Mary said. Her shoulders seemed to straighten.

Relief swamped through him, shocking him. He didn't know her; what did it ultimately matter to him if she hated him on sight?

But he wanted her. Not in the way that most people would assume. Oh, she was a very attractive woman. But for someone like him, being constantly surrounded by whites, blues and browns, he needed something more. Something warmer, hotter. Red-gloves didn't come up to places like this to live. Fire didn't catch easily on a rocky hilltop.

"Then what is it?" he asked, realising she wasn't going to elaborate.

She didn't turn around. Instead, she slowly withdrew her hands and hunched her shoulders. "I'm here to *marry* you. The least you could do is acknowledge me when I turn up at your door."

Quinton blinked.

"I sound stupid, I know I do. But you're meant to be my husband—no matter how much of a business arrangement this may be—and it would have been nice if you had even *noticed* me."

She didn't sound stupid. But she did sound . . . spoiled. She hadn't given him *time* to say anything. He'd answered the door and wondered why the hackney driver was hovering behind her, and then she'd told him to pay the man and stormed inside. Maybe he should have greeted her first. It would have been polite.

"I'm sorry, but you didn't really give me much time." He didn't want to start this marriage apologising, but she clearly needed placating. He wasn't about to let her tread all over him, though.

Quinton had seen her before, after all. She'd only been eighteen then, full of fire and spirit. She'd captivated him, but he had soon realised it was as much her vivaciousness as her ability. Mary had not even noticed him. So much so that no recognition had dawned on her face when he'd answered the door. Back then, he'd been just another face in the crowd. Someone to dance attendance on her, as she'd thought she'd deserved. Being the niece of a very powerful man had given her a false sense of her own importance, and he'd known that, but he hadn't cared. Her confidence had lingered in his memory, her burning smile along with it. And so when her uncle's note had reached him, he'd snatched at the opportunity to 'make a wife out of his wayward niece'.

"You were meant to . . . " her voice trailed off and she turned around. Her skin was a light, honey brown, the smooth contours hinting at an interesting mix of ancestry.

"I was meant to what?"

She shook her head, but he thought it was more at herself, rather than him. Quietly, she said, "You were meant to pay attention to me instantly."

Quinton was at a loss for words.

"But, that was the former me. The me who thought she was invincible, who would never have agreed to marry a stranger and live in a small town on the top of a hill that was only accessible by airship."

"I don't know what to say." What *could* he say? That in those few sentences she'd managed to convey her utter dissatisfaction at being forced into marrying him?

She laughed, but it was acidic. The flames danced in the fireplace. "What is there to say? That you got a bad deal?"

Quinton frowned. She was not the girl he remembered. But then, she'd been a *girl*. It had only been a few years since he had last seen her, but she had been tempered through fire—whether it was her uncle's or her own, he didn't know.

Mary wanted to scream at herself. Had she learnt *anything*? Hadn't she just shown she was as spoilt and selfish as ever? She had stormed into her future husband's home, angry because he hadn't fawned over her the minute he saw her. What did that say about her?

"I can imagine this will take a bit of adjusting to," Lord Smitherson said. She hadn't even introduced herself, she realised. But it was a bit foolish to worry about that now. They were to be married.

"I am sorry. I was behaving like a child." She sat down and hung her head, staring at his bare hands. She wondered what colour gloves he wore. Those hands looked strong, though. Long fingers, with a faint dusting of dark hair.

He came to stand before her, then bent one knee and knelt on the ground. He tipped her chin up. Her skin tingled. "I understand you were in some difficulty, and had to marry quickly. Your uncle did not say what happened, but it is easy to guess."

Heat rose up her cheeks, flushing her face. Shame, she realised. She'd never thought to feel it.

"Look at me," he said, voice soft.

Mary raised her eyes and met his, a strange, silvery colour. Almost metallic. He was handsome, she realised. Very. She should feel lucky. She would have, mere months ago. Married to a handsome lord. Someone who would pet and coddle her. Look after her, laugh at her exploits.

She thought she'd been engaged to a man such as that. And look where she was now.

No, she wouldn't be satisfied with just a pretty face. Not this time. But she didn't have a choice; he could be a monster and she'd still be stuck with him.

I'd set him on fire first, she thought and was startled at herself.

Lord Smitherson's expression was sincere, his fingers warm against the skin of her jaw. "I do not care what happened before. You will be my wife and I will treat you with respect. If you have any interests you wish to fulfil, I will try to ensure that you are able to. We will be living in a rather isolated town—it would be good if we could get along."

Get along.

Wonderful.

Mary was feeling rather shaky. And embarrassed. She was a married woman, had been for days now. And yet Lord Smitherson, Quinton, as he'd asked her to call him, had yet to come to her as a husband did his wife. And it was becoming very urgent that he did so.

Deciding it could not be put off much longer, she went in search of her husband. Quinton spent a lot of time in the lower levels of the house, leaving her free to follow her 'interests', as he said. But there wasn't much to interest her here. She'd found it easy to keep entertained before, with parties and gatherings and teas, but here, even though those options were available to her, she was indifferent. Mary didn't need to sit and listen to gossip, or discuss dresses and the gentlemen on offer. Those things were . . . empty. She needed something of purpose. She just needed to work out what that was.

The first day she had spent exploring. The house was beautiful; nothing like its forbidding exterior. Warm, sumptuous hues decorated the interior: reds, yellows, oranges and splashes of blue and purple. She felt bathed in visual warmth. And then there were the charming little mechanical creatures, the birds and butterflies and beetles. They walked and flew and even sang. It still astounded her.

But playing with these gorgeous objects did not allow her to understand or know her husband better. Not when he was absent most of the day.

Heading downstairs, she followed the directions of a servant. Stepping onto the final landing, she realised she was in the lowest levels of the house. The earth seemed to feel heavy atop her. It was warm here, surprisingly so. She could feel the source of heat tugging at her, insistent, almost as if it was alive. Frowning, she realised that the servant's directions, and her ability, were leading her in the same direction. Her feet whispered over the stone floors, and finally she came to the heat's source. It had to be a forge, she realised. Sustained, controlled heat, always burning, moulding, creating. It was as if her skin had come alive: tingling, excited.

Opening the door, she saw Quinton standing next to the forge, wearing a large apron made of something sturdy. The scent of flame, hot metal, graphite and male reached her. Flickering shadows were cast over his face and body as he worked on something centred on the bench in front of him. His shirt stuck to his body with sweat, and she realised he was very healthily built. Her eyes drifted to the fire, even though she found the view of her husband working more appealing than she had anticipated. It was as if the flame was a friend, welcoming her.

Stepping fully into the room, she cleared her throat and Quinton seemed to startle. But his hands were gentle as he placed his work on the table. "Mary?" He raised an eyebrow.

What could she say that wasn't too obvious?

"I wondered what you did all day," she managed, licking suddenly dry lips. She saw his eyes focus on her mouth. Maybe he wasn't completely unmoved by her, as she had feared.

"I make things," he said, shrugging. She could feel heat suddenly emanating from him, and she stepped closer. In the flickering light, she could see he was blushing. It was almost sweet.

Looking down at his work, she realised *he* made the strange birds and butterflies that decorated the house. His fingers had made those delicate, beautiful things. A half-finished mechanical cat lay between his hands; spirals and swirls and wires of metal crafting the creature with lavish attention. What would it feel like to be the centre of that kind of focus?

She shivered.

Quinton frowned. "Are you all right?"

Mary smiled. "Yes, of course. I didn't realise you made all those lovely sculptures."

He shrugged. "It is part of me."

Fire was a part of her, like breathing. How could making strange little mechanical birds be a part of him?

"What glove colour are you?" she asked, staring at his hands.

His strange eyes met hers. "Grey."

"Grey?" She'd never heard of someone with that colour before.

He came around the desk to stand in front of her. "It is metal. It is not common."

No, she thought; he was anything but common.

"Well, I imagine the two of us should work quite nicely together." She nodded at the forge and then looked at him again.

She received a faint flicker of a smile.

Quinton smoothed back his hair. "Is there anything you need?"

Mary smiled again, hoping she looked more confident than she felt. Leaning up, she wrapped her arms around his neck, pulling herself up on her tiptoes. She kissed him. Warmth tingled from his lips to hers, and her eyes fluttered shut. Tilting her head, she opened her mouth, suddenly hungry for him, for his taste and his touch. A low groan reached her ears and then suddenly, he was hugging her, lifting her, carrying her to a chair, where he set her down.

"Mary, we're in my workroom."

Feeling flushed and slightly frantic, she reached for him.

"Mary?"

"What better place could we be?"

Afterward, Mary lay cuddled on his bare chest, feeling a kind of contentment she hadn't expected to find in Mercury, or ever again. Quinton was a kind man, she realised; careful and thoughtful of her, and he also made the most wonderful pieces of art.

Not only that, he'd made her cry out not long ago. In a rather lovely way. Her supposed fiancé had never managed as much. She had been such a fool.

Strong fingers feathered through her hair. "Mary, was that . . . acceptable?"

Startled, she looked up at him. They were on the floor, the stone probably hard against his back, but he didn't complain. She was wrapped in warmth from him and the forge.

At her look, Quinton muttered a small "never mind," and tucked her back against him. It was peaceful, lying like this in the semi-darkness. Listening to his breathing and her own, feeling her heartbeat against his . . .

Ticking?

Frowning, she pressed her ear harder to his chest. There it was, a distinctive *tick, tick, tick* rather than the predicted *thump, thump, thump.*

She jerked backwards. "What?"

Quinton reached an arm out towards her, but she wrenched back, scrambling away, tangling her feet in her discarded dress.

"Mary?"

Clutching the cloth of her blue skirt to her chest, she felt herself trembling. "You don't have a heartbeat!"

"Mary, I can explain—"

Fear took hold of her. What had she let into her body?

"You let me have sex with you. What are you? Are you even *human?*"

"Mary—"

She began to unravel, like kindling falling from an unprotected hearth. "What *are* you?"

Quinton flinched. "I'm human."

Mary yanked her clothing around, trying to find her bodice so she could dress herself. "Humans don't tick!"

He tried to grab her arm, but she ducked away. Unable to find the bodice, she stood, holding the dress in front of her like a shield.

"I have a mechanical heart."

"A *what?*"

"A mechanical heart. See this scar? It is where it was inserted." He ran one of those long fingers down his chest, highlighting a smooth, pale line she had not noticed before.

Clutching her dress with one hand, she pointed with the other, the warm colour of her skin starting to burn. "You're a monster!"

Mary sobbed until her eyes were so swollen she could no longer open them. At first, she had cried with rage at her husband, screaming and hitting the fire-hued silk pillows that been scattered across her bed. She had used every bad word she'd ever learnt in combination with his name. Then she had cried with wrath at her uncle, for forcing her to marry such a man. She'd gripped the comforter and hugged it to her body, refusing to leave her bed except for when certain bodily functions were too hard to ignore. Finally, Mary had cried at herself, for being so judgemental. After all, hadn't she railed at the way people thought of her because of a simple act she had done? How a foolish part of herself had been discovered and remarked upon?

That had spurred her out of her bed, much to her maid's relief. Looking in the mirror had been a shock, although she'd barely been able to see her reflection as her eyes had been so swollen. She was such an idiot. It was not Quinton's fault he had a ticking heart, rather than a pumping one. It was difficult to understand how he could be alive with that horror inside of him. But if it was anything like the little birds and beetles, then perhaps it wasn't as bad as she imagined?

It still made her uneasy, a sick feeling settling in her stomach, when she thought of having lain with a man with a false heart. But then, he had shown her he was kind, whereas a fully flesh and blood male had told her he loved her and would marry her, while being a husband to another woman.

Clearly, she wasn't the best judge of what was acceptable and what wasn't. She feared she'd made an entire mess of her life. Touching her stomach, her eyes barely open, she hoped that she would be the only one to pay the price.

"I'm sorry," Mary whispered from the doorway.

Quinton looked up from his days' old newspaper—it took that long to reach Mercury at times—and met her gaze. He could have pretended he didn't know what her apology was for, to simply brush the matter away with a flick of his hand, but her words had echoed through his head and metal heart too much for him to forgive so quickly.

So Quinton said, "I can't help what is inside my chest."

Mary took a step into the dining room. "I thought as much."

She looked wan, her eyes still puffy and her face slightly blotchy. It had been two days since the debacle in his forge. He hadn't been able go back and finish the cat; the memories were too raw.

"There aren't many grey-gloves because—for some unknown reason—we are often born with defects. Sometimes is it just a club foot, or deafness, other times it's more serious. A broken heart."

Mary dropped into the chair opposite him with a plop. Her warm skin had paled, making the red in her cheeks and around her eyes more noticeable. "A broken heart?"

Quinton laid the paper down on the mahogany table in front of him. For some reason, despite his anger, he wanted her to understand. To see he was no *monster*. "There was something wrong, something the sawbones couldn't fix. My father was a grey-glove like me. So he built me a new heart."

Mary said nothing for several seconds. "Did he have a defect as well?"

"He was deaf in one ear."

"I'm sorry."

"You don't have to be sorry for that. It was no one's fault, his disability. And he saved my life—gave it to me twice. Not many fathers can do that for their children."

Mary's fingers twitched, the red of her gloves twining around itself over and over. "Can we start over?"

"How about I show you something?" Leaving his paper on the table, he stood and headed out the door, Mary following behind. He led her through the halls and up to the second floor. His room was next to hers, but she had never entered his chambers. Perhaps she never would. The thought gave him a pang.

"In here," he said, opening the iron door with a wave of his hand. Weak light shone in the room, but it was enough to illuminate the space he was headed towards. A heavy bed occupied the centre of his private space, and he strode past it. He stopped in front of a niche holding a glass bell jar. Within, suspended on a metal rod, was a replica of his heart.

"Something like this is what keeps me alive." It was the shape of a human heart, with copper tubing and a sturdy casing over half the organ, designed so the internal workings were obvious to someone who wanted to know how the life-saving device was made. Inside was a small pump, powered by cogs and wheels. This one, however, wasn't ticking.

Mary stared at the replica organ for what felt like aeons to Quinton. What would she say? How much more might she revile him?

A red-tipped finger extended towards the curve of the glass, almost wonderingly. "It's amazing." She looked up at him. "But this one isn't working."

Quinton lifted the cover of the jar and touched the tip of his finger to the heart. It began to pump, a ticking sound filling the quiet.

"You power it yourself?"

"My ability does. So as long as it lasts—and my other organs— then so will my heart."

Mary reached out and touched his chest, where he'd shown her his scar. "I'm sorry I called you a monster. You're not. You never were. I just panicked, wondering how a man could have a fake heart. But my ability is part of me; I can't help but want to be near fire. It sings in my blood. Like everyone else, your ability is part of you; but unlike everyone else, yours is built into your very being."

A sizzling feeling ran through him from top to tail. If he'd had a normal heart, he was sure it would have pumped faster.

"You can accept me?" he asked, removing his finger from the replica and replacing the jar lid.

She reached over, clasping his hand, holding it tightly. "I can. You and your clockwork heart both. But can you accept *me*? I've been horrible, and selfish."

She had, but she was trying. It was more than most wealthy, privileged people would have done, man or woman. "You have had a tough time. I am not what anyone would have imagined, I know."

"You are *more* than I had expected, or deserved." With that, she released his hand and stared at the ground between them. An expensive rug lay at their feet. "You don't know everything about me."

"I know that you are willing to try," he said. "It is enough." It would be. They would have trouble; two strangers married a little over a week, of course they would. But he hoped she would settle down and accept his solidarity, his sturdiness, like that of the mountain and its ore beneath their feet. Just as he might be able to bask in her warmth, her inner fire.

"It might not be." She raised eyes to his, dark brown irises wary. "I'm pregnant."

He shrugged. "I had thought as much." It did not matter to him. He was glad; if their firstborn was a child not of his blood, he may not have to go through what his father had. If anything, it had been a relief when he'd worked it out.

"*What?*"

Now it was Quinton's turn to offer her comfort. He gently touched the curve of her jaw. "You're the niece of a very powerful man; a niece who is reported to have almost as much power in her gloved hands as her uncle. Most mistakes or pranks would be forgivable. But a child out of wedlock? Even your uncle would have had difficulty with that one. If you had just been caught having an affair, it could have been hushed up. Many women take lovers before marriage, no matter what the popular belief may be."

"Then why did you agree to marry me?" she all but wailed. "What would inspire you to want a woman carrying another man's child?"

He grasped her hand and pulled her towards the bed. He sat down and tugged her hand, until she sat next to him. Quinton wanted to be eye to eye. "I saw you once, years ago. You were warmth and fire and laughter and wit. It captivated me. Part of it was your ability; fire with metal. That is a combination grey-gloves dream of. We are too much of the earth to want to be with a brown-glove, and water can corrode metal, so a blue-glove is not ideal, either. And a red-glove is not something I can find in a town like Mercury—which suits my ability but not yours. So when your uncle's letter came, I jumped at the chance."

"We met before?" She raised a hand to her mouth. "And here I was, on the first day, acting like a brat because you did not pay me any attention. And yet I hadn't remembered our first meeting."

Quinton shrugged. "You were young."

"I was selfish. Self-involved. I thought I was invincible. It's a shame it took someone else to teach me I was nothing more than a balloon of pride."

"We are each invincible when we are young. Imagine how I was with my mechanical heart." His lips quirked in a half-smile. Her eyes lit at this, but then the spark died.

"But that doesn't explain why you do not care that I am pregnant."

"It was a relief. My firstborn child will not be at risk of having my ability—of having a potential fatal illness because of it. I don't know why it affects grey-gloves, but it does."

Her eyes grew wide, locked on his face. "You really don't mind."

He took her other hand in his own, held them both tight. "I really don't."

Mary smiled, but it crumbled, giving way to a sob. She flung herself at him, wrapping her arms around his chest and pressing her face to his ticking heart. He ran a hand over her hair, trying to sooth her upset. He wasn't sure what he had said, but he had heard pregnant women could be emotional. Mary certainly was that.

"Mary?"

She raised her tear-stained face, staring at him, her eyes searching for something unknown. Then she kissed him. But it wasn't like last time; there was no desperation in it. Just sweetness and acceptance. He tilted his head, deepening the kiss, shifting her so she sat across his lap. She let out a gasping breath and then cupped his face in her hands.

"Quinton?"

"Mmmm?" He was wondering how he might remove her bodice. If she'd let him. He hoped she would. This time would be better, he thought. In a real bed, under the sunlight.

"Quinton?"

Realising that she may not approve of him ogling her, especially after their last experience, he met her eyes, fearing he still might see rejection.

"Yes, Mary?"

"I think I just fell in love with you."

SEVEN MONTHS LATER

"I'm going to kill that lying, ratting bastard!" Mary shouted.

The midwife cast an anxious look over her shoulder at him, but Quinton just smiled. He knew he wasn't the ratting bastard in concern.

Mary's face was red and scrunched in pain as she bore down, obeying the midwife's instructions. The room was sweltering hot, but that's what red-gloves needed when they required comfort. With each yell, the flames in the room blazed higher. They'd had to remove anything combustible from the other hearths, and warned their neighbours they may have some unexpected fires. It was a side effect of Mary being who she was. She'd also been stripped naked, in case her skin caught fire, but thankfully that hadn't happened yet. It was also why the midwife was another red-glove.

Downstairs, Mary's uncle paced and sweated, ready to prevent any conflagration from blazing out of control. He was also here to support his niece, although Mary had remained stubborn and refused to forgive him entirely, even though her pairing with Quinton had gone 'unexpectedly well', in her uncle's terms. Quinton felt slightly disconcerted at having one of the most powerful men in the realm hovering like a distressed father. But then, Mary had a way of unsettling even the most calm.

Mary wailed, "When will it be *over?*"

The midwife peered between Mary's legs and muttered something to herself. Then she looked up at Mary, sitting in the birthing chair, which Quinton had made himself, so it wouldn't catch fire. "I can see the crown, milady. Just push when I say, and hopefully not much longer."

Mary's eyes met his, hers slightly wild. "I'm never doing this again!"

Quinton smoothed her hair, careful not to linger. He could be burnt if she lost control. "That's fine, my love."

"Push!"

Mary screamed, her whole body straining with the effort. If he wasn't at risk of being burnt alive, he would have held her. On her final push, her hands, which were gripping the arms of the birthing chair with white knuckles, caught fire.

And then there was one of the most wonderful sounds he'd ever heard.

A baby's cry.

"You have a daughter," the midwife announced. She wiped the infant's face with a cloth and then took it over to a small table to give it a more thorough wipe down. She returned, their baby wrapped in soft fabric. Even though the babe's face was wrinkled like a prune, he didn't think he'd seen anything more beautiful in his life.

Mary lay panting. She reached a flickering hand out. "A daughter?"

Quinton stepped forward, "Your hands, my love."

Gasping, Mary glanced at her fingers and the flame vanished. "Can I hold her?"

"Of course. If you keep that," the midwife nodded at Mary's hands, "under control."

Babies often didn't show signs of their ability until a few weeks after birth. Some did: Mary had burst aflame; Quinton had made all the metal in the room dance. But a baby may not necessarily share the ability of the parent, so caution was often the best approach.

Mary smiled, a weak, tired expression, as the babe was passed across. Blue eyes looked around blindly before focusing on Mary. One arm emerged from the blankets, waving a small fist. Quinton smiled. Mary looked wondering as she ran a finger across the little knuckle. And then the second arm emerged, but there was no hand, no fist.

Mary gasped. "What's wrong with her?"

Frowning, Quinton leaned forward, staring at the baby. He felt a tug in his chest, a jump in the rhythm of his clockwork heart.

The midwife *tsk*ed. "Your babe seems otherwise healthy, but we can get a sawbones to check. Missing limbs—they are not uncommon."

But neither are they common, Quinton thought.

"It's my fault. I did this to my child!" Mary burst into tears.

Reaching forward, he pried the infant from her arms, holding the babe close to his chest. His heart rattled a little, then settled back into its original pace.

Quinton smoothed his free hand over his wife's hair. "Mary, love?"

"If I hadn't been such a stupid—"

"Mary?"

She stopped, tears streaking down her face. "She only has one hand, Quinton. For most of us, even people like my uncle, our abilities come out strongest through the skin of our hands. How will this affect her? This is all—"

He gave the midwife a look, and the woman hurried over to the far side of the room. She couldn't leave yet, as Mary still needed her assistance, but at least she was far enough away that she may not hear them if they spoke quietly.

"Mary, it isn't your fault."

"How can you know that?"

Quinton smiled at his wife, then his child. "Because our daughter is like her daddy."

"But—" Then Mary's eyes widened. "She's not yours," she whispered, obviously trying to work out where their daughter's ability may have come from.

"No, but grey-gloves appear from time to time randomly."

Mary was staring at the both of them, at him holding the precious bundle of wrinkly, tiny humanity. "How can you be sure?"

He tapped his chest. "I could feel it."

She sat up, alarm across her features. "Are you okay? Did it affect—?"

"I am fine. And our daughter will be, too."

"But you said they have defects. Will her heart be all right?"

"Like the midwife said, we can get her a sawbones. But there is usually only one problem. Mine was more severe than most."

Her alarm eased, but Mary still looked miserable, staring at their babe with sadness. "But her hand . . . "

"Will be fine." Quinton smiled down at the little bald baby in his arms. He ran a finger over her tiny left arm, touching the blunt tip. "Daddy will make you one."

THE VENETIAN CAT

CHERITH BALDRY

"If you had given me thumbs," the cat observed, "we would have finished this task much sooner."

Ser Raniero Foscari glanced up from his workbench and gazed at the cat seated opposite him, idly batting a globule of mercury to and fro with one delicate paw. "If I had given you thumbs, *carissima*, you might by now be lying at the bottom of the lagoon. I made you soft and frisky and frivolous. I made you *safe*."

The cat flicked out, for a moment, the tip of a rose-pink tongue. She was small, barely more than a kitten, a confection of silk and fur and curled shavings of silver, with upswept feathery ears. Her eyes gleamed true emerald. Ser Raniero remembered the nights of her making, so long ago, nights when raging grief had made his hands tremble so that he could scarcely control them for the precise work.

Now he bent his head again and took up a thin pair of tweezers. With them he edged one hair-fine silver wire into its proper slot, and dabbed down a rod which fused the connection with a brief hiss. His aching shoulders relaxed and he let out a sigh. "Done."

"Really?" The cat leaped to her paws and padded across the bench, skilfully avoiding the debris of Ser Raniero's equipment, and sniffed curiously at the device. "Will it work?" she asked.

Raniero shook his head. "I don't know. And there's only one way to find out."

He took a flat disc of silver that lay on the bench beside him, and fitted it over the complex innards of his device, the spider's web of silver wire and ceramic connectors. Once the disc was in place, the artefact seemed no more than a silver mirror with a particularly elaborate scrolled border.

In its dim reflective surface Ser Raniero caught a glimpse of himself: his thin hawk's face, with a scar running down his left cheek. His hair was dark, tumbled curls frosted with silver, and he wore a black woollen robe with white bands at his throat. *Add a pectoral cross, and I might be a priest,* he told himself wryly.

The cat stood on the bench beside him, diamond claws flexing in and out, whiskers twitching with scarcely controlled impatience. "Are we going to do it now?" she asked. "Tonight?"

Raniero took in a long breath and let it out. "Tonight."

The cat sprang up to his shoulder and perched there, digging her claws hard into the thick wool of his robe. Raniero rose too, and crossed the room to a massive oak cabinet that stood against one wall. Opening the door, he took out two vials, one clear crystal with glints of silver dancing inside it, and the second dark as the juice of mulberries. Secreting both inside his robe, and picking up his mirror-device, Raniero headed for the outer door.

When he reached it, he stood with his hand on the latch, turning back to survey the four walls that for so long had been his kingdom. In the centre, several oak tables had been pushed together to form a square with a space in the middle. The light, from lamps set behind globes of water, was concentrated on the bench where he had been working, throwing the corners of the room into shadow. On the tables stood hissing alembics fogging the air with vapour, strange constructions that sprouted bits of metal and intricately blown glass, pallid cultures that seemed to slide out pseudopodia just in the corner of Raniero's eye. Scrolls and leather-bound books were piled carelessly wherever there was space.

Only I know how much of this is camouflage, he thought. *And not even I know whether I shall ever see it again.*

Ser Raniero paced through the halls and down the staircases of the Palazzo Ducale until he reached the balcony that overlooked the Great Courtyard. Below, torches were flaring, the fizzing actinic flames cold and glaring against the ancient stonework. Musicians were tuning their instruments, playing scraps of melody now and again on archlute, baryton or viol.

Ser Raniero paused, looking down with sick disgust at the

crucified man at the centre of the yard. He had been there since that morning; amazingly, he still lived, straining upwards for a gulp of air, only to collapse again with a groan of agony from torn muscles and shattered hands and feet.

Why does she do this? Raniero asked himself. *And why this cruel parody?* But he was afraid that he already knew the answers to those questions.

He realised that he had delayed too long when trumpets sounded from the top of the stairway. Light burst from clouds of what might have been taken for fireflies, until they ended their transitory lives in a shower of scent and a metallic taste on the air. By their uneven flames a crowd of masked courtiers poured down into the yard: men and women dressed in silk and velvet, lace and feathers, their eyes a feverish glitter behind their masks. Ser Raniero slid back into the shadows, watching, waiting for the way to clear.

Then the Duchesa came. She stood at the head of the stair, tall and superb in purple velvet so dark it was black in the folds. Amethysts glowed on her fingers and at her throat. Her mask was a tall headdress of feathers dyed purple with golden beads that fell about her shoulders like a shower of coins. At her girdle hung a golden key studded with precious stones. With stately tread, gripping the folds of her gown in one hand, she began to descend.

On either side she was flanked by a winged lion formed of gleaming brass. Their wings clashed together as they raised them above their shoulders. The curled gold of their manes was liquid fire and their eyes gleamed burning cinnabar. Their claws clattered on the stone steps as they kept pace with their mistress.

But half way down the stair the Duchesa paused. Though Raniero was sure he had not moved or made a sound, she turned and fixed him with an imperious gaze.

"Ser Raniero, come here."

Obediently Raniero started forward. He sensed his cat quivering with apprehension on his shoulder, and whispered, "Silence, *carissima.*"

The lions turned towards him, their heads raised alertly as Raniero approached, the furnace of their crafting still incandescent in their eyes. Raniero sensed their patient watchfulness as their glance swept over him before they continued down the stair beside the Duchesa.

Raniero followed her down until they stood together at the foot of the stairway. "At your service, Serenissima," he said, bowing.

The Duchesa regarded him; she was an inch or so taller than he. The lower part of her face beneath the mask was white, her mouth thin and set. Her eyes were cold and direct.

"I think not," she responded. "What you serve, Raniero, unless it be the art we share, I do not know, but I am sure it is not I. Why were you lurking in the shadows there? And what is this?" she asked, flicking with one finger the silver surface of the mirror device.

Raniero's stomach cramped with fear, but he strove hard to keep his voice steady as he replied. "A mirror, as you see, Serenissima. A small gift . . . "

"For me? Ah, no, Ser Raniero, I see it in your face. Can it be that you have found yourself a friend at last? And there I thought that you saved all your devotion for your little cat. At least since my sister's unfortunate . . . demise."

Raniero did his best to keep his face indifferent under her taunts, and was vastly relieved when she waved him away.

"Go to your little friend, then. And may she have much joy of you, for truly I have none."

Ser Raniero bowed again and stepped back, though he could not resist halting again to ask, "Serenissima, can you not put that poor devil on the cross out of his misery?"

The Duchesa's mouth curved in a smile. "Certainly, Ser Raniero. I intend doing that very soon."

At that moment the musicians struck up and the heaving mass of courtiers transformed themselves into the whirling patterns of a dance. A man in scarlet tights and padded doublet, wearing the horned and sneering mask of a devil, reached out his hand to the Duchesa and drew her into the measure.

Raniero pushed his way through the dancing courtiers and made his escape out of the Porta della Carta into the Piazetta where the air was cold and clear, filled with the tang of the sea and the sound of waves slapping against the quayside. The few passers-by walked quickly, their heads down; no one wished to attract the attention of the Duchesa or her retinue. Only at the far end of the Piazza did blazing torches and the faint rhythms of fiddle music betray some small festivity.

Ser Raniero paid little attention to any of these, pacing swiftly and silently beside the wall until he reached the entrance to San Marco. The doors were open, but the interior was dark and silent, except for a faint gleam of candles towards the high altar.

In the narthex, the cat jumped down from Raniero's shoulder. "Must I come in?" she asked. "I don't like to see it."

Raniero stared at her. "*It?*"

The cat shrugged uneasily. "You know what I mean. I'll stay here and keep watch," she added. "Call me when you need me."

"Very well, *carissima*," Raniero murmured. He bent to caress her, a long stroke that began at the top of her head and ended at the tip of her feathery tail. The cat pushed her head into his hand.

"I trust you, Raniero," she murmured.

I wish I trusted myself, Raniero thought. Then he straightened up and strode into the basilica.

Ser Raniero headed for the candlelight near the altar. As he drew closer he saw, as he had expected, that the candles were clustered around a bier enclosed in a dome of crystal. At the foot of the dome lay little offerings: posies of flowers, sweet cakes, with here and there a gleam of silver from a wealthier pilgrim.

Raniero remembered his encounter with the Patriarch only a couple of days before.

"This has gone on far too long," the elderly priest had said. "The people are treating her as a saint. What the Holy Father will say if it ever comes to his ears, I shudder to think."

"I can assure you," Raniero had responded, "that you won't have to put up with it much longer."

Now as he reached the bier, Raniero saw something he had not expected: a young man, kneeling at its foot with his golden head bowed over his hands, the glitter of tears on his cheeks.

"Lady, you are so beautiful," he said in an aching whisper that reached Raniero clearly in the silence. "If you could rise and speak to me, I would serve you all my life."

After a moment, Raniero recognised him: Lucio Contarini, the youngest son of that great house, who had just reached the age when he could take his place on the Great Council. His presence shocked Raniero: here, alone, and suffering such grief.

He may be a romantic fool, to give such devotion to an image. But he's a decent lad, and of good family. I wonder if he might be useful . . .

Raniero edged forward silently until he had a clear view of the body on the bier. On the drapery of white samite lay the form of a woman. Her eyes were closed, her hands pressed together in prayer. She was gowned in white silk, with pearls stitched over the bodice, translucent as tears. Her face was pure beauty, save that the skin of face and throat and hands showed no warmth of flesh, but all was silver, cold and rigid.

Ser Lucio started, as if he had just realised he was not alone, and looked up at Raniero. He showed no embarrassment at being found weeping. "I come here every day," he said simply. "No living woman can match her."

There were many such, Raniero thought, *who knelt at her feet when she was alive. It takes a strange devotion to do it now.* Aloud he said, "None could, or can," and was alarmed to find his voice shaking.

"She seems like an image cast in metal," Lucio continued. "Is it really true that this is the body of Rosalba, who would have been our Duchesa?"

Raniero nodded. "It is true. The . . . malady spread over her body, entrapping her in silver."

Lucio rose to his feet, looking down at the body on the bier with a troubled expression. "I have never heard of such a malady."

For a moment, Ser Raniero was torn between his need to act and his growing sensation that this young man was part of the pattern he had fought so hard to weave. "I will tell you a story," he said. "It began more than twenty years ago, when Donna Serafina was Duchesa, and I was tutor to her twin daughters . . . "

With a touch on Lucio's arm, Raniero drew him to a bench beneath a pillar, not far from the bier, and sat beside him.

"I taught them languages and mathematics," he continued, "and together we began to explore the art that since I have made my own." Since Ser Lucio seemed bewildered, he explained, "The juncture between the human body and spirit, and the crafting of metal and fabric . . . the point at which the doctor meets the alchemist and the craftsman, and fuses all their skills into one. I found it—still find it—fascinating.

"Rosalba spent less and less time with me. As the elder twin she studied statecraft and the duties of the Duchesa with her mother.

But Vittoria shared my passion for the new art. We developed it together until eventually she set up her own workshop. But I still shared my discoveries with her, though, God help me, I failed to notice that she never shared any of hers with me."

"And then?" Lucio asked.

Raniero paused for a moment, the memory of what came next threatening to surge up and overwhelm him. *Rosalba loved me. I would have been her Consort. But then . . .*

"Then Donna Serafina died. And before Rosalba could be confirmed as Duchesa, she fell ill. Her body weakened, though her mind remained clear. And silver gradually spread over all her skin, until she became as you see her now. At last her grieving sister placed her here, with that impermeable crystal dome above her, and in the fullness of time Vittoria became the next Duchesa."

He could not keep the bitterness out of his tone as he spoke the last few words, and he saw that Ser Lucio had understood. *The boy is not such an idiot as I thought at first.*

"Are you telling me that the Duchesa murdered her sister?" Lucio asked.

"I have no doubt of it," Raniero replied.

The young man shuddered, gripping his arms about himself as if he was cold. "I wonder she can bear to see her here," he said. "So beautiful still, and knowing what she did . . . "

"Bear it?" Raniero let out a crack of laughter. "She *gloats* over it. Her sister's body is a perpetual memory of her triumph."

Tears welled into Lucio's eyes again and he blinked them back. "I remember . . . " he began. "No, not *remember*, for I was but a babe at the time. My father told me how his brother Francesco and his wife Bianca raised a rebellion against Donna Vittoria. But they were discovered, found guilty of treason and permitted to kill themselves. Though my father said they were fools, perhaps they knew what you have just told me, and could not bear to serve such a woman."

"That is very likely."

"And there is nothing anyone can do now," Lucio said. He sounded desolate.

"Oh, never say that, boy." Raniero felt a fierce satisfaction. "Vittoria despised me from the beginning, because she found me easy to deceive. Perhaps then she was right. But she despises me still, and that is where she has made her mistake. For though it has taken me twenty years, I have discovered two things: an antidote to the poison, and a way to get into that crystal dome."

"A way to . . . " Ser Lucio's voice shook. "Ser Raniero, are you saying that Donna Rosalba *is not dead*?"

"It depends what you mean by dead," Raniero retorted. "Vittoria thought that she had entrapped her sister's spirit in a body frozen to metal, inside impenetrable crystal. She wanted Rosalba's suffering never to end."

Lucio's eyes widened in horror. "A mind so trapped would be insane!"

Raniero's mouth twisted. "I said that is what Vittoria *thought* she had done."

Before he could say more, there came a scuttling sound from the doors into the narthex, and the eerie yowl of a hunting cat. He rose and peered across the basilica, thinking that he could discern a single glimmer of light. Seconds later, he saw movement in the darkness that resolved itself, as it reached the circle of radiance cast by the candles, into his cat, racing towards him with some glittering creature clutched in her jaws.

She dropped the thing at Raniero's feet; he stooped to examine it. It looked like a crab, or perhaps a spider, built of gold and crystal with segmented legs and bulging, many-faceted eyes on its upper body. Though its carapace was crushed, it still lived, its limbs twitching.

"Kill it," Raniero said. He did not ask himself why the glittering thing had come there. If its purpose was evil, the damage had been done.

Instantly the cat slammed down a paw, diamond claws digging deep into the creature. Its legs spasmed, then the whole thing collapsed and disintegrated with a tinkling sound into rings of metal, the bulbous eyes rolling away like marbles into the shadows.

For a second Ser Raniero had the sensation of something incorporeal whipping past him and escaping through the open doors into the night beyond.

"I've wasted time," he said. "We must proceed."

Ser Lucio, who had joined him once more beside the bier, was goggling in fascination at the little cat, who stared impudently up at him, then opened her mouth in a wide yawn, showing her pink tongue and a set of filed steel teeth. He opened his mouth to speak, then closed it again.

"Cat got your tongue?" Raniero asked.

"It . . . it's beautiful!" the young man stammered.

"*She's* beautiful," Raniero corrected him. *In the name of all the saints,* carissima, *don't speak now, or we'll be here all night.*

"I like cats," Ser Lucio said, squatting down and holding out a hand. "Will she come to me?"

The cat answered by turning her back on him and padding up to Raniero, tapping one forepaw imperiously on the ground.

"True, *carissima*," Raniero said. "It is time."

He slid the cover off his mirror-device and set it, the open side down, on top of the crystal dome. At once the elaborate scrolled border untwisted itself and became a set of tendrils that fastened onto the shining surface and began digging their way through. Raniero's heart beat faster as he watched, and he felt his palms begin to sweat.

Hairline cracks radiated from the device, spreading rapidly from the centre to the edges. The cracks grew wider, more crevices branching from them, until the whole of the dome seemed to be covered with the frost-flowers of winter. Seconds later it collapsed in a soft cascade, the shards of crystal mounding themselves in shining heaps around the bottom of the bier and on the body of the woman who lay there. Raniero caught the silver device as it fell, and laid it aside.

"Quickly now, *carissima*," he murmured, brushing away the shards of crystal that lay scattered over Rosalba.

The cat leaped up and crouched on Rosalba's breast, while Raniero sat on the edge of the bier and drew from his robe the vial with the mulberry-coloured liquid. He unstoppered it and, raising Rosalba's head, poured the contents between her parted lips.

For a moment that stretched out for Raniero like a century, nothing happened. Then he heard a stifled exclamation from Ser Lucio, and saw that the silver colouring of Rosalba's hands was fading, sucked back like a receding wave. White skin flushing pale rose appeared in its place, over her hands, her face, and her bosom at the opening of her gown.

"Now!" Ser Raniero whispered.

His cat stretched forward until her face almost touched Rosalba's. Raniero sensed again an incorporeal presence, bridging the gap between the woman and the cat. The cat collapsed, limp and lifeless, while the woman's breast began to rise and fall with deep, slow breaths. Rosalba, true Duchesa, opened sea-green eyes and looked around.

"I am here," she whispered.

Mingled laughter and tears pulsed in Raniero's throat, but he forced them back. He wanted only to look at Rosalba, and rejoice in her beauty, her intelligence, in all good things that together they had restored. He realised that he had been braced for failure, and hardly knew what to do with success.

But in the midst of his joy he was aware of coming desolation, like an animal crouching in the dark, ready to spring. *It is over . . .*

Rosalba reached out a hand to Ser Raniero, who took it and raised her. She swung her legs down from the bier and stood up, the cat sliding away to fall limply to the floor. As she took a step forward she stumbled, so that Raniero had to steady her with a touch on her elbow.

"I'm sorry," she said, smiling into his face. "It seems so strange to have only two paws—I mean, feet, and no tail."

She gazed around, exultation in the gaze that paused a moment, faintly puzzled at the sight of Ser Lucio, then returned to Raniero.

"I must see my sister," she said.

Vittoria's voice spoke from the darkness. "And so you shall."

Rosalba whirled, gasping, and Ser Lucio let out a cry of alarm as light blazed out, dazzling the three beside the bier. Enraptured by Rosalba's resurrection, they had all been deaf to the stealthy approach through the basilica.

When his vision cleared, Raniero saw that they were surrounded by a circle of guards. In one hand they held torches, fizzing with silver-blue light, in the other, drawn swords.

Vittoria stood on the far side of the circle, still masked, still resplendent in purple and gold. Her two brass lions flanked her, with burning eyes and claws. Though she was hard to read beneath the mask, Raniero sensed that she was struggling to beat down massive astonishment and, perhaps, fear.

"Ser Raniero," she said. "Did you really believe you could keep a secret from me? You are such a poor liar. I knew that the mirror you carried was more than it seemed. I confess I had no idea of its true purpose. My congratulations."

"You sent that scuttling thing after me," Raniero said, not troubling to hide his disgust. "Did you entrap the spirit of the poor devil you tortured to death? If so, he is free now."

Vittoria shrugged. "No matter. Its work was done. And now . . . "

At her gesture, the guards began to close in, forming a tighter circle around the bier. Ser Lucio stepped close to Rosalba's side, pulling a jewelled dagger from his belt, a futile gesture against so many swords.

"Kill them all," Vittoria said.

For a moment the guards hesitated, out of reluctance or bewilderment. The lions stirred, their shoulders flexing so that light dazzled from their arching wings. Raniero tensed, waiting. But in that moment's pause Rosalba stepped forward.

"Vittoria," she said softly. Reaching out, she unfastened the ribbons of her sister's mask, and cast it aside.

Raniero caught his breath as the two women confronted each other. He could not remember the last time he had seen Vittoria unmasked. In her face he could see the ruin of the beauty that lived fresh in Rosalba now. A beauty marred by twenty years of power and corruption, yet he could still discern there the passionate girl who had grasped too greedily at life and knowledge.

"Vittoria, do not do this," Rosalba said. "There is no reason why you and I should be enemies."

Something convulsed in Vittoria's face, and she let out a crack of laughter. "No reason? You do know what I did to you?"

"I know." Rosalba's voice was calm. "But if you will withdraw to the holy sisters of Corpus Domini . . . "

"A convent?" Vittoria's laughter rose more shrilly. "You would send me to a *convent*? Are you completely stupid to think that you have anything to bargain with?"

Rosalba turned her head, her gaze encompassing the ring of guards. "They are witnesses to this," she pointed out. "And they know who I am: their true Duchesa. If I die here, will you kill them all to be sure of their silence? And what will you say to Giulio Contarini when he asks what has become of his son?"

The guards shifted uneasily, glancing at each other. Raniero could see that Rosalba's words had reached them, even if her sister was impervious.

Vittoria paused, then with a savage gesture she spoke to the guards. "Get out. Wait for me in the Piazza."

Clearly the men were glad to go. They filed out through the doors, taking their torches with them, so that the basilica was left in the dim light of the candles, and a blood-red glimmer from the eyes of the brass lions. The smouldering light woke a glint of gold in the beads of Vittoria's discarded mask, and the jewelled key that hung from her girdle.

Lucio eased a pace away from Rosalba's side, but his dagger remained in his hand, the blade pointed at Vittoria.

"Now." There was a calculating look in Vittoria's face and Raniero wondered with renewed apprehension what plan she was hatching now. "Tell me, dear sister, setting my fate aside, what are your intentions?"

Rosalba too seemed aware of an unspoken meaning behind the question, but she answered it readily. "I will take up my duties. Raniero will become my Consort, and with God's blessing we shall have daughters."

"You *fool*!" Vittoria spat out the words. Her voice was laden with satisfaction as she added, "As Duchesa, you can never wed Raniero. He is sterile."

Rosalba's eyes widened in outrage. "I don't believe you!"

"Ask him."

Raniero took a pace back as Rosalba whirled to face him, her hands outstretched. "Raniero, tell me it isn't true!"

The crouching beast had pounced, and Raniero felt himself sliding into an echoing darkness. *I would have told her*, he thought, *but not now, not so soon . . .* "It's true we cannot wed," he responded, his voice rasping in his throat. "I am too old for you, too scarred, too twisted by many griefs . . . "

"Don't tell me that, Raniero!" Rosalba interrupted. She took his hands in hers, and her touch woke such deep anguish in Raniero that he thought he would cry out, yet he remained silent. "Do you think I don't know what you are? For twenty years I lived at your side. You held me, stroked me, whispered encouragement when I would have despaired . . . I loved you first when we studied together, I loved you when I was your cat, and I love you now. I will have no other."

"But Serenissima—"

"Don't call me that!" Rosalba stamped her foot. "I am Rosalba! Rosalba!" She stood close to him, her skin flushed, her lips red and trembling, unshed tears glittering in her eyes.

"My dear . . . under whatever name, my very dear . . . " His heart breaking, Raniero broke her clasp and took a step back. "You must have a Consort who can father children. And Vittoria is right: that man is not I. There is something about my art . . . whether it is the hours of toil or the airs of metal and fire in the workshop, or maybe because the winning of knowledge from the great unknown demands something in return. For whatever reason, I am sterile. Have you never wondered why your sister has never borne children? For twenty years she had her Consort, and countless lovers, and yet never a child? You must marry a man who can give you daughters."

As Rosalba gazed at him, Vittoria's harsh voice broke the silence. "So dramatic. And really there is no need. Renounce it all. Go with Raniero to another city; wed and be happy. I will send you money."

To his shame, a spark of hope woke inside Raniero, though he crushed it down immediately. *I cannot truly believe she will let us go. She can never be secure while Rosalba lives.* But there was a tiny consolation in seeing indecision in Rosalba's face.

"Rosalba," he said, "you have seen what the city has become under your sister's rule. For twenty years she has tried to destroy all love, all laughter, all delight, save for the perverted forms that please her. And she has no heir, so who is to rule here, if you do not? The Dukes of Padua, of Verona, or Milan or many more, will squabble over your city as dogs squabble over a bone."

After a long-drawn-out moment Rosalba nodded, and turned back to Vittoria. "No," she said.

While she waited, Vittoria's long white fingers had begun to toy with the golden key. Now she raised it to point it at Rosalba. A starburst of white light spat from the end of it.

Quicker than Raniero, Ser Lucio dragged Rosalba aside. A tiny dart whipped past her and struck harmlessly against the side of the bier.

Vittoria raised the key to strike again. But at the same moment the two lions, who had flanked her in silent stillness all this while, turned with ponderous grace to face her. Their eyes blazed and gouts of fire came from their jaws with a roar that rolled like thunder, echoing through the basilica.

Vittoria shrieked as her gown became a sheet of flame, enshrouding her. Her hair flashed fire, then crisped. She fell to the ground, her limbs writhing, blackening under that inexorable blast.

Raniero took a pace back; even though he had half-expected this, he was sickened and shaking. Ser Lucio had turned his face away. But Rosalba, her face white, her mouth set, went on watching until her sister's last anguished struggles faded and her rasping cries sank into silence. The lions let their fire die, and crouched at Rosalba's feet.

"Dear God . . . " Raniero whispered.

Lucio was gaping. "What happened?"

Gently Rosalba let her hands rest on the heads of the two lions, caressing their golden manes. "My thanks, dear friends," she said, looking down into the fierce faces. "You have kept faith for so long."

"Serenissima." One of the lions spoke, its voice creaking as if rusty from long disuse. "It has been our joy to serve you."

Ser Lucio turned swiftly to Raniero, sudden understanding in his eyes. "They are..?"

"Your uncle Francesco Contarini and his wife Bianca," Raniero responded. "I crafted the two lions, and Rosalba, in her cat form, visited them in prison. When they agreed to our plan, she took them poison for a more merciful death than Vittoria would have allowed them."

"I entrapped their spirits and bore them to the workshop," Rosalba said, her eyes brilliant with memory.

"And I gave the lions to Vittoria," Raniero finished. "They have guarded her for twenty years, until Rosalba could return. I did not expect it to take so long."

Rosalba stooped toward the lions, still stroking their curled golden fur. "Now go," she commanded, "and be free, or stay and serve me. It is your right to choose."

Neither of the creatures moved. "Serenissima, we are yours always," one of them said.

Rosalba bowed her head, then stepped away from them to face Ser Lucio. "I owe you thanks, too," she said.

Lucio bowed his head. "My life is yours, Serenissima."

"Then take him," Raniero said. "You need a young man, one who is worthy of you, and here is one who loves you."

Ser Lucio let out a gasp, but Rosalba paid no more attention to him than to the body of the cat, still lying beside the bier in a heap of silk, fur and feathers. Instead, she whirled on Raniero, her face filled with outrage.

"I cannot wed you, so you would throw me into the arms of the first man who presents himself? What do you think of me?"

"As a woman who will have every man in Venice scrambling to wed her," Raniero retorted dryly. "You would do well not to hesitate, before the daggers are drawn."

"And this is what it is to be Duchesa?" Rosalba asked bitterly.

"You know it is." Turning to Ser Lucio, Raniero went on, "Lucio, can you take her now, knowing what you know? It will be difficult."

Lucio faced Rosalba. For a moment Raniero was afraid that he would fall on his knees and kiss the hem of her gown, but he stood fast, his gaze full of grief and understanding. "I have loved you all my life," he said simply. "I will go on loving you until I die."

Rosalba hesitated for a long moment, then reached out and took his hand. "You may escort me to the Palazzo. We will speak of this further, but I promise nothing." Turning to Raniero, she added, her voice shaking for all her efforts to control it, "I wish I could hate you. But I cannot, and for that reason you must leave Venice tomorrow. I cannot be near you if we are not to wed. I am not my sister. There is no way that you and I can be together."

Without waiting for Raniero's reply, she turned away and led Lucio out of the basilica. The two lions rose and paced gravely after them.

Ah, carissima, *you are wrong,* Raniero thought, watching them go. *I always knew it would come to this.*

When he was sure that Rosalba and Lucio had left, Raniero pulled the white cover from the bier and draped it over the blackened remains of the woman who had called herself Duchesa. Then he gently gathered up the body of the cat and lowered himself to the floor, with his back against the bier and the cat on his breast.

He took from his inner pocket the second vial, the one where silver glinted in its walls of crystal.

"God's blessing on you, Rosalba," he murmured.

Then he unstoppered the vial and drank down the contents. The pain was swift and agonising, and he could not suppress a groan. But when the darkness rose to claim him he was able to embrace it like a friend, breathing out his last breath in silence.

Moments passed. The cat stirred, twitched up his ears and opened eyes that glinted emerald as he looked into the dead face of Raniero. A ripple passed through his body and the tip of his tail flicked to and fro.

Then the cat leaped to the ground, a tiny mote of gleaming silk and silver in the dark reaches of the basilica. He arched his back in a long stretch, flexed diamond claws, and gave a sudden leap as if for the pure joy of movement.

At last he whirled to face the door to the narthex, raced across the shadowed reaches of the floor towards it, and slipped out, following Rosalba, on the trail of love, always.

THE WRITING CEMBALO

GIO CLAIRVAL

LAKE COMO, 1822

The dead man at Alessandra Maroni's feet looked like a demigod. She pictured him as the half-human, half-divine Achilles, who had come to rest after a battle under the walls of Troy, waiting for a shepherdess to find him and take him into her arms. Except that Achilles could pretend the title of demigod because of his parentage. This dead hero, instead, resembled a half deity because two of his limbs were missing.

He had one very handsome leg—muscled and long-boned—that hinted at a stature beyond average. The other leg lay across a boulder five steps away, the mangled upper thigh mercifully turned toward the lake that shivered and shone ten yards below.

Resting on his belly, full head of hazel hair in disarray, the man displayed one sole arm that ended in an aristocratic hand, palm up as to collect the thin rain that sizzled on the fragments of copper and steel scattered all about. His body had been blasted free of its clothes. A few black swaths of fabric, caught in the leafless bushes, waved in the wind like crow wings.

"Madame Venturin?" Alessandra called.

She glanced up and down the path that led from her mansion on the lakeside toward the village on the hills, where the brand-new Skyroad Station had risen before the explosion. The mule path, squeezed between mountain and water, appeared to be deserted, apart from her French governess, panting as she hurried to cover the distance between them. Farther up the path, the upper half of another corpse wore a tattered Austrian uniform jacket. Alessandra frowned at the colours of Emperor Francis.

A sudden gale shook the rare olive trees. She pulled her pelisse around her. In the dimming light, burning red pieces of the blasted dirigible studded the mountainside.

Alessandra, after leaving home for the opening party,had rushed ahead of her governess, and was five hundred yards away from the zeppelin station when the explosion occurred. A rock had shielded her, but the ringing in her ears was only starting to decrease now. Silence had fallen on the lake after the tremendous noise and the distant cries that had followed the blast. Now night birds began to chirp questions.

As soon as she reached Alessandra, Madame Félicie Venturin cried, "Oh, Seigneur mon Dieu!" The governess straightened skirts that didn't need straightening. "Poor souls. There's nothing we can do, ma chérie. Let's go home."

Alessandra pointed a finger to the body.

"Who's that?" Félicie asked.

"A dead man missing a leg."

"I can see he's one leg short, not to mention one less arm, but why do you find this corpse so interesting when there will be a choice of cadavers if we walk up to the station? Which we won't." Félicie dabbed the corners of her eyes with a large handkerchief and studied the black soot marring the fine cloth.

Alessandra shed no tears. If one listened to the doctors she helped at the hospital, she had the temperament of a stretcher-bearer in the battlefield. She should tell the governess that the dead man made her think of Achilles, but the Frenchwoman lacked imagination.

"Phaethon," Félicie said.

"What?"

"He's Phaethon, son of Apollo, struck down by Zeus's bolt. The hot bits of metal surrounding his body are the remains of his immortal father's chariot."

"Félicie Venturin, you will never cease to surprise me."

With our middle-aged Frenchwoman, appearances were deceitful. Under a vaguely military broad-collar redingote, she wore a grey high-waist dress with a chemisette filling the bare neckline for modesty, when in fact the governess professed libertinage as an art. Nevertheless, she had thrown her hands up when Alessandra insisted on wearing *trousers* at the Skyroad Station inauguration ceremony. "Why don't you stick faux moustaches to your upper lip while you're at it?" she said. "You'll look like a dweller of the island of Lesbos."

"Félicie, you are the most conservative woman on Lake Como, possibly in the entire Kingdom of Lombardy-Venetia." This oft-repeated statement was far from true, but Félicie never failed to fire back: "That's why your mother, that saintly woman, asked me on her deathbed to look after you."

Alessandra huffed. Her trousers seemed a sensible choice now.

She couldn't pull her gaze away from the corpse. "He's magnificent, don't you agree? And so helpless. Well, so dead."

Félicie nudged the body with the toe of her ankle boot. "Oh, I see why this one fascinates you. Your dead gentleman has a lovely derrière." That was all Félicie, trying to divert her protégée's attention from the macabre scene. As if Alessandra, at five-and-twenty, wasn't able to control herself.

A fat raindrop hissed on an incandescent piece of copper. Félicie sighed. "We can do nothing for a corpse. Come away."

"Wait! There must be injured people needing immediate assistance."

"The entire village is already there."

The governess started down the path toward Villa Adele, the Maronis' mansion. Alessandra grabbed her by the arm. "We can't leave him here."

"We can and we will. Do you want me to carry him? Who do you think I am, Hercules?"

Alessandra considered the governess: if Félicie had been a piece of furniture, she would have been a floor-to-ceiling wardrobe. "Come on, Hercules." She grabbed the cadaver's unique bare foot. "Half of him is missing, so you'll be hauling a quarter of his weight only."

"We could chop his head off, too. The head is the heaviest part of the body. Then it'd be easy to drag him all the way down and bury him in the park."

The corpse chose that moment to say: "Sabotage."

"*Il est vivant,*" cried Félicie.

Alessandra jumped, although, as usual in tough circumstances, her mind cleared at once and calm settled upon her.

"Help me," she ordered, sliding her hands under the man's armpits (the missing left limb had been severed midway between shoulder and elbow). Together they flipped the not-so-dead gentleman face up.

Alessandra's heart gave an extra beat. *Bruno Castelli!*

Meanwhile, the governess was busy covering the maimed body with her redingote. "Poor thing, to have his right limbs severed!" she commented, as if Alessandra hadn't noticed by herself. "And I know his face."

"He's the engineer who built the prototype zeppelin."

"*Oui,*" Félicie said. "His mother is some Austrian royalty."

"Countess von Mansfeld," Alessandra said, "but his father is Italian."

As Alessandra bent to lift the *signor ingegnere*, she recalled him, last Saturday, tall and seductive in a waistcoat that enhanced his elegant build, as he spun her around in the ballroom, bowing at the end of the waltz, begging for the privilege of visiting her parlour next week, before being whisked away by the blonde wife of the universally hated Chief of the Austrian Police in Milan.

She squeezed Bruno's shoulder lightly. "Don't worry, Signor Castelli. You'll be fine."

He smiled and slipped back into unconsciousness.

"Alex! Are you all right?" Her brother's shouting jolted Alessandra out of her reverie. Fabio, along with most of the mansion's male servants, was running up the hill, his unbuttoned hunter-green overcoat flapping behind him. Five years younger than Alessandra, he wore his curly golden hair short. Colonel Maroni, their only parent left after Mother's death while giving birth to Fabio, did not hide his hope to see Italy become a unified and independent state soon, and Fabio supported Father in every possible way. Luckily, the police did not take the younger Maroni's revolutionary sympathies seriously, as the youth was in the habit of piling up debts and bisexual love affairs like that George Gordon, Lord Byron. Alessandra loved Fabio very much.

"Take his arms," she said. "I mean, his arm."

Fabio leaned to whisper in her ear, "We cannot have this man in our house."

"He's injured."

"He's a spy."

Alessandra's nerves fluttered.

"A spy?"

"I can't believe it," Félicie cried. "Such a charming man. Are you sure?"

"We are certain."

Alessandra stomped her foot. "Fabio Maroni, a wounded man is a wounded man, and our family has always chosen honour over safety. Now lend a hand, as honour demands."

Fabio, his Adam's apple moving up and down, crouched to do as he was told. Meanwhile, the pillowy Félicie displayed a surprising agility by sprinting down the path. She soon disappeared inside the mansion.

Colonel Maroni, lean and greying, met our small committee at the door, an anxious Félicie hovering about, a handkerchief as vast as a foulard pressed to her mouth. On her order, the impassive Maggiordomo had gone to fetch the family doctor.

The three Maronis retired into the library on the ground floor.

There, sitting in an armchair upholstered with a delicate Chinoiserie, a petit-point embroidery of swallows and apple-tree flowers, an additional personage was to be found: a purveyor of mechanical toys, but also of the weapons and explosives necessary to the cause of independence. The Dutch gentleman, Jozef Van der Payn by name, had fine features, straw-yellow hair elegantly grizzled at the temples, and an agreeable embonpoint straining the buttons on his red-brocaded vest. Upon seeing the Maronis (through his sole eye—a black patch concealed the other), Meester Van der Payn rose.

"It seems I missed all the entertainment," he said lightly.

"Please, Meester, people died."

"I beg your forgiveness, Signorina, although I think the death toll will be minimal. The police were to keep the crowd away and the explosion occurred before the doors were scheduled to open for the guests."

The Dutchman scratched his neck under the high collar." Posterity will side with the winners, and I can't imagine the Austrians keeping the north of Italy for long. But maybe it wasn't a political act. Perhaps the bomb bore the signature of the partisans of the railway instead of the insurgents."

"Or both," Fabio muttered loud enough to be heard.

Jozef glanced sideways at Fabio and turned to the older Maroni. "Do you believe in the future of zeppelins, Colonel?"

Judging by the sudden colour on Maroni's cheeks, the question had taken him by surprise. To Alessandra's knowledge, the Dutchman had always been discreet, never mentioning the obvious use of pyroglycerine, the experimental stuff he smuggled out of a laboratory in Turin especially for the colonel (who, not being on active service, wasn't supposed to procure and stock explosives).

"Yes and no," was the curt response. Colonel Maroni's slight frame appeared to fill the room, an effect created by his booming voice.

Fabio shuffled his feet. "And what about yourself, Meester? Do you think zeppelins are the best means of transportations we could dream of?"

Father knitted his eyebrows and joined thumb and forefinger several time in rapid succession—the Family's secret sign for *be careful*.

A just precaution. The door to the guest room, across the entrance hall, was open, and Castelli might have come to. Unless Father meant they should be careful around the Dutchman. Fabio gestured the footman who was serving vermouth to leave and pull the door behind him.

Anyone could be a spy today, but if Alessandra had to lay the blame at someone's feet, she would have chosen Jozef Van der Payn's Hessian boots instead of Bruno Castelli's buckled evening pumps—those were the shoes he'd been wearing at the ball.

No. Bruno could not be a spy. It must be a rumour circulated by some jealous man, maybe the Chief of the Police himself. Perhaps the strapping Castelli was indeed the blonde signora's lover, and the cuckolded Chief planned on sending him to the infernal Spielberg Fortress in Moravia, where so many patriots suffered. And here he was, poor Bruno, maimed and unfairly suspected of spying. Alessandra twisted the delicate linen handkerchief in her hands.

"I'm not interested in flying machines full of gas," said Van der Payn. "Besides today's explosion, something tells me they are dangerous."

Fabio rose to the bait. "They're not as much dangerous as they are Germanic."

Her impetuous brother had missed one more opportunity to keep his mouth shut.

Van der Payn picked up the horsewhip that had been resting across his thighs and tapped the heel of his boot. "Colonel, I wonder whether the cause of modern transportation would be better served by Tom Hepherson's locomotive."

"I've had the opportunity to see a locomotive at close range at the Stockton and Darlington Railway Line in England, and the machine greatly impressed me."

"The train is the future, Meester," Fabio cut in. "If only we could fund the railway instead of these zeppelins. I mean, an industrial line running from the steel factories on Lake Como to Milano. Imagine the—" Fabio never finished his sentence: the footman had pushed the door open for Dr Ruffa. Everyone rose.

Dr Ruffa set his black bag on an ebony table. "He'll live. What is left of him. Both leg and arm were severed very neatly, likely by sheets of hot steel, and cauterised in the process."

"Poor man," said Alessandra.

"He's rich enough to buy the best prostheses," said Félicie Venturin, entering. She'd apparently been standing behind the door.

Dr Ruffa sniffed. "He surely would need prostheses, but he refuses to let me put him on the list—"

"Why?" Fabio voiced everyone's surprise. How could a crippled man reject the latest products of Swiss precision?

"I don't understand either," said Ruffa.

"Can he be transported?" the colonel asked abruptly. "Shouldn't that man be cared for in hospital?"

Alessandra pulled her shoulders back. Discussions with her father had taught her to keep herself straight as a rod, in a way that made her tiny and slender frame seem a few inches taller. "Papa, the journey would be overwhelming for a man in his condition." She hushed her brother by the sheer strength of her gaze. "What do you think, Doctor?"

Ruffa cast a quick glance at Colonel Maroni. "Yes. Better let him rest here. I'll see him tomorrow."

Everyone followed the doctor as he stepped back into the entrance hall.

"It's settled then." Alessandra took a pile of towels from a passing handmaid. "I'll do it, Lucinda. I can take care of our guest myself."

Colonel Maroni bristled. "Wait, Sandra. Is that proper—?"

"Papa, I've been visiting the hospital for the last two years. The doctors let me help him around." She pictured Bruno in a wheelchair, his bright green eyes dulled by resignation. She would not let it happen. She knew what to do around mutilated persons." Are you saying I'd faint or something?"

"Of course not, but—"

Madame Venturin set a gloved hand to Colonel Maroni's forearm. "Monsieur, aren't you happy that your daughter is finally showing some interest in the male variety, even if the specimen is missing a limb or two? A glance at the man informed me on the presence of all his attributes."

Colonel Maroni blushed up to the roots of his greying curls. "Madame—"

Félicie pursued the attack. "You surely don't want our *demoiselle* to keep dressing in . . . britches? Next thing, she will want to be called 'George'. Come, now. I'll serve you a cup of hot chocolate in the yellow room upstairs. Nice and thick, as you like it."

"Fél—Madame, wait—" The rest of Father's words were lost up the stairwell. Everyone knew Colonel Maroni was on the brink of proposing to the spirited Frenchwoman.

Alessandra wondered if Castelli's well-known wealth impressed the governess more than his intact attributes. Wouldn't hurt to check those out, though. For Science's sake.

She pushed the door to the guest room open and stopped.

Bruno Castelli stared at her, emerald eyes full of wonder, as if she were some celestial apparition. The expression softened his sharply cut features.

Her heart pitter-pattered. Her legs went weak at the knees, but she had to pursue her mission with courage. For a few seconds, she couldn't remember what her mission was. Ah, yes. To wash her patient. She took a deep breath. Showing embarrassment was out of the question. She dumped the towels on the bed and grabbed a glass. "Would you like some water?"

She filled the glass while desperately trying to come up with a subject of conversation. *Any* subject.

"Signore, do you know this is the highest latitude where the olive tree grows? A few kilometres to the south you won't find any. You would have to journey all the way down to Liguria."

"It's the temperate climate of the lake." He sounded distracted.

"Yes, but it's chilly in winter." She fluffed out a pillow and then the other, and repeated the operation." Oh, I know most Austrians believe elephants scratch their hides against the palm trees of Piazza del Duomo in Milano."

"Signorina, perhaps most Austrians think that by adding an 'A' or an 'O' to any word they can speak Italian, but I was born in Milano and I consider myself as Italian as my name. I know Northern Italy is not the north of Africa."

"Our Germanic friends think it is the south of Austria."

He clutched the sheet. "Are you testing my pro-Italy sentiment?"

On impulse, she sat down on the bed. "Can I ask you something?"

"Anything," he said in a guarded tone.

"Why are you refusing prostheses?"

He blanched.

"I refuse prostheses because I would be half-man, half-machine."

"But your mechanical limbs wouldn't have a mind of their own; they would obey *you*."

He spoke very quickly. "Fact is the surgeon *intimately* joins the artificial limb to the long filaments on one side of the nervines. Oh, I shan't mention the fact that a few neurologists deny the existence of the neural cells that supposedly command movements. Nobody knows how these nervines work exactly, or how the electric impulses travel down the filaments, for that matter. My point is this kind of surgery is both an indignity and an act of faith."

Wondering if Bruno was ever going to breathe (logorrhoea from some painkilling narcotic, surely), she held her tongue.

"Apparently," he continued, "nervines have an affinity with copper coated with thungserius. Through their filaments, these neural cells colonise the layer of the metal, which acts like an amplifier, transmitting the electrical impulse to the mechanism that replaces the muscle, and the prosthesis moves."

Now Alessandra allowed herself a short huffing sound. "I attended a lecture at the hospital."

"I stand chastised, signorina. Of course you are familiar with the concept."

"Allow me to insist, signore. You decide you want to move your arm, and the arm obeys. It's all. You would be almost . . . normal again.' Oh, God. She didn't mean to sound so insensitive."

"You don't understand!"

The violence of his tone startled her.

"It's a . . . contamination," he cried." Man and machine. Joined."

"Bruno, you must think that mind and matter are unconnected, as in Descartes' philosophy." *Oh, my goodness.* She'd called him by his first name.

He recited: "'I am a substance the whole nature or essence of which is to think, and which for its existence does not need any place nor depend on any material thing.'"

"Descartes permitting," she said,"I wouldn't be so sure that mind and matter are separate. Take the nervine cells—"

"Never!" His hand swiped the night stand, knocking over the glass. He stared at the water dripping on the carpet. "I am sorry. I did not mean . . . "

"I understand, Bru—signore. You are already maimed, and being part machine would make you feel even less whole."

Bruno blinked twice. "Precisely."

Alessandra's hand flew to her mouth. "I did it again, didn't I? I was being callous . . . "

"You were merely trying to state a hypothesis." He extended his hand, touched hers, and pulled away just as quickly.

The brief contact made Alessandra's heart jump in her chest. She struggled to keep her voice level. "Signore . . . "

"Signorina, I've been wanting to ask . . . Would you do me the honour . . . " He paused.

Was he going to . . . ? It must be the narcotic speaking. Her head swam. Why was her heart racing? She'd always hated the idea of getting entangled in a marriage. She had always believed she would marry Science only. She even bought faux spectacles to discourage suitors, and she routinely defined herself as a Bluestocking to fend off those who liked bespectacled women.

She waited for him to continue, his big green eyes filling her field of vision.

"Did I tell you about the memoirs I wanted to write? I intend to purchase an automaton to do the writing in my stead, under dictation. I hear the Swiss have made wonderful progress." His eyes shone. "I shall need assistance. Would you do me the honour of helping me in this endeavour?"

Alessandra inhaled. "Of course."

He closed his eyes, apparently thinking no more words were needed, for which she was grateful.

Jozef Van der Payn paused in the destruction of the *arrosto con patate*. He bared his small teeth in a smile, a civilised form of menace addressed to the new man in the house, Bruno Castelli, who sat à la place d'honneur, at the colonel's right hand. "What project keeps your mind occupied presently, signore? What will the next mind-shattering invention be?"

"I›ll be writing my memoirs, along with scientific observations."

Alessandra blurted, "Our guest is interested in acquiring a mechanical device that prints words under dictation. I've heard about a Swiss machine—"

Bruno put down his fork.

Jozef rubbed the bridge of his narrow nose with two fingers. "I know a watchmaker in Geneva who has fabricated an automaton called 'the Writing Cembalo'."

"Quaint," Félicie said.

Fabio sniggered. "A cembalo?"

"A musical instrument?" the elder Maroni marvelled. "Like a harpsichord?"

Alessandra leaned forward. "But, as the word indicates, a clavicembalo has keys, a keyboard. How—"

"No keys. No keyboard. The name is a poetical licence. A Swiss joke, you know."

The dining companions chortled. Switzerland's border being thirty kilometres away, everyone knew most of the Swiss, like the natives of Lombardy, were hopelessly down-to-earth and seldom facetious. One had to push east, to Venice, to find jolly people and mandolins.

Jozef twisted his portly upper body to scrutinise Bruno with his sole eye, bright blue and glinting. "Should I procure one, signore?"

"I love your bread machine," said Félicie, who hadn't spoken much so far, being busy guzzling Barolo. "Although those copper arms . . . kneading dough are a little unsettling. Now, dear Jozef, that writing device must be a real marvel."

"It is, Madame, and its value is such the automaton is not for sale. I can only hire it to the Signor Castelli."

Alessandra had rarely seen a smile smoothing Bruno's billhook-sculpted features.

"For sale or rent, it doesn't matter," he said, his smile broadening. "Please, Meester, by all means, do procure the Writing Cembalo. I'm always eager to see a new machine."

"So are we," the colonel said. Father had stopped being suspicious of 'the Austrian spy', since Bruno had no contacts with the exterior in a month, and the two of them spent hours discussing the respective advantages of the railway and the skyroad. "The Maronis are a family of engineers."

"Except me," Fabio said. "I hate machines."

Jozef patted his mouth with an ivory-coloured napkin. "Oh, really? I didn't know."

Alessandra was sure the napkin had been hiding a sneer. Her stomach somersaulted. The Dutchman knew something about her brother. Something—she suspected—she would not like.

Three weeks passed in a blur, as she endeavoured to instil optimism and hope in her patient's melancholy spirit. (He *will* change his heart, she thought, and he will accept prosthetic limbs—for . . . love, if not for scientific reasons).

One sunny morning, the noise of a carriage pulled her to the window of her parlour on the first floor. Jozef Van der Payn's sturdy black berline, drawn by four black horses, stopped before the entrance. The Dutchman alighted from the cabin and made a great show of smoothing his midnight-blue coat. Two dust-covered footmen, who had been riding on the open hooded seat behind the cabin,leapt down and busied themselves unfastening and taking down a large crate secured on top of the carriage. The valets carried it inside.

Family and guest gathered in the library. Fabio declared he wasn't interested in another of the Dutchman's circus automata, and sulked in his quarters.

Alessandra kept her gaze on Bruno, but his lovely green eyes were riveted on the crate, which stood taller than she.

Jozef relinquished his coat to one of the lackeys, rolled up his lace-cuffed shirtsleeves and inserted a chisel under the nailed lid to pry it open. The valets, like in a practiced choreography, moved forward to receive the lid in their hands as soon as it came loose. Alessandra couldn't see the contents because Van der Payn had ordered the crate to be placed with the opening facing the other side.

Jozef leaned forward. A slim arm emerged from inside the crate, and he took the hand. The automaton rose of its own accord. "Ahhh!"sighed the house personnel, who had tiptoed into the library.

In the middle of the room stood a very tall creature with strikingly fine features, in an empire-line dress of pristine white, with small neat puff sleeves and no modesty filler to conceal the square-cut décolleté. The automaton's fair hair was tied up in classic Greek style. Everything *très à la mode*.

"It's a woman!" Father and Bruno cried, while, at the same time, Félicie said, "It's a doll."

"It's a machine," Jozef said. "The best Writing Cembalo I could find."

Bruno stood frozen to the spot. Alessandra had seen the same expression on his face when he had first beheld her upon regaining consciousness after the explosion.

Félicie stepped up to the contraption and pinched its bare upper arm. The automaton didn't react. The governess, owl-eyed, murmured, "It's soft and warm, like—"

"—living tissue, yes." The Dutchman nodded. "A perfect imitation of life. Her name is Daniela." He extended a hand toward Bruno. "Daniela, the signor Bruno Castelli here will be your master until his work is finished."

The automaton moved her head with a slightly mechanical stiffness. "Good morning, signore. I am happy to serve." Daniela's voice, low-pitched, sounded older than its apparent age of six-and-ten or so.

Bruno stared. "Thank you, Meester. She looks *perfect*."

She? Alessandra wondered. She had always despised possessiveness as one of the basest sentiments, one that found its origin in the animals' territorial instinct. A rational woman, she considered such agitation of the human psyche unbecoming. Jealousy was beneath her, yet she couldn't control a pang of bitterness at the idea of Bruno revealing his innermost thoughts to that feminine-looking device.

As days and weeks passed, Bruno's fascination with the automaton grew to worrying heights. He shut himself up in the library, alone with the Cembalo, every afternoon.

When she stood outside the closed door, despising herself for her petty eavesdropping, Alessandra heard him dictate descriptions of India's picturesque landscapes and the colourful people he'd encountered there. He interspersed his narration with long lists of components he'd used to build his contrivances. He added testing protocols and recounted his achievements, his failures. The inventor's passion gave his voice intonations she never heard when he talked with her.

As soon as the master stopped his flow of reminiscences, saying, "Go," the machine spouted back words at inhuman speed. Where the syntax had been altered by the shortcuts of spoken speech, the Cembalo created harmony. When a generic vocable bled the sentence of its vigour, the automaton spilled the perfect term. If Bruno hesitated and failed to express his full thoughts, garlands of complete sentences wreathed the air. Alessandra expected a snake made of letters to slink,writhing and worming, through the crack between the door and the Venetian tiles, to creep at her feet.

Bruno told her that, at the end of a working session, after the editing phase, the machine spurted out printed pages neatly folded in four.

Every evening, he would quit the library, a bag overflowing with paper slung across his back, and, leaning on his crutches, he would hop across the entrance hall to his bedroom. Sometimes, Alexandra watched him through the door left ajar. His hand worked quickly to smooth the folded papers out against his thigh, after which he stacked the pages up on his night stand. Then the nocturnal revisions began. Quill in his left hand, he filled the margins of every sheet of paper with symbols the Writing Cembalo would recognise. An archipelago of ink dots stained the bedclothes.

In the morning, she often found him asleep under a blanket of paper leaves. Her help was never needed: Bruno declared himself perfectly happy with the Cembalo's work.

Alessandra, waking up in the dead of night after spells of slumber, could hear Bruno's crutches tapping on the tiles downstairs. His muffled voice reached her as he prepared the following day's dictation. The friendship that had been blossoming between them seemed to have waned. His mind and heart dwelled with the automaton.

This madness had to stop.

Such a complex machine, she reasoned, must be easy to disable.

The day she was supposed to accompany Bruno to the public library for his research, she asked Father to replace her, under the pretext of a terrible migraine. The colonel surveyed her attentively, as his daughter had never suffered from headaches, but he went.

Fabio was out on horseback. She waited for Félicie to leave the house with her handmaid, heading for the market. The crunching of the pebbles under the two women's feet had just faded when Alessandra pushed open the door to the library.

The scene under her eyes made her recoil in surprise. Van der Payn's bulk leaned over the automaton, which sat on the table, holding up its cotton shift to bare its chest. A metallic lid was visible on the Cembalo's stomach. Under it, she saw the slot whence the prints came.

"What are you doing?" Alessandra asked as soon as she regained the use of her tongue. She hadn't known the smuggler had been visiting.

Jozef swivelled; his azure eye widened, but after a second, he recovered his composure. He set a chisel to the automaton's stomach and popped the lid open. "Paper jam," he explained.

"Jam? Of paper?"

"I mean that a sheet of paper is stuck in here. I thought "jam" would describe the problem well enough." He extracted his fob watch and put it away. "Castelli sent a servant to query me. The Dutchman had taken a room at the only hotel in the village, for the duration of the hire.

"Nice of you to come on such short notice, Meester."

Interested despite herself, she approached to see what the man was doing.

He dug one hand into the Cembalo's bowels. "Drafted thing! I can't get it—Can you please pass me those pincers?"

Alessandra complied.

He manoeuvred the pincers, deftly, gently. "Got it. Now I'm going to pull it out very, very slowly . . . There!" He extracted a scrap of paper from Daniela's inside.

Alessandra drew closer. The sight gave her pause. "Is . . . that . . . flesh . . . around the mechanism? Real flesh?"

"Yes, that's why she understands human speech."

"So it's half human?"

He waved the scrap of paper about. "In a way." He proceeded to close the lid, which slipped into place with an audible *click*." I will now take my leave, with your permission, signorina."

"Has the Signor Castelli ever seen it . . . *her* with the lid open?"

"I don't think so. Daniela never malfunctioned before." He scrutinised Alessandra. "Are you getting enough sleep, signorina?"

"Not much, Meester." She felt herself blush.

Alone in the library, after seeing Van der Payn out, she unsheathed the little knife strapped to the garter on her left thigh—the weapon of the Giardiniere, female conspirators against the Austrians—and ordered the woman-machine to hike her chemisette up. Even with the lid visible on her stomach, the automaton still looked human enough to remind her of one of the dead patients the doctors autopsied at the hospital, except that this one gazed at her hands as she inserted the knife in a notch.

"Daniela, are you . . . ? Are you . . . ali . . . ?"

"Paper."

"What?"

"Some paper is still stuck."

"Oh." Alessandra flipped the lid open and inserted her hand in the aperture. All her scientific interest couldn't prevent her from wanting to gag, although her repulsion couldn't keep curiosity at bay. She groped for the paper. "Got it."

"Funny."

"What?"

"A woman's touch. It's different."

Two sheets of paper came out, each folded in four. Alessandra slipped them into her apron front pocket and left the library.

In her bedroom, she read the papers. Her heart thumped so fiercely she had to recline. She untied her dress without calling the chambermaid and lay in the darkening room. Sleep eluded her. She finally struck the flint and lit a taper.

The first paper related a conversation between Father and Fabio, about the Carbonari's insurrection that should soon inflame the Lombardy-Venetia, the blasting of all the zeppelin hangars in the Como Province, and the detailed plans of the first Italian locomotive.

The second paper recounted the construction of the automaton called Daniela.

At the break of dawn, Alessandra tiptoed into Félicie's bedroom and put a letter on her night stand, after which she went downstairs to knock on Bruno's door.

"May I come in?"

Without waiting for an answer, she pushed the door, a candle in hand. Bruno jerked awake. Seeing her, he nearly choked.

She spoke in a firm voice. "She grew up in Biertan, a Saxon village in Transylvania. Her mother was a mail woman and her father used to work in a mine until he was fired."

"Who?"

"Her father sold her to a gentleman who took her to Geneva, promising he was going to marry her, but the man sold her to the watchmaker instead."

"What are you talking about?"

"The watchmaker forced her to drink litres of a beverage containing thungserius and, after rendering her unconscious, inserted various mechanisms in her body."

"That's . . . "

"There are no words for it." Her voice sounded like ice in her ears. The *signor ingegnere* professed to feel horror for flesh contaminated with mechanical parts, but he'd been using this poor slave . . . He couldn't know, she reasoned. Nonsense. An engineer should have suspected.

Alessandra lowered her head as to charge the enemy. "She was on the brink of death for weeks, suffering horribly. And now you are using her to write your memoirs."

"Where does this tale come from?"

Alessandra held out a sheet of paper. Bruno read it in a silence punctuated by exclamations.

"It's in Daniela's print, all right."

"She printed her story for me to find." Yes, Alessandra thought, Daniela had waited for Jozef to leave, and she seized the occasion to make her predicament known—to a woman. She didn't trust Bruno enough to reveal her story to him.

"I can't believe it."

"Bruno, I've seen how she's . . . made inside. Of metal and flesh."

Words spilled out like waves of accusations. Bruno's eyes filled with anguish. "I didn't realise . . . "

"Why are you doing this? Are you working for the Austrians?" She pulled out the second paper. "You've been eavesdropping and dictating information to poor Daniela—"

"I would never do such a thing! Do you believe your father and Fabio would talk about insurrection when I'm within earshot? I don't blame them. Mother's origins make me the perfect suspect. But I'll tell you something: your father likes me all the same. I know he does. We've been working together. Show him the drawing; he'll recognise the prototype locomotive we—"

"You must have instructed Daniela to eavesdrop and print what she hears, and you retrieve those reports every day, along with your notes. An accomplice, a servant, surely, brings them to the police."

"You have me wrong . . . " His voice faltered.

Alessandra felt through the light fabric of her skirt the small knife she kept in her garter. "Prove it. Prove you're not a spy."

"I love my country!" he cried. "Why would you believe anything I say?"

She wanted to believe him. She was tempted to trust those big eyes expressing the innocence of a man who knew little about the human soul, despite having travelled the world; that adorable slightly unfocused gaze, turned inwardly, with the occasional sparkle betraying faith in the only certainty possible: strings of causes and effects, a vision of the world like a perfect mechanism that only needed a little rust inhibitor and oil coating to function smoothly. Moreover, Bruno's disinterest in politics was, she reckoned, genuine, and he was too intelligent to let himself be used by the police. She had never seen in him the anguish of a man victim to blackmail and, as it was, she didn't think he could be bothered with reporting to the police—

She felt her resolve slacken.

"I would not lie to you," he whispered in her ear.

"Bruno, I . . . " She let herself sink onto on his bed. Drifting.

His lips brushed softly against her neck and, not content with tasting the soft skin behind the ear, moved along a winding lane to one eyelid and then the other, both receiving salves of quick, small kisses, and then the exploring lips ventured across the cheekbone. If the journey to the corner of her mouth had burned a hot trail, the hesitation on the hill of her lower lip brought a brief coolness. Still, when his tongue, a stubborn scout, gently forced a passage between the double white gates and reached its twin, heat radiated everywhere, including uncharted territories. From now on, Alessandra stopped trying to memorise every sensation (even in the interest of Science!) and lost all ability of coherent thought.

"Mission accomplie!"

The exclamation, proffered by a deep contralto, caused Alessandra to jump upright. "Madame!" she began.

By candlelight, Bruno's face took on an interesting shade of coral.

Alessandra smoothed her dress while her trembling calmed. "Is it time already?" To Bruno, she explained, "I sent Madame Venturin to call everyone to the library at 6 o'clock." She helped him rise from the bed, passed him the crutches, and together they followed the governess.

In the library, Alessandra stood in the centre of the room, facing the small assembly. "Father, I apologise for disturbing you at this early hour."

"Speak, Sandra. What must be done must be done."

"The hour is sad when we come to distrust one another," said Félicie.

Josef lowered his head. "You were saying adieu with that kiss, then?" He slapped his own mouth.

"A kiss?" cried Colonel Maroni.

"I am sure it was metaphorical," said Alessandra. Félicie's liberties with the portly Jozef came as no surprise, and the Dutchman had probably spoken up on purpose, just for the pleasure of sowing trouble.

"I did not kiss him!" Félicie protested. *"He* kissed *me* as I was trying to test his political convictions."

"Madame!" The Colonel's face was a study in indignation.

"Dear, someone had to immolate herself on the altar of truth."

Alessandra raised her voice. "Shall we go back to the truth now? There's a spy among us."

The Meester, eyes narrowed, glanced at the elder Maroni.

Father straightened. "Well, something I know for sure is that it is not I."

"Of course not, Father," said Alessandra. "You were jailed; your fortune was seized."

"And restored," said Jozef.

"It happened to scores of patriots," said Alessandra. "The Austrians end up restoring the seized fortunes because they cannot rule Lombardy against the Lombard aristocracy. Not for long. And the first deal a spy gets is *immunity*, whereas your whereabouts are under constant surveillance, Papa, and your passport has been revoked." Alessandra smiled at him. "But I would believe you anyway."

Fabio, who'd kept his tongue so far, rolled his eyes heavenward. "This is ridiculous. Are we going to dole out suspicion and trust according to filial or romantic love?"

"Why not?" Félicie said.

Fabio cast a defiant glance at Jozef then looked sideways at Félicie. "And who will rule *you* out, Madame?"

"Daniela rules her out," Alessandra said. "When I retrieved a jammed paper from her ... stomach, she said that a woman's touch was different, and she sounded genuinely surprised. I believe that, before me, no woman had ever retrieved a paper from her ... er ... printing inside."

"It's just an assumption," said Jozef.

"Yes, but a very plausible one," Alessandra retorted. "And it is not I, for, besides being a woman, and because I am one, I'm not told everything, and the police gets the information anyway."

Fabio turned to Jozef. "It's you, then."

"Not so," said Félicie. "I know because, on Alessandra's instruction, I put the question to the Cembalo."

"And what was the Cembalo's answer?" asked Father. "Who is it then?"

Before Félicie could reply, Bruno Castelli spoke. "I, too, have been retrieving printed paper from Daniela, every night."

Everyone turned to face him.

"I know it's not you," said Alessandra.

"You do?" said Fabio. "So you know what the Cembalo said to Madame Venturin?"

"Madame hasn't told me yet. But I know the Signor Castelli is not a spy."

"Why?" the old and the young Maroni asked in unison.

"Because I love him."

"I've never heard more stupid a line of defence," said Fabio.

"Stupid, maybe, but winning," said Félicie.

The silence draping the small assembly could have been cut with a sabre.

Fabio, very pale, rose, bowed stiffly from the waist to Father, but avoided Alessandra's eyes and left without a word, his gait that of a much older man. Then Van der Payn took leave, too, his sole eye glinting with mischief. Madame Venturin piloted a stunned colonel to the door. At the threshold, the latter said; "My own son, a spy . . . I often wondered." And he let himself be led away.

"I never suspected," said Alessandra. Her heart ached.

Bruno put his arm around her shoulders. Together they made their way to the window. Outside, a zeppelin floated in the whitening sky, a single strand of lights shining like opals across the hull. It reminded her of Phaethon and his father's chariot of the sun, but this silvery vessel carried the cold moon to the other side of the world; it would never burst into flames.

The strong arm that rested on her shoulders slid down to encircle her waist. "Alessandra, I cannot bear to hold you with just one arm any longer."

His hand cupped hers, full of promises. He would be whole again. She would get used to the touch of a mechanical limb.

The zeppelin continued on like a pale balloon.

"One day," he said, "a railway will follow the Silk Road. We could see the dawn in Cathay."

"I'd really enjoy a trip on one of your zeppelins. Dirigibles dance so freely among the clouds . . . "

"True. But the steam train is out of this world."

SOUTH, TO GLORY!

D.G. WHITE

15TH FEBRUARY, 1878: BAVARIA

"My Darling Ashlynne, words cannot describe the feelings of loneliness and regret which well up in my bosom at the sight of the locket you gave me ere my departure to this lonely, desolate, ice-blown, god-forsaken shore."

At the thought of ice, Preston Featherstone shivered. He leaned out of his overstuffed chair, grabbed the poker and gave the fire a few experimental pokes. It came to life gratifyingly fast. Preston turned to his manservant. "What do you think, Bunny? A bit thick?"

Bunny shook his greying head. "I think not, sir, although I would counsel against your somewhat reckless use of the word 'bosom'."

"For goodness sake man, this is the nineteenth century. A chap ought to be able to say 'bosom' to his fiancée without fear of her fainting." Preston waggled his whisky tumbler by way of punctuation. "As far as she's concerned I'm a rugged Antarctic explorer. That should grant me some licence, surely?"

Bunny did not comment.

Preston sipped his drink and leaned back in his chair. "Right, let's press on. Ahem: *Nothing in England could have prepared me for the violence of the climate beneath the Antarctic Circle. We lose men daily. Our local Inuit guide, Umbopo, believes they are being lured away by the spirits of the Ice Forest; the one I mentioned in my last letter, if you recall. Despite our having to flee*

*from the terrible snow-spiders, I have assured the expedition we
are men of science and fear no paranormal terrors. Incidentally, it
is quite lucky I had time to write this letter. Normally I wouldn't
write until we'd established camp for the night but I had a spot of
time as we had to backtrack to pick up several of Bunny's fingers,
which had dropped off from frostbite . . . "*

He broke off at the sound of a polite cough. "Yes, Bunny?
Problem?"

"I'm not writing that, sir."

Despite a general reluctance to abandon the feudal system,
Preston had long ago learned the wisdom of retaining Bunny's
good favour. He took his valet's outburst on the chin. "Why ever
not? Dash it all, I have to ramp up the drama somehow. It can't be
snow-spiders every week, you know."

"Doubtless, sir, but I would prefer that our return to England
from," Bunny glanced around the inside of the Bavarian ski chalet,
"the South Pole be achieved with all of my digits intact."

The man has a point, Preston conceded. "All right, what about
this: *I only just had time to write this letter as we have stopped
to mend a puncture on one of the bicycles. Bunny ran over a
particularly sharp penguin.*"

"I wouldn't run over a penguin, sir."

"And you haven't, that's the beauty of it." Preston beamed.
"Right, that ought to do it for this week. Just finish off with: *I
look forward to the day I see you again, hopefully with all limbs
intact (mine, not Bunny's) even though I am travelling over the
most rugged and dangerous yeti-infested land in the world. Hugs,
kisses and whatever-else-I-can-get-away-with-under-the-stairs,
your fiancée, Preston.*"

He glanced over at Bunny. "And you can write that last bit with
your eyes closed. I'm not having you taking literary liberties with
my betrothed."

"Very good, sir."

"You'll go into town and post it first thing tomorrow morning.
Same address in the Falklands. They'll have it franked for me and
send it on to England, as usual."

"Very good. Shall I take one of the bicycles, sir?"

"That might be wise," Preston agreed. "Give it a bit of an airing
before that photographer chappie shows up."

Preston had to admit, finding a photographer who couldn't speak a word of English had been a stroke of luck on his part. He and Bunny had been holed up for several months now in the south of Bavaria while the world at large (or at least Ashlynne and the members of Preston's Club) were under the impression they were attempting to be the first men to reach the South Pole by bicycle. The scheme depended largely on their not being recognised, and this had proven quite an effort. The thought lowered Preston's spirits. "They said I was a fool, Bunny!" he declared, apropos of nothing.

Bunny paused mid-lick and peered at him over the envelope. "Beg pardon, sir?"

"Those rotters at the Club, going on about exploring and suchlike. They said I was a fool!"

"You are a fool, sir."

"Yes, but they don't know that! They were just saying it. Hah! I showed them, didn't I? They were completely gobsmacked when I told them about this little jaunt. I say, you should have seen the look on Ashlynne's face when I showed her the plans for the rocket-powered zeppelin bikes! I thought she was going to show me her ankle there and then, I tell you. When I get back from 'Antarctica', Bunny, she'll be a dead cert, honestly." Preston paused, lost in salubrious thoughts.

"The photographer will be here on Thursday, sir," Bunny reminded him, "That should give us time to send the photographs to the press and be back in England for Ascot."

Preston's eyes twinkled in the firelight. "That's the plan."

16TH FEBRUARY 1878: A SLIGHTLY DIFFERENT BIT OF BAVARIA

"Are you sure about this sir?" Bunny asked, a note of caution evident in his voice as they looked down upon the sleepy hamlet of Baden-Humpen.

"Of course I am," Preston replied. He fastened his goggles over his eyes with a snap. "We've got to test the bally things out sooner or later."

"Naturally sir, but might I suggest we do it somewhere other than the main street of the village? It may attract attention."

Preston hated it when Bunny used logic; it felt like he was cheating somehow. "Bunny, face facts. We have to post that letter."

"I could post it perfectly well, sir."

"And we have to test the zeppelin bikes. What could possibly go wrong?"

"Need I remind you, sir, that if you are recognised it will spell the end of this entire endeavour."

"Really Bunny." Preston fixed him with a stern glare. "No-one will know who we are. We went all the way to Paris just to make the reservations for the chalet. No-one knows we're here and I don't know anyone unfashionable enough to know any Germans, so no-one's going to tell them either. Good Lord, it will be fine. And you're forgetting the speed differential. We'll rocket in, post the letter and be out again in a flash."

Bunny still seemed doubtful. "Perhaps I should go alone?"

"Nonsense. I've been itching to try the bike ever since the gin ran out. Oh, make a note," he said. "We need gin as well."

"Sir . . . "

"Really Bunny, the whole point of this escapade is to make me look dashing to Ashlynne. I can hardly do that whilst hanging onto the bike for dear life, can I? I've got to practise until I can ride this contraption around in the proper English manner."

Bunny raised a questioning eyebrow.

"While smoking a pipe, I mean." This seemed to Preston a natural end to the conversation. He patted the big silver gasbag above his head, checked the rockets strapped to the back of the bike, seated himself firmly in the saddle and pulled the ornate brasswork lever on the handlebars. From within the bowels of the frame he heard the whirr of clockwork. "Tally ho!"

Nothing happened.

Then, everything happened.

One minute Preston was stationary, and the next he was clinging to the handlebars as the bicycle leapt forward over the snow. Lightened almost to the point of weightlessness by the balloon full of hydrogen above it, the contraption skipped over the surface of the snow. As it rushed beneath them, the fine Bavarian powder offered almost no resistance to the skis on either side. The rockets lashed to the frame at the rear of the bike roared with a continuous stream of fire. Preston hunched low over the handlebars to avoid being blown off. His pipe streamed cinders as it remained clamped between his bared teeth.

Preston and his bicycle rushed towards Baden-Humpen like a particularly English avalanche. Bunny followed at a safe distance, albeit without igniting the rockets. The two odd-looking machines and their riders, the first screaming and the second silent, with a look of grim fatalism, careened onto the main street of the small town. They swept past the tall-gabled houses with alacrity. To Preston's extreme relief, as he entered the main street, the rockets cut out. Unfortunately this did little to affect his overall speed. He attempted to dodge pedestrians and several horse-drawn sleighs with varying degrees of success. His progress down the street was marked by shouts, screams and the astonished whinnying of more than one horse.

Preston's gaze was drawn to a carriage which had stopped by the post box. Preston, whose mental list of improvements to the bicycle now included a very large section on brakes, found himself heading straight towards the carriage and the short but statuesque brunette who stepped from it. In desperation, he wrenched the handlebars and somehow managed to turn ever so slightly, missing the young lady but hitting the carriage instead.

The bicycle stopped. Preston did not. Instead he catapulted over the carriage and into a fortuitous snowdrift. The crash, which had severely holed the gasbag, had also allowed the exhaust from the rockets to come into contact with the escaping hydrogen. The bicycle and the carriage exploded with a violence few in the village had seen before.

Preston pulled his head out of the snowdrift, dazed and confused. Before him stood the young lady, her dainty hand paused to place a letter in the box while around her rained the charred remains of her carriage.

"Oh, hello Ashlynne," said Preston, and fainted.

16TH FEBRUARY 1878: THE SLEEPY HAMLET OF BADEN-HUMPEN

When Preston awoke he wasn't sure what was going on. He remembered something about rockets, and he was cold. This was the limit of his thinking capacity at present. Preston knew when he was beaten. Rather than try to think his way out of things, he sat back and let the conversation wash over him.

"I'm terribly sorry, ma'am, but he insisted on coming with me."

Something prodded Preston in the buttocks. "That's all right, Bunny, it doesn't look like he's *compos mentis* anyway."

"Quite how you can tell is something of a mystery, ma'am."

"Don't be cheeky. What are we going to do? That was the Baron's coach. He'll not be pleased."

"I think we should get the twit out of here as soon as possible. Tell the Baron it was a gas leak from one of the horses."

Preston lost interest at that point and let his mind drift off, although a nagging voice was wondering exactly who this Baron was. Another voice was wondering why Ashlynne was here. As far as he knew she was supposed to be in England, training for the British Olympic Sewing Team. He was musing on this when he felt a pair of arms lift him up and put him back on his feet. Someone slapped his face, hard.

"I say!" Preston began, but he was cut off by a tall man ranting in German. He decided to let him go on as long as he wanted.

After a while the tirade ebbed.

"I say, hello, what?"

This seemed to send the tall man into paroxysms of rage. His face and bald head went a deep shade of purple and the ends of his big handlebar moustache quivered. He launched into some more of what Preston could only assume was choice Teutonic invective.

Bunny stepped between them. "*Entschuldigung, Mein Herr,*" he said. "*Sprechen Sie Englisch?*"

"*Ja!*" shouted the man. Shouting seemed to be his default setting.

This will be the Baron then, Preston decided. "Jolly good," he declared, extending his hand. "Preston Featherstone, don'tcherknow."

He received another slap in the face.

"I say, a chap's only trying to be decent."

"Decent? You have destroyed my carriage! That carriage has carried the Von Kleckervalffs for two hundred years!"

"Oh. Well, probably time to get a new one then." Preston was nothing if not a modernist. He frowned, trying to remember. He wished everything would stop spinning around. "I say Bunny, is this true? Did I destroy his carriage?"

"Indeed, sir."

"That doesn't sound like something I'd do." He thought about waking up in the snowdrift. It was all a blur before then. A sinking feeling overcame him. "Was I drunk?"

"No, sir. You were riding a rocket-powered zeppelin bicycle."

"Ah," he beamed at the young lady, who looked uncomfortable. "That does sound rather like me, being a big, rugged, manly explorer and all." He became aware that the Baron was staring at him. "Yes?"

The Baron gestured at the wreckage. "What are you going to do about it?"

Preston was still too dizzy to think straight. "Nothing," he declared. "That is at least until you can tell me what you're doing poncing about with my fiancée."

The Baron stopped in mid-growl. He turned to Ashlynne. "*Your* fiancée? But this is *my* fiancée."

"I beg to differ."

"Oh, *ja*? Well I beg to differ with you."

"Now look, I don't mean to be pedantic but we can't both beg to differ. It's just one of those things. Still, there's an easy way to settle this. We'll ask her."

Both men nodded and turned to face the young lady.

"Ashlynne," Preston called to her.

"Tallora," the Baron called to her.

The lady didn't move at first, then with precise, definite steps she moved to the Baron's side. "*Buongiorno, mio amato*," she said in flawless Italian.

Preston was gobsmacked. "Well I never."

The Baron turned to him in triumph. "*Mein Herr*, may I present the Contessa Tallora Dee, of Tuscany."

Preston didn't move, just stood there with his mouth open until he received a nudge in the ribs from Bunny.

"Lord Featherstone offers his apologies," said Bunny smoothly. "He's had a rather long day."

"I say, have I?"

"Yes," Bunny hissed from the side of his mouth.

The Baron's face grew dark again. "I do not care about the length of his day. He has ruined my carriage, and I will have satisfaction." He slapped Preston's face for a third time.

"Would you mind awfully not doing that?"

"Yes, I would mind. I challenge you to a duel, sir, with Schlagers."

Preston wasn't sure what a Schlager was, and didn't much care. "Perhaps some other time," he said, making a show of consulting his pocketwatch. "Come along Bunny, best be off, by Jove."

No-one moved. Preston glanced at Ashlynne, or Tallora, or whatever she was calling herself. She had a look of pleading in her eyes that seemed to be willing him on. As he looked at her he felt something stirring within him. Without thinking he felt himself adopting a heroic pose and saying in a rather brash voice, "Schlagers, eh? Alright, what time? Dawn, I suppose?"

He heard Bunny's sharp intake of breath.

"Perhaps in England, but not in Bavaria," snapped the Baron. "Here, we duel at noon."

"Noon? Jolly good, gives us time for morning tea. Huh, and all the chaps in England said you lot were uncultured. Fancy that, eh?"

There didn't seem to be much more to say. After a bit more staring the purple leached out of the Baron's face and he left in a huff, trailing his (or Preston's, depending on how you felt) fiancée behind him. When he was out of sight, Preston's legs give way beneath him and he fell back into the snowdrift.

"Bunny," he asked in a small voice, "what just happened?"

16TH FEBRUARY 1878: BACK AT THE CHALET

Deciding that the snow was too cold, Preston swapped it for a bathtub back at the Chalet and shivered in that instead. He was in the mood for some heavy thinking. This was a depressing prospect. He'd never been particularly good at it, so he was glad when the door opened and Bunny walked in with a towel.

"Ah, Bunny. How are the preparations?"

"Your valise is packed. I have sent one of the staff into town to book us two tickets to Paris on the 11:30 train."

Preston nodded and slid further under the mass of bubbles in the tub. "Excellent. Let old Baron whatsisface stand out in the snow, I shan't be there."

"Indeed sir, although if I may be so bold it does rather smack of running away."

Preston was shocked. "Bunny, I am a complete coward. In the whole time you've worked for me have I ever faced up to anything?"

"No sir."

"Quite, and I don't intend to start now. Plan B: The Falklands. We'll hole up at one of Daddy's depots."

Bunny left the towel draped across the back of a chair and turned to go.

"Bunny," Preston said, "I wasn't imagining things, was I? That was Ashlynne?"

"I really couldn't say, sir."

Before Bunny could reply further there came a knock on the bathroom door.

"Well really," frowned Preston. "Whoever that is send them away. A chap's trying to take a bath, for heaven's sake." He felt around under the suds for the soap.

Bunny opened the door. Through it stepped a pensive-looking Ashlynne.

Momentarily forgetting his lack of clothing and position in the tub, Preston scowled. "It's you, is it? Still Italian I suppose?"

Ashlynne walked in and sat on the chair. She took a deep breath. "Preston, there's something I need to tell you."

Preston thought this was the understatement of the century. Unfortunately he chose to communicate this via a snort which sent bubbles everywhere, lessening the impact to a large degree.

"I'm sorry about this morning," Ashlynne said. "The Baron thinks I'm out buying a new hat to replace the one you set on fire. I came to explain." She stood and toyed with Preston's toothbrush on the ledge below the mirror. She took a deep breath. "Preston, I am not on the Olympic Sewing Team as I may have told you in the past."

"I beg your pardon?"

"No."

"But what about the gold you won at Helsinki for the hundred-metre long stitch? Dash it all, I've seen the medal."

"A clever fake made up by the Foreign Office."

Preston stared at her, agog. "How the bally heck did you get access to the Foreign Office? I seem to have enough trouble with the Post Office, and I'm a Lord and everything."

Ashlynne sighed. She rubbed her temples. "I am a spy, dear. I go all over the world, protecting Britain from her enemies."

Preston considered this. "Oh, very well."

"What?"

"Well, fair enough then. I'm not against women having careers. Everyone's got to do something, I suppose."

"You mean you're not angry?"

"Not particularly."

It didn't seem as though Ashlynne had been expecting this. "Why not?"

Preston looked up at her from his bath. "You called me 'dear'. I'll forgive a lot for that."

There was a pregnant pause. Ashlynne bit her lip and leaned in close. "That's . . . good, dear, because there's another favour I need to ask . . . "

16TH FEBRUARY 1878: HIGH NOON

Preston stood in the main street of Baden-Humpen. "Bunny, explain to me exactly what I'm doing here again?" He gave his sword an experimental swing.

"You're waiting to engage Baron Erich Von Kleckervalff in a duel in order to give your fiancée the distraction she needs to steal the plans for the proposed German invasion of the South of France."

Preston gave the sword another swing. "That's what I thought." He grimaced, then turned. "So, what's the plan?"

"Sir?"

"Bunny, I rely upon you to come up with these things."

His valet said nothing, and Preston began to feel a nagging doubt. He tried to jolly things along. "Clearly, I shan't be fighting the duel, shall I? No doubt you have cunningly arranged for this village's examples of whatever the German version of urchins are to start an avalanche or something so the duel may be called off."

Bunny looked doubtful. "I don't think so, sir," he replied. "I haven't had the time. This was all rather last-minute."

"Well don't look at me. If Ashlynne hadn't started making cow's-eyes we'd be well on our way to the South Atlantic by now."

Bunny declined to comment further and seemed to take an inordinate amount of interest in his fingernails. Preston inspected his sword. "So this is a Schlager, is it? Nicely weighted."

"I hadn't realised you were a sword aficionado, sir."

"I'm not. Did a term of fencing at Eton, but passed it up to take on advanced monocle-polishing."

"Perhaps a bad choice, under the circumstances?"

"Not really. I needn't remind you who took gold in last year's English All-Comers Monocle and Spectacle Tourney. Proudest day of my life. Unlike today."

He looked over at the building opposite. This was, apparently, the hotel containing the Baron's apartments. Quite a crowd had gathered. They cheered as the Baron exited.

"Good Lord Bunny, is he wearing lederhosen?"

"It would appear so, sir."

"But it's nearly freezing."

Bunny nodded. "Baron Von Kleckervalff is a Junker, sir."

"He's an oik."

Both men fell silent as the Baron strode through towards them. "So!" he roared in a way that Preston really wished he wouldn't. "You do have some spirit. I have lost twenty Guilder." He turned to his retinue and flicked one of them a coin.

"Yes, well, sorry to disappoint old bean, but you're dealing with Englishmen here," Preston told him. *When you're in it up to your neck Preston old boy,* he told himself, *keep swimming.*

The Baron glared at him. He glanced at his sword arm. "At least you know your way around a sword," he barked. "The last fellow I fought barely knew how to hold it."

"You pick your opponents well, I see."

The Baron turned an acute shade of purple. "Are you trying to insult me, *mein Herr?*"

Preston turned to Bunny with a smile. "Was I trying to insult him?"

Bunny nodded. "Indeed, sir."

"Enough!" the Baron roared, "My blood is up! Sir, take your place, and may God have mercy on your soul."

Preston decided that enough was enough. "Bunny, I'm running out of options here. Unless I'm very much mistaken it appears I'm going to actually have to fight this bally duel."

"My sincerest condolences, sir."

"You must have some sort of plan, surely?" Preston was grasping at straws.

"I did have one, sir."

Thank goodness, Preston thought. "What?"

"Run, sir, run like hell."

Preston liked to think of himself as a sporting chap. Unfortunately, sport for Preston and his social circle generally involved cricket, which was also one of the slowest forms of animal life on the planet, or grouse shooting, which involved shotgunning small birds from the comfort of a wicker chair. This was not, he now realised, the best training for being chased about the high street of Baden-Humpen by a homicidal maniac with a sword. Quite early into the duel it became obvious to Preston that the Baron was a great deal fitter than him, and he had the nagging suspicion that he was going to lose. The duel started fine, by Preston's reckoning, as all he did was run around the village square with the Baron in hot pursuit. The Baron's seemingly excellent health, coupled with his own disgraceful state had made this a short-term option only. Preston soon found himself turning, panting and wheezing, to face the Baron. He glanced hopefully at Bunny, but his valet seemed intent on staring at the Baron's hotel.

"So, you stop running, eh? Now we fight!" The Baron was smiling and not even breathing hard. Preston knew that his only hope lay in action. He screamed, closed his eyes and slashed the Schlager randomly about in front of him. At the same time he lurched forward.

The sad thing was that, untrained and unscientific as this method as, it could have worked. Preston figured that actually being attacked was the last thing the Baron would be expecting. He was right. The Baron immediately sprang to one side. Unfortunately, Preston had his eyes shut. This meant he carried on regardless through the centre of the square, only stopping when his progress was checked by a large statue of Bismarck. Preston's Schlager hit it in the arm, cutting it deeply but then refusing to come out again. Preston tugged at it but it wouldn't budge. He tried to ignore the Baron's peals of laughter.

"I say," Preston asked hopefully, "I suppose that's that then, what?"

"What do you mean?" The Baron seemed quite pleased with this outcome.

"My sword's stuck in this jolly statue. I can't fight you now. I expect we'd better call it a day."

The Baron laughed again in a manner that Preston had decided was definitely worse than his near-constant yelling. *"Mein Herr,"* the Baron chuckled, walking forward to loom over the Englishman, "I still have my weapon. I see no reason to stop the fight."

Behind the hulking form of the Baron Preston saw Ashlynne emerge from the Baron's hotel. *Thank goodness,* he thought, *that's that.*

Except she wasn't alone. In fact, the short, chubby chap with her seemed to be holding her arm behind her back, while her face was a mask of pain.

"My Baron! My Baron!" the chap yelled as he pushed Ashlynne forward into the square.

The Baron turned. "What is this?" he demanded. "Who are you to mistreat my fiancée this way? Unhand her at once, swine!"

Preston agreed wholeheartedly with the sentiment, but the other chap obviously didn't. "Apologies my Baron," he reported, "but I caught her in your rooms. She had picked the lock to your cabinet and was looking at the War Plans!"

There was silence for a moment, then the Baron barked, "Bring her here."

The chap pushed Ashlynne forward until she stood before the Baron. "Contessa Tallora," he said, "perhaps I now begin to see why the *Englischer* recognised you. Admit it, you are a spy."

Ashlynne glanced at Preston, who shrugged and looked meaningfully at the sword still firmly wedged in the statue.

She sighed and hung her head. "You win, Baron," she said in English with no trace of an Italian accent. "I'm with the Secret Service branch of the Foreign Office." She straightened and looked him in the eye. "We know all about your plans for the south of France."

Preston saw her flinch as the Baron reached out and stroked her face. "We have ways of dealing with spies," he growled. "The Kaiser's men in Berlin will be pleased to get a new source of information. But I cannot send you to them untouched. Honour demands satisfaction." With the tip of his sword he motioned to the old scars on either side of his head. "Duelling scars from the Gymnasium. Properly treated they are a mark of honour. Left to bleed, they fester and pucker." He stroked Ashlynne's face again, this time with the steel of the blade. "No-one steals from me," he whispered. "Not ever."

Perhaps it was the sight of the steel blade next to his beloved's tender skin, Preston didn't know. What Preston did know was that the Baron, who had heretofore seemed such a monstrous figure, was going down. He reached into the pocket of his waistcoat. "Oh, Baron," he called casually.

The Baron turned, only to be blinded by a powerful flash of light from Preston's hand. He cried out in pain, dropped his sword and clapped his hands over his eyes. Immediately Preston ran forward and grasped Ashlynne around the waist. "Come on," he told her. "No time to lose!"

"But what of the plans?"

Preston kicked the short tubby chap next to her in the crotch. "Grab them!" he cried.

"He hasn't got them. They're still upstairs."

"Oh." Preston said to the unfortunate German. "Terribly sorry." He turned back to Ashlynne. "You'll just have to remember them."

They started running down the main street.

"I don't understand," panted Ashlynne. "What did you do back there?"

Grinning, Preston opened his hand to show her the shiny circle of glass he held. "All-England Monocle-Polishing Champion, remember?"

Ashlynne laughed, which was the best thing he'd heard in months." Come on," he told her, "the fun's not over yet."

Behind them he heard the Baron's cry of rage. "You can run, English swine, but you cannot hide."

"Technically that's true," Preston panted to Ashlynne as they neared the end of the High Street, "but I think he'll find we can run jolly fast."

"How . . . ?" she began, but before she could finish Bunny came pedalling around the corner astride the one remaining rocket-powered zeppelin bike.

"All aboard!" he cried. "Five miles to the Swiss border and freedom."

Ashlynne took a seat on the handlebars while Preston stood behind Bunny with a foot upon each of the contraption's skis. With a grunt at the extra weight Bunny pushed off down the slope.

"Any particular route?" he asked.

"Just aim towards Switzerland," Preston yelled over the increasing roar of the wind. "It's quite large, you can't miss."

Behind them Preston could hear a strange chuffing noise. He glanced over his shoulder and his mouth fell open. Behind him he could see the Baron sitting atop what seemed to be a steam-engine on skis. On either side of the boiler, two large paddlewheels churned up the snow. At the front stood the Baron, half-hidden behind a wicked-looking circular assortment of rifle barrels.

Preston decided the most English response at this point was to extend two fingers skyward. In response the Baron raised the collection of barrels and bellowed incoherently. With a whir and a spurt of escaping steam the barrels began to revolve. Bullets spat out of them in a wide arc. Abruptly the firing stopped. Preston stared as the Baron began hitting the barrel with a gloved fist.

"Jammed, eh? Sucks to you, Fritzy!" Preston yelled.

"I wouldn't gloat quite so quickly if I were you, sir," Bunny warned, holding onto the handlebars with one hand and his hat with the other, his legs pedalling furiously.

"Whyever not?"

Bunny nodded upwards to where the large silver gasbag sat. It looked rather deflated. It was now obvious what the Baron had been shooting at.

Preston returned his attention to their forward path, peering over Ashlynne's shoulder as she perched delicately on the handlebars. At the bottom of the hill they were currently rushing down there loomed a much steeper slope.

"Over that hill is Switzerland," Bunny wheezed, panting heavily. "With the zeppelin intact we might have been able to make it. Now . . . " he trailed off.

"Damnit, use the rockets!" Preston cried.

"I can't, sir, not with you standing directly behind them."

Preston looked down. Bunny was right, of course. From his position on the skis, his legs were directly in the path of the rocket exhausts where they were clamped on either side of the bicycle frame. He swallowed and looked over his shoulder. The German contraption seemed a lot closer now, and it looked like the Baron had almost cleared the jam. He swallowed hard and made his decision.

"Well then," he said in a small voice, "I'm afraid there's only one thing for it."

Bunny looked shocked. "But sir!"

"I'm afraid I must, Bunny. For England. I may never see you again." Preston held out his hand.

Reluctantly, his eyes wet with tears, Bunny shook it. "Sir, this is the bravest thing I've ever seen you do."

"Not really," said Preston as he yanked Bunny off the seat and sent him tumbling into the snow. "I'd say it's about normal."

Bunny cried something incoherent as Preston leapt onto the saddle and pulled the rocket lever. They came to life in an instant, kicking the bike up the hill at an amazing rate. Ashlynne lost her hold on the handlebars and crashed back into Preston's waiting arms. They crested the hill, their speed causing them to momentarily take flight, passing high over the astonished roof of the Swiss guardhouse. "You see?" Preston whispered with a smile into Ashlynne's delicate, shell-like ear. "All's well that ends well, eh what?"

LADY PRESTO MAGNIFICO AND THE DISAPPEARING GLASS CEILING

KATRINA NICHOLSON

Destitute.

Penelope Sanbourne didn't want to face it, but that's what she was. With her father dead and no inheritance save his unpaid bills, the only things of value she owned were her dress—an expensively tailored purple and black costume designed for a magician's assistant—and her steamer trunk. It was purple-painted and chugged along behind her, spitting steam from its tailpipe as it rattled over the cobblestones.

It was evening and most of the shops were shut. Her rooming house loomed out of the fog ahead, dank and dark in the yellow gaslight. Her ground floor lodgings were small, pokey and airless, and there was no furniture apart from a pair of rickety cots, but it was a place to sleep. Come tomorrow she wouldn't even have that. Her landlady, Mrs Cutter, was a charitable woman. However, charity only went so far. Apparently her father had not paid the rent in three months.

She extinguished the trunk's boiler, lit the lone candle sitting on her father's trunk, and began to undress. Her wrists and elbows screamed as she twisted to undo her own corset. A terrible end to a terrible day. After the theatre owner who had contracted her father refused to let her take over his magic show, she'd spent the entire day scouring the West End for someone willing to take a chance on a nineteen-year-old lady magician. She'd been derided, propositioned, rejected, and laughed at. She possessed some of the most ingenious illusions in London, but no one wanted to see them unless they were performed by a man.

If only she had a little money, she could buy herself more time to find a situation. Unfortunately, though her father had been one of London's most popular illusionists, he was also a degenerate wretch whose money tended to go up in smoke. Penelope tried in vain to tamp down the wave of resentment that arose every time her thoughts turned to the man who had raised her. Reginald Sanborne had made his way in the world via natural charm and stealing his daughter's magic tricks. He lived for the adulation of the audience and sought a similar high offstage by chasing the dragon. Two days ago he'd lain down on a couch in his favourite opium den and never got up again. Some deeply buried part of Penelope had never given up hope that he would one day love her as a father should and was sorry he was dead. The rest of her was simply angry.

She blew out the candle and lay down on her cot in her nightdress, seething. She was sure she would not sleep. But in the middle of the night she was jolted awake by a scraping sound on the other side of the room. Penelope's blood ran cold. Was someone there?

Dim yellow gaslight seeped through the open window, revealing the silhouette of a hatless man who was quietly digging through her trunk. Her rage surged forth once again. One of her father's creditors, no doubt, fed up with waiting for payment, had decided to help himself to her things. She slid silently out of bed and felt in front of her in the darkness for a weapon. Her fingers closed around her wand.

"You there! Get your hands off my things!" Penelope shouted, stabbing the wand into the centre of the silhouette.

"Bloody hell!" a deep voice exclaimed in surprise as the wand sank into flesh.

Penelope let loose all her pent-up feelings in a vicious series of stabs. "Out! Out! Scoundrel! Cur! Bastard! Thief! Get out!"

"Ow! Ow! Christ! Stop it!" protested the voice as she drove the shadow back through the darkness.

The backs of his legs hit the sill with a strangely hollow thump and Penelope shoved him in the chest, toppling him backward through the window. She slammed the casement shut and shoved her wand through the handles.

Danger past, she slid down the wall, shaking, and curled her arms protectively around her knees. The situation had become intolerable. Tomorrow morning she would give up her dreams of becoming an illusionist and take whatever employment she could secure.

Edwin Forrester lay in an undignified heap outside Penelope's window and attempted to collect his wits. Apparently two years fighting the Russians in Crimea wasn't enough to prepare him for a battle with one fiery-tempered girl in a nightgown. Penelope Sanbourne was small and slight with modestly styled brown hair and downcast blue eyes. He had followed her around all day as she meekly accepted being turned away time and again. He'd felt sorry for her. She couldn't help being a woman any more than she could help who her father was. But who would have thought she was such a spitfire inside? If she was able to fend off a midnight intruder with nothing but a . . . what had that been? A hat pin? Then clearly this assignment wasn't going to be as easy as he had thought.

Covertly retrieving the command engine Reginald Sanborne had designed and sold to the Crown before he died should have been as simple as pinching it from Penelope's rooms while she was out. Unfortunately, Penelope carted everything of value around with her in a self-propelled steamer trunk. He hadn't wanted to scare her but he had had no choice but to attempt a nighttime break in. In light of its spectacular failure, Edwin realised he would have to try a more direct approach.

After the incident with the midnight intruder, Penelope spent the rest of the night underneath the window clutching the weaponry from the sword cabinet illusion. She half-hoped he wouldn't come back and half-hoped he would, if only so she could exact revenge for the scare he'd given her.

Eventually dawn came and it was time to vacate her rooms. She stacked her father's trunk on top of her own and went out into the world.

Penelope emerged onto the cobblestones in the pink early morning light. She looked up and down the lane, wondering which direction she ought to go. Would it be better to seek a situation as a serving girl in a tavern? Or try her hand as a seamstress or shop girl? Then she looked directly across the road at the run-down old theatre. It had been shut up for years, but now there was a poster pasted across the splintered wooden doors.

NEW ACTS SOUGHT. APPLY WITHIN.

She stood uncertainly in the street while tradesmen and labourers swirled around her on their way to work. Surely an application from her would not be welcomed. But if she did not apply, would she not always wonder? She crossed to the wide wooden doors, pulled one open with an awful rusty shriek, and went inside. The foyer smelt of dust and mildew. The dark red carpeting was grey with dust and the place was lit only by a few candles, despite the fact that there were gas sconces on the walls.

"Hello?" Penelope called, propping the door open with her trunk, partly for light and partly because she was afraid of being trapped inside.

"Ah! Hello!" a deep voice called from the dark doorway at the top of the balcony stairs. "I'll be right with you."

A man emerged from the gloom, candle in one gloved hand. He had a handsome face, clean-shaven and cheerful. He was probably five-and-twenty and wore no hat. His softly curling brown hair was unfashionably long—almost covering his ears. His waistcoat and trousers were grey, probably to hide the dust, and matched the silvery colour of his eyes. Despite his apparent good health, he leaned heavily on a cane, favouring his right leg as he clomped noisily but energetically down the stairs.

"It's a terrible racket, I know," he said ruefully. "But there's no help for it."

Penelope recognised the gait. She'd seen it before on soldiers who had returned wounded from the Russian War. The recent introduction of airships and clockwork cannons to the battlefield had spared many a young man from an early demise atop a cavalry horse, but there were still an unfortunate number who returned despondent and missing a limb. Not that this young man seemed to be letting his injury get to him.

"You have a false leg?" she asked.

"Yes, but enough about me. You are here to audition your act, correct?" he asked.

"Yes. Penelope Sanborne," she said, stiffly offering her hand and wondering if he was going to throw her out once he found out what she did.

"Not Reginald Sanbourne's daughter?"

"The same."

"Then you must be an illusionist as well."

"Yes, I go by the name of Lady Presto Magnifico."

If he thought the idea of a lady magician strange, he didn't show it. He smiled sunnily and pumped her hand rather than kissing it, as if she were a man. "Delighted. Edwin Forrester. I own this theatre, shabby as it is. I've inherited it from an uncle, you see, and I'm hoping to fix things up. Now, do show me your magic. I am all ears, er, eyes, as it were."

Edwin perched on the edge of the ticket counter, wooden leg sticking out awkwardly in front of him, and invited her to regale him.

***

"I can see that you are a discerning audience," Penelope said. "Therefore I must confess to you that what you are about to see contains nothing whatsoever of the occult."

Edwin watched as she removed her top hat and displayed its white velvet lined interior to him. "As you can see this is a perfectly ordinary hat."

She set the hat brim-down on the ticket counter. "And yet—" she rapped the hat sharply with her wand. "Voila!"

Penelope pulled the hat away to reveal a very realistic looking clockwork rabbit cloaked in white velvet sitting on the counter. Edwin leaned forward eagerly, staring at the rabbit. It had transformed itself from her hat lining. That much he was sure about. He also suspected that this device was the basis of the clockwork cannons currently used by the British Army, which assembled themselves from seemingly ordinary steamer trunks. Here, at last, was Reginald Sanbourne's work.

"Extraordinary!" he exclaimed, taking up the rabbit and inspecting it. It was extremely cleverly designed, with tiny, intricate workings of clockwork and springs. "What else have you to show me? I wish to know how everything works."

Penelope regarded him through narrowed eyes. "A magician never reveals her secrets, sir."

"Not even to the owner of the theatre to which she is under contract?"

Penelope frowned. "I suppose a man in such a position may pick up a thing or two. However, if he truly wishes to learn the art of magic, there is only one way to go about it."

"And that way would be?"

"Why, to become my assistant, of course. I will have need of one once I am contracted."

"Then consider yourself contracted," Edwin replied, extending his hand to seal the bargain. It would be no hardship to spend a day or two on false 'rehearsals'. Penelope would teach him how her father's devices were constructed and he could study her in more detail, so that when the affair was concluded he could see to it that she was given an appropriate situation. Providing for her was not part of his assignment, but Edwin could not in good conscience leave such a remarkably brave woman in even worse straits than her father had.

"You will not regret this, sir. Truly," Penelope said, pumping his hand enthusiastically. Edwin grinned at her. He felt his spirits lift with the contact and it suddenly occurred to him that he could get himself into trouble here if he wasn't careful.

Penelope moved into one of the dressing rooms backstage and they began their preparations for the act, filling the wings of the stage with props and boxes fetched from her father's old theatre. Edwin himself was living out of one of the other rooms, which was entirely improper, of course, but Edwin sensed that Penelope was glad to have someone to watch over her. He felt guilty for that, as it was no doubt his own unexpected midnight appearance that had put the fright into her in the first place.

Over the course of the next week, Penelope instructed Edwin in such magical tasks as freeing himself from a sack, disappearing from a box, and being stabbed-through with swords. The more Edwin learned, the more he began to regret the fact that their show would never be performed in front of an audience. The deception and sleight-of-hand appealed to his spy's heart, and it impressed him that complex illusions such as the Mummy Case were in reality no more difficult than hiding behind an open door. Penelope never lost patience with him when he stumbled or fumbled and she made sure to adapt the performance to accommodate his inability to properly bend his right leg.

The only shadow that loomed over Edwin's time with her was the increasing pressure he felt from his superiors as time passed without his securing the command engine. The engine, which allowed clockwork devices such as cannons to perform tasks without the aid of a human pilot, would be highly desirable to Russian agents as well as the Crown. Edwin had seen neither hide nor hair of the thing so far. Was it possible that the Russians had gotten to it before him?

He was entirely absorbed by such dark musings when Penelope burst into the theatre, cheeks flushed with excitement, followed as always by her trusty steamer trunk.

"Edwin! I have wonderful news!" She cried, climbing the steps to join him on the stage.

A new trick? Perhaps involving your father's new command engine? Edwin hoped.

"I've secured us a commission! We'll be performing in front of a real audience tonight!"

"A performance? Tonight?" Edwin repeated, stomach sinking. "But . . . "

"I know it's short notice, but I ran into Mrs Cutter, my former landlady, this morning. She is hosting a soirée for her charitable foundation this very evening and the entertainment she had secured sent word that they would be unable to accommodate her. It seemed the perfect opportunity to launch our act, as Mrs Cutter is quite well-to-do. What do you think?" Penelope asked, beaming.

I think I am going to be ill, Edwin thought. Now that the prospect of appearing onstage was real, it turned his brain to mush. He was accustomed to lurking in the shadows. As the disabled male assistant of a female magician, he would have no hope of escaping scrutiny.

"I confess I may have given her the impression that you are the magician and I your assistant. Simply to get our foot in the door, you understand. Once they see the act, our sexes won't matter. I am sure everything will work out."

It will be a disaster, Edwin moaned inwardly. But there was no getting out of it now, not if he wanted that engine. He reluctantly let her lead him backstage to begin their rehearsals.

Penelope peeked around the ratty curtain. She and Edwin had tidied up the theatre as much as possible after their rehearsals, but it was still somewhat shabby. The guests, in their evening finery, stood out like peacocks in a chicken coop. She hadn't realised that there would be quite so many of them, or that some would be nurses and young patients from the newly founded Great Ormond Street Hospital. They packed the house, babbling excitedly as they settled themselves. Penelope was simultaneously thrilled and nervous. This was her big chance . . . but how would the audience react?

"How is it looking out there?" Edwin asked from behind her. He was dressed in an elegant grey suit that had belonged to her father. The trousers were a little too short and the jacket a little too tight across the shoulders, but in the shadows cast by the gas stage lights, no one would notice. He perched his top hat rakishly on his head and grinned at her, not quite managing to hide his nervousness. No doubt this would be embarrassing for him, but he was determined to make a success of his theatre. Perversely, his anxiety swept hers away. He had been so kind and accepting. She could be confident enough for the both of them.

"It's a full house," she told him, adjusting her own top hat and smoothing the sleeves of her purple gown, making sure her various accoutrements were accounted for inside. "And we are going to astonish them."

With that, she reached into a concealed pocket inside her sleeve, removed a packet, and threw it hard into the middle of the stage. A cloud of purple smoke burst forth. She stepped onto the stage and appeared from inside the fog as if by magic.

"Ladies and gentlemen," she boomed in her biggest voice. "I am Lady Presto Magnifico, daughter of the world-renowned Lord Presto Magnifico and practitioner of the art of magic!"

The crowd went quiet as she smoke cleared, revealing not the man they were expecting, but a woman in a multi-layered purple and black dress. "Is that a lady?" one of the children loudly asked his nurse. Penelope ignored him. She couldn't let them think for too long or everything would fall apart.

"Behold! Not even the flames themselves dare deny my power!" She whipped her wand out of her sleeve and waved it dramatically at the lit gas lamp on the wall. As if responding to her magic, the flame dimmed down to almost nothing as Edwin twisted the valve backstage. The audience gasped.

"I have drawn the flame into my wand," Penelope said, swiping her other hand over her wand hand to cover the fact that she was using her thumb to strike the match at the tip.

The audience murmured in wonder as she drew slow hypnotic circles in the air with the flaming end of the wand. "Watch how it responds to my call. See how it takes root where no ordinary fire could survive!"

Penelope tapped the wand sharply on the lid of a jar, the movement extinguishing the match and knocking a tiny hole in the lid, causing the phosphorus inside to burst into flame.

The audience gasped and applauded automatically as Penelope swept the jar off the table and held the contained flame aloft for their appraisal. Their eyes followed it involuntarily and Penelope grinned, knowing she'd won. Not one of them was thinking about the fact that she was a woman now.

From backstage, Edwin watched as Penelope kept the crowd riveted with colour-changing milk, a host of clever card tricks, and a coin whose face changed inside the pocket of a child volunteer. He couldn't help but be proud of her. Not everyone could have withstood the kind of scrutiny she was under. He wasn't at all sure he could, and he'd been shot at before. Then came his cue: "And now, to assist me with my next trick, please welcome Mr Silver!"

Edwin bit back a smile at the name, which Penelope had chosen based on the colour of his eyes and wardrobe. Taking a deep breath, he stepped out onto the stage, remembering her instruction to keep his arms spread wide as he presented himself to the audience. He gritted his teeth as they applauded; trying to remind himself that no one was interested in shooting at him, regardless of how exposed he was. He stepped inside the sword cabinet and let Penelope 'impale' him with half a dozen carefully placed blades. As he watched the awestruck faces of the children in the audience, Edwin found he was starting to enjoy himself, especially with Penelope smiling at him like that. By the time they clasped hands and took their final bow, he had been completely carried away on the wave of well wishes generated by the crowd. Penelope 'vanished' them in a cloud of purple smoke, and every member of the audience leapt to their feet in a standing ovation.

Edwin kept hold of Penelope's hand as they ran backstage, hiding behind the curtain to watch the crowd break up. They were all smiling and chattering about the show.

"You've done it! You've really done it!" he exclaimed.

"I know, I almost can't believe it," Penelope admitted, leaning into him as if to share her success with him.

"This calls for celebration. Let me take you to supper."

Penelope smiled. "You're forgetting that neither of us has any money."

"That was before we secured a commission," Edwin told her, removing the banknotes Mrs Cutter had given him from his waistcoat pocket.

Penelope was thrilled when their commission was able to buy them a meal of roast capon and wine at a rather richly appointed inn. There was a crystal chandelier in the dining room and a liveried waiter to attend them. As the wine level in the bottle decreased, warmth and well-being spread through Penelope's body. She found herself smiling at Edwin and cherishing the smiles he gave her in return. She could scarcely believe that after being miserable for so long, she'd finally found someone who appreciated her for herself.

They went for a late walk after supper, strolling around the lake in St. James's Park, Penelope's steamer trunk trundling along behind them. Gas lights stood out as yellow orbs in the quiet darkness. Edwin made a valiant showing, but after a while Penelope noticed that be began to lean more heavily on his cane. His face had taken on a pinched look and his right hand kept drifting toward his thigh.

"You are in pain," Penelope observed.

"I'm sorry. It's just rather more work dragging this old wooden thing along," Edwin admitted.

He hadn't tried to pass it off as nothing, which Penelope was glad of. It gave her a chance to be of use to him.

"Sit down. I may have just the thing."

Edwin dropped gratefully onto the edge of a stone fountain as Penelope opened her trunk. She lifted out the tray at the top which contained mundane magical props such as cards, handkerchiefs, and coins. Underneath was the mother lode which, until now, Edwin had not been permitted to see. Here was the rabbit hat and the coin that switched faces, the phosphorus fire and something else—something large and man-shaped. Edwin gasped when he saw what it was.

"This is the other Mr Silver, my automaton assistant," Penelope said. "Or he will be once he's finished. A friend who does waxworks is making his face. She'll deliver it tomorrow."

Mr Silver's current face was made of a shiny silvery metal fashioned into a sort of masquerade mask. Its body was composed of clockwork joints and gears protected by metal plates.

"Mr Silver, sit up please," Penelope ordered.

With a whirring of clockwork and springs, the automaton raised itself to a sitting position inside the trunk. *The command engine* Edwin thought. *It's inside Mr Silver's head.*

"That's incredible!" he said aloud. "Where did you get it?"

"I made it, of course," Penelope replied as she removed a small packet of tools from the trunk.

"*You* did? I thought your father was the inventor!"

"You and everyone else in London," Penelope said bitterly as she began loosening one of Mr Silver's legs. "Father couldn't have lit so much as a lamp on his own. Not that he would ever admit it. He took all of my best work for his show and passed it off as his own. I was fed up, so I kept Mr Silver here a secret. Why do you think I take my trunk everywhere?"

The reality of what she was saying crashed through Edwin. Penelope had invented the clockwork rabbit and the chemical boiler. Not Reginald. "You saved my life," Edwin whispered.

"What?"

"In Eupatoria. I was collecting battlefield intelligence for Baron Lyons when a cannonball struck my leg. I was bleeding alarmingly fast . . . the lads were sure I would die. Had the field hospital been in a tent behind the lines, I would never have made it. But the new, lighter chemical boilers had made it possible to construct airships that floated on gas which would not burn. There was an airship hospital directly above us. I lost the leg, of course, but kept my life."

Penelope took his hand and squeezed it. "I'm so glad, Edwin. But it is a coincidence that my little inventions bear some resemblance to the army's machines. I don't see how I can be responsible for your rescue."

No, of course she didn't. She had no idea that her father had sold her inventions. He had nearly given himself away.

"You're right, of course," Edwin said, bringing the back of her hand to his lips for a kiss. "I was carried away, that's all. With automatons like this, there would be no need for a flesh and blood man to be exposed to cannon fire at all."

"I suppose you're right," Penelope said thoughtfully, looking down at Mr Silver. "But I had a more immediate use in mind for him tonight. Roll up your trouser leg, please."

Edwin froze. "You . . . you want to see my leg?"

The sight of his mangled limb had already driven away his fiancé. He and Mary had been friends since childhood and their mothers had arranged for them to marry. He wasn't sure what had hurt more: Mary's rejection, or the fact that his mother now thought him too broken to be a good match. He was enjoying Penelope's company so much. He couldn't bear to think of what might happen when she saw the ugliness that was his right leg.

"If it's alright . . . " Penelope said uncertainly.

Splendid. Now she would assume he did not trust her if he refused. Well, there was no help for it, then. Taking a bracing breath, he rolled up his right trouser leg, exposing his mahogany leg. It began with a bowl shape attached to the scarred stump of his thigh and ended in a carved foot shape hidden inside his right boot. There was a crude hinge where his knee should have been. He held his breath as Penelope carefully undid the strap and removed the leg, revealing the puckered red skin of his stump.

"Just as I thought," Penelope said, gently running her fingers over his tender flesh. "Your poor leg is being rubbed raw. I think I have some India rubber that will help."

There was no trace of disgust on her face as she fashioned a new cap for his false leg and attached it to his stump. It fit much tighter than the wooden cap, which would reduce rubbing. He was about to thank her when he realised she wasn't done. Instead of re-attaching his old leg, she brought over the leg she'd removed from Mr Silver.

"I realise it's a little unorthodox," she said as she strapped it on, "but I think you'll get along much better with a proper knee joint. This one is spring loaded. The energy you put into it through the power of your stride is then used to straighten the leg, giving you a more even gait. There. Try it out."

Edwin stared at the new leg as Penelope hauled him to his feet. He took a step forward, watching the gears in the knee turn, winding the spring as his thigh muscles tensed and unwinding it when he relaxed. It was remarkable. He walked back and forth in front of the fountain without falling over or even needing the aid of his cane.

He looked at Penelope, who stood watching him with a smile on her face. "Well now, that seems to be working out rather wel—"

Her words were cut off as Edwin stepped up to her on his new leg, took her face in his hands, and kissed her. She stiffened in surprise at first, then relaxed into him, her arms twining about his neck and her weight pressing against him. He was able to support it—and his own—thanks to the new leg.

"Penelope, thank you," Edwin said, resting his forehead against hers. "This . . . I . . . you really are most extraordinary."

"It's nothing, really, compared to what you've done for me," she whispered, toying with the curling hair at the back of his neck. "Thank you for everything, Edwin."

He didn't want to release her, but it was getting late and there was always the risk of being set upon by footpads if one lingered too long in the park after dark. They walked hand-in-hand back to the theatre, Edwin's cane stowed away in Penelope's trunk, and let themselves in the rear door. Edwin was just beginning to wonder whether it had been too improper to kiss her, when the reasons he'd inserted himself into her life resurfaced like a bucket of cold water to the face. Penelope's room was in shambles. Her father's trunk had been pried open, its contents scattered, the cot overturned. Someone had been looking for something, and this time it hadn't been him.

Penelope took in the devastation with a kind of detached horror. Why did these things keep happening to her? Creditors. Destitution. Midnight intruders. What next? Kidnapping? Murder? She didn't notice she was trembling until Edwin gathered her into his arms.

"Wait here," he said, guiding her to sit on the edge of her cot.

Penelope watched him set things to rights. Part of her wondered distantly why he didn't alert the police, but she didn't want to say anything that might lead to Edwin running off to fetch a constable and leaving her here alone. When he finished tidying, Edwin turned to look at her, a question on his face.

"Stay with me," she told him. Even having him down the hall would be too far.

She lay down on the cot, turning on her side to make room for him. Edwin lay beside her and pulled her up against his warm chest. He wrapped his arms around her waist and laid his hands on hers, giving them a reassuring squeeze. With his body surrounding her, she was finally able to relax.

"I've no desire to go to my own room," he said, "but I am a little concerned. About the impropriety of the situation. For you, I mean."

"Nonsense," Penelope muttered sleepily. "We've still got all our clothes on."

Though in truth she'd rather not have. She wanted to take Edwin inside her and never let him go. *So this is what it feels like to be cared for,* Penelope thought as she drifted off.

She awoke the next afternoon to find that Edwin was gone. Worried that something had happened to him, she rose—still clothed—and went looking for him. She found him on the flat roof of the theatre, peering down at the street from behind the chimney.

"What is it?" she asked, coming up behind him and tucking her body up against his.

"See for yourself," Edwin said, sounding amused.

Penelope peeked around the chimney and saw two groups of people milling about in front of the theatre. The first group was made up of women and children from the middle classes. They were lined up in front of the door. Across from them were a group of sour-faced men. Husbands and wives, judging from the way they were shouting at each other.

"What is going on down there?" Penelope wondered.

"Well, it seems that they—" he pointed to the women and children, "have heard of the lady magician from their friends and want to see the show tonight. And they—" he pointed to the men, "object to their wives having funny ideas put into their heads by lady magicians."

Penelope watched as the crowd grew in size and anger. More people, attracted by the noise, had joined in or just stopped to gawk. There had to be more than three hundred people down there.

"Oh dear," Penelope said. "I seem to have single-handedly destabilised the Empire."

"Nonsense. It will be at least a fortnight before word of this reaches the colonies," Edwin said, grinning. "Besides, I seem to recall that you had assistance."

"What are we going to do?"

"I may have a friend who can help, but you will have to trust me."

Edwin let himself out the rear door and Penelope busied herself with her work, affixing the wax face that had been delivered that morning to the body of Mr Silver and trying to ignore the seething crowd outside.

Penelope had finished her modifications and was pacing the foyer when she heard a sudden hush outside. She was just reaching for the door when it burst open on its own. Edwin ducked inside.

"Penelope, I must tell you something before—"

He was interrupted when two footmen in royal livery threw open the double doors with a flourish and the strains of *God Save the Queen* began outside. Then, accompanied by a collection of guards and attendants, Queen Victoria swept into the shabby foyer. She was six-and-thirty but still bright-eyed and glowing on the arm of her dashing husband, Prince Albert. She wore a voluminous emerald gown and blue sash while the Prince had on an imposing red military coat and medals.

Stunned, Penelope dropped to the floor in a curtsey and stayed there. The Queen glided forward and stopped in front of Penelope. "We are very impressed with Sir Edwin's account of your work, Miss Sanbourne. I understand it is thanks to you that our forces were able to take Sevastopol last month. Well done."

"Yes," the Prince added. "We look forward to seeing your demonstration and I am sure Sir Edwin's father looks forward to equipping his airships with your latest invention."

His airships? Penelope thought. But that would mean Edwin's father was Lord Ashbury, commander of the airship navy! And that Edwin was a member of the nobility. She suddenly felt hopelessly inadequate. It was one thing to play at being noble onstage, and quite another to actually *be* high born.

"Oh, er, thank you, your majesties," she managed to stammer before the royal couple swept off with their entourage to commandeer the balcony.

She felt Edwin take hold of her elbow and guide her backstage. Once they were safely in their rooms he turned to her with an apologetic look. "I'm so sorry, Penelope. I did not mean for you to be blind sided."

"So it's true, then," Penelope said, feeling her desolation shift to ire. "You are the son of a lord!"

"The youngest," Edwin clarified. "Though Father wants rather less to do with me now that I am unfit for battle."

"You lied to me. You let me believe we were equals. That we could—" Penelope cut herself off before she gave voice to the embarrassing admission that she had been envisioning a future with Edwin. "And what is this about my helping to capture Sevastopol?"

"Your father has been selling your inventions to the Crown. Your rabbit is the basis for our clockwork cannons, and your steamer trunk provided the chemical boilers needed to power the airship fleet."

"So it was not a coincidence after all," Penelope said numbly.

"No. We also paid him for the command engine in Mr Silver's head, but he died before he could deliver it."

"That's why you're here," Penelope realised, feeling doubly betrayed. "You're not a theatre owner at all, are you?"

"No. I am Prince Albert's spy and procurement agent in matters of technology."

Penelope reached behind her, found a trunk, and collapsed onto it before her knees gave out.

"Is anything you told me true?" It was the closest she would allow herself to get to the real question on her mind: whether the tender feelings he had to shown her were a lie as well.

Edwin crouched awkwardly and took her hands, encouraging her to look into his earnest silver eyes. "Penelope, nothing of what I have told you of my thoughts and feelings is a lie. I may have entered your life on a pretence, but I have no wish to leave it."

Her eyes filled. She wanted to believe him, but how could she trust anything he said? She pulled her hands roughly from Edwin's and fixed him with an angry glare. "And if I wish you to go?

Edwin paled, hurt flashing in his eyes. "I wish you would not. There may be some danger presented by your father's injudicious dealings and—"

"I am perfectly able to defend myself against creditors. Now if you will excuse me, I have work to do."

"Surely you will still need my assistance during the performance."

"No. The *true* Mr Silver will serve me quite well."

Edwin turned to look at the automaton. He seemed startled to note the machine's resemblance to himself, right down to its suit of clothes and the shape of its waxwork face. She regretted having made the automaton over in Edwin's image. It was like a brilliant beacon proclaiming her regard for him.

"I expect Mr Silver will be needing his leg back," Edwin said quietly.

Penelope almost said yes just to hurt him, but could not bring herself to do it. "He will get on well enough as he is. Come along, Mr Silver."

She swept out of the room, the clockwork man following her with the odd gait of a man with a wooden leg.

For Penelope, the performance was a blur. She shoved aside all of her hurt feelings and threw her heart and soul into the act. The Queen's arrival had settled the conflict among the mob. No man would dare protest her performance now that it had been tacitly approved by the monarch. The women and children were free to watch with rapt attention. For them, she was performing illusions. For Prince Albert and the Queen, she was demonstrating her scientific prowess. She hoped they would be impressed enough to offer her employment. It would allow her to sever her ties with this theatre and its fraudulent owner.

"And now, for my final trick, I will run Mr Silver through with this blade," she said, holding up a wickedly glinting medieval sword. "And yet by the power of my magic, he will remain unharmed."

By the power of my building sword holes into his abdomen, Penelope thought, and stabbed her automaton, thrusting the blade in up to the hilt in full view of the audience. On cue, Mr Silver closed his glass eyes and sagged realistically. There was a horrified silence from the crowd. From where they were sitting, the automaton was indistinguishable from a real man. She allowed them to savour the moment before drawing the blade back out and showing them its bloodless surface.

"Not a drop of blood," she intoned mysteriously. "And behold! He lives!"

At this command, the automaton straightened and opened its eyes to a chorus of gasps followed by a storm of applause.

"Take a bow, Mr Silver," Penelope instructed.

Mr Silver bent at the waist, spreading its arms as if to capture their cheers and whistles. At her 'thank you,' he disappeared backstage.

Penelope drank in their adulation for a few moments more, then vanished in her characteristic puff of smoke. As she emerged backstage, her sense of well-being was immediately dashed by cold fear. A strange man with a thin moustache and a hard face was waiting for her. He held a pistol on Edwin, who stood frozen at the back of the room near the rear exit. With his other hand, he drew a second pistol and thrust it into Penelope's face.

"Where is engine?" the man demanded. He was dressed as a member of the upper classes, but his heavy accent gave him away as a Russian agent.

It was not creditors after all, Penelope realised. "I don't know what you mean," she said aloud to buy herself some time.

"You have engine, yes? Give to me or I kill him," the Russian told her, cocking the pistol he held on Edwin.

"No, please, I—" Penelope began, covertly reaching up her sleeve. "There's no reason to *attack him!*" she shouted, hoping to distract the Russian and bring her automaton into the fray on their side.

Edwin moved forward too soon and the Russian pulled the trigger. With a loud *bang* the pistol went off. The bullet took Edwin in the centre of the chest, knocking him back against the wall.

"No!" Penelope shouted, flinging a powder packet into the Russian's face. He screamed as purple smoke erupted, dropping the pistol and clawing at his eyes.

Penelope snatched up the pistol, and struck the screaming Russian in the face. Tears streaked down her cheeks. "You have killed him! You filthy, murdering cur!" she yelled as the Russian crumpled to the floor.

The door burst open and Edwin rushed in, followed by a handful of royal guards and the royal couple themselves, both of whom seemed invigorated by the commotion.

"Penelope!" Edwin exclaimed when he saw her. "Are you hurt?"

Penelope looked from Edwin to the figure slumped against the door across the room, which, now that the red haze had cleared from her eyes, she noticed wasn't bleeding. In the dimness, they had both mistaken Mr Silver for Edwin.

"Thank God!" Penelope cried, throwing her arms around Edwin's neck. "He's a Russian spy. I thought he'd killed you."

"There now, everything is perfectly fine," the Queen soothed as Edwin squeezed Penelope tightly. "Guards, please remove this man to the Tower."

The guards hauled the unconscious Russian away.

"It appears we have not managed to keep the secret of the engine nearly so well as I had hoped," Albert mused.

"I suspect the lovely Mr Sanbourne was unable to resist the lure of doubling his profit," the Queen said, frowning.

"I can't believe you were accosted by a Russian spy," Edwin said to Penelope.

"I can't believe it wasn't you he shot," Penelope replied.

"Are you sure you're all right?" they asked together.

Victoria and Albert exchanged a knowing look.

"We will leave you alone shortly to work things out," Albert said. "But first we wanted to offer you a position."

"We have had trouble inserting reliable spies into Russia," the Queen continued. "It occurs to us that in addition to providing us with the results of your experiments, you might use your show as a cover to allow Sir Edwin to collect information."

"If, that is, you're willing to work with me," Edwin added.

Penelope looked from Edwin to the royal couple and back again. It was all so sudden. But such an offer would surely never come again.

"Thank you, your majesties. I accept," she said with a curtsey.

"Excellent!" Albert exclaimed.

"Well, we shall leave you to it," the Queen said with a wink in Edwin's direction. She took Albert's arm and they left Penelope alone with Edwin.

"I'm sorry I lied," Edwin said, taking her hand. "Will you forgive me?"

"Yes," Penelope said, surprised to find that it was true. When she had thought him dead, her hurt feelings had been drowned in a wave of regret.

"Since I am to assist you in your magic, I thought it prudent to learn a trick. Would you like to see it?"

"Very much."

Edwin reached behind her ear and with a clumsy flick of his wrist, extracted a ring—a silver band set with an amethyst—from his sleeve and presented it to her. Albert had given Victoria a ring on the occasion of their betrothal fifteen years ago. Dare she hope this ring carried the same sentiment?

"Penelope, you are an extraordinary woman. But it would be improper for me accompany you into Russia, loving you as I do, without making you an offer." Edwin awkwardly lowered himself to one knee and looked up into her face with an expression of undisguised hope. "Will you accept me, flawed as I am?"

"Your sleight-of-hand does leave something to be desired," Penelope joked. "And of course I will expect you to be more forthcoming with your truths in the future, but otherwise . . . " she crouched down to Edwin's level and took his face in her hands. "Edwin, you are perfect. Of course I will accept."

Edwin beamed, taking the ring from her and slipping it onto her finger. Their lips met and locked, their bodies crushed tightly together. They could not get close enough.

"Perhaps now we shall have a repeat of the other night," Penelope said against Edwin's lips as she tugged him by his lapels toward her cot. "But this time, with slightly more impropriety and slightly less clothing."

"Nonsense. It is not at all improper for Mr Forrester to bed Mrs Forrester. It is simply a matter of timing," Edwin replied, and they tumbled together onto the cot.

PRACTICALLY PERFECT

RAY DEAN

The dock was busier than he remembered it when he'd left a few weeks before. As tourists pushed and shoved their way off the barge and onto the quay, Patrick Marshall refused to join in with the jostling crowd, far more disconcerting than the currents. He stood back and waited for them to clear before he tried to disembark. A young woman at the back of the pack tripped over the hem of her fashionable skirt and nearly fell to her knees. It was only the quick thinking and nimble feet of a nearby fellah that prevented her from injury. She was all a-flutter with pretty embarrassment and thanks until she caught sight of the dark-skinned hand on her elbow. With a fearful gasp she pulled away before scuttling after the rest of her group onto the sandy trail to the tombs.

The heavy scrape of a crate across the floor of the boat brought him back to the matter at hand. Turning, he lent his own strength to the task, taking the bottom of the crate and lifting it. He met his old friend's eyes over the rough-hewn boards that fashioned the top of the crate. "Let's make quick work of this, Rabah, and we shall have a few hours to ourselves before my meeting with Miss Wardlaw."

"We would have had more time to ourselves if we had but purchased a ride into port on a craft of greater speed and," he ground his teeth together as he struggled to lift the crate higher between them, "space."

Together they set the crate on the back of a wagon and walked back up the gangplank to get the next. "And you know that if we had purchased a ride on the *Zephyr* or the *Boreas* we still would have been forced to take the train from Cairo or get right on this same barge." Patrick pulled a crate toward him and waited for Rabah to do the same. "The priests still won't let the airships travel over Egyptian sands. Covering the sun angers the sun god, Ra."

"I would rather a shorter voyage, especially with the weight of our cargo. But I am always glad of time to sit and talk with you, old friend." Rabah grunted as they lifted another crate between them. "Do you think it wise to wait?"

As they hefted the second crate over the edge of the boat and stepped down the gangway, Patrick gave his friend a curious look. "She won't be expecting me for another few hours. I know she likes to be punctual, but really, Rabah-"

"The man at the head of that group." He looked towards the gaggle of tourists that were now only beginning the ascension to the better-known tombs. "That is Halen Crawford." They braced their feet as they lifted the second crate onto the first.

"I thought he looked familiar." Patrick groaned as a muscle in his back gave a twinge. "He's leading tours now?" He barked out a laugh. "He always was a stuffed shirt; now he's paid to sound like he knows what he's saying. We'll never get him to keep quiet." Patrick wiped a kerchief over his brow. "What does he have to do with my appointment with Frances?"

Rabah was already crossing back onto the boat with a smile twisting at his lips. "While you've been away, Mr Crawford has decided to court Miss Wardlaw and—" Startled at Patrick's sudden push past him, Rabah watched as his friend attempted to lift the last crate on his own.

"Come, Rabah, let's get this done."

Together they loaded the final crate onto the wagon at the end of the quay and Patrick climbed up onto the wagon's seat. With a jerk, he unlocked the brake, startling the donkeys.

Rabah rushed to the side of the wagon, gesturing at the small pile of bags huddled on the pier. "What about your belongings, old friend?"

"Bring them when you can. I have to go." With a quick flick of his wrists, he sent the donkeys off at a quick pace, and sent a half-hearted wave over his shoulder.

Frances shielded her eyes from the blinding flood of sunlight as she tried to gauge the hour. Patrick was due back soon and as hard as it was to admit the uncomfortable truth to herself, she was looking forward to his return.

Leaving her maps on the camp table, she crossed to the top of the stairway and peered down. Daoud, their *reis*, was hard at work supervising the bucket brigade. Her shadow fell over Daoud and the foreman lifted his head.

He smiled his great smile as he raised his hand. "*Sitt*, we are making progress."

She smiled back at him. Even though they were old friends, he always referred to her with the honorific 'lady'. "I see. How much longer do you suppose it will take,Daoud?"

He gestured, a wave of his hand like a wise old conjurer that made his words seem all the more important. "We will finish when we finish, *Sitt*."

"Yes, well . . . " she removed notebook from the breast pocket of her vest and noted the date. "My father is due back in a month and he'll expect progress, Daoud. More progress than we've achieved."

Nodding his head, the thick turban protecting his head from the worst of the punishing sun, he turned back to the workers and hurried them along.

Frances knew it wasn't his fault. In fact, the very reason they had to remove water from the tomb was the only reason they found it in the first place. Winter rains had flooded the Nile's banks higher than anyone could remember, and when the waters receded, they'd taken more than just the normal scree that collected at the base of the *wadi*; several large boulders had broken apart from the force of the waters and had revealed the entrance to another tomb.

A number of notable Egyptologists had all raced to claim rights to excavate the tomb, but the Antiquities Department, in an excited rush, had given the rights to the man who had discovered it. Thomas Wardlaw had been the first to arrive on the scene and with his daughter in tow, had recorded the first indication of a tomb: the flat, levelled cut of stone that marked a stair.

What had been a clamour in the scientific community turned into a trickle as everyone realised that the tomb was still buried . . .

under water. The floodwaters had receded back to the normal banks of the Nile, but the same water that had revealed the tomb choked the stairway it had revealed. When Thomas had exhausted all the conventional methods of removing the water from the tomb's stairway, he sent Patrick to look for a solution, any slightly-less-than-crazy scheme that would help them reveal the tomb's treasures. Unable to suffer the wait at the steps of his discovery, Thomas had returned to Luxor, hoping to arrange investors to back their excavation. He knew when that when the solution presented itself, it wasn't going to be cheap.

Thomas had been hesitant to leave Frances behind. While he left much of the excavation details to her when they were together, he was always at her side. Even though he told her she had his every confidence, she knew that he was still unsure of her, because she was his daughter, not his son. "After all," he'd declared, "all the men will be doing is removing water from the tomb . . . not anything of circumstance. So this should be easy enough for you."

There in the safe cover of the tent, she didn't have to hide her eyes from the sun, but still she ducked her head so that no one would see the moment of weakness that had her rubbing at her eyes.

As he approached the dig site, Patrick pulled up short on the reins and fought the headstrong donkeys as a steamer-sled cut across his path. The contraption, built to convey baggage for the throngs of tourists that scattered the sands, belched black smoke from its final set of stacks. The inky cloud choked the donkeys and Patrick struggled to control the beasts and keep them in place. The group of tourists served by this track-fed monstrosity was led by the same pompous jackanapes that he'd managed to avoid at the pier. He had a feeling his luck wasn't going to continue to hold out. Cutting across the sand like an oversized sidewinder, Halen Crawford's gaggle of well-dressed ladies fluttered behind him. With their expensive hats covered in silk flowers and feathers, they resembled a spring basket of colourful blooms that would have been very much at home in his grandmother's foyer.

Once the group had cleared out of his way, he made short work of the remaining journey. Recognising the distinctive set-up of tents, Patrick set the brake on the wagon and handed the reins to one of the Wardlaw labourers. He slid to the ground and moved to stand behind Frances, who had her full attention focused on the approaching mass.

One of the dragomen from Shepherd's Hotel was trying in vain to keep up with Halen's ground-swallowing steps, stopping from time to time for the ladies to run after him, their hems lifted high enough to allow for some speed, but low enough to hide their petticoats. Halen presented himself at the tent with characteristic aplomb, his wide white grin shining beneath his kepi.

"So good to see you, Miss Wardlaw." The rounded vowels and the hiss of consonants gave his inflection more of a snakelike resonance than Patrick had originally given him credit for.

"Mr Crawford." She lifted her chin and looked over the group trailing behind him. "I see you're on a tour."

"These delightful debutantes are from Mrs Weatherbee's School for Young Ladies on their World Tour." Head bobbing and fan fluttering ensued as the aforementioned females reformed in their little knot. "I thought they might enjoy seeing a woman hard at work." His toothy grin and grand hand gestures did much to thrill those in his charge and equally set Frances on edge if her ramrod straight backbone was any indication. "Come, ladies, and meet Miss Wardlaw."

They surged forward in a formation that any military commander would have envied, almost completely penning Frances in her tent.

"She's quite the little helper for her father. A woman with a wide variety of skills and is-"

"Quite busy, thank you, Mr Crawford." She turned a somewhat polite smile on the masses. "Ladies, if you will excuse me, I have quite a bit of work to do. Mr Primer, just a few hundred feet further into the *wadi*, is due to bring a sarcophagus out of the tomb," she lifted her pendant-watch and a true smile stretched across her lips, "in a few minutes."

The promise of a piece of treasure had the ladies all a-twitter with excitement. "Oh, may we, Mr Crawford . . . please?"

"Well, I did want you ladies to see the Wardlaw Tomb and-"

Patrick couldn't stay quiet any longer. "It's still underwater, Crawford." He felt Frances tense as he made his presence known.

"There's nothing to see unless you want to stare at buckets of muddy water."

Halen looked from Patrick to Frances and back again, his mind visibly whirring with various arguments for both avenues of action. With the pressure of the young ladies of the tour group waiting anxiously behind him, and the rather insistent regard of Patrick, Halen felt the world hemming him in. With a burst of uncharacteristic energy, Halen skirted the table and grasped Frances' arm, drawing her out into the light of the sun.

It took a moment for her to extricate her arm from his grasp after they'd come to a stop, but Frances managed to do it with a minimum of fuss. "What do you want, Mr Crawford?"

He gave her an indulgent smile. "Come now, Frances," his tone tried to coax her into a smile. "We rarely have any time alone."

She looked up at him with narrowed eyes. "That is by design, Mr Crawford." She continued on before he could interrupt. "I have work to do, sir . . . and you have a group of young ladies to mind."

"You know I only conduct these confounded tours to be near you, my dear." He side-stepped to block her view from Patrick and the other men at the work site. "And when your father returns from Luxor, you and I will ask him to set a date for the wedding."

Frances seemed almost frozen to the spot and Halen's expectant smile dwindled to a waxy grimace.

"Frances?"

She blinked at him. "My father has explained your proposal, and while I am honoured at your consideration, I can only hope that you will understand that we are not suited in such a manner."

"Not suited?" Halen's voice climbed up his vocal register. "Your father accepted my suit, Frances. He has given me his word." Halen followed her as she marched past him back to her camp table, sputtering his displeasure. "This won't do, Frances. Really, you can't act like this and expect me to understand. I am far from pleased."

Stepping around Patrick, she picked up her notebook. "I don't act to please you, Halen." She held up her own finger to mirror his posture and cut off his words. "I act the way I want to."

"You'll think differently," he asserted. "You'll think differently when we're married and you've my household to run." He snatched her notebook away and tore a few pages from it. "I'm saving you from this . . . this . . . masculine sham of a life, Frances. Once you're my wife, you'll see the truth of my words." He threw the notebook down at his feet where it made a hollow thud as it came to an abrupt stop in the sand. "You'll see."

Patrick stopped short when he felt Frances' arm connect with his chest. Without sparing him a look, Frances stepped up to Halen and tilted her chin up to meet his angry glare. He didn't tower over her like Patrick did, but the look she gave him seemed to shrink him down to the size of a mouse.

"What I see now, Halen, is the idiocy of your offer. When you asked my father for permission to court me, I felt a certain . . . curiosity about the idea. I had wondered what it would be like to have a man court me. It was momentarily interesting. I had no idea that you had entered into an 'agreement' with my father. That does not make me think any better of you. Rather," she straightened her spine another fraction of an inch and seemed to look down at him further, "I now consider you an inconvenient bore."

The words may as well have been yelled, instead of the soft, enunciation of her thoughts, for they had the same effect. All movement in the vicinity stopped. The young women Halen had been squiring gaped in shock at the exchange, and more than a few fans forgot to flutter in reaction, even in the stifling heat. The workers turned toward the camp, their expressions studies of concern for their young *Sitt*. But those most affected by the sudden outburst from the normally staid young woman were the two men standing closest to her.

Unable to make any argument, Halen resorted to the first words that came to mind. "Just you wait until your father comes back." He wagged his finger at her again and seemed lost when she didn't move or reply. Left in that uncomfortable silence, he pivoted on his heel in the sand and trudged off with his tour group.

"Well," Patrick couldn't help the choke of laughter in his voice as Halen nearly tripped over a discarded parasol as he traipsed along with his beruffled ladies. "I don't think he was expecting—"

"Speaking of expecting," Frances whirled around to face him, her finger poking into his chest, "you didn't send word to tell me exactly when you'd be coming back."

Patrick backed up a step and she advanced, "I thought it would be better—"

"Oh!" she gasped and poked again. "You thought it would be better . . . what?"

"Better if I just came home." He captured her hand in his and held it still, his fingers gentle, his hand warm. "Are you really angry with me, Frances?"

Her bluster disappeared and her shoulders slumped. A moment later she recovered herself and withdrew her hand from his. "Just tell me you brought it with you."

Patrick shook his head and smiled. "Back to business." He gestured at the crates on the wagon. "One water pump for the Wardlaw Excavation . . . done."

A moment later he was moving, her hand pulling at his sleeve. He kept pace with her as she ran to the wagon, not wanting to give her any reason to let go. It was only when they'd reached the vehicle that they slowed to move through the cluster of her workers. Rabah, who had made his own way to the camp, offered her a steadying hand. She eagerly took it and set her booted foot on the wheel to lift herself up. A sudden slip drew a gasp from her. A heartbeat later, two hands caught her boot in their steady grip. With a slight boost, she was safely atop the wagon. Turning to thank her rescuer, Frances met Patrick's warm brown eyes.

Rabah cleared his throat and handed her the jimmy. She gave him a smile and nod in thanks. Inserting the metal tool between the lid and the wall at the centre of the box she pushed down and was rewarded with a loud squeak as the nails pulled free of the crate. Another few pushes and she stood back as Rabah removed the lid and handed it down. Inside the crate was a mass of metal pieces and joiners. Frances pressed her hands to her chest to contain the wild beating of her heart. Giving her men and wide smile, she fairly bounced on the balls of her feet.

The workers had emerged from the stairs and Daoud made his way to the front of the group to stand beside Patrick. "Well, *Sitt?*"

Reaching into the crate, she removed a few pieces of the pipe and felt their weight. "Once we've put this together, Daoud, your men will be able to lift the water from the tomb and we'll finally be able to dig!"

The men sent up a rousing cheer and Frances handed the first two pieces down to Patrick. Once he took the pipes from her and moved away, she found herself clasping her hands together as if she could hold onto the warmth of his touch. It was a silly notion and she shook herself out of her reverie. Fanciful thoughts were something that those prissy little misses on Halen's tour could afford. If she wanted to be taken seriously as an archeologist, it would take more than her certificate from the *Institut Francais d'Archeologie Orientale* and a father who was an Egyptologist; it would take years of dedication to make even a small mark in the history books.

Once the pieces were all handed down and laid out near the mouth of the stairs, Frances joined Patrick beside the blanket covered with parts of the water pump. "I've only read about these," she admitted. "But you've seen it in action?"

He nodded as he rearranged the placements of some of the parts to match the diagram he had drawn out on paper.

She tilted her head to look at the drawing and then reached out and took the same part Patrick had just moved, turning it around in the other direction.

He gave her a sharp look and turned the piece back and moved on. "What was that with Crawford?"

"He's decided that we should marry." She looked at the diagram again and moved a pipe at the corner of the blanket and switched it with one in the centre. "I decided that he'd lost his mind."

Patrick watched her rearrange the position of a valve. "I think he'd be a good husband." He heard her gasp and while she was distracted, he put the other piece back in place. "If you weren't who you are."

She opened her mouth to argue and then closed it again, looking down at her hands placed primly on her knees. They both held the marks and scars of hard work. "I'm not what you would call a proper young lady."

Her tone bothered him more than he'd care to admit and he turned to look at her as the plans in his hand dropped to the blanket. "What does that mean?"

She picked up the paper and looked it over. "Those girls at the dig today," she sighed. "The perfect dress, the perfect hair; I'm sure they even know how to dance and sing and play musical instruments . . . they're probably all practically perfect."

"Frances," he began, grinding this teeth together, "where did you get the idea that—"

"Well my father has certainly said it enough," she picked up two joints and set them together. "He thinks that I'm hiding myself away because I don't think I'll make a good wife. And then there was Halen-"

"Halen the a-"

"Patrick!" She scolded him with her voice but her eyes were bright with laughter. "I'm not worried about something as silly as that, really, but—"

"I really wish you wouldn't listen to people like Halen Crawford." Patrick tried to fit two pieces together, but the edges didn't match. Another attempt yielded the same result. "What does he know about you anyway?"

Frances leaned over and gave the part in his left hand a half turn. The two pieces fit snugly together on the next try. "Halen and I have known each other for years."

Patrick gave her a smile. "I've only known you for two, and there's something I can tell you without a doubt." He handed the joined piece to her and watched as she easily set it into place. "You would be a great success in anything you did, because when you decide to do something . . . you, Frances Wardlaw, do it."

"And if I wanted to be an Egyptologist . . . *and* a wife?" She handed a pipe to Patrick and exchanged it for the piece in his right hand.

He put the two parts together with a quick twist. "Then you'd make a success out of that too, Frances."

She gave him a satisfied nod. "All right then." She picked up a U-shaped pipe and joined it with the collar already in her hand. "Then I'm deciding we need to get this thing put together. I want to dig tomorrow!"

"Yes, Miss Wardlaw." Patrick gave her a mock salute that earned him a cuff on his shoulder.

"You know what else I've decided, Patrick?" She looked over at him with a regal lift of her chin and a quirk at the corner of her lips.

"I'm afraid to ask."

Her eyes flashed in a moment of playful anger before she continued. "I've decided that you are going to come to the *Aswan* and share a meal with me."

"Tonight?" He prayed that his voice didn't show the strain of his emotions.

"Of course, tonight," she answered him. "We need to celebrate! Because," she handed him a handful of bolts, "I missed you while you were gone, Patrick. I missed you a lot."

He looked down at the metal joiners in his hands and tried to remember how to breathe. "I missed you too."

The Wardlaw labourers lived in a nearby town. In the cooler winter months, when excavations peppered the sands along the Nile with makeshift collections of tents, the towns in the nearby areas were nearly empty of men. While some of the more well-known digs brought their workers in from Cairo or Luxor, Thomas Wardlaw preferred giving work to local men. They were loyal and their families were appreciative of the work. They sometimes came to watch the men work in the tombs, their babies and small children playing beneath the tents the men pitched to shield them from the sun.

Patrick, who usually stayed on the *Aswan* with the Wardlaws, had opted to stay with Rabah and his family in the village while Thomas was gone. Even with the number of servants living on the shallow-bottomed boat with Frances, he couldn't help but feel that there was a potential for rumours to circulate and he wouldn't dream of causing her family any discomfort or shame.

That, and the fact that sitting with Frances, alone, at every morning and evening repast would be too tempting for him. He was bound to say something stupid . . . perhaps tell her exactly how he felt. So, for tonight's celebration, making the journey to the Wardlaw *dahabeeyah* gave him ample time to remind him to keep his thoughts and his words to himself.

When Patrick arrived at the quay, freshly bathed and in a clean suit of clothes, Frances was waiting for him, her hand resting lightly on the deck rail. Even in the twilight he noticed the slight tremor of her fingers and hoped she wouldn't notice that his hands were clammy as he took her free hand in.

Her lips parted then closed as she watched him lower her hand, though he didn't let it go. "I've asked Tures to serve tea in the parlour."

He nodded, but didn't say anything, waiting for his heart to slow to a steady rhythm.

Frances wondered what to do. She wanted to take her hand back, because in a moment or two, she was going to do something stupid like giggle, or prance about like a silly schoolgirl . . . or throw herself into his arms.

It was the night that provided her the escape she wanted. The bright moonlight overhead was suddenly doused and a large slowly moving shadow slipped over their heads. Leaning back, Frances could see the soft lanterns of a large dirigible coasting low in the sky. In the night sky, the aerofoils were all but invisible apart from the moonlight sliding along the curved canvas bodies of the airship

They sailed the air at night, giving tourists an unequalled view of the Nile and the villages along the way. "When did that start?" Patrick's question startled them both.

"A few weeks ago. The tickets make them too much money to turn down." To Frances, they blotted out the romance of the moon and her silvery light. "At night they can be called illusion, a trick of the human eye. They avoid the embargo on airship travel over Egypt while they can remain more illusion than cold reality. If the Crown allowed them to fly over the sands, in no time we would have no sky left to gaze upon."

She turned to Patrick, only to find him a few inches away, his eyes focused on her face. "Patrick, I—" She blinked at him, wondering where her words had gone.

"Yes, Frances?" His tone was honeyed and warm, the light of the lanterns dancing in his dark eyes.

"I wanted to say, that is, I thought . . . "

He stepped closer, his hands closing around her upper arms to steady them both. "Yes, Frances?"

Her eyelids began to close as she rose up on the tips of her toes in her boots. "Thought that I, and you . . . "

His breath brushed against her cheek. "And I?"

She shivered. "That we—" As Frances leaned closer she saw a sweep of motion over Patrick's shoulder. "Look out!"

Patrick instinctively curled his body around hers, trying to protect her. The defensive movement did nothing to protect him from the vicious blow he took from behind. Patrick staggered as pain pushed away all conscious thought.

Frances panicked. She saw their attacker clearly as the airship moved further away and the moonlight fell unfettered to the ground. Halen Crawford lifted his weapon to swing again and Frances tried to push Patrick out of the way. With her sudden shift, she knocked her parasol from its resting place against one of the rails, and the long shaft and serviceable canvas cover tangled with Halen's feet. With a yelp and a muttered oath he fell to the deck, hitting his head, and slumped unconscious.

Patrick leaned heavily against her. She tried to manoeuvre them towards the gangway, but he staggered and a moment later they both fell heavily into the waters of the Nile.

Her shout was immediately answered by the crew aboard the *dahabeeyah*. The *sufragi* who had been awaiting their appearance was the first to the rail, calling for help. Servants and sailors rushed down the gangway and the two young men who dove immediately into the water soon had both Frances and Patrick safe on the quay.

Many disappeared up the gangplank to find dry clothes and towels, and a few remained to assist Frances.

The young woman was muttering to herself as she rolled Patrick onto his side. "What did that article say? Godey's . . . or Peterson's . . . page 500 or so . . . what did they say to do?"

"*Sitt?*" Tures moved closer. "What do you mean?"

Frances barely looked at the girl over her shoulder. "I read an article about drowning . . . how to make them breathe . . . I read an article." She fought with his unresponsive body, trying to push him into a position that might jog her memory. "I just need to remember. I just need to . . . " The search of her mind finally yielded the right information and Frances grabbed a few towels and thrust them under Patrick's back before she straddled his chest and pushed to expel the water from his lips. Her clothes had soaked up enough water that they glued to her limbs, rather than allowing her free movement, but she pushed the thoughts from her mind as she concentrated on reviving Patrick.

She counted the number of repetitions and was about to turn him again when water spurted out from between his lips and she pushed again, near frantic. "Please, Patrick. Breathe!"

Gasps turned into coughs and Frances snatched up a cloth to wipe Patrick's face. "Frances?"

"Yes, Patrick?"

He smiled at the owlish look of her eyes, still wide in shock and fear. "What happened?"

"Halen is what happened," she asserted, and saw Patrick's confusion grow. "He hit you!" Turning her head, she glared at Halen's unconscious form with a rancour she had had never turned on any other man in her twenty years, but the slight tremor of Patrick's hand on her arm drew her attention back to his pale face. "Don't ever . . . *ever* do that again."

His smile was distracting. "Well, I hadn't planned on a jealous suitor cracking me over the head," He shook himself slightly. "But I wasn't asking about him."

"Then what?" A cooling breeze across the Nile brushed against her damp stockings and she realised where she was sitting. "Oh dear."

"Frances-"

"Patrick, I had no choice!" She struggled to find a way to rise, but there was little she could do without pulling her skirts even higher on her legs. "What you must think!" She tried another method to get up but found herself confounded by the puzzle.

"Frances!"

She froze and stared back at him, her cheeks warm with embarrassment. "Yes, Patrick?"

"I'm not arguing!" He smiled when she didn't move. "I'm not upset." She continued to stare at him, her eyes filling with tears. "And I think after you saved my life, I owe you something, including my discretion."

"Well," she sputtered. "I really wasn't the one to save you." She turned from one side to the other looking for assistance from the sailors who had so bravely jumped into the water after them, but all the sailors and servants had disappeared into the night, leaving them alone. She turned back on him, high colour in her cheeks from frustration. "And you're lucky I remembered that article from one of my Lady's magazines," she all but scolded him. "You, who are so fond of making fun of my one little vanity!"

His lips curled in a smile even as raged at him. His free hand idly smoothed over the back of hers, trying to calm her sudden tirade. "You're right, I'll keep quiet about them in the future."

"See?" She gazed down at him triumphantly. "That's exactly what I've been trying to tell you, Patrick."

"Yes, Frances." He grinned up at her, enjoying the bright light in her eyes. "Now, I have something to say to you." She sat still for a moment looking at him. Convinced that he finally had her attention on him, he nodded. "Frances, I think—"

She stopped him short. "Patrick, let me tell you what I think." She smiled when he waited for her speak. Wrapping her arms around his neck, she leaned closer. "I think you're practically perfect."

SMUGGLER'S DEAL

MARILAG ANGWAY

The *Emese* fell from the sky.

There had been a contingency scheme. As a steam-powered carrack, the airship was lauded with safety measures beyond the flight requirements: rotational sails, twice the backup supply of stone-fuel in the engine room, a more-than-seasoned crew. There were cannons aplenty for distance shooting, blunderbusses ready for closer combat, and protections upon the high metal plating that ran across the ship's body.

To be sure, any skailor worth her salt would have praised the hardiness of the *Emese*.

But any skailor worth her salt would have also acceded that projectile acid was an exceptional circumstance. Contingency or no, the ship was bound to deteriorate, and do so quickly.

So the *Emese* continued its involuntary descent, tipping further on the direction of the bow, making it much harder for the ship's captain—in fact, for anyone—to hang on.

Aura strapped herself to the ship with a set of ropes. By her side, her navigator had been the first to take the plunge, her plump figure spilling overboard faster than the downward plummet of a cannonball. All of the clock-makers had scrambled out of the engine room, some hanging onto the masts, others climbing them in order to reorient the sails. The attempt at the sails worked somewhat; the speed of the plummet had slowed. But that did not stop the *Emese* from further tipping to the side.

As frightening as the situation was, Aura could not bring herself to fear for her life. Instead she felt a great deal of anger and a strong desire for murder. Bounty hunters were not required to kill their bounties, and Aura was known for her leniency in that department. However, she was damn sure that if she survived this defeat, she would not be against a slow and painful murder. Heck, she might even *enjoy* it.

Damn that Frederick Newgate!

Aura lamented the state of her ship's turul figurehead. One of the wings had snapped off, and she found no end to the irony of her choosing a bird as her airship's mascot. Clearly the *Emese* was not fit to fly the skies at that moment.

The captain positioned her body against one of the rope ladders, all the while pulling her emergency glider open. She looked up and saw the *Marchioness* looming closer, its dark, metallic hull gleaming victorious in the morning sun.

The *Marchioness* hovered in the sky.

She had just emerged the decisive victor of a dangerous game. The minute the new cannons had been set in play, there had been no hope for the *Emese*. Still, the time between the fall and the extractions had been limited, and it took more than two trips to retrieve the crew from Aurora Gaigna's ship. The *Marchioness* was known for its skilled wingmen, but even so, her captain had expected a more efficient rescue.

Frederick Newgate remained still, his eyes taking stock of the captured *Emese* skailors. One by one, the last of his men arrived on deck, securing the last of their involuntary passengers. There were surprised yelps, a couple of fisticuffs, several whimpers of untold injuries.

His eyes narrowed. "She's not aboard," Fred said.

"No, Cap." His first mate, Darcy, was struggling to hold onto a rambunctious, curvy female who was screaming bloody murder at him. Darcy grimaced, though he gave no other indication of discomfort towards his captive. "We got everyone but. The navigator was hardest to get at, but Hoshe's got more nerve and skill than a Pernatan clock-maker. He went in after her right quick."

Fred looked away, biting down his frustration. "Send another set of wingmen down. *Find her*, Darcy. Without Aurora Gaigna . . . "

"Due respect, Cap," Darcy grunted, finally managing to subdue the woman, who seemed to understand the gravity of the situation, "sending any of us *now* would be suicide. It's too far down, and there's no saying what's below us. The Old World—"

"Is the least of our worries. We can't leave her in the Old World for the things below to get at her."

"Cap, you've been watching the ship," Darcy said, "It's gone now. No turning back. Besides, without their captain, they're no good, right? That's what we wanted!"

"Like hell we'd be no good," snapped Darcy's prisoner. "The authorities'll hear about this!"

Fred ignored the woman, his stare still on his first mate. "We are smugglers, Darcy, *not* murderers. One does not waste the life of a highly-decorated bounty hunter. Take the helm and watch the skies. I will signal for you."

"What? Cap—"

Fred silenced him with a stern look. Darcy's objection caught in his throat, and he immediately bellowed orders to the men. The woman looked at the horizon. Her mouth was a thin line, which loosened briefly to say something quietly to Darcy. The first mate grinned. "Oh, like as not he'll get her alright."

Fred did not hear the rest of the exchange. He hurried towards Darcy's open locker, pulling the flyer out and spreading the metallic hinges wide. The wing fabric was old, frayed, but Fred had no time, and he knew the risks. He put the contraption on his back, secured the fastenings around his waist, rushed to where he could still see the falling airship. He climbed the ropes to the side, his feet planted firmly upon the bulwark. He checked his jacket and found his flare secured underneath his shirt. Good.

Frederick Newgate took a deep breath, and flung himself from the *Marchioness.*

Damn Frederick and his damn ship and his damn acidic cannons!

Aura woke to infuriated thoughts, which did nothing to lessen the pain she felt all over her body. She groaned and tried to sit up, only to find that she was pressed to a thick tree branch, ropes a wild tangle around her. She could see broken branches above, evidently disturbed by her fall. She expected a ship to be hovering somewhere near the clouds, but she saw not even a speck of it, heard no noise of its geared engines.

Moving had been a pain, and she winced when she plucked at her glider, tattered and torn from the impact with the tree. It would be useless to her now, though she thanked the heavens that she'd managed to escape. Aura tried to turn her head, but found that it was too painful to do so.

She heard movement and tried to place it. Something below spoke to her.

"Trust you to be difficult about the whole thing."

Aura saw rough hands reach towards her. She could barely move, could not stop the hands disentangling her from the tree, could not even hold an objection when they began rubbing at her bruised muscles with something cold, gelatinous, and smelling of mint.

Blasted smuggler, she thought before losing consciousness once again.

Damn this woman!

The bounty hunter had gotten herself tangled up, which made it difficult for Fred to retrieve her. He suffered the pain silently as he climbed down the tree with the woman slung over his shoulder. Had she been childlike or wraithlike, this would not have been such an issue. Aurora Gaigna, however, was neither child nor wraith. In another circumstance, he would have appreciated having such a woman in his arms.

Clearly that appreciation did not apply while stuck up a tree.

Fred gently placed her on the ground, pulling at his pack in order to get at his salves. He knew there would be relief in them, but judging from the great height she had fallen, no remedy was better than taking her to a physician. He unbuttoned the woman's trench coat, turned her around, and loosened the ties on the back of her corseted waist.

"Sorry, a necessary disrobing," he muttered, exposing bruised flesh.

Fred knew she couldn't hear him, but the one-sided conversation alleviated his worry somewhat. He had never really set foot upon Old World soil. The dirt at his feet, the brush of the tree-bark, the crisp smell of natural plants, it was all very strange, almost menacing. The floating cities gave warnings about the world below for a reason, and the dangers on the ground far surpassed that of the sky. Pirates and bounty hunters could be fought, for they were human—for the most part. The Old World, however natural it was, bred things that were no longer human.

The thought of encountering trouble hurried his hand. Fred set the salve aside and picked up the flyer.

"No good," he said. During his downward glide, one of the wings had torn away. He ripped the fabric from the other wing and used it to rub the rest of the salve on the woman's skin, making sure not to press too hard or move too far down. He re-laced her clothing and turned her to face him. She breathed steadily.

She would survive, he thought with relief. The bounty hunter would be furious—murderous—when she woke, but he could handle that. Aurora Gaigna had chased Fred across floating cities on and off for enough years that he was used to her presence.

This time, though, he had leverage.

He looked around, saw that he was in a shaded clearing. Parts of the *Emese* could be seen littering the area, though the ship itself must have fallen elsewhere. He made to examine the clearing further, but the rustling leaves stayed his movements. Beneath him, the ground rumbled in an odd rhythm.

Fred had no time to react when the brush was invaded by a troop of automata. One of them shot him with a dart, and he was too slow to react. He felt the pinprick, winced at the numbing pain travelling from his neck and spreading to the rest of his body.

He fell to the ground.

The world grew lighter with each subsequent blink.

"You look more intimidating in the propaganda," a voice said beside her. Aura registered it as gruff and male and altogether *too familiar.*

"Holding firearms does make me seem a bit more malicious," she rasped. She wriggled and found that she could move. "Take note, I'm a much better markswoman than the posters give me credit for."

Her arms were tied in front of her, her legs as well. Every time she moved, it felt like her entire body was being subjected to a wrestling match against a pack of sharp needles. And the needles were winning.

She steadied herself upon the cold, metal bars at her back, fighting off the stabbing pains erupting from her legs and forearms. When she tried to scoot away from the man beside her, she found that she could not. Aura looked down.

"Ah, yes," he said, his voice irritatingly unconcerned. "I wasn't actually planning on getting in this spot of trouble, but there it is."

Aura traced a long metal chain that looped around her tightly-wrapped wrists down to the ground and back up to the wrists of a tied-up smuggler. He was smiling at her, from the tops of his amused, green eyes, down to his wide, crooked grin. He looked bruised, though his face did not show any mark of pain. She saw the chains behind him circling one of the metal bars, and was relieved that it had not been done to her. The chain that connected her wrists to his was inconvenient enough.

"Frederick Newgate," she said his name fully, spitting every other syllable out with venomous intent. For a moment, she had forgotten the immense soreness all over her body.

But the moment passed once she realised she was cuffed to a man and they were both imprisoned within a dimly-lit, nondescript room. Somebody had taken her trench coat and rid her short, chestnut hair of pins. There were no firearms upon her person. She wanted her revolvers, desired the security of feeling them around her waist. She patted her black boots down and frowned. They had taken her favourite derringer as well. And, she realised, it was *damn cold* without her coat.

"Fred, really," the man said. "Anyone who's read my file knows that the surname isn't real."

"You shot my ship," she said, though her attention was no longer on him. If she could find anything upon her person, anything at all—ah, her boot. The derringer wasn't there, but maybe . . .

"A matter of necessity," he said. "Why be chased by a beautiful woman when you can meet her head-on?"

Aura ignored him. She planned to do so for some time, until she heard him say softly, "I *am* sorry about your ship."

Thoughts flooded her head, her crew fallen, her ship in tatters, her turul figurehead . . . all of them lost. She had travelled with her skailors on the *Emese* for almost a decade. Aura's crew had been formidable, the *Emese* a technological marvel; yet it took one smuggling ship to bring it all crashing down.

Her temper flared, and with excruciating effort, she aimed her elbow and attempted a jab. A hard one.

It never landed. A scuffle ensued, as much of one where two captives were chained to each other. Aura landed on the man's lap, the chains becoming a tangled mess between them. She pushed off by reflex, which only worsened the situation, and it took some moments of struggle before they were sitting side by side once more. Her face burned with annoyance and embarrassment.

He laughed, which further incensed her. Yet she had noticed his pained breathing as they fought. Like her, the smuggler was putting on a brave face. "You deserved that," she said.

"Look. We're stuck here, so best make friendly and work together, yes?"

Aura sniffed. "Friendship is hardly something I'm willing to offer. Not unless you'd perish happily for it."

"Funny how propaganda never seems to mention your temperament, Aurora Gaigna," he said. She decided not to chide him, and instead gazed at her surroundings.

Metal bars inside a metal prison, polished stone floors that seemed to vibrate with warning. The place was sturdy and unbreakable, and Aura had no equipment with her that would be able to cut through any of it. There were gas lamps near the door, illuminating both the prison and the room in a limited fashion. She needed to contend with two locks, one on the prison, and the other on the outer door. She returned to searching her boots, her fingers reaching to the inside of the leather.

The open bars gave her a view of a small window opposite the door, though very little light came through that. The gas lamps seemed low on fuel, the flames flickering constantly. There was a wooden table with several chairs on the other side of the bars, a couple of plates and cups littering the table's surface. The plates and cups were full of food, uneaten and—from the smell that occasionally wafted towards her—rancid.

"The interesting thing about the automata that captured us," the man said, understanding her gaze, "is that they have a keen awareness of what food is, but no idea what to do with it. Whoever made them did so in a hurry, with no thought to configuring them with human capabilities."

Aura's fingers caught at the snag inside her boot, and she tore away at the leather. She pulled a long, metal instrument out and began to pick at the locks around her feet. Frederick whistled.

"Captured by automata. *Lovely*." As if she needed more bad news to come her way. She heard the *click* of the lock as it opened. She kicked the chains to the side and began to work on her hands.

Frederick continued to observe her in silence. This scrutiny made Aura uncomfortable. Normally, her black coat covered most of her freckled skin and hid the unladylike muscles on her arms. Even though she had long since stopped caring about the strict, modest fashion of the Society cities where she had grown up, she felt her thin, laced corset and her fitted leather pants were hardly proper in *any* one-on-one interaction with a man, bounty or no.

"It was not on my list of things to accomplish," he replied. "Though no doubt we can get out of this."

She stared at him. "Why are you even here? Last time I checked, it was my ship that dropped from the sky, not yours."

"Exigent circumstances. Besides, I had to make sure you were alive."

"That defeats the purpose of shooting me down, doesn't it?"

"Don't you start, too. I've heard enough of that from Darcy."

Click. The shackles fell off.

Frederick beamed. "Great, now—wait, *wait*!"

"This is how the situation is going to end," she said, positioning herself close enough that it was clear what her intentions were. Her hand moved toward the captain's neck, the metal pick close to his skin. In all her time spent chasing him across the skies, this had been the closest she had gotten to him. She ignored the unsteady beat of her heart, ignored the heat rising up her cheeks and the sweat developing on the palms of her hands. "I am going to leave—quietly—but before that, I'm going to cut your throat."

Frederick pressed his head as far back as he could in an attempt to break free of the pick's dangerous end. There was already a small scratch at the side of his neck, where the pick had nicked his skin. "Aurora Gaigna does not kill her bounties."

"There is a first for everything." Aura had lost her crew and ship for this. She would be damned if she *didn't* end his life at that point. She pressed in for the kill.

The next thing he said was spoken quickly, yet she heard every word of it. "What if I tell you your crew is alive?"

She loosened the pick's pressure on his neck, though she did not remove her hand. Aura faced him, her eyes narrow, her lips pursed.

"Speak. Quickly," she whispered, the cold air mingling with her breath, causing light swirls to rise.

"Your skailors are alive," he repeated slowly. He was still stiff, but the desperation and rush had left him. "All of them."

"That changes nothing. You could be lying, or they could be half-dead." Why would he save her crew?

Better yet, why would he try to save her life?

"They are alive and well," he said. "And do recall that I have an *airship* to get us out of this."

"I'm well aware of the ship situation, thank you," she said drily. The cold metal kissed her skin. She shivered in spite of her attempts to suppress it.

"Then you know that the only way you can get skyward is through me."

"With the proper incentive, I'm sure your men can be bought."

Again, Aura wanted to slap the annoying, pretentious smile off his face. "Alright, humour me. Why is my crew alive?"

That was when he snaked his hand up her wrist, knocking the weapon away from her. He went for her neck, but she moved on reflex, kicking away as she backed out of his reach. Aura was hardly surprised at his retaliation, but she had underestimated his speed. The pick landed near his side, and Frederick pulled it towards him, dangling it from his fingers. He winked at her and began to undo his chains.

She wanted to scream with frustration, but she did not want to bring the automata's attention upon them.

"The aim was to slow you down," Frederick said as he struggled with his chains, "not to kill you. There was never any intention of leaving you and your crew stranded on the Old World."

The chains on his hands sprang free. He rubbed his wrists, returning some colour upon his pale skin. "We were to hold you and your crew for leverage. When I realised you'd gone under with the ship, I had no choice but to go after you. Unfortunately, the disturbance might have alerted the Old World's . . . ah . . . inhabitants."

Aura stood a few feet from where he sat. "And you expect me to cooperate with you in exchange for my skailors?"

"Better. You get your crew and a way out of the Old World. I'll even drop you off at Pernata with the funds necessary to buy you a new ship. I hear the clock-makers there are the best."

"The *Emese* was already a Pernatan ship. She cost me several high profile bounties, one or two of which were higher than *yours*. You cannot possibly match her price."

"In my sort of business, I can afford a new ship without much strain on my resources," he said.

That gave her some pause. As a bounty hunter, she was used to receiving offers of bribery from the people she caught. None of them could ever really match their bounties, however. Frederick Newgate had practically doubled the price on his head, especially if he was offering her an airship from the most technological city in the sky. Coming from a smuggler, the deal was too good to be true. "What would you get out of this?"

"You must agree to stop hunting me."

She stared. "I haven't dropped a bounty since I began this trade."

"You did say there was a first for everything." Frederick had finished with the chains on his legs. He held up his open hand to her, the pick lying on his palm. "If you want, you can kill me and escape. But where would you go? It could take days, months, *years* before another ship flies directly above us. On the other hand, you can have your heaven-sent instrument, unlock the shackles at my back, and take my deal."

There was no telling what was beyond the metal prison. With the risks outside, keeping the man around might be a benefit.

She plucked the pick from his hand, approached him. She felt him tense again when she crouched over by his side, when her hand brushed his shoulder. Then he heard the *click* behind him, and he let out a sigh of relief. "Thank you."

"This is not an agreement by any form whatsoever," Aura said, her lips close to his ear, "If we don't survive, the entire deal is moot."

He grasped her outstretched hand and pulled himself up, his other hand holding onto a prison bar. Frederick cut an interesting—heck, *impressive*—figure: broad-shouldered, lean-muscled, tall. He was slightly shorter than her, though not by much, judging from the height of her heeled boots. If there was another scuffle between them, a proper one, she wasn't sure who would win. She hoped it didn't amount to that, but one could never be too prepared.

"Trust me," Frederick grinned, as though reading her mind. "I wouldn't *dream* of getting into that kind of wrestling match with you."

What an infuriating man.

"Now," he turned his attention toward the prison door. "About escaping . . . "

Three blunderbusses greeted them as the outer door swung open.

Fred's reflexes won, and before Aurora could impulsively attack, he pulled the bounty hunter behind him, his body covering hers from the weapons targeted at them.

"Frederick," Aurora said, trying to push him aside so she could stand beside him. "Those are *blunderbusses*. The only thing you've done is prolong *my* death by a few seconds."

The figures that were pointing guns toward them were nothing more than simple automata. One was clothed in a short, tattered cape, as though its creator had remembered that it was designed to mimic the human figure. The other two remained sleek and bronze and nude, creations with hardly a care for the exposure of their metal skins.

Not that it was uncomfortable to stare. Unlike the rumours going round above the skies, of clock-makers inventing automata that lived in flesh bodies and possessed human thoughts, these crude figures were less than human.

Human and machine stood their ground, the silence and movement dragging on like the long and inconstant rhythm of a broken clock. Fred sized up the automata.

They had entered a large chamber, yet there was hardly any room to manoeuvre with the automata before them. Two of the blunderbusses had sharp bayonets attached to the barrel. Fred would need the proper timing to be able to avoid both bayonets, but that would not prevent the shots.

Without warning, the bayonet automata lunged at them. Fred had expected it, ducking down and turning to his side. The blade ripped at his sleeve, nicking his arm. He couldn't see Aurora behind him, but felt her move out of the way to the other side. There was a yelp, then impact of metal on metal. One of the bayonets had hit the wall, right near Aurora's head. She was pale and shaking, her face caught between relief and astonishment. Their eyes briefly met. He knew she was still recovering from her fall, and the healing gel wouldn't fix the injuries on her back completely. Aurora's movements would be limited, yet she was shaking her head, refusing his help.

If it were up to Fred, he would have tried to fight his way toward her, to shield her from the automaton. It would have been a reckless thing to do, and probably not something the bounty hunter wanted. Fortunately for both of them, he didn't have the choice. He had to leave Aurora to fight her battle.

The second bayonet automaton was still gunning for him, and the third one had moved toward him with precision, the blunderbuss raised and aimed for his torso. Fred avoided another close swipe with the bayonet, getting just behind the automaton and pushing it toward the one with the readied blunderbuss. A shot was fired, knocking Fred down, bruised and cut, though otherwise unscathed. The second automaton, however, was not so lucky. The bullet had exploded in the machine's chest with the smell of burnt wires mingling with gunpowder. It fell onto the floor with a crash, the blunderbuss rolling from its metallic fingers.

Fred didn't wait for the other automaton to reload. He leapt toward the gun, pointed it up, clicked, and fired at the second automaton. He fell backward from the recoil, but was satisfied to see that his shot had been true. The automaton went down just as quickly as the first.

He picked up both blunderbusses, checked the barrels. "There's one shot left on each. You can have—" Fred looked around for Aurora.

The bounty hunter was nowhere to be found.

Aura was more than displeased to find herself imprisoned once again. It was humiliating enough having been chained to a man inside a prison, but being strapped on a table like a cadaver was much worse. Her skin prickled with discomfort from the wires that were clamped on her arms and stomach. Aura's Society upbringing was telling her how uncouth her position was, while the bounty hunter in her was chiding herself for getting into such a pickle in the first place. The only saving grace was that she still retained her clothes, or at least, what was left of them after her tussle with the automaton.

The machine that had dragged her away stood by the exit. Two others hovered over her, peering down with human-like curiosity. Aura blinked twice, and her eyes narrowed.

One of the automatons was wearing her trench coat.

She remained still while the automata examined her. Once they moved away, she had opportunity to scan the room for aid.

Looking had been a big mistake.

There were a few other tables in the room, smooth and shiny, with crooked, spidery legs made of brass or copper. Some of the tables were empty, while others were draped in white cloth. A few were occupied by human bodies. Only, unlike Aura, they were showing much less skin and more bone than she was comfortable with. From the decaying state of the skin and the rotting smell wafting from the occupied beds, she guessed that these humans had been imprisoned for far too long.

She twisted at her straps, desperation kicking in. One of the examiners returned to the table. It didn't get very far before something outside diverted its attention. The bayonet automaton turned toward the only exit.

Aura ignored the distraction. She struggled again, this time realising that she was loosely bound. She manoeuvred her hand towards her side pocket where she had placed her pick. Her fingers stretched and pulled at the pocket lining, reaching, reaching . . .

Something smashed onto the metal door. The booming crash echoed in the chamber, making the walls sing. The three automata had their full attention toward the exit. The one with the bayonet reached for the door's handle.

Aura didn't wait to see the result. She pulled the pick out of her pocket and moved it around. She placed the sharp end of the pick upon her straps and began cutting. The room, meanwhile, had been invaded. Alarms shrieked all over the premises. The smell of gunpowder had become more pronounced as shots were fired.

She looked up to see a bayonet swinging toward her arm.

"I could have handled myself!" shrieked the siren of a bounty hunter as she pushed herself off the metal table, free of her restraints. "Behind you!"

Fred swung around to find a clothed automaton standing there, its long, sword-like arm prepared to eradicate him as though he were some fly and it a swatter. He didn't give the machine much chance to do so; the blunderbuss went off, and the machine tumbled. That left one more.

Unfortunately, he'd run out of bullets. He dropped the bladed gun and mentally thanked the automaton at the door for falling so quickly. It was a pity it had already fired its first shot. The burn near his shoulder would hurt abominably later, but the adrenaline was keeping him steady on his feet.

The automaton wasted no time in its offensive. It swung at Fred. He ducked. The whooshing sound gave him indication of how strong the swing had been, and he knew that if the punch had hit its target, there would be one smashed skull and one dead Frederick. He scurried out of the automaton's way. It was slower than the blunderbuss-carrying automata, though the difference was slight.

He found Aurora rummaging through the clothed automaton's coat. "What are you doing, woman? Get to safety!"

She ignored him.

Fred cursed at Aurora's tenacity, then cursed again as one of the automaton's legs connected with his torso. The hit sent him flying across the small, circular room. Acute pain burst in his upper body as he slammed onto a wall. His eyes blurred, his head swam with dizziness, and his legs threatened to collapse beneath him. He faced the pain, doggedly telling himself that dying was *not* a good idea.

There would be no way to match the automaton's speed as it

lunged at him for one fatal kick. Fred closed his eyes, awaiting death.

It never came.

Instead, he heard a shot. The automaton turned away from him. Fred steadied himself on a nearby table, clutching at his chest. He looked up to find Aurora Gaigna standing by a table, her eyes hard, back straight, legs planted a few centimetres apart. She wore the trench coat that had been on the fallen automaton, sleek and black and every bit as menacing as it had been in her pictures. Both of Aurora's arms were raised as though she was at a firing range, the automaton her target.

Without flinching, she fired five more rounds into the machine, all directly at its chest area. There was a spark and a hesitation, but the machine still moved toward her. Fred tried to tell her to stop, that it was no use. She needed something stronger.

The woman pulled another revolver from her coat, cocked it, and shot six more rounds.

The automaton fell, its circuits broken, the gears that ran in its torso burned.

Fred gaped at the damage and looked at the woman who had approached him. "That . . . was beautiful."

She met him with a grimace. "How did you find me?"

He grinned. "Years of you tailing me have given me some valuable experience."

"In what?"

"In learning how to hunt the huntress!"

They heard rhythmic clatters outside the chamber. Aurora holstered her revolvers and pulled Fred upright. "It's not over yet. Our antics must have alerted more of them. Can you still move?"

Fred blinked. "Is this you worried about me, Aurora?"

She let go of his arm and scowled.

He laughed. Fred gazed at the walls, at the high ceiling, at the solitary ladder secured at one side. His laughter ceased, and he winced instead. "Now *that* is going to be one painful climb."

Climbing the ladder was an arduous process. Every time Aura lifted her arms to reach for the next rung, her back wailed with agony. Once or twice during her ascent, she had fumbled her hold, which would have resulted in a fatal accident if not for Frederick pushing her up every time she slowed.

The automata had filed into the room, some beginning their own climb, others attempting to shoot them down with more blunderbusses. Thankfully, they had reached a point that the guns became ineffective. Blunderbusses were known for their explosive nature at close proximity, but they were useless at long range.

No, if anything was a threat, it was the automata taking to the ladder.

Aura did not need Frederick's agitated coaxing to know that they were still in danger. She could already see the landing above her, and it took two more reaches for her to make it to the top. She gritted her teeth and pushed her body up, her legs skipping several rungs at a time. When she made it to the landing, she looked out into the open.

The view of the Old World was breathtaking. For as far as Aura could see, there were colours of red and orange, yellows and browns scattered on the horizon. She imagined they were the trees she'd heard adventurers speak about, that these were the marvels most floating city dwellers could only dream of.

But Aura was not interested in the marvels of the Old World, nor was she particularly keen in staying to explore. She turned her gaze to the skies in search of Frederick's airship. "I don't see anything!" she said after an initial scan.

Frederick's arm shot up from below, his fingers wrapped around a pistol. Aura stared at it. "You had that the *entire* time and didn't bother to use it?"

"It's a flare, you impulsive bounty hunter," he said, his other arm reaching the landing. Aura caught a whiff of singed flesh, and her eyes focused on the wound Frederick had sustained against one of the automata. "Shoot it in the air," he said, resting his arms upon the landing.

She accepted the pistol and did as he suggested. The bright sky thundered and sparked red. She waited.

Nothing happened. Below, the automata gained speed as they climbed. Then . . .

"There!" Frederick rasped. He laughed and pointed. "Just in the nick—"

His laughter stopped as one metallic hand clamped onto one of his legs, which were still planted upon a rung. Aura caught his outstretched arm with both of her hands. She tried to pull the pale Frederick back up. It was no use; the automaton's grip was more powerful than hers.

She caught the panic in his eyes, knowing that even if he fell, she might still be able to make it up onto the ship herself. And if he had been telling the truth and her crew had survived . . . it would take little effort to commandeer his *Marchioness* and turn the other pirates to her cause. Wasn't that a better option at this point?

Aura cursed. *Blast this damn smuggler!*

The automaton pulled again, and Fred slipped. Aura reached for the derringer that had been hidden in the folds of her coat pocket and shot it right at the automaton's head. The force of the bullet threw the automaton back, and all but its arm ripped away from the pressure. As it fell, the automaton exploded below, causing a cloud of smoke to rise up and engulf them.

The force of the explosion almost wrenched Aura away from the landing, but for her grip on Frederick. She fumbled and groaned as the derringer slipped from her hand.

The *Marchioness* had made its way down, lowering another ladder. This one was less rigid and more treacherous, but at that point, Aura didn't care. She pulled at the flexible rung, and climbed.

She reached the bulwark and rolled onto the deck to give Frederick space to collapse, clutching at her stomach to prevent herself from vomiting. Frederick followed suit, hitting the deck of his ship shoulders first and yowling with pain. Aura heard triumphant yelling and the pounding of several feet, but that had been the extent of her awareness. She didn't see the men and women scrambling to pull ropes and set sails and turn gears. She didn't catch the sight of those acid-throwing cannons, prepped and shooting at the automata below, most of the machines now a mess of broken metal and sparking wires.

Somewhere along the lines, she lost consciousness. Again.

She opened her eyes to lamplight. She heard the distant roar of thunder, felt the cushions beneath her move as the ship moved. She brought herself up and touched her bare feet to the ground, the cold, familiar texture of metal plating soothing her soles. She closed her eyes, savouring the sense of airship flight.

Then she remembered whose ship she was on, and her eyes flew open.

"Rested now?"

Aura turned to her side to find Frederick grinning at her. He had changed into more comfortable gear: less regal, less adventurous, but still impressive—and alluring. When she looked at her own clothes, she realised that she was wearing far less clothing than she wanted.

"Why am I in undergarments?"

"Hardly," Fred said, eyeing her. Aura's gaze eventually held his, and he shrugged. "The gel I administered could only do so much to assuage the pain. Once its effects wore off, you were back to writhing in pain. In order to apply more gel in, we had to strip you down."

"I don't remember this."

Frederick sighed. "Of course not. My ship's doctor had to douse you with sleeping draughts. It was the only way he could get to work. And before you start threatening my life, I would like to mention that I was not responsible for stripping you naked, enviable a task that may be."

"Hardly comforting," Aura said, feeling the silken fabric of her too-short breeches. "This isn't really *me*."

"It was all we had at the time," he said, though he didn't sound at all apologetic.

"I can barely breathe in this new corset, and I hardly think squishing my innards is the way to go with mending broken ribs," she snapped. "Get this thing off me."

Frederick's eyebrow rose. "Really, Aurora?"

"I—no." She had caught her mistake, but she did not blush. Instead, Aura made to get up. Nausea and dizziness clouded her mind, and she stumbled.

The man stood close to her. She wasn't sure what caused her immediate difficulty of breathing, the corset or the smuggler. Either way, it was most inconvenient. One hand steadied her at the small of her back while the other was holding her hand. He remained there, his face close, too close.

"Ah." The tension, however brief, broke. "Your crew. I suppose you'd want to see them."

He quit himself of the cabin in rapid strides. Dumbstruck at how easily—well, relatively more easily—she could breathe, she hobbled over to the chair away from her bed, pulled on her trench coat, and walked out.

The *Marchioness* hummed in the sky, its engine emitting a steady rhythm of whirs and beats, the gears peddling with amber fuels. On the deck, men and women mingled peacefully enough, as though the previous events had all been one funny accident.

The inside of Captain Newgate's cabin, however, was far from harmonious.

Fred had changed his mind about the bargain he had struck. When he told Darcy of his decision, the first mate was more than argumentative.

"You've gone *soft* on her, Cap," Darcy accused.

"If you're looking for a denial, there isn't going to be one," Fred said mildly. After the ordeal on the Old World, he was more than happy to have escaped with nothing but a patch on his scarred shoulder and some wrapping around his wounded ribs. If Aurora Gaigna so much as questioned his previous arrangement, he was of the mind to let her go without as much as a struggle.

So it surprised him that the bounty hunter was more than willing to enter into an agreement once she had approached him.

"Why?" he asked, sitting behind his desk. Aurora stood before him with the same determined confidence she exhibited when she was shooting at the automaton below. It was *damnably attractive*. He suppressed this distracting thought, choosing instead to focus on the conversation.

"Far be it for me to make deals with those I hunt down," she said slowly, fingering the sleeves of her coat, "but I know who to thank for the safety of my crew. And as much as I hate to admit it, you saved my life."

He shook his head. "You are more than entitled to blame me for everything that's happened."

"Yet you went back for me. Twice, may I add." There was a twinkling in her brown eyes, one he found almost as striking as her posture. "Apparently, you were so adamant that you jumped off the ship with an unreliable flyer."

"A lapse in judgment, come to think of it," he murmured.

"All the same," she continued, "consider this smuggler's deal made."

Something bothered him still, and it was only a few moments later that he realised what it was. "You don't look at all worried about letting me go."

Aurora chuckled. She eased her stance and approached the desk, her hands touching the surface of the wood. Frederick opted to step out of his chair, to stand before her as well. "I am not the law, Frederick Newgate. I follow the prices, and you were willing to offer me a higher one. If you *want* to bring ethics into this, consider the situation at hand. Had you been a crueller man, you'd have left me to perish with the automata. So forgive me for being a little more lenient in the matter."

"Ah. Well, if you put it that way . . . "

"Now, if you don't mind," she turned to face him. Her eyes caught his, and he closed the gap between them. "I—"

"I've a present for you. To solidify our newfound friendship."

He watched her brows furrow in curiosity as he pulled a small package from inside his jacket. Fred stood patiently while she unravelled its contents. Aurora whistled when the packaging revealed a new derringer. She ran her hand over the surface, admiring its make.

"Now this is a pretty piece," she said.

"Your derringer came in handy," he admitted. "I imagine my predicament made it doubly painful to have lost it."

He raised his arms in alarm when Aurora pointed the derringer at him. Perhaps giving her a weapon had been a bad idea after all . . .

"Damn smuggler," she laughed.

He relaxed his shoulders. Aurora put the derringer away, still smiling. She leaned toward his face and whispered, "Mark my words, Frederick Newgate, the next time we meet . . . "

"Oh, I can imagine what the next time is going to be like," he said, whispering back as he pulled her toward him, his lips meeting hers.

THE TIC-TOC BOY OF CONSTANTINOPLE

ANTHONY PANEGYRES

1. THE NEST, CONSTANTINOPLE 1886

He wonders whether he'll ever read a fresh newspaper again, especially *The Commonwealth Times* with news from England, the country of his Mother's birth. It has been three days.

Four newspapers lie strewn over the lounge room table like points of a compass: *The Paleologos Times*, *The Venetian*, *The Commonwealth Times* and *The Gallic News*. Neophytos had read newspapers daily with his mother, at least three articles in full from each and the opening few lines of all articles over the first ten pages.

"Even though you can't go out *there*, Phyte," (Phyte was her preferred sobriquet for him). "You need to be aware." Mother had said that often. Neophytos disobeyed only once, a thin scar on his face running down from below his right eye reminds him. She had mentioned buying other newspapers in languages she never knew: Ladino, Arabic, Turkish and Armenian. "But you can learn, Phyte."

"My mind's already overflowing," he replied.

He wrenches himself up, turning the spanner clockwise. Phyte's hands, as always, feel awkward and cold when touching his bolted breastplate.

Outside, in the background, sounds occasionally whir away and then end with percussion, like the finale of Tchaikovsky's 1812 Overture, the one his mother used to play on the phonograph.

Venetian Bombs! Newspapers report regarding the symphonic noise. *The Venetian* though, ignores the other front-page headlines, never mentioning the bombing or the clock-men who fix The City's walls all day and night. The Venetians don't have clock-men nor Greek fire. Their invading ships are often ablaze in the harbour. Neophytos wishes he could see them. '*Flames of Hope*', states the headline in *The Paleologos Times*. The boats burn in a colourful array: lemon and orange, sapphire and ruby. Signs that *Panagia*, the Virgin Mary, is guarding The City as she has eternally. *The Venetian* claims that *Madonna* is guiding their unerringly accurate cannonballs.

Phyte strides over to the faucet, and turns the handle in vain hope. Nothing, not a drip. An aqueduct must have been struck. He puts his mouth over the tap's nozzle, and sucks. The only taste is metallic, acrid. His lungs require water: steam and clockwork. He will wind down without it, no matter whether he wrenches himself up when the morning street callers wake him, selling their round *koulouri* bread and roasted chestnuts and sour cherry juice.

A convivial knock on the door, four gentle beats. He knows the routine and tiptoes to the back room. This time there are calls in Greek and a "Professor Stevenson!" The surname sounds outlandish, every syllable uttered with an exaggerated clarity not found in English. His mother won't come to door with her usual poise, she won't lead them upstairs and away from him, she won't sound her polished articulate self, despite not speaking in her mother tongue.

Phyte waits, knowing that they can't see him. He doesn't want to be tossed into some research lab, or worse. When the clockwork scientists from the University of Constantinople leave, he races upstairs, past his mother's lifeless body with that bruise encircling her dented eye socket. He softly opens the shutters to watch them depart, strolling down the street, genial Byzantine hand gestures reflecting their worries and doubts.

He will need, somehow, to make his way through those unseen and seen dangers of the streets. He rubs the scar on his face. There is no ideal time for flight, not since the French invented street lamps.

"Why can't I leave?" he would ask every few days.

"We've been over this. You're unique," she would answer, stroking his hair or patting his arm. "People fear the different. And when people are afraid, they're dangerous."

"What am I then?"

"Like in all those myths: a hybrid." Her gaze would intensify at this point and she'd wave her hand as if dismissing something trivial." But you're no monster, no minotaur or harpy. You're part clock-man, part flesh. I couldn't just let you pass away, could I? Not my own son."

She said other things too. But the one he always recalled was: "Phyte, in a way, you're new species. In nature, if one species competes with another they become a threat. If they're a similar threat, one species attempts to destroy the other. Nature is survival. *Eat or be eaten*, as they say back home."

It was only his lungs and breastplate, she assured him, that were different. But when he had clambered down to the ground that day over the balcony, from these very shutters, faces had stilled and stared, even the hawkers. The glares bore down on him from all angles, wherever his eyes met. Soon he was backed up against the pomegranate juice stand, the city folk encircling him like hyenas: not cackling though, more murmuring. He thought of breaking through. But where could he go? With panic his breathing heavied and dragon-like steam exhaled from his lips. The murmurs turned menacing. He heaved nervously, fogging the air about him.

Then Mother came, swooping down like a double-headed Byzantine eagle, brushing away people from both sides of her, berating the crowd to give him air. They knew her. "A recovering patient," she shouted as she barraged through. "Step back, he may be contagious." She swept her arms around him and led him home.

Once inside their home, door closed, she struck him with a letter opener, slicing his face. Juice gushed out a moment later. "Fool. You're alien to them!" she said and for the first time he wondered how deep her love went.

Survival: eat or be eaten he thought as she dabbed his wound with salt water before stitching it up.

The incident cemented an animosity toward whoever *they* were—*out there*. In the newspapers the characters were different, that of fable or story. *Out there* they were real. Nevertheless, the yearning to break away grew. He never ventured out again but he also never stopped asking to see the world beyond the shutters.

What happened to her? He wishes he could recall. *Did he see orange?* Sometimes when the world turns orange he forgets. He returns to the body and holds her hand, now stiff and cool.

"Ponty," Phyte calls out while inspecting his caged rat. Starved of liquid, old Ponty has slowed down. Phyte wrenches him up but his small lungs need water. "C'mon, Ponty," he says. Pet in hand, he slides open the shutters and kisses the rat before placing him on the ledge. "You'll have to go, Ponty. Find water. We'll meet again."

From the other side of the balcony railing a wild rat pauses before approaching, whiskers and nose all a-twitch. *Why doesn't it scamper away as rats do when caught naked in the open?* Its focus is his rat. Ponty stands there listlessly as the wild rat leaps on to its back, teeth gnashing. A spurt of red, and Ponty's eyes flare orange as both plummet from the railing, vanishing from sight.

The next day, the knocks on the door sound heavier, belligerent. He pockets his wrench and races upstairs rather than to his usual hideaway. "City Police!"comes the call. His hands tremor as he opens the shutters. "City Police! Open the door!"Neophytos squats on the ledge. The front door breaks open with a boom.

Heavy boots gallop up the stairs. He leaps from his nest, grabbing the railing and swinging himself downward, hoping that the faces that must by now be looming above, don't spy him. *Dead,* he hears. Then *Murdered.*

Phyte hits the ground, rolling heavily. He rises and, like clockwork, jogs steadily *tic-toc, tic-toc, tic-toc* through the town. To the East are the woods, pine and fir trees beyond The City's walls. *Tic-toc, tic-toc, tic-toc.* He doesn't glance back to see if they follow. He doesn't look sideways to see if people glare. His mind fades while he steams onwards. *Tic-toc, tic-toc, tic-toc. The woods, remember the woods.* It is the one thought he can cling to. His legs moving: *tic-toc, tic-toc, tic-toc.*

At the gateway out of The City's red walls stands a string of guards strapped in leather armour and boots and helmets, muskets raised. But the traffic is dense and he does not slow and he does not quicken. *Tic-toc, tic-toc, tic-toc.* Out the gate and down dung-stained pathways, teeming with horse and carriage, oxen too, and even the occasional heavily laden camel, donkey and mule. Then the woods appear to the side.

There is no sign of anyone seeing him veer into them. No shouts or curses. He heads into a world of shadows and blades of light, the dry ground full of nettles. It is all mechanical now, all *tic-toc, tic-toc, tic-toc* . He can't even think of water. His mind is empty. His legs *tic-toc, tic-toc, tic-toc* until he is deep within the woodlands.

Tic-toc, tic . . . toc, tic . . . toc, tic . . . .

2. The Compound

Water splashes over his face, a little seeping past his lips. Another bucketful follows. This time he reacts, sucking it into his lungs. His eyes flare open. Men in long, scarred leather jackets and overworn leather pants, air-masks off their mouths and hanging around their chests, babble away in a foreign tongue above him. He readies to thank them in *Lingua Franca*—a bastardised Italian spoken in the Empire's ports and harbours, but stops on realising his wrists and legs are tied. Then he is being carried through the air like a spitted paschal lamb. Dogs, all with studded collars, bark away by their sides. They are tied up just before the nettles beneath him surrender into a downward sloping tunnel of concrete.

A few strap their masks over their noses and mouths as they pass through damp passages with several closed doors on either side. Eventually they stop by an open door. They untie him, then hurl his body onto a dirt floor.

They leave, bolting the door behind them.

Phyte's night eyes adjust. A figure lurking in the shadows doesn't respond to Phyte's timid greeting. He raises his voice and it echoes off the deaf walls. Keeping an eye on the figure, he scans his surroundings. Next to a water-filled trough, a musty—yellow paillasse is scrunched up against the wall, and there's a pit in the corner for his bowels. But besides the wet subterranean air, which frees up his lungs, there is no stench of human waste.

Phyte steps closer to his cell mate, and discovers the *whirrs* and *tic-tic-tocs* of a nearly-dead clock-man. Some plates, torn loose, hang limply from his metallic torso; springs jut outwards.

In an untried experiment, Phyte grapples with bolts as he strives to re-attach metal plates. The wrench was left on him and he uses it wherever possible. But the clock-man doesn't toc the way they did when marching past his home. He kisses the icy plates repeatedly. After all, kisses were proven miracle workers in all the English fairy tales mother read to him as a child.

Eventually, lips blue, he collapses asleep on the dank paillasse.

Hours later, the clunk of the door being unbolted awakens him. He's not sure of the time. Two people, clad in a higgledy-piggledy leather assortment enter, their muskets lowered at him. The female has a ceramic bowl and spoon in her other hand, and the male, a heavy-looking leather bag. Phyte considers snapping a neck, fleeing. But even if he evades the muskets, he imagines there'd be a labyrinth of warren-like passageways, brimming with armed guards.

Besides, *she* is unique: a thin face swallowed by a dangling nose, and a wooden cross hangs around her neck. Starved of female company outside of his mother, his gaze is magnetised by her. "Here," she serves him a warm bowl of *trachanas,* a heated cereal mixed with goats' milk. He wolfs it down. A subtle, almost medicinal tang, is the only difference from his mother's recipe.

She smiles, which softens him. The male guard—she calls him Djoto—stands next to the clock-man, his iron jaw and bell-like chin a hedgehog's coat of sharp whiskers. His breathing mask is strapped on as he removes an array of prickly tools from his bag. A wire from his ear connects to a palm-sized disk that he attaches to the clock-man's chest. He scribbles in a journal and starts to unscrew plates.

"Where are you from?" Phyte asks in Greek. When they don't respond, he asks in Venetian, French and English. She laughs and says something to the man who prattles back. Not Turkish or Arabic or Slavic or Wallachian or Armenian either; he would recognise those sounds, sounds that rippled by occasionally outside the shutters. Languages, Neophytos thinks, are like waterbodies: they gush or trickle along, some ebb and wane, others wallow deeply and a few skim along the surface. This language is resilient and pure like the mountain lakes in the stories he's read. Perhaps they're Magyar or from further afield, Georgians?

"Neophytos," he says, pointing to himself.

She doesn't reply. Djoto hammers away at the clock-man, now lying on the ground in a jumbled array of springs, metallic parts flailing outwards from his body.

The whirrs are erratic, grinding and painful.

The clock-man should tic-and-toc to the right beat.

Steam and adrenaline teem through Phyte and, despite the musket, he hurtles over and sweeps Djoto away, scarcely registering the guard's gawping eyes. Phyte shoves springs back into the body, adjusts metallic plates. He pulls out his wrench.

He notices Djotos' spanner clearly, shiny and modifiable, as it slams into his temple. There's a blaze of orange before darkness swallows him.

On awakening, Phyte gingerly raises his fingers to his temple. Swollen and soft like a ripe persimmon. The female guard hovers over him, musket targeting his face.

Phyte imagines her twitch with curiosity as he crawls over to the pile of screws and cogs, springs and metal plates. He reaches for his wrench in his long pockets. It's gone, taken. His mother once said that Brits never cried like emotional Levantine folk. Phyte is unsure of what he is, Brit, Levantine or something else, and tears slip as he battles on gathering scattered parts.

"They don't feel," she says in Lingua Franca. He cringes but her hand is tender on his shoulder. "Clock-men don't feel or think."

"What will you do with me?"

"Research. But we'll be careful with you," she rubs his shoulder. "You're a good boy."

The ignominy. He is a young man, seventeen.

"I'm Irema."

Over the next few days, he flinches as Djoto pricks his skin, chokes as tubes are shoved down his airways and brought back up, winces as his chest plate is hammered on and he sees orange as Djoto sedates him with blows. The arms are the worst: Djoto is especially fond of raking welts across them with a fork-like tool.

Phyte, however, is accustomed to pain and fever, *and* recovery from both. A growing boy required new chest plates. Mother was an ingeniously busy lady. She had told him proudly, "Now that you're big enough, provided you exercise and stay lean, this last one should last."

3. FRIENDSHIP

Djoto and Irema obsessively scrawl away in their journals. Other than that, the pair are as different as liquid and dry air. Irema arouses him in the mornings with warm sponges and *trachanas*, no matter the belting from Djoto the evening before.

"As you can imagine, there's a number of clock-men here. But there's only ever been three of your kind—and now only two," says Irema one morning, armed with her musket, leading him out of his cell for the first time

Is this a fragment of the underground puzzle?

Traces of steam loop and shimmy from the bases of doors they pass by. The steam isn't affected by any breeze. It does not betray a means out.

They arrive at an open room, with a desk and chair and shelves behind it. Two newspapers lay on the table along with quills, an ink jar and paper too. One newspaper's script is foreign but the other, which he picks up, is *The Venetian*.

"You read Italian?" Irema asks.

"Mother taught me plenty. Life was a regime of exercise and lessons . . . And newspapers. The latter became more of a passion."

"You must have felt so alone."

"We had Ponty though." And he describes their pet and his pint-sized chest-plate.

He sees Irema suppress a smile. "This isn't to hurt you," she says, manacling him to the desk. "I'll be back in a tic."

She returns, a rat in her hands, "A friend brought him in after a scouting trip in the woods yesterday. Got to him before the dogs did. We were going to hide him from Djoto for a few days—but now maybe longer." Irema raises him up and Phyte sees what he has hoped for, the glint of his brass chest-plate. Ponty squeaks when released, he stands there regarding Phyte before scurrying up his arm to perch on his shoulder. Phyte kisses him as the manacles are unlocked.

"He'll stand up for food," he says. "And he'll follow me anywhere."

"Watch this," she says, lifting Ponty from his shoulder and placing him on to the tabletop. She pinches the rat's back. Ponty's eyes flash orange as he twists, almost biting her nimble fingers. "Did you see that? Did you see his eyes?"

There's nothing odd about it. When Ponty angers his eyes change; so do Phyte's at times. "All living creatures view things in orange on occasion," his mother had told him. Yet Phyte had never seen mother's eyes that way.

Phyte doesn't reveal that though.

The outing becomes a daily routine. Irema jots down Phyte's every behaviour. Ponty sits on Phyte's shoulder while he reads the newspaper, interpreting the tale-filled world outside. Today's headline is: *Valiant Venetians Depart*. Phyte reads:

Our valiant Venetian troops only depart from their courageous stance against the fallacious Christians of Constantinople as they now prepare to defend the entirety of Christendom from the infidel Moors of North Africa.

Phyte knows better: the clock-men and Greek fire have triumphed.

"Pleasing news for you, I suppose," says Irema. She coughs as she hands him her tobacco pipe. "It's the steam," she says with a wave of her hand.

Phyte inhales, enjoying a warm, soothing sensation, which he savours all the way down into his lungs.

"Are you sure that you've never smoked before?"

"Mother and the headlines never really engaged in smoking."

"Well then, it's time you were educated. Try the mastic flavoured weed from Chios and afterwards the sweet-wine leaves are from Crete."

Phyte, who can form rings out of his own steamy breath anyway, blows smoke rings in a care free manner to impress Irema, who hastily sketches images of them in her journal.

The daily excursion evolves. Phyte accompanies Irema on her morning rounds, her musket casually levelled at him the entire time, notebook in the other hand. Ponty scampers by their side or gets a lift. They see at least a dozen clock-men, some split open, some whole. In the distance he hears the clanking bolts over doors, the ringing of large hammers, the staccato chimes of smaller ones. Phyte infers that although the compound is vast, it's not, at least, an infinite sprawl.

One sole door, Irema never opens.

"What's in there?"

No matter how he asks it's always the same response: "That door's *not* for you."

Phyte knows Irema is all notes and scribbles but, unaccustomed to trips and company outside of his mother, he feels closer to her with each passing day. One morning, as they puff away on honey and fig flavoured tobacco from Sicily, he discovers something tantalising about the way Irema leans back in her chair, legs crossed and lying over her desk rather than under it. When Phyte reaches for more weed, he allows his arm to linger over hers. She looks at him oddly, eyebrows cocked. He kisses her cheek, she winces, perhaps in pain, perhaps not, so he aims for her lips. She springs away, her nose longer than usual as her face curls around it with loathing.

He swallows, "Is it me? Is it my steam?"

Irema nods.

It's juvenile but when they return to his cell he buries his head in the stench of the paillasse to avoid her. He feels her sit nearby. "We're simply different, Phyte. But we're friends." She massages his neck and shoulder. "And I have somebody I know you'll like. One last surprise."

Rejection initially clouds him. He hopes for signs of change. Is the pistachio flavoured tobacco from Aegina a deliberate deviation? When she casually crosses her legs is it for her or for him? What are the lyrics to the songs she ululates so bitter-sweetly?

Overtime, he accepts that they are what his mother intimated—a separate species. He needs to remain close to this separate species though. He needs a means out.

4. Research

Phyte and Irema nibble on the tips of salted pumpkin seed shells to split them open for eating, then toss the remains around the room. Their giggling at the mess emboldens him. "What happened to the third one like me? Did Djoto ram too many tubes down his throat or did he damage his breastplate? I always thought that the medication in the *trachanas* fought off infections."

"Clever boy," she says, avoiding his eyes. "Djoto took the breastplate off. He was dead before we could get it back on . . . despite the *trachanas*."

Phyte, finished with the seeds, still grinds his molars. "Am I next?"

"Possibly," she says, sweeping the shells on her desk into a pile with a newspaper. "Not for a while, I hope. We're working on the clock-men first."

When will the research be taken too far with him? Months, days or mere hours?

"Help me slip away."

When she doesn't reply, the room transforms to orange. Phyte's hands become burning fists. He strides over to the wall and pounds it. Earth and paint crumble away. He veils his pride at the imposing dent, fashioned by his now inflamed knuckles.

"Calm, calm," whispers Irema, scribbling away.

Her other hand fingers her musket, a precaution of course. He doubts she'll use it.

"You're a tough boy. Almost as strong as a clock-man."

"I'm not like a clock-man."

"Is that what your mother told you?" She vigorously shakes her head. "Do you think I could breathe steam with just your lungs? Your eyes are stiller, you blink less, you work on steam. It isn't just your lungs. You're a myriad of alterations."

It makes sense. His previous escape outside when younger: the way they scrutinised him. His lungs need water; his heart, the occasional wrench-up to keep it *tic-toc*ing.

A few days later they stand before the *other* door. She motions him to pull off the bolt.

"Djoto's cruel, Phyte. He doesn't see you as human."

"As if I don't know that. But what about you?"

"My notes now indicate otherwise. The many adjustments aside, you're certainly human. So now,' she says gravely performing the Orthodox cross, two fingers and a thumb, right to left, "I have three souls to protect: mine, *yours*—" She opens the door. "And hers. Her name's Nea."

Inside, a girl, perhaps in her late teens, lies on a paillasse. It's as if Irema has vanished. Phyte doesn't register her watching from the doorway, quill moving rapidly over paper. It is hard to peel his eyes away from the girl and her pale olive skin that he fancies would darken in the sun. Her eyes blink slowly as she looks up at him, her gaze almost mechanical, so perfect.

Everything occurs rapidly as if he has been wrenched up into overdrive. One arm loops around her waist, the other tingles against her cheek. He finds himself firm, no sign of trembling. She talks as if they are in the same gentle current, being caressed along in the same direction. He doesn't feel a need to hold back on anything, there's an ease and confidence, as though they are linked components.

"There are many more like us," Nea says. "At least that's what Father said. Professors from the university and clock-man technologists have been doing it on the side for a while."

"Doing what?"

"Saving lives. Enhancing them, too."

He has so many questions.

"Didn't your mother tell you anything?"

"We read the newspapers."

Nea scoffs. "The real news never hits the papers. Steam lungs and the wind-up hearts were the remedy." He brushes a hand through her hair, and feels above her midriff. A plate is in the place of her breasts. "All covertly. A ban took place on all research—not surprising after all the deaths at the university."

Her eyes are the key. Eyes that are sure, not like all the ones he has seen twitching and flickering and blinking this way and that: unsure of their desires, unsure of themselves.

Irema pointedly taps the door. He whispers to Nea, "I'll come for you."

His paillasse is hard against the wall. His arms are marred by heavy welts.

"Djoto took things too far last night" she says, scooping *trahanas* from his bowl. Phyte winces as she smooths the dollops over his arms as a salve. "You blew steam in his face for it." She laughs at the recall.

"His *research* seems excessive."

"Rumours are that Djoto's father, a merchant from Tbilisi, was badly maimed by a clock-man near the city-walls—an accident of course, but those sorts of things can fester in the hearts of the young, like mould. When he was older and understood that clock-men have no consciousness, he'd nowhere to place his anger. I s'pose now he has." Irema waves a rough hand towards his bedding, "There's no need for your paillasse to hide the tunnel."

"You know?"

"Ever since you hit the wall outside. It's useless. Surely you understand that sideways will just take you to other rooms."

Phyte does know. Determination had blinded him over the past few days, ever since meeting Nea. "I need my wrench."

"Phyte," she says, dismissing the notion.

He holds out pleading arms. "Before I go, I'll need my wrench."

Irema presses closer, her breath tickling his ear, "The entrance is too heavily guarded but there's another way out." It turns out that she's been excavating a little herself. An old mine shaft. "If you escape," she whispers, "Head east, deep into the woods, far away from us. The team never venture there. I promise to take care of Ponty."

That evening Djoto arrives earlier with Irema; a clock-man trails behind them. Djoto, brows rising and falling gleefully, babbles away in Georgian to Irema. He has not bothered to strap on his mask and, for the first time, Phyte, sees his mouth: not cruel but full lipped; it is the teeth behind them that are cruel, small and tight and tea-stained.

Irema claps Djoto's back in a congratulatory way. However, while Djoto is occupied, searching through his painfully elaborate toolkit, her face falls in warning.

Djoto rises from his kit and barks at the clock-man. The clock-man arrives. "This is the first non-Byzantine clock-man."

Another command and the clock-man, all well pronounced *tics* and *tocs*, marches over to the far wall.

"Now watch." He yaps another instruction and the clock-man punches the wall. Puffs of dirt and dust mist through the air; its fist is all the way through to the equivalent of its metallic wrist.

Djoto yells again and the clock-man marches over to Phyte. "A sweetener before the pain," Djoto hocks up phlegm and spits at Phyte, aiming for his face but falling short, the slime landing on Phyte's neck.

Another command. The clock-man strikes Phyte, quick and sharp, in the midriff. Phyte sees orange. Everything feels knocked.

He drops to the floor, knees up to his chest as he coughs up bloodied water.

Djoto leans over Phyte and yanks his hair back. "The first stage was to construct a clock-man," Djoto jerks Phyte's head up. "The second stage is to recreate your kind, but there's no need for you to live through that. We've another hybrid."

He mutters something and the clock-man clamps down over Phyte's upper arm and yanks, dislocating Phyte's arm from his shoulder socket.

Phyte writhes on the floor long after they leave.

Later, lying there, eyes closed in hope of diminishing the pain, he travels far away in his thoughts. For most of his life he yearned for more, the outside, freedom. He admits he may have once been better off in his mother's safe confines.

He groans as somebody pinches his face and then his cheeks sting from repeated slaps. He opens his eyes. Irema's concerned face hangs over his. She must have slipped back inside. "You need to stay conscious," she says. "Bite down on the sleeve of your good arm when I tell you to. Can you make it to the wall?"

He hobbles over with her aid. "Bite down," she says as she teases more sleeve into his mouth. She extends his forearm and rotates his shoulder towards his body. His scream is muffled as it takes three rotations before his shoulder clicks back in. She drops his wrench on to the floor. "Your door is open and so is hers, but not for long. A lit oil lamp waits for you just outside."

There's no time to thank her as she abruptly leaves. It occurs to him that she will know where he hopes to go if they are to meet again: the east side of the woods. That she knows alarms him. Their friendship fails to ease his sweltering anxiety. He sees orange as he wrenches himself up. He gulps water out of the trough, like his mother once taught him, down the other channel and into his lungs.

5. THE CHASE

"Quick, the door's open," he tells Nea. The wrench is in his hand. Thickish liquid drips off it.

Their first brief kiss is one of shared steam as they leave the cell. On the floor, just outside, lays Irema, stagnant, her eye socket a shattered mess of blood and gunk and bone. Nea kneels over her. "What happened?"

"I . . . I don't know. I don't remember." Phyte glances at his wrench. "We need to hurry."

Everything appears as Irema said. He swivels the lamp about but there is no movement of steam; it hangs like a static miasma blanketing the passage's ceiling above them. They are unseen and unheard as they crawl over dirt in the torpid air of the old mine shaft, squeezing past fallen rocks, catching their clothes on rusted nails and splintered wood, grazing their skin. There are other shafts interlacing theirs but still no trace of air. *Is it the right path?* He allows himself to be carried only by the hands of hope as he leads on, grunting now and then. Then there is a wisp of steam moving through the air. Further on and more tendrils follow in the same direction, coalescing into a foggy pathway. Invigorated, they both crawl quicker. They arrive, up unsteady foot-rungs. Steam above them rises and sneaks out through the spaces between a heavy iron door and its frame. Together, they struggle with that moist door. They heave with their backs and it gives a little; surface debris slides off it as they grind it open.

Light forces his eyes closed for a moment. Nea laughs between puffs of steam.

"Hush, we still have a while to go eastward."

In the distance a solitary dog barks. Phyte can't see anything past the conifers: all fir trees and pines. "Keep that way—no matter what. If we're separated I'll find you."

They set off at a jog. The only sounds they make are the crunching of nettles underfoot and their steady breathing. Phyte hopes any noise is drowned out by the bird-song of the woods. His guts burn and his shoulder flares, but he trudges on.

Another dog barks a long way off, at a higher pitch, more of a yelp.

Phyte works with the beat instilled in him: *tic-toc, tic-toc, tic-toc.* He knows Nea does the same beside him. There is an admirable symmetry in the way that their soles hit the ground, an organised beat. He's always liked that, the beat more than the rhythm. It's soothing, regular.

A third dog joins the chorus, with a series of yaps, louder and a little closer.

Steam flows from their mouths, water escaping their bodies as they sweat in the dry day's heat.

The pack carries on well behind them. There is no doubt now that they're the noises of the hunt.

"East," he says. "Keep going eastward."

He stops. About ten yards further on she realises and turns back. Phyte jabs eastward. She nods. He watches her resume her run, then he tears off his shirt and sets off northward, allowing the shirt to trail along the ground as he goes. The dogs' excited barks mean they are only just beyond his vision. He ties his shirt around a rock and hurls it as far westward as he can, looping it low to avoid the branches, then jogs on.

He's steaming up, he feels his mind begin to wane at the edges. *Tic-toc, tic-toc, tic-toc.* He turns back briefly. It's worked, and all three dog calls grow distant. They've found his shirt off the trail.

He continues on. It's downhill; a good sign, he imagines. He hopes for water, he hopes that dogs can't swim and that his lungs will breathe more freely. He doesn't clamber down the slope but jogs in time, *tic-toc, tic-toc.* His boots begin to squelch over the clammier ground. Pines give way to other foliage: poplars and oak trees and weeping willows. He's read in *The Commonwealth Times* that weeping willows live near water and he soon hears evidence for it, the *sher* of running liquid. The dogs behind sound clear again, combatting the growing noise of the brook. He looks back—they're only fifty yards away and gaining.

In the distance he eyes a metallic gleam, water.

"Never run from a dog," his mother had always said. "They sense fear."

He thunders along. *Tic-toc, tic-toc, tic-toc.* He doesn't see the fallen branch. It clips his boot and he tumbles down. When he rises the dogs are nearly on him. He turns, wrench in hand, slowly stepping backwards.

The dogs, all wearing studded collars, race towards him, paws leaving the ground as they fly through the air. He stops before a weeping willow, using its trunk to shield his back. The dogs steady when they approach. A brutish, bristling dog drools and the other two bare their lips, revealing mottled gums and canines. Phyte readies his legs and his wrench. One of the smaller dogs comes in first. He connects with a boot to its neck and it yelps and tumbles backward. It recovers and the two smaller dogs semi-circle him. The larger one snarls behind them.

The smaller dogs leap at him. The one he kicked avoids his boot this time and latches on to his calf. Everything is orange as he connects with the wrench, a strike to its eye socket. It crumples to the earth as the wrench is jerked from his hand on impact, spinning out of his reach through the air. He fogs up the air around him, panting and heaving as the bigger dog plunges in, snapping but missing his stomach. The animal's weight sends him plummeting. On the ground, he's consumed by the stench of dog breath, snarls and growls, and the sickly feeling of blood streaming down his legs. The fog and steam leave him and he is all mechanical, a flurry of strikes with his one good arm. He does not know how long he struggles, how long he launches out with his fist.

The last he remembers is that his wrench is somehow back in the blood-soaked hand of his good arm as he drags himself brook-wards through damp leaves and dark soil. There are no more snarls and barks.

6. REFUGE

Once again, water revives him, not splashed this time but trickled into his mouth. He is being wrenched up. Two faces appear above his: Nea's comforting, certain glance and an old man, dressed in black, with lined skin and mossy white hair and beard. There's a kindness to his face, a dreamy look of a younger man, a sense that he is sweet-tempered and soft-edged.

They are in a yard of sorts, a hut nearby and the woods surrounding them. The monk makes the sign of the cross over his face.

Phyte is told that there are sleeping mats inside while they carry him into the hut. He has so many questions. All Nea says is, "We're in the Eastern side. We're safe, Phyte." He drifts off into a deep sleep. Now and then, during his slumber, Djoto's face appears, as does his Mother's and Irema's and he sweats and squirms, but Nea's eyes always materialise and he quietens.

When Phyte properly wakes, the monk is standing over him. "He's up. Glory to God." Nea comes and holds his hand.

His legs are heavily bandaged but he attempts to rise. "Rest," says the monk. "You've been out again for days."

They stay with the ascetic who has fruit and nut trees, chickens too, a beehive further off in the woods, along with goats which produce milk and cheese and yoghurt. The monk feeds Phyte and crafts him a walking staff. "Just don't go beyond the brook."

Phyte grows stronger each day. He feels the tug of the world beyond, not the human world but of the world beyond the brook. *Why shouldn't they go there?*

He approaches the monk as he lights a candle in a tray of sand at the hut's entrance. It flares up like a ship's beacon in the desert.

The monk offers Phyte a candle.

"Why are you caring for us? asks Phyte, lighting the wick. "You don't know what I've done. What I might do."

The monk touches Phyte's chest plate. "I don't busy myself with the sins of others, or judge my brother."

Nea steps in and gazes at the flickering flames.

"We can't stay here," says Phyte

"Where will you go?" asks the monk.

"There isn't really anywhere else, Phyte," says Nea.

"We can build our own place like this. Live our own lives," says Phyte.

The monk lays one calloused hand over Phyte's and the other over Nea's. "Stay as long as you want. Forever if need be. You were sent for a reason."

The weeks roll on. The brook flows, and Phyte wrestles and shares steam-laced kisses with Nea there, out of the old man's sight. They divide the chores; Phyte's palms harden through his gathering of firewood, he learns how to milk the goats and also ensure that the chickens are safely sheltered each night. By the end of the month though, the goats' milk is low and the chickens need feed.

Phyte watches as the monk packs a hamper: a flask of water and a flagon of wine, many sealed pots of honey, the comb within, cheese too.

"What are you doing?"

"The City's a while away. Food and drink's for me. The honey's to sell for chicken fodder as well as seeds for the yard. We'll start a patch."

"I should go," Phyte's obdurate hands are on his hips. "Let me go."

The monk waves dismissively.

"Why shouldn't I?"

"They'll spot you in a minute—they'll see your steam—your eyes. Isn't this better than prison? Why do you want so much?"

Phyte marches outside to speak to Nea, who is whacking almonds off a tree with a staff. "Can we trust him? How do we know that he won't simply trade us in?"

When he turns back to look at the hut, the old man, with his bag and walking stick, has already left and is moving off down the path.

"We can manage, the two of us. Wait a minute," she says, tugging at his shirt, preventing him from following the monk. She dashes inside and returns, placing the wrench into his hand. "Now run."

A hint of the monk's black robes ahead. He begins his chase, *tic-toc, tic-toc*. His world plunges into orange. Wrench out and ready, his arm itches to bring it across the old man's eye socket, ending the risk to his, now their, survival. The monk has cared for them, as his mother did, as Irema did. *Tic-toc, tic-toc*. He is not far now; he can see the walking stick and the robes fanning in the breeze. *Perhaps I can see other than orange?* The monk turns around, his face exposed and open in greeting. *Could I request something from The City instead?* He could ask for pipe weed or a newspaper, he hasn't read *The Paleologos Times* for a while. His hand, gripping the wrench, is all aquiver.

IRONCLAD

M.L.D. CURELAS

NORTHERN CALIFORNIA, 1872

Jessica peered out the stagecoach door, ignoring the driver's proffered, sweaty, hand. She wished, not for the first time, that her boss had sprung for the expense of a steam coach, with all the luxuries that came with it, like clockwork drivers and footmen. But in the aftermath of the War of the Southern Rebellion, federal troops had come to the state to combat the Indians, and clients were few. The profits from this small job would stretch even further if costs were kept to a minimum. Understanding the need for economy, however, did not soothe her tender posterior.

She stepped off the stagecoach, one crimson boot skimming over a steaming pile of horse dung before landing safely on the warped wooden planks masquerading as a sidewalk. She released her death grip on her skirt, allowing the rich fabric to swirl around her ankles, kissing the ground and sending up a cloud of dust. Peeling off her gloves, she examined the hotel in front of her.

When the driver dropped her trunk beside her, Jessica laid a hand on his arm. "I'll need assistance to my lodgings."

The man squinted at her. "This here is the only hotel in town."

Jessica pushed a stray lock of raven black hair behind her ear, and smiled. "I believe there are rooms above The Painted Lady?"

"Yeah, but that's the—" The driver stopped talking and his mouth hung slack for an instant. "Oh."

"I'll pay you for your time, of course." Not waiting for his stammering acceptance, Jessica strode towards the brothel, a pastel pink building that would have seemed sweet and innocent on the Bay, but in this dusty town, where white was a bold colour, it was shocking and rude.

The swinging doors were a cheerful lavender, and smooth beneath Jessica's touch as she pushed on them. She waited a few minutes in the entryway, allowing her eyes to adjust to the dim interior.

At the sound of her name, Jessica turned. A tall woman came out from behind the bar, laying a towel on the counter.

"Jessica?" the woman repeated. "I'm Eliza. I thought your coach was arriving later! I would have met you at the stop."

"We made good time. There wasn't any rain to slow us down." Jessica clasped Eliza's hands and kissed her on both cheeks, European fashion. "The driver has brought my trunk."

"Of course." Eliza glanced over Jessica's shoulder. "Up the stairs, last door on the right."

Jessica arched her back, discreetly working the kinks out. She was exhausted, but she had a job to do. "Daisy has left?"

"Yesterday. Her mother has taken ill." Eliza clucked, eyes twinkling. "Rather worrisome, sudden illnesses like that."

"Yes." Jessica forced a chuckle, although she didn't find the sudden illnesses of mothers to be the least bit amusing. "How fortunate that I was available to come and help you out. I understand Daisy has important patrons."

Eliza looked toward the stairs. "Ah, there is your driver. I'll show you to your room."

When the stagecoach driver had left, Eliza cupped Jessica's elbow and guided her to the stairs. "Now, you mustn't worry if you only entertain one person tonight, Jessica. The Painted Lady has been well compensated in anticipation of such an event."

Jessica sighed, one hand rubbing her hip, thinking of the jouncing coach ride. Apparently the economy of the company did not extend to bribes.

The bannister was dust-free; a royal purple carpet lined the stairs. The Painted Lady, Jessica thought, must entertain a lot to afford its upkeep. A row of doors lined the upper hallway, gaslight lanterns dotting the walls. Due to years of training and experience, she perused the hallway for any potential threats. Was that a person's shadow at the end of the hallway? A saloon girl? Or someone else?

She thought she heard the rasp of a wooden door rubbing against carpet. A curious girl then. Perfectly natural. There was no reason for Jessica to believe that anybody suspected her true reason for being at the brothel.

She willed her heartbeat to slow, and kept her voice calm. "I'm relieved to hear that your establishment won't suffer financially, Eliza."

Eliza shot her a fleeting glance. "Daisy is one of our more popular girls. She's quite busy. Ah, here we are. You're right next door to Otto, so it should be fairly quiet for you and your guest. Guests."

"Otto?"

Eliza smiled, dimples appearing in her cheeks. "I'll introduce you."

The door next to Jessica's room stood open. Eliza stopped and rapped on it. "Otto?"

"Good afternoon, Miss Eliza." A tall, broad figure filled the doorway.

Jessica's eyes widened. A clockwork man! His joints moved with the characteristic jerkiness of his kind, but silently, indicating well-oiled gears and springs. Jessica calculated the expense of the oil needed to maintain the clockwork man in a town where dirt, grime, and dust were so pervasive, and whistled in appreciation. Her father would have given his eyeteeth to examine such a specimen as Otto.

Otto turned to her. His glass eyes looked real, as did the thatch of dark hair on his head. "Good day, Miss Jessica. I hear that we are to be neighbours."

"Yes," Jessica smiled. He was handsome by any standard, mechanical or organic. "I just arrived."

"Otto entertains our female guests," Eliza said. "I know it looks exorbitant, but we actually lost money when we had male hosts on staff." She lowered her voice. "Otto has better stamina."

"Oh." Jessica stifled a giggle, and held out a hand. "Nice to meet you, Otto."

"The pleasure is all mine, Miss Jessica." The clockwork man took her hand. His skin was hairless, perfectly smooth, and the colour of aged ivory. It was the best replicant-skin that Jessica had ever seen; most of the clockwork men she knew had smooth metal plates covering their gears. "My evenings are seldom full." His thumb stroked the sensitive skin on her inner wrist, and to her annoyance, Jessica felt a wave of heat roll over her body.

She extracted her hand from his grasp. "You must excuse me, I have to freshen up after the long coach ride. I'll see you later, Otto."

He bowed his head and retreated into his room.

Eliza laughed and opened Jessica's door, handing the key to Jessica. "He's a marvel, isn't he? The latest in clockwork men. A wonderful gadget."

Jessica managed a smile. "Thanks, Eliza. When should I come down?"

"We start entertaining at seven." Eliza nodded. "Have a pleasant afternoon, Jessica. You may want to take a nap."

Jessica shut the door and leaned against it, waiting for her body to cool. Now was not the time to get flustered by a little male attention, especially the attention of an artificial man. Never mind that Otto was the most sophisticated clockwork man she'd ever seen . . . and being her father's daughter, she knew good clockwork.

A servant rapped at the door, bearing a tray laden with dishes. Jessica lifted the lid of one, revealing several dainty cucumber sandwiches—cucumber! Her mind boggled at the expense of shipping that by steam coach. The Painted Lady operated as if having federal troops stationed in California hadn't driven up the price of, well, *everything.*

Once she had devoured half a dozen of the tiny sandwiches, Jessica was able to concentrate on the task at hand. She would have, at most, two nights to accomplish this job. She could only envision it taking that long if her mark did not appear this evening.

After peering out into the hallway, Jessica locked her door and opened her trunk. She pawed through dresses, underclothes, lingerie, and nightdresses, tossing them haphazardly aside, caring little if they landed on floor or bed. A modest jewellery box rested on the bottom of the trunk. She set that on the floor, leaving the trunk bare. Jessica hooked her fingers around the edges of a knot that marred the golden plank, and heaved. Within a couple of minutes she had worked the board free, revealing the space beneath the false bottom.

Jessica took out the hand cannon first, loaded it, and tucked it beneath the plump feather pillow on her bed. Next came the medical equipment: the syringe, vials, and stethoscope. The top drawer of the bedside table would do for now; she knew many soiled doves who had similar paraphernalia in their rooms. Her gold pocket watch, which contained a tiny photographic camera within its geared innards, also came out. Spyglass, badge, and portable steam-powered telegraph remained in the trunk. If she needed those, it would be because the job had gone to hell. And that shouldn't happen—how difficult could it be to seduce a scientist?

The last item removed was a thin, plain envelope, the colour of bone, with a scarlet wax seal. After a moment's hesitation, Jessica also placed this in the top drawer of the bedside table. Then she replaced the false bottom and pushed the trunk over to the armoire.

She placed her small jewellery box on the top shelf of the armoire. Cunning tools and gadgets were concealed in her necklaces, rings, and bracelets, even her earrings. Wonderful accessories that people expected to see on a woman, needing no explanation for their presence. Next she hung up her clothes.

With the aid of a button hook, Jessica removed her boots. The heel of the right boot popped off into her hand with a gentle twist; she removed a piece of paper that had been folded into a square. She clutched the paper for a moment, unease fluttering in her stomach. Being found with this particular piece of paper could ruin her life.

Shaking her head, Jessica grabbed another pair of boots, the ones she intended to wear that night. She didn't have anything to worry about. Her mother had died so long ago that Jessica was the only one left who had known her. It would take quite a detective to uncover her origins. The job hadn't been compromised.

She sprung open one of the heels and inserted the paper into it. Closing the heel, she set the new pair of boots onto the floor of the armoire.

And then, finally, Jessica collapsed onto the bed.

Humming, she reached down the front of her dress, wriggled her fingers into her corset, and dredged out a battered photograph. Jessica studied the image. A man, aged about thirty, wearing goggles and a laboratory coat, stared out of the grainy image. She'd been examining the photograph for a few days now, since her boss had assigned her this job. She thought she'd recognise him in person.

She put the photograph into the bedside table, curled up against the pillow—fingertips brushing the hand cannon—and shut her eyes.

Promptly at seven she descended the stairs, dressed in a sapphire blue gown with a modest neckline and a very long train. The sleeves were tight from her wrist to elbow, and slightly puffed from her elbow to shoulder. It was the height of fashion and very respectable, all the way down to the front hem . . . which ended at her upper thighs. Her stockings and garters were sheer white, her boots a blue to match the dress. Jessica's black hair was caught loosely at the nape of her neck, with a few tendrils curling about her cheeks. Her only adornments were a golden locket and a sapphire ring.

Many eyes followed her progress down the stairs, but not the ones she wanted to see.

After spending ninety minutes flirting with the men, Jessica had a better idea of how The Painted Lady could afford its upkeep. Soldiers. Officers. She sipped from yet another cup of tea, studying them from the corners of her eyes. The presence of a military fort in the town had not been in her dossier for this assignment . . . yet it did make sense, considering the occupation of her mark. And the men who weren't officers or soldiers, who were they? Not farmers, she judged, eyeing their well-cut clothes. More scientists? But that didn't add up. She'd been near most of the men at one point or another, between singing, dancing, and socialising, and those suited men didn't smell of coal, oil, or chemicals.

The lavender doors swung open.

Jessica's eyes flew to it, as they had all evening, and a soft sigh of relief spilled from her lips when she saw it was him. Taller than she'd expected, and better looking than the picture she had—of course, the picture wasn't a full body shot, and he wore goggles in it—but it was definitely him. The puzzle of The Painted Lady's patrons would have to wait.

Jessica rose from the arm of the chair and drifted over to him; he had not ventured far into the room. "Dr Brown?"

Startled blue eyes flicked to her. "Good evening." His gaze swept down her body and back up, lingering at a few spots. "I don't believe we've met."

"I'm Jessica. May I pour you a drink, Dr Brown?"

The scientist frowned. "No need for such formality. I go by Wes here."

"Certainly, Wes. Now, what I can I get you?"

"Oh . . . " Wes turned his head, looking over and around her. "I usually keep time with Daisy."

Jessica *tsk*ed. "Daisy's mother took ill, and Daisy has left to nurse her." Daisy's mother's illness had cleared up immediately upon receipt of the steam coach tickets to the Bay, where reservations at The Palace Hotel awaited them. The client had wanted to ensure that Daisy would not be tempted to renege on the agreement. It was a pity that her boss hadn't negotiated a larger fee, Jessica mused, since the client had to be loaded. Her posterior would certainly have appreciated it.

Wes blinked. "In that case, I should be delighted to have a drink with you, Jessica."

Jessica beamed up at him, and curled an arm around his elbow. She wrinkled her nose at the faint odour of coal that hung about him. He must have come straight from his lab.

She deposited him into a chair, then strolled to the bar. Otto had replaced the bartender.

"I see you have met Wes," Otto said. "It must have been hard to wait this long for him."

"What do you mean? I'm here to entertain gentlemen." Jessica snapped her fingers. "I forgot to ask what he wanted to drink."

"Our dear doctor always orders the same drink. I have no difficulty recalling his preference." The clockwork man pulled a glass tumbler from the shelf and held it beneath the counter where the kegs were stored. "You remarked earlier on Daisy's important patrons, yet have ignored several of them. When Wes entered, you immediately went to his side, something you have not done all evening."

Jessica's eyelids drifted to half-mast, and she regarded the clockwork man through her lashes. She was sure the other women had noticed her behaviour—it was their job, after all. But for Otto to notice . . . Had the clockwork man overheard her conversation with Eliza that afternoon? And, more importantly, how much had he inferred from that conversation? She forced a trilling laugh. "What an active imagination you have, Otto!"

The clockwork man blinked at her, looking puzzled, if a mechanical construct could be said to have emotion. His eyes flickered, and his expression lightened. He leaned across the bar. "I understand," he said in a low voice that sent shivers running up her spine. "I risk your cover by saying so much."

The smell of oil filled her nose, sparking happy memories of her father's machine shop. Forcing aside the pleasurable feelings Otto aroused in her, Jessica said coldly, "I don't know what you're talking about."

Otto nodded. "Of course."

Avoiding his gaze, she concentrated on his movements as he filled the tumbler, enjoying the slight jerks that marred the otherwise steady motions. Reluctant admiration for Otto's reasoning skills filled her—there weren't many people, men or women, who could out-think her—but they posed a risk to her right now. Her Leyden jar would have been ideal for the situation, for the electricity would wreak havoc on Otto's metal body and intricate gears, but she had not brought the bulky apparatus with her. She drummed her fingers on the bar. Perhaps the hand cannon? She shook her head. Ignoring him was the safest course—she doubted her boss could afford to replace him.

Otto handed the full glass to Jessica.

She sniffed. "Sarsaparilla?" She cursed under her breath. She'd been hoping for a little alcohol to grease the task ahead of her. She twisted the ring on her finger. Time for plan B.

"It is what he drinks," Otto said. He cocked his head at her. "Would you like an iced beverage? Your cheeks are flushed."

"I'm fine, thank you, Otto." Jessica clutched the drink to her chest. "I should return to Wes, before one of the other girls poaches him."

The clockwork man nodded. He leaned over the bar again. "I am sure you will be more comfortable away from the soldiers, given the circumstances."

"Circumstances?"

"The war that they wage against your people."

Jessica's mind blanked for an instant. With effort, she focused on her facial muscles, quirking an eyebrow. "Otto, nobody is waging war on my 'people'." She injected concern into her voice. "Have you had a diagnostic recently?"

Otto frowned. "I apologise. Your hair . . . eyes . . . facial structure . . . I assumed . . . "

Jessica smiled weakly. She did not need a bored clockwork man taking such an interest in her. No one involved with this job would appreciate the attention. "Why, Otto, are you *flirting* with me? And while I'm working too. Shame!" She playfully slapped his wrist.

Otto's eyes swirled. "Ah. Discretion."

Jessica saluted him with the glass. "Thanks for the drink."

She knew that he watched her leave. When she had settled on the arm of Wes's chair, she glanced over her shoulder at the bar. Otto had propped his elbows on the dark mahogany surface and was staring at her.

"The clockwork man is amazing," Wes said. He sipped at the drink and peered around her to the bar. "I'd love to examine him up close. He's a sophisticated machine."

"Would it prove useful for your research?" Jessica asked. She ran her fingers through Wes's hair, massaging his temples.

"Maybe." He grabbed her hand. "No more talk about work. Let's go upstairs."

Keeping her hand gripped in his own, Wes stood, drawing Jessica to her feet. Clasped hands held high, as if they were stepping onto the dance floor, they went upstairs. Jessica led Wes down the hall to her room, and waved him inside. As she closed the door, a single, dark shape appeared at the top of the stairs. She scowled.

Jessica arranged a smile on her face as she turned back to Wes. He wasted no time. Wrapping his arm, still holding her hand, around her back, he pulled her to his chest and kissed her.

He was a good kisser, Jessica thought in surprise, especially for someone who spent so much time in the lab that his only female companions were those he paid for. However . . . there was work to be done. She pulled away. "Another drink, Wes? Something . . . hot, perhaps?"

Wes regarded her from half-closed eyes. "In this heat?"

A more genuine smile spread over her face. "Do you know that drinking a warm beverage on a warm day helps cool you more than a cold one?"

"Hmmm . . . yes, I see how that might work. Fix some tea then, and we'll test your assertion."

On the chest of drawers next to the washing pitcher and bowl there was a copper and glass steam kettle. It wasn't pretty, but she supposed attractiveness had been sacrificed for the sake of convenience. Jessica had seen one in a judge's office once, but had never operated one. She measured tea leaves into the kettle, poured water from the pitcher, and, moving with a sureness that she didn't feel, used the flint striker to ignite the boiler.

"Is that safe?" Wes asked.

"Perfectly," Jessica said, hoping it was true. She turned back to him. "That will take a few minutes to come to a boil. Where were we?"

Wes smiled. "You were in the process of losing your clothes."

Jessica arched a brow. "I don't remember that. But you're correct, it is a trifle warm in here." A true lady's garment would have had a million tiny buttons down the back: impossible to undo without help. Jessica had borrowed this dress from a saloon girl. All the buttons were down the front.

She wasn't sure how to be seductive about taking off a dress, so Jessica undid them matter-of-factly, keeping her eyes on Wes. He seemed to like it, his cheeks flushing. With a final flick of her fingers, Jessica worked the last button open, pulled her arms from the tight sleeves, and let the dress fall to the floor.

Other than being chillier, standing there in her corset, pantalettes, and stockings didn't feel much different from her usual work clothes. It certainly wasn't as shocking as her men's trousers and vests. The hoity-toity types in San Francisco would probably prefer her in her undergarments—at least they were feminine.

The tea kettle shrieked.

Grabbing the thick towel that lay on the chest, Jessica picked up the kettle and poured tea into the delicate china cups. "Sugar, Wes?"

At his affirmative, she added two lumps. At the same time, her pinky finger deftly flipped open her sapphire ring. A slight jiggle of her finger sent a trickle of powder into the cup. She stirred, closing the ring with another flick of her pinky.

Jessica carried the two cups back to the bed where Wes sat propped against the brass headboard. She handed him the doctored cup, took a sip from her own. "And now for the experiment."

Wes nodded, taking a hearty gulp from his own cup. He lowered it and blinked at her. His pupils were dilated, the blue iris almost entirely swallowed by black. "I feel . . . strange." His eyes drifted shut and his head lolled against the headboard.

Jessica kissed his cheek. "I do apologise, but I need something from you." She turned from him, opening the top drawer of the night stand. The opiate he had ingested would ease the use of the serum she would inject into his bloodstream.

Her hands were caught in a vise-like grip. "Really? And what would that be?"

Jessica's head whipped around. Wes's pupils were still dilated, but only just. The opiate was wearing off. "But—you can't!"

"I take pills to combat such tactics. I'm not stupid, and neither are my investors." His eyes were shrewd. "Who do you represent?"

Jessica tugged. He tightened his grasp, and she had to clench her jaw to keep from gasping again, this time in pain. "I don't know who the client is," she said, "but I am a Pinkerton operative."

"Pinkerton? Pinkerton hires . . . ?" His eyes swept over her half-naked body and his lip curled with disdain.

Jessica straightened, bringing her knee up into his groin. Wes gasped. He let go of her as his hands moved down to the offended area, and Jessica dove around him, shoved a hand under the pillow, and grabbed her hand cannon. She rolled off the bed, twisted, and landed facing Wes, hand cannon pointed at him. His hands were still cupped protectively over his groin, but his blue eyes watched her.

"Pinkerton doesn't, in fact, hire—" she pointed her finger to the floor, where the faint sounds of the piano and laughing men and women drifted through the boards. "I was willing to play nice to get the blueprints, but since the drugs won't work, we'll do this the hard way."

Someone knocked on the door. Jessica didn't take her eyes from Wes. "Who is it?" she asked, making her voice as throaty as possible. "I'm a little busy at the moment."

"It is Otto. I was wondering if I could be of assistance?"

Wes opened his mouth and Jessica rammed the muzzle of her hand cannon against his cheek. "Shhh." Relief swept over her. With Otto's logic gears and strength . . . Hell and damnation, what was she thinking? Raising her voice, she said, "No, thank you, Otto. We're just fine here."

After a moment of silence, Otto said, "I have excellent hearing, Jessica. I am offering to help you with your . . . work."

Her seduce-and-drug-the-scientist plan was unravelling before her eyes. Her boss would have a fit if she brought a civilian, even an artificial one, onto the case. Unless . . . Jessica narrowed her eyes and scrutinised Wes. His eyes were wide; his forehead beaded with sweat. Fear.

She sighed. So, the clockwork man and the scientist weren't playing an elaborate game with her. "Come in then, Otto."

The clockwork man entered, shutting the door behind him. Jessica tossed him the key, and he turned it in the lock, leaving it there.

The hand cannon was still directed at Wes, but Jessica made sure to keep the clockwork man in her field of vision. She was reasonably certain that he meant her no harm, but made of metal, powered by gears and springs, he was a lot stronger than her. If he wanted to cause trouble . . . well, her increasingly not-so-simple job would get interesting in a hurry.

"How do you think you can help me, Otto?"

He ignored the question. "Is it true you are a Pinkerton operative?"

Otto's voice was childlike in its excitement. Jessica's lips twitched. A fanatic. The knot in her stomach loosened. "Yes. I have my badge, but for obvious reasons I can't show it to you at the moment."

Otto nodded. "I have always wondered if perhaps my skills are wasted in my current occupation. If I help you, do you think you could provide a letter of recommendation to your employer? I enjoy investigating."

Which explained his lurking about in hallways and eavesdropping. "Yes. *If* my mission is successful." A clockwork operative! Jessica smiled, imagining the hefty bonus for recruiting an agent of Otto's strength and abilities. *And* she would have an opportunity to see him again. "Your plan is . . . ?"

"There is a saying that you catch more flies with honey than vinegar."

"I like honey," Wes said.

Jessica's eyes didn't waver from the scientist. Her wrist ached. "What if honey doesn't work?"

"I am strong enough to break bones," Otto said. Something whirred and Jessica risked a quick peek. Otto's pupils were contracting, focusing on her arm. "He hurt you. I see the bruising."

Telescopic lenses? Jessica wondered. She'd have to ask him later. Maybe while she was at it she'd ask him how he could sound angry, as if he had emotions.

"I said that I like honey!"

Jessica took a deep breath. "Thank you, Otto, for reminding me of my options. I do have some honey." She lowered her hand cannon. "But first, Wes, I need to ascertain that you have the information I was hired to find. Your research—are you developing a steam-powered, armoured tractor?"

Wes pinched the bridge of his nose. After a few moments of silence, he looked up at her, resigned. "What do you want?"

And here it was. Jessica picked up her long-forgotten tea cup and gulped the contents, grimacing at the tepid liquid. She put the empty cup back down on the bedside table. "I have a job offer, in writing." Jessica opened the drawer of the bedside table and removed the ivory envelope with the unadorned scarlet seal. "From the organisation that engaged Pinkerton. They will accept copies of the plans in lieu of employment. And they also demand the name of your investor."

Wes stretched out a hand for the envelope, but Jessica held it out of his reach. "I also have this . . . " She leaned down and grabbed the heel of her right boot. With a sharp twist the heel swung open and the compact, folded square of paper plopped to the floor. Jessica scooped up the paper, snapped the heel back into place, and straightened. "Another offer from a third party," she said, handing both the envelope and the thick fold of paper to Wes.

"You're betraying Pinkerton?"

It shouldn't have hurt so much to disappoint a mechanical man. Jessica shook her head. "I've given the scientist his job offer; my task for Pinkerton will be completed when I relay his response to my boss. I'm simply providing Dr Brown with another . . . option."

Otto hummed, eye lenses whirring lazily, but made no other response.

Wes popped the seal of the envelope with a fingernail and scanned the contents. He read it again, more slowly. The corner of his mouth curled upwards and then he threw back his head and laughed. When the guffaws had tapered to chuckles, he tucked the letter back into the envelope, which he slid inside his shirt.

"An invitation to clown school?" Jessica asked, irked.

He shook his head, and unfolded the thick square of paper. After reading it through twice, he refolded it with slow, precise movements, and tucked it into his shirt with the envelope.

"Do you know who Pinkerton's client is?" Wes asked.

"I suspect," Jessica said, "that the client is Army Intelligence. They worked hard to keep the organisation's identity a secret, but," she shrugged, "they're easy to spot once you know what to look for."

"And the other?"

Jessica's mouth pinched at the corners. She hated divulging her own secrets. "That's personal."

Wes nodded. "My investors are a new intelligence branch of the government, independent of the Army or Navy Intelligence offices. They call themselves the Secret Service."

The men in suits downstairs. Government agents. Her breath hissed out. Nothing could ever be simple.

"The colleagues of the Army officers are your investors?" Otto asked, coming to the same conclusion. "But why are they developing it here instead of the East coast? Would they not want these armoured tractors for use in case the unrest in Europe affects us?"

Jessica gave Otto a look of approval. She'd never interacted with a clockwork man so capable of thinking outside its programming. Hell, she knew a sad number of flesh and blood people who couldn't think their way out of a cardboard box. "Well, Wes?"

Wes squirmed, cheeks flushing. "The second letter confirms a rather uncomfortable hypothesis I've had for some time now."

He'd never come out and say it. "Otto, they're going to use the tractors—"

"Oh!" the clockwork man blurted. "The Indian campaigns." He paused, then repeated in a much softer voice, "Oh."

"I imagine an armoured tractor will be useful on the lava ridges," Jessica said.

Wes grunted. "If I can figure out the wheels. I need it to crawl, to gain traction, not roll . . . " He cleared his throat. "My apologies. Yes, I suspect my research will be used on our own soil first."

"Against the Indians," Jessica growled.

"As you say. Against the Indians," Wes said.

Otto placed a cool hand on her shoulder. "What have the Modoc offered you to desist with your research?"

Wes looked her straight in the eyes. "Not enough. Not enough for the repercussions I'd have to face."

Jessica sagged, relishing the chance to lean against Otto, who wouldn't bend, or wilt, or break. She hadn't thought that her mother's people would be able to come up with enough money to bribe the scientist—and what else could they offer? They had no land, no appreciable wealth.

Otto squeezed her shoulder. "How likely are the Modoc to initiate peace talks?"

Jessica sighed. "There have been talks, but they won't return to the Klamath reservation." She shrugged. "But I believe there will continue to be talks, as long as their fighting ability remains somewhat equal to that of the Army."

"I won't sabotage my own research!"

"Now, Doctor, nobody suggested anything of the sort," Otto soothed.

Yet, Jessica thought wryly. But what additional honey did Otto have to offer?

"I am the only one of my model," Otto said. "My inventor has patented his work, of course, so I cannot show you much, but a look at my arm servos and gears should prove illuminating to one interested in clockwork mechanisms."

The comforting presence of Otto's hand left her shoulder. Otto stepped closer to Wes, rolling up one pristine white sleeve. He grabbed his left wrist with his right hand, twisted, and removed the left hand from its arm, revealing dozens of tiny, interlocking gears, clicking and clacking as their teeth moved against each other, shiny cams, and springs.

Wes craned his head. He pursed his lips, a low whistle escaping. Jessica goggled at the exposed gears. Even with a tinker for a father, Otto's gearwork was beyond her comprehension. He was beautiful.

"What materials does he use?" Wes asked, leaning close to Otto's arm.

Otto cocked his head and hummed. "I cannot say. You may have a photograph."

Wes nodded, his fingers twitching. "I need a pen," he muttered. He pulled a jeweller's loupe from his pocket, held it up to his eye, and squinted at Otto's exposed gears. Sighing, he rested against the headboard, returned the loupe to his pocket, and crossed his arms over his chest. "With a gear system like that I could . . . the patents . . . my research . . . The trade is acceptable."

Jessica relaxed her jaw as tension ebbed from her body. She thumbed open her locket.

"Trick jewellery?" Otto asked. His pupils dilated, whirring.

"Yes," she said. She pressed a button, and the innards of the locket expanded on a tiny accordion. "Hold out your arm, Otto."

Jessica held the locket up to her eye, and peered at Otto's arm through the tiny lens. Making adjustments with the minuscule knobs, she brought Otto's arm into focus. Then, holding her breath, she depressed the clasp. The camera clicked. She took two more photographs, to ensure that at least one would be of sufficient quality and clarity for their purposes, then tapped another button to close the camera.

Shutting the locket, she turned to Wes. "I can develop those photographs tonight, and have them for you tomorrow."

Otto harrumphed. "One."

Jessica nodded. "One," she repeated. "Thank you, Otto."

Wes slid out of the bed, adjusted his shirt and trousers. "Under the circumstances, I will refuse the employment offer of your client, and the demand for blueprints." He held out a hand.

Jessica clasped his hand. "I'm sure once the client is informed of your investor's identity, your refusal will be accepted." She hesitated. "And the other?"

"Thank them, certainly, but they needn't worry about paying me. Coincidentally," Wes said, winking, "my current research is floundering. It may be years before I can find my way to a solution."

Jessica closed her eyes briefly, concealing the surge of emotion that overcame her. "That's certainly tragic," Jessica said. "Be sure to talk with Eliza on your next visit to The Painted Lady. I'm sure she can cheer you up."

Wes raised her hand, brushing his lips across her knuckles. Releasing her hand, he turned to the clockwork man. "Otto, a privilege to meet you."

The two shook hands. "I hope your clockwork research is successful, Dr Brown," Otto said.

When the sound of Wes's footfalls on the stairs had faded, Otto cocked his head at Jessica. "So, partner, when do we head back to the office?"

Jessica's pulse pounded in her neck. The smell of oil surrounded her, and she could just hear the gentle clicks of his gears. "Only business partners?"

Otto's eyes dilated, and Jessica detected a hitch in his clicking. "But I am not human. Miss Eliza says I'm amusing, but I am only a tool. I can't be a companion."

"You're the only being I've met that's smart enough to keep up with me. And you—you are kind. And steadfast. I don't care what these people think." Jessica smiled. "To answer your question, we don't have to leave until tomorrow, after I give Eliza Wes's photograph for safekeeping."

Otto cupped her elbows with his cold hands. "I find the idea of being more than business partners . . . pleasing."

With a husky laugh, Jessica grabbed a fistful of Otto's shirt and pulled his head down for a kiss.

THE LAW OF LOVE

ANGELA REGA

I woke to a young woman's hand winding the key inside my chest. One . . . two . . . three . . . the levers that pulled down made my eyelids flutter. Four . . . five . . . six . . . my heart was beating. I was alive once more.

Flashes of sunlight streamed through the glass I sat behind. I must have been here a long time; the sun had heated my porcelain and fish-scaled skin.

I blinked a few times. The woman saw I was animated.

"There!" she said, as pleased as if she had made me herself. She yanked her hand out and zipped my chest back up.

Where was I? Where was my father? I ricked my head left and right, absorbing my surroundings. I was poised in a seated position on a long wooden plank suspended on the back of a false wall. On either side of me were dolls of all shapes and sizes: kewpie dolls with kiss curls, aristocratic ladies clutching umbrellas and wearing ornate bonnets, dolls with ebony hair, porcelain skin and silk kimonos, and me.

Although we were all different, the young lady with dark yellow teeth that had woken me up made sure to have us all seated in the same position: legs and arms outstretched, heads facing the front glass. I blinked twice and admired the view. I had never seen such a large window, the ones in my father's house being small enough to let a branch or a bird in, but never an entire street. I froze. Two girls in navy blue frocks with white piping around the collars pressed their faces against the window, peered in, then ran away, leaving little circles of fog on the glass. The wonder of the view made me forget my confusion. Perhaps my father would come soon.

A whirring sound came from my right. I turned my head to see a porcelain doll with long, red hair and green eyes like sparkling emeralds.

"Welcome to Chapman's Doll Orphanage," she said, raising her whole arm up as if in a salute and bringing it straight back down into her lap.

"You are very pretty. Sorry you can't bend your elbows."

"You are an unusual little doll, so green and scaly in parts. I'm Colomba; what's your name?"

"I don't have one."

Colomba lifted her arm. Because her fingers were fused together in porcelain, she put her whole hand into the string tied around my wrist to read my story.

"Your father made you from mermaid scale and his skin, he named you Daughter. That must be why you have the faint smell of the sea about you. I've been there once. The scales on your arms are so . . . green!"

"My father loved a mermaid once, but she returned to the sea."

"Your father's a doll maker; I saw him deliver you in a bag. I have no idea who made me. One day I woke up to Missy Yellow Teeth winding me up."

My father had sold me? If I had tears I would have cried. I had seen him crafting a new doll in the likeness of his latest lost love. I let my chin droop to my chest.

With a stiff arm, Colomba patted my shoulder awkwardly.

"Nice to meet you, Daughter."

"And you, Colomba, but I am no longer a daughter."

"Names don't matter. Whoever buys you will give you a name. Shh . . . Miss Eugenia, Yellow Teeth is coming. She doesn't know I can speak."

Miss Eugenia sauntered over to where Colomba and I were seated, and stood between us and the large glass window, her bony hands firm on her hips.

"I placed you near the counter for a reason! There are too many redheads in the front window! If you keep walking off like that I won't wind you up! Christmas is only two months away. Wouldn't you like to go to a good home?"

Colomba didn't answer, but nodded her head up and down compliantly. Eugenia pursed her thin lips together, picked my friend up by the foot and left her suspended so that the pantaloons under her skirts were in full view. "There! Now don't move!" She and placed her back in the small armchair at the counter.

"Now . . . the new doll." She crept back towards me and I hoped she would not hang me upside down, too. She peered into my face, her head cocking to one side then the other as she stroked the scales on my right arm. "Not a pretty one, that's for sure. God made them and he paired them in two but I'm not sure which God made you." She put me back down. "No good child will want you."

I cried, but of course nobody comforts a doll—there are no tears to shed. My father had sold me and I was no longer who I thought I was. I wanted to be near Colomba but Eugenia insisted on keeping me on the long wooden bench next to other dolls that didn't want to speak to me.

"You're so ugly," a boudoir doll sneered at me. "Nobody will ever buy you." The other dolls along the bench stifled giggles. It was true; my body, half covered in green scales was different to their perfect all porcelain skins.

Soon they were gone, sold to spoilt children and ladies that wanted them to sit in their middle of their beds surrounded by soft pillows. But I remained.

Each day Eugenia wound me up, and each night I would spend my night staring through the window and watching the world go by. Christmas had passed and no children pressed their faces against the glass with the same anticipation as before.

That was when I saw him. And he saw me.

He was dressed in a long black overcoat, top hat and black trousers, a gold monocle chain hanging from his shirt pocket. He stopped opposite me, one hand pressed against the glass shopfront. Our eyes connected and for a brief moment I wasn't sure if he was repulsed or attracted by me but he didn't blink. Then he adjusted his top hat, tilted it to a greeting and kept walking.

"Oohhh, he likes you," Colomba said from her armchair and she raised her arms straight up in front of her because she couldn't lift them sideways to show her excitement.

"Who is he?"

"Oktave, a poet and musician of sorts."

I felt the desire for my clockwork heart to beat faster but it stayed at its usual rhythm.

"How do you know him?" I asked her, but already Colomba was articulating her legs to get out of the chair and didn't answer. It was those blue eyes like one of my father's medicine bottles that kept me entranced. When he had walked away, my heart was left with a longing. Nobody had looked at me like that before.

Eugenia asked him twice if he was sure it was *me* he wanted when he came into the shop to purchase me at full price the next day.

"She's due to be wound at sunset," she said to him as she handed him his change.

"Of course."

"Don't forget."

"How could I? I'm besotted with her smile."

He picked me up and held me close to his chest. I pressed my porcelain ear against it and heard the heart beating behind his chest bone. *Glugg ug. Glugg ug. Glugg ug.* Oh the beauty of that rhythm! So different to my *tick tick tick.*

We walked together, me in his arms. The streets were wide and colder than I imagined but I had never ventured further than my father's house and then awoke behind glass. The world was damp with leftover rain, and smelt dank. A mouse scurried past Okatave's foot and the sound of horses' hooves trotting over cobblestones echoed in the distance.

We stopped at a large wrought iron gate. Oktave pushed the gate open and it creaked itself shut behind us we proceeded up a path.

"Welcome home," he whispered, opening the door. I wanted to stare as there was so much to behold in the salon but I had been programmed to blink with each pull of a lever. A painting of a beautiful woman with an emerald dress and ebony hair in long ringlets hung from the back wall. He stared at the picture for a moment as if paying homage and then sat me on the velvet divan.

"I've always wanted to make love to a mermaid," he said and kissed my blinking eyelids. Oh the wetness of his large lips on my dry eye sockets. To feel them so lubricated! He lifted my scaled arm and brushed his tongue against it. I creaked a little.

"And you can never speak of our love, little doll. It will be our secret."

I was joyous and wanted to shout it out to the world but all the dolls I had come to know had either all been sold and Colomba still sat in armchair at the counter. There was nobody to tell.

We passed the blustery winter nights with the same ritual. He would bring me to the divan, caress my body with his large hands and move against my body until his heart almost stopped beating, his eyes rolling back in his head. I was small, dwarfed by the bulk of his body on mine. But what wonder to be loved!

Then he would bathe himself clean with the little jug and basin he kept at the side table, wind me up while my heart was still warm with his love and seat me at his bedside table to keep vigil while he slept.

It was right, what Colomba had said. Whoever owned you would give you a name. Now I had so many: my little dark one, my dear one, my darling.

I wondered what happened to her. Had a man as fine as this bought her? Or was she some toy of a spoilt child that cut her hair and yanked off her limbs?

I hoped she had been as lucky as me.

It was the first balmy night of spring when daylight lengthens that I noticed Oktave did not seem himself.

Night approached, but still he made no move to retire to the divan and make love to me. I fluttered my eyelids, waved my scaled arm up and down in his direction but he didn't notice.

Instead he paced the salon, checking his fob watch, combing his hair.

That night, he didn't call me anything. I had no name.

My blinking slowed, my limbs stiffened. I tried to look up to see the plaster ceiling rose but my head was too heavy.

I became woozy at the moment the woman from the painting entered the room.

"My love," Oktave said and swept her into his arms. My head drooped and I could only lift it high enough to see feet and Oktave's hand undoing the laces of her boots.

The floor seemed to be liquid, the walls rippling and then everything froze. My heart was slowing down and soon would stop. He had forgotten to wind me up and had called her what he had never called me—my love.

My eyelids opened on the first creaking wind of the key. How it hurt. His hand in my chest; he held my heart. I blinked and looked up to see his face staring intently in mine as he wound me awake. I creaked and whirred a little. I was stiff. I needed oiling and care. I needed love.

He sat me on the divan while he sat at his writing desk, quill in one hand, the other, under his chin. He was deep in thought. I knew that expression. My father kept the same expression when he wrote love letters to the mermaid that had returned to the sea.

Oktave was writing letters of longing. With one hand, he stroked absentmindedly at my skin; with the other he held the quill. His eyes never left the words on his page. The letters were not for me.

I never needed pursuing, only winding up.

Pursuit is the law of love.

I heard a crackle and hiss from the fireplace. The fire was on; winter was already approaching again. I had been asleep for many months.

I looked out the window at the blur of the gaslights lining the street. Would he caress me the way he did before? Call me my darling, my dark one?

That night he loved me but not with the same abandon. I saw the unfinished letters on the desk, the inkpot open. His mind and heart were elsewhere, but from the way he moved against me, I knew I had satisfied his desire for release. He left me on the divan and went back to the seat at his desk, his back towards me.

If I could have run for him to pursue me, I would. Would that make him fall in love with me in the same way he loved the lady from the painting? Her emerald green dress was reminiscent of the colour of my scales.

I couldn't run. My father had not made me that way. I could walk slowly, but my knees didn't bend, just like Colomba couldn't move her arms. I was not meant for pursuit.

The law of love would never apply to me.

He writes letters that she never reads. They lay strewn across the desk, some drafts crushed into balls, others made into paper cranes. The more he crumples and rewrites, the more he seeks solace in my arms.

Now he places me by the fire. I am so close that it burns the scales on my arms but he doesn't notice and I do not care. As long as he loves me, caressing me with his large hands, his voice barely a whisper, the weight of his body squashing mine, I am happy. May she never come back. I watch with hope as he throws some of the crumpled letters into the fire.

We passed many nights like this, until the bitter, short nights began to lengthen. I grew comfortable in the habit.

Then, one morning, a letter arrived. He paced the room, drawing the curtains open and shut and opening and closing the front door. Was it from his love? Perhaps, he would forget about her and learn to love me as he loved her? He had grown used to my body; we had our routine. But neither is habit the law of love. Still, I lived in hope.

He was not prepared the day the woman in the painting arrived. She knew how to string him along. She had come later than expected, at the height of spring.

The gate creaked open as the sulky trotted up the path. Oktave swooped me up, pressed me to his chest and raced down the stairs. He would show her that I was a ticking doll. Alive and in love! He would declare our love!

He ran past the front door and raced with me down the narrow staircase that led down to a room I had never seen him go. Down, down, down, it was dark and smelt musty. He brushed a cobweb off his face. At the bottom of the stairs was a small door that reached the height of his hip.

He crouched down, opened the small door and stretched his arm inside as if reaching for something. He dragged a large cardboard box across the floor towards us and pulled open the lid.

I wanted to scream but I had been made to not raise my voice louder than a bell or a tinkle. Inside was a mass grave of dolls; headless torsos, arms and limbs tangled and twisted together, hair matted and knotted. Some eyes shut.

There was one reminiscent of my red-headed friend, Colomba. Her eyes were frozen open and stared blankly at me. Then I saw what was common with all of those intact—their chests were unzipped, their hearts ripped out, their empty cavities filled with sawdust, others filled with straw. A small mouse scurried out of the chest of the red-headed doll, and Oktave coughed as the wood dust charged the musty air.

The pain in my heart made me release a sound of grief. Oktave cocked his head and looked at me with curiosity; perhaps he would change his mind? It was the longest moment between heartbeats. He bit his bottom lip and shoved me inside, his hand squeezing my chest and pushing me down to make me fit into that cardboard grave.

I coughed and splattered as tendrils of the matted hair of decaying dolls choked my dry lips. I wanted to cry but no tears came. Oktave had not kissed my eyes in a very long time.

Then his face looked as I had never had seen it. It was desparate. Violent. Oktave pressed the palm of his hand into my face and pushed me further in. Then he turned the lid and left me enclosed in darkness.

I heard his footsteps down the narrow staircase and the door open.

"My love!" he shouted.

I lay between the sleeping dolls that would never wake; squashed between superfluous limbs, rotting moth wings, mouse droppings and the heaviness in my heart.

He'd not enough time to rip my heart out and had left it ticking.

It wouldn't be too long. Soon I would be at one with my sisters when I required winding. A little mouse scuttled delicately across my face. I mourned Oktave had not removed my heart, leaving me empty for the little mouse to fill the void.

LOVE IN THE TIME OF CLOCKWORK HORSES

REBECCA HARWELL

The funeral of Gregory Samuels was a torpid affair as only a handful of relatives who had not yet forsaken this side of the family attended. On the way home, his daughter Clara Samuels wished to head straight to the stables where the last of the Samuels' clockwork horses was housed. Her brother Aiden, however, wished to see a judge.

"He was not in his right mind when he wrote that damned thing," Aiden said. He stuck his head out of the carriage's window into the smoke-filled air of lower New Boston and called to their driver, "To the East Side. Judge Higgins's residence."

The driver, a spindly man whose jacket had lost several of its burnished buttons, gave a loud, "Ay, sir," and reined the two ancient clockwork horses off the main cobblestoned street and down a filthy little alley, claiming it was a shortcut to the Queen's Bay. This was the east bank where New Boston's upper classes danced, courted, and generally wasted their lives in other utterly boring pursuits.

Clara frowned. She looked down at the faded paper she clutched with her father's scrawl across the top. "He left Desert Steel to me. No judge will overturn this will, let alone interrupt his supper to read it." She tried to sound certain, but the corset under her drab black dress itched, and her makeup had long been ruined by tears.

She only wanted to see her father's horse, and her brother would not get in her way.

Aiden gave a patient nod, which only served to make her angrier. "The racetrack is no place for a woman, especially one of your birth. If you won't give that thing up to be sold for scrap, I will have Judge Higgins rule it mine. Maybe then we will be able to keep the manor for a few months longer, and start rebuilding your dowry."

A stream of curses rose in her throat, but highbred ladies did not swear like dock workers, as her mother used to say, so Clara allowed herself only a sour glare. She had hoped that when her father had to use her dowry to climb his way out of debt it would put off an inevitable loveless marriage to a gentleman. Unfortunately, her brother, it seemed, did not want a spinster for a sister. Clara would have to find a new excuse to avoid the unappealing binds of matrimony for a few years longer.

Judge Higgins, another man born of old blood, lived on the east side of the Queen's Bay. The carriage jolted as the clockwork horses, both of a model several years out-of-date, fitted and started on the bridge that spanned the brown waters. The engines of the automobiles driving by churned and blew out clouds of black smoke. Clara wrinkled her nose.

"Wish it had been proper to get an auto for the funeral." Aiden sighed. He also watched the metal machines pass them by as their driver coaxed another few steps out of his horses. "I hate these old-fashioned things. Unreliable."

Clara pressed her lips together, ignoring him as she watched the fine curves of manors come into sight on the near side of the bay.

Back when times were good, her father had owned a stable full of clockwork horses, and he took her there every Sunday after church, much to the chagrin of her mother. Desert Steel was his last, the only one he refused to sell off when business went bad, and Clara knew she would see him cared for. Her father had left the horse to her for a reason, after all. She was not about to let Aiden sell him for scrap metal.

The judge lived in an impressive manor. A cobbled drive lit by gaslights led up to red double doors. When the carriage stopped, Aiden stepped out. He turned and offered a hand to Clara. She stared at it for a moment, then decided her pride was not worth ripping her new skirts. She took his hand and climbed down. Aiden rang the bell, and a servant appeared.

Judge Higgins was, unsurprisingly, in the midst of supper. If Aiden wanted to challenge the will, he could have done it at a more reasonable time, not the hour after their father was put in the ground. He smiled at the maid and told her it was a matter of the utmost urgency that they see the judge.

Judge Higgins was not pleased. He came into the lamp-lit study with his napkin still around his neck. Clara graciously averted her eyes from the tall man. The judge realised his *faux pas* and removed it, before sitting down behind an impressively large desk.

"It couldn't have waited?" he asked gruffly.

Aiden nodded. "Thank you, your honour, for seeing my sister and I. Today, we buried our father, Gregory Samuels. He left a will in his lock-box at the bank. As much as I wish to honour his final wishes, I do not believe he was in his right mind when he wrote it."

"You came to see me about a will? On a Sunday?" Judge Higgins looked Aiden over as if he couldn't quite believe it. Aiden nodded vigorously, and the judge sighed.

"Well, let's have it."

Clara rose and handed him the will. She remained standing as the judge looked over the single page of handwriting. He snorted, then glanced at Aiden. "I suppose the part you take issue with is that your father left a clockwork racehorse to your sister?"

Aiden nodded again. "We have lost much since our father's business went under. He sold the other horses. We need to sell this one as well, something my sister doesn't understand."

Judge Higgins sighed and handed it back to her. "It is a tight will, if an unorthodox one." When Aiden opened his mouth to protest, the judge held up a hand. "Miss Samuels here is the rightful owner of the clockwork horse known as Desert Steel. I won't hear any other nonsense on the subject. If you need to sell it, I am sure you can convince her to part with it."

Aiden muttered something under his breath that neither Clara nor the judge could hear. She didn't mind. Clara's small smirk had turned into a triumphant smile, one that she wore out the door and into the carriage.

"You don't have the funds to keep it, Clara," he told her for the tenth time over the *clip-clop* of the clockwork horses' hooves.

Clara sighed. She straightened in her seat, adjusted her petticoats, and looked her brother in the eye. "I know. That is why I'll run Desert Steel in the first race he qualifies for. The winner's purse will keep him stabled for a few months."

Aiden shook his head. "So that's it, then. You're just going to abandon your studies at the university and go off and join the racing business? Why can't you put your efforts into finding a husband and settling down?"

"Because I have no interest in dull gentlemen and I am now the owner of a race horse who will soon be a winner."

Now, she had only to go to the bad side of town to find a jockey.

Clara Samuels wasn't a proper lady, something her brother had never ceased to remind her of. For one, she was twenty-one years old and had never had a serious marriage proposal. Some might say it was because of her sallow complexion and the way the tip of her nose turned up. In truth, her sad lack of suitors had more to do with the fact that on every introduction to a gentleman, she flat out told them that she wasn't looking to marry. She hated the thought of being tied down to one house, to one man, for the rest of her life. A compromise was reached in her family that she would attend a prestigious local university for young ladies and search for a husband after she graduated. Until the day of her father's funeral, she had engaged purposelessly in her studies. No more. Now, she had a charge and a mission to keep him.

Of course, another reason someone might claim Clara was not a proper lady was because she did outrageous things like walking alone on the west bank as the last glints of sunlight shone off the opalescent oil stains in the Queen's Bay.

She held up her third-best petticoat to keep it from trailing through the mud that dotted the wooden walkway, though she wished she had a free hand to politely cover her nose from the eye-watering stench that arose from this side of the bank.

Turning off the main street, she headed into the darkness toward an old stable.

Barkley's had seen the height of its glory not long after the Civil War. Now a rundown building with two chimneys on top, one spewing a black cloud and the other a white one, the stable was patronised by those who ran cheap clockwork horses for quick cash. Clara sucked in a breath and entered.

A gruff man who watched her with far too much interest for her taste directed her to a stall at the end of the first row. At this time in the evening, the stable was quiet. Her shoes clopped over stone, rousing the clockwork horses from their trancelike naps, the closest thing these creatures needed to real sleep. A few curious heads peeked over the metal doors. Steam hissed out of their flared metal nostrils as she passed them by. Most of the horses here were nearly falling apart, their owners trying to squeeze a few last wins out of the beasts before selling them for scrap.

Clara stopped in front of the final stall. Inside the door, a figure in trousers was hunched over, tinkering with a gear in the right foreleg of an average-looking clockwork horse. This one was tinged black, with bright orange eyes from the fire hidden deep within the workings of its chest.

"Mr Woodward? Joseph Woodward? My name is Clara Samuels. I have a business proposition for you. I was wondering if you might have some time to discuss it."

"It's Jo." The figure rose and turned around, and Clara let out a very unladylike gasp as one of the most beautiful women she had ever seen held out a callused hand. "Most people make that mistake."

Clara stared for a second before she remembered her manners. She grasped Jo's hand lightly and shook it. She knew she should glance down modestly, but she could not stop looking at the woman before her.

Jo stood a head shorter than her, and wore breeches and a shirt, both stained with grease. It was men's gear, but it fit around her curves in a way that made it more feminine than the skirts Clara had on. Her hair was raven black and clipped short, framing her tanned face. Dark eyes that hovered between gray and blue watched Clara with a hint of amusement, and her blush deepened.

She mentally told herself off. She was a lady and a racehorse owner now, and she needed to act the part instead of letting herself get flustered at a pretty smile. Clara cleared her throat. "My apologies, Miss Woodward."

"Just Jo. We don't stand for formalities around here." She gave the clockwork horse behind her a slap on the metal plate of its hindquarters and left the stall, closing the iron gate behind her. "So, you have a business proposition for me."

"Well—yes," Clara said, stuttering a bit. She took a moment to get a hold of herself and stared past Jo's left ear as she spoke. Those eyes somehow managed to turn her tongue into a knot. "I need a jockey. Your record is impressive, and I'd like to hire you."

Jo leaned up against the stone wall. She took a case of cigarettes out of her pocket and offered one to Clara. Heat rushed to her face again as she stammered out a *no thank you*. Jo shrugged, lit one from striking a match off her boot, and inhaled. "I haven't run in any real races. You'd know that, so you're not looking for a Mechanics' Cup or some other big affair where they let off fireworks in the winning horse's name afterward. You're a highbred lady looking at the dirty races."

"Yes," Clara admitted. In the past week she'd been over every race on the east coast that Desert Steel might run in. Any respectable race required a track record that her horse didn't have. "I just inherited him from my father. He didn't have the funds to keep the horse, and neither do I. My brother wants to sell him, and he will if I don't get enough money to house him for a couple more months. I need a quick win, and I think you're the jockey to do that." Her voice rose in pitch, her desperation filtering in.

Jo looked at her for a long time, and Clara had to stop herself from squirming under that dark gaze. "What are the terms?" the woman asked slowly.

Clara paused for a moment, temporarily forgetting what she had rehearsed on the walk down here. "Um . . . thirty percent of the purse. I can offer you fifty dollars if you don't win, as compensation for your time."

She smiled and shook her head. "Don't let anyone around here hear you talking about compensation. In this world of clockwork racing, you only get paid if you win."

"Does—does that mean—?"

Jo nodded. "Against my better judgment, but I like you. Send me the details of the race, as well as the address where you're keeping the horse. I'll want to work with him for a few weeks before I race him. Deal?" She held out her hand again.

Clara was almost overwhelmed by the rush she felt at those words. She held onto those feelings, as warm and tantalising as they were, for only a moment before she buried them underneath propriety and took Jo's hand like a wellborn lady.

The race was to be a "dirty" affair, as Jo had called it. It was scheduled at a run-down track north of New Boston with a semi-legal status that would have curled the eyelashes of a more respectable woman. Although after meeting Jo, Clara was reevaluating her definition of the term. Jo could hardly be genteel, yet there was something so charming, so electrifying about her.

When her thoughts were not consumed by the jockey she had hired, she worried over university work and her finances. The payment to reserve a spot in the race had depleted her coffers so significantly she was unable to hire a mechanic. Jo had reassured her that she'd have no need of one. She could get the old clockwork horse up and running. "Besides," she'd said, "it might not be tradition, but it's always better when a horse's jockey and mechanic are the same. If you know how he's put together, you'll know how he'll run."

Two weeks after their initial meeting, she had sent Jo the address of the old stable her horse was housed at. The stable's owner had graciously allowed the rent to be postponed, as her father had been a good customer through the hard times. Jo showed up early on a Saturday morning.

Clara had spent the better part of the evening prior deciding what to wear. Part of her wanted to put on the fine saxony dress whose maroon overcoat contrasted nicely with her blonde curls. However, thinking back to Jo's simple clothing, perhaps she would make a better impression in something—less flashy. Not men's clothes, though. Clara still had some shreds of propriety left.

She settled on a thin gray dress with no petticoats and a modest corset. Pairing it with her rain boots and her hair in a simple bun, she left the manor with her oldest parasol and walked to the stable.

Jo was already there. As Clara rounded the corner and opened the door to the stall, the jockey was running her hands down the outer metal plating of Desert Steel's left foreleg. The clockwork horse responded to her touch by leaning into her. Steam ruffled her short hair as his nose brushed the top of her head.

"He's a beauty." She wiped her greasy hands on her shirt and stood. "An older model, but he's been kept up and oiled well. I've recalibrated a couple of the malfunctioning gears. The plates on his left hindquarters need to be hammered straight, and I'll have to alter the saddle plate for someone my size. But he's a good horse."

Clara only faltered for a moment under that intense gaze. "Yes. He was always my father's favourite. Do you think he can win a stakes race?"

"Your father would probably turn over in his grave if he knew you were putting this horse in a stakes race. Only one horse, the winner, survives. The rest go to the track, which sells them for scrap."

"He would get sold for scrap either way." Clara looked over the stall. A thick carpeted mat covered the bottom, stained with grease from where Desert Steel had rolled. The horse himself was a coppery colour. The constant turn of gears made it seem as if he was always moving even when he stood placidly. He shone brighter, his flaming eyes clearer than Clara remembered. "He likes you."

"He's got good taste," Jo said with a smile. "I think he can win. He'll be racing for his life, and he won't give up that easily. When's the race?"

Clara told her it was in a month's time, and Jo nodded. "Well then, we'll be seeing a lot of each other."

Clara tried to speak, but her throat had gone suddenly dry.

They did indeed see a lot of one another. Jo came to the stable three times a week during the afternoon. It meant that Clara had to race home from her classes, change into something suitable, and run to the stable to see her, and she did so. Without money to hire a carriage or auto, she was becoming quite the athlete. She only wondered what the neighbours thought of her hiking her skirts up and jogging down the street in her rain boots.

Desert Steel grew perkier by the day. After a week of repairs, a grease-stained Jo emerged from the stall and told her that he could be ridden. Her next visit, Clara watched as the jockey cinched a leather saddle around the horse's midsection plates and climbed up. They took him to the track out back and ran him a few laps. The awkward *clop* of the clockwork horse's walk soon turned into the smooth drumbeat of his gallop.

After slowing him to a walk, Jo led him over to the edge and jumped off. She grinned up at Clara. "I think you might have a stakes winner here." Clara could only smile in return.

If she was honest with herself, she knew there was now more to this affair than a race, a clockwork horse, and a jockey. There were feelings that she had only ever read about in novels, the ones her brother would tease her about when they had been adolescents. It wasn't proper, she knew, but ignoring them wasn't making them go away. Whenever Jo flashed a smile or looked her in the eye, Clara's insides melted.

She tentatively brought the subject up the week before Desert Steel's first, and possibly only, race.

Jo was in the stall, tinkering with one of Steel's knee joints. She looked up and saw Clara standing at the door. "Nice to see the university hasn't swallowed you whole yet. He'll be ready for Saturday. Just fixing a couple of parts that have been bothering me."

"Jo, are you married?" The question slipped out before Clara could think better of it.

She frowned. "No. Why?"

"It was nothing," Clara said as heat rushed into her face. "I was . . . curious."

Jo stood up and leaned on the other side of the stall's gate. "Why are you curious?" Her eyes seemed to grow larger and deeper as they regarded a very red-faced Clara.

"Like I said, it was nothing." She swallowed, and then the words came tumbling out again. "It's just, you're a woman, and you're a jockey. You wear breeches. I—just—"

A long moment passed before the corners of Jo's mouth slowly turned up in a small smile. "It's all right. My family came on hard times. My father used to be a dockworker, but he was injured. It fell to me to put food on the table, and the only thing I've ever been good at is tinkering and riding. I got a shot, disguised myself as a boy, and went for it. I've won enough races now that no one who hires me cares that I'm female."

"Your parents, they must be proud of you." The moment she said it, Clara regretted her words as a shadow passed over Jo's face.

"They died of the fever two years ago. Now I'm just trying to save up enough to go west and see what's out there."

"But why?" She hoped the edge of anxiety in her voice went unnoticed. "You seem to have a good life here."

Jo shook her head. "I don't want to live out my life in the house my parents died in. Besides, in New Boston you have to be respectable and get married. I won't be young enough to ride forever, and I have no plans of marrying a man."

"Why not?" The final question slipped out in a whisper.

Jo looked at Clara, her smile broadening. "I think you know why."

Clara swallowed, bid her jockey a good evening, and left before her treacherous tongue could say anything else. True, she did suspect why. Such things were never discussed in high-class circles. If you were fortunate enough to be a woman born of good blood, then you had a duty to marry and carry on the family name. Even if it wasn't something that you found . . . appealing. The lower classes did not have the same restraints. What Clara's friends would look down upon with disdain and disgust, the working class shrugged and let be. A woman like Jo would never need to marry. Clara was not so free.

And if she was? She had never considered any kind of relationship besides marriage. It was simply out of the question. Now, however, at night she lay awake in bed thinking about a future that could never come to pass.

The day of the stakes race arrived. Clara, wearing her best gown, purple over grey petticoats, rode in a clockwork carriage down to the track. Her brother had insisted on the carriage. Even if he was not willing to accompany her to such a reputation-ruining event, he did not want his sister to be gossiped about any more than she already was, so he paid for the ride.

At the track, Clara dodged drunken men and fancy ladies with their cheap perfume. She ignored the lewd comments thrown her way with a turn of a parasol, and made for the ramshackle stables where Desert Steel was temporarily housed. The hems of her skirts were soon stained with greasy sludge, and she did not want to even consider the state of her shoes. It was not perhaps the best choice in clothing for such a place, but Clara had been working hard to remind herself that she was, in fact, a proper lady, and dressing the part was vital to her success.

The clockwork horses she passed blew out steam, their glowing eyes holding a menace that she hoped she was imagining. Next to these iron beasts, their withers and legs thick and strong, Desert Steel looked almost fragile.

Jo fastened the last of the saddle straps. She wore black breeches and a grey shirt. Her number, an eleven printed in flourished script, hung on her back. Clara took in a sharp breath. She was beautiful.

"He's ready to run," Jo said. She stroked the interlocked metal plates hiding the clockwork underpinnings of Steel's neck. "I think he'll win."

"Purse is five hundred dollars if he does. That's a hundred and fifty to you." Clara avoided Jo's eyes. "Enough to start your new life in the west."

"Yes," Jo whispered. She strapped on her metal riding hat and grabbed the electric spur from the shelf, hanging it in her belt. It was a wand of arm's length, with a tip that gave enough of a jolt for a clockwork horse to take notice. "I suppose I'd better start planning my departure."

"Yes," Clara said, hardly realising she had just parroted back Jo's words. "You had better." Her heart sped up, and her breath came shallowly. Suddenly, the screeches of gears and grunts of the horses and angry voices of owners and mechanics faded into nothingness, and the entire world was only the thin gate that stood between Clara and Jo. Even Desert Steel faded until all she saw was a strong jaw, short hair, and eyes as deep as the blackness between stars. She bit her lip, trying to bring herself out of it, but the urgency of the race was gone.

Jo opened the gate and stepped out in one fluid movement. One arm curled around Clara's waist. The other combed fingers through her hair and brought her face down to meet Jo's lips. Clara forgot that she was a proper lady standing in a public place. Fire raced through her. She relaxed in Jo's arms, strong arms that held her in a way she had never been held before.

Jo pulled away. She let go and stepped back. "I'm sorry. I just—I shouldn't have. Not here. It isn't proper—"

Clara kissed her. She surprised even herself when her arms reached out and brought Jo back to her. She never kissed much before, only a peck on the cheek after an evening out walking with a gentleman. This was different. She wanted to stand there forever, feeling Jo's warmth against herself.

They slowly parted. Clara blushed as some men in the stable whistled and others gave snorts of disgust. She stared at her skirts for a long time before she realised she was breathing heavily. She glanced up. Jo's face was wearing that inscrutable look again.

"I'd better get Desert Steel out there," she said softly. "I don't want to miss the start of the race."

Clara looked at her for a long moment. "Yes," she finally said. "Good luck."

Jo cracked a smile. "I won't need it."

It took an enormous amount of willpower for Clara to turn around and leave the stall. She walked quickly through the stable and outside. It was a rundown place, with a pitted metal track, seats that might fall apart if you sat on them, and an announcer who looked as if he would pick your pocket if you turned your back. Clara made her way through the scant crowd to the owners' box. It really was only a box, with a metal guard rail around a dozen perfectly ordinary seats in the middle of the rest of the stands. She sat down.

Her father would be happy to see his horse running in a race, even if it was something as bawdy as a stakes race. He had always loved to watch Desert Steel run. Clara wondered what he would think if he knew what had transpired back in the stable, or that she was wishing right now for Desert Steel to lose. Without the winner's purse, he would get sold for scrap, but it meant that there would be no money for a ticket to the west.

She fiddled with the edge of her gloves as the horses lined up, the announcer droned out their names, and the gears in the starting gates began to turn. Desert Steel glinted copper amid the dark metal of his eleven competitors, but her eyes were focused on the grey-clad figure in his saddle.

Was it her imagination, or did Jo smile at her just before the pistol went off?

Desert Steel was a streak of copper fire pounding against the metal track. The iron horses were larger, and their jockeys threw out dirty tricks to clear the field, but Jo was well versed in these kinds of races. Clara held her breath as Steel wove in and out of the other horses, dodging kicks and sideswipes. He rounded the final turn ahead by a nose, and when the second pistol went off, it was Jo who reined the lead horse to a stop.

There were no fireworks, no winner's parade. A shady-looking man in a trench coat handed Clara an envelope, startling the life out of her.

"Good race," he muttered and left, yelling to a boy to round up all the losing horses to be sold. As if they heard his words, the clockwork horses still on the field bucked and pulled against their harnesses. Their jockeys stung them over and over with their electric prods until they settled down.

Clara sat there, clutching the envelope of money in her hands. One or two men eyed it, but the hard look on her face must have dissuaded them from trying something. She waited until the stands cleared, until the lone maintenance worker went out to the track. A cranking sound filled the air, and the gaslights around the track went out, leaving her in the near darkness of dusk.

"Desert Steel is being taken back to your stable," a voice said behind her. Clara jumped up and turned to see Jo standing there, grease smudged across her face and shirt. Her number was still pinned to her back. "He's a cocky fellow. He knows he's won, and now that he has a taste for it, I bet you'll get a few more winners' purses out of him." She glanced down at the envelope Clara still clutched.

"Oh, yes." She dug into the thick pile of bills and pulled out roughly half. Clara held it out without looking at her. "Here. You earned this many times over."

Jo took it, flipping through the stack. "This is enough for a train ticket to California and a month's room and board."

Clara voice sounded only slightly choked as she agreed. "You'll be able to fulfill your dream of going west, and I have enough funds to keep Desert Steel for a while longer. If you're right about him being a winner, there will a lot more races in my future, and adventure in yours." She glanced up briefly. "Good fortune go with you, Jo."

"And with you, Clara Samuels." Jo turned to leave, tucking the money into her waistband.

Clara watched her walk through the maze of seats. She reminded herself that this was probably for the best. She was a respectable lady after all, and respectable ladies did not associate with women like Jo. They did not run off and leave their families. They did not spend their lives unmarried. They went home and attended formal dinners, paid attention to their studies, and eventually wed a gentleman and raised his children.

As the words sped through her mind in her brother's voice, Clara realised how truly awful such a life sounded. Before she could think better of it, she gathered up her skirts and ran through the seats after Jo.

She turned around just as Clara began to speak. "You shouldn't go alone to California."

Jo's face was unreadable. "Why not? I can take care of myself. I've been doing it for a long time."

"Yes, but what will you do there? How will you earn any income?" Before Jo could respond, Clara took both of her hands in her own. "You could have a clockwork horse to race. You said that Desert Steel was a winner. Prove it. Race him in the west."

"There aren't any real races out there," Jo said slowly.

"There will be something. He wants to run, even if it is in another bawdy affair like this one."

"And what about his owner?"

Clara kissed her, quickly, but with a passion that surprised even herself. She broke away, saying "His owner will be there, cheering the pair of you on, if you wish." She waited, part of her terrified that Jo would say no, and the other half terrified that she would say yes.

"I'd like that." Jo squeezed her hands. "If you pack lightly, we could be on a train tomorrow morning."

Travelling on a Sunday wasn't proper, but standing there, holding the woman she loved, Clara wasn't the least bit concerned with what was and wasn't proper. "I'd like that," she repeated.

THE WILD COLONIAL CLOCKWORK BOY

NICOLE MURPHY

There was no doubt about it—his arm was beyond his ability to repair.

Cursing, Jack Doolan released the broken limb. It fell down and crashed into the log he sat on, sending a rain of splinters into the air. *Probably dented now*, he thought and scowled at the glistening metal. He used his natural hand to lift the mechanical marvel high then let it slam back into the wood again because the violence suited his mood.

He'd done everything he was supposed to do to protect his clockwork arm and yet here he was, hours from the nearest town, days from a reputable mechanic, and it was seized and useless.

The nearest mechanics were in Goulburn and Queanbeyan, but they could only service the most basic of machinery. The first mechanic of any real note was all the way in Parramatta, but Jack couldn't trust them to do the job right.

No, to get his arm fixed, he'd need to go all the way into Sydney Town. All the way to her.

He'd have to go see his wife.

He lifted the metal hand and let it fall again, and watched the splinters fly with satisfaction. If his hand worked he'd have punched the wood, to get out the frustration of having to see Kate again.

Sitting here hitting a log wasn't going to solve the problem. The sooner he got to Sydney, the sooner he could leave again.

The sooner he'd be unable to resist her, and unable to refrain from breaking her heart again.

Clumsily, one-handed, Jack packed up camp, got on his horse and started the long journey east.

Kate gave the key a twist and stepped back. The mechanical cockatoo shuddered, and then the wings started to flap. It lifted slowly into the air and flew a circle around her workshop.

Perfect, she thought. An absolutely shame that Lady Griswold couldn't keep better care of her plaything, for such a beautiful piece of engineering deserved the best. But Kate carefully cleared the white powder that had stopped up the mechanism, restoring it to its former glory and when the time came and the bird was again returned to her for maintenance—and she was sure it would be— she would do it again.

The cockatoo—brilliantly painted metal in white and pink— landed in front of her. Kate picked it up, gently placed it in its gilt cage and put the cover on. It wasn't smart to call attention to the wonder she held.

She carried it out to her front room and it seemed her timing was perfect. A shadow passed over the building, blocking the sunlight that streamed in her front windows. A thud on her roof suggested the anchor had found purchase and then through the glass panes in her door she saw a rope ladder fall from the sky.

Kate put the covered cage on her counter top and opened the door. A horse and cart had stopped in the middle of the road and the horse was still being brought under control. The cart driver glared balefully above him but there was nothing he could do. The craft of the sky were the conveyances of the rich and thus would always be more important than mere land-based vehicles.

She looked up and smiled at the sight of the very dapper Mr Smythe, Lady Griswold's man, clambering down the swaying ladder. Above him was the bulk of the Griswold dirigible.

Mr Smythe set his feet on the road and stood still for a moment. Kate imagined him saying a prayer of gratitude. Then he turned and walked toward her, ignoring the glare of the cart driver.

"Mrs Doolan," he said in his crisp British accent. "Good day to you. I take it the work has been completed?"

"It has, Mr Smythe." She took him into the store, closing the door behind them and locking it. A lot of money was about to exchange hands.

She pulled back the covering so Mr Smythe could see the cockatoo.

"It looks good as new."

"It is." Kate hesitated and decided something had to be said. "I hope that Lady Griswold will make a greater effort to keep the internal workings clean. It will help the cockatoo to work for longer."

"I will pass that message on," Mr Smythe said. He reached into his vest and pulled out a packet which he handed over.

Kate hefted the packet in her hand. It felt the right amount and she'd prefer not to count in front of her customers. Besides, Lady Griswold's husband was the head judge in New South Wales and she'd be a fool to be anything but scrupulous.

In this at least.

"Thank you, Mr Smythe," Kate said. "I look forward to doing business with you in the future."

She locked the door behind him and stood in her storefront, waiting for the rope ladder to be pulled up, the thud of the anchor disconnecting from her roof and the shadow of the dirigible moving away.

When it was gone she went into the hallway, closing and locking the store door behind her. Then she pulled the lever, setting the traps she had laid out in both the storefront and her workroom. If anyone tried to break in, they'd be thwarted.

She unlocked another door and pulled the string to turn on the pale electric light bulb. She went carefully down the stairs and groped in the dark for the second string to turn on the next light.

It cast a sullen brilliance over her basement as she knelt by the large chest against the wall and withdrew the key from the ribbon around her neck. She unlocked the first lock, and then proceeded to activate the pulleys and slides that had to be moved in a certain way to allow the lid to open.

Finally, the last click sounded and she hefted the heavy wooden top. Next, she removed the piles of clothing that looked for all the world like the precious cargo she was protecting.

Including her wedding dress. Every time she handled it, Kate remembered the dreams of that day, the bliss that followed, and then the eventual disillusionment.

When she got to the base of the box, another series of levers and slides were enacted to remove it. In the real bottom sat piles of notes and coins.

Her retirement money. Kate needed to save to ensure her comfort in her declining years. Her good-for-nothing husband certainly wasn't going to help with that.

Kate counted out the money Mr Smythe had given her. She wasn't surprised to see that in fact it was more than she'd asked for—Lady Griswold was buying her secrecy.

Kate kept some of the money aside—she needed to live now—then she put the rest in with her collection. It was looking a healthy amount. Perhaps it wouldn't be too much longer before she could afford to travel to America. Study under some of the great craftsmen. Become a true master of her art and ensure she would never want again.

Best of all, she doubted Jack Doolan would ever come to her there.

She put everything back in the box, reset it and relocked it. As she stood, she heard footsteps above her head. She froze. Someone was in her storefront.

She listened to the pattern of the steps and realised that whoever was up there was skilfully avoiding her traps.

Only one person could do that.

She tossed the key to the trunk over into a dark corner of the basement and then stood in the middle of the room. Moments later, a man's silhouette appeared at the top of the stairs.

Kate's heart thudded so loudly she was sure it could be heard. Seeing him did what it always did—cast her back to the first time she'd set eyes on Jack Doolan.

The moment she'd fallen in love.

He walked down the stairs and she watched him reappear in her life—first his dust-covered boots, then his worn trousers. She noted his mechanical hand hung loosely by his side and quickly ascertained that this was the reason for his visit.

She lifted her chin. Good. She could treat this as a business transaction and nothing more.

She was sick of the pattern of their marriage. He'd come back, and they'd see each other again, fall in love again, have a wonderful reunion and Kate would convince herself that this time, they'd work it out. But then the call of the bush would become too strong, Jack would disappear and Kate would once again be heartbroken.

No more.

His torso appeared, and then his shoulders. Finally, his face, and Kate silently cursed.

He was still the most beautiful man she'd ever seen. Dark eyes. Straight nose. Full lips. Strong jaw and brow. Curling black hair. The face of an angel, that unfortunately was bound to the form of a devil.

Jack stopped at the base of the stairs. His eyes travelled slowly down her body and Kate was glad she was in her work clothes—a serviceable blue dress, covered in a voluminous white apron, with oil and grease stains all over it.

Yet when his gaze met hers, that familiar heat was there and Kate had to fight against her own body's reaction.

Curse him to hell.

"Jack."

"Hello, Katie." He smiled and Kate clasped her hands together to stop herself reaching for him. "I've missed you."

I bet you haven't, Kate thought. *Not until you needed me.* "What have you done to your arm?"

He winced. "I took care of it. Did everything you said to. But the darned thing has seized and I can't fix it."

"Come upstairs." Kate walked past him, but noted his intelligent gaze scanning the room. He'd see the trunk. He'd undoubtedly come up with a reasonably accurate assumption of what was in there.

She could only hope her bushranger husband wasn't able to open it and steal everything she had.

Well, he wasn't any more. At least, she chose to believe he hadn't returned to his former life. He had been a bushranger, in Victoria. He'd not been very good at it and had been arrested, tried and imprisoned before his twentieth birthday. When he was released he'd come to Sydney in the hopes of leaving behind his reputation.

The wild colonial boy.

She didn't know how he supported himself in the bush, and she didn't want to know.

At the top of the stairs, she disconnected the traps and went into the workshop. Jack followed. She cleared a space on the counter and pointed to it.

"Put your arm there." Then she busied herself getting her lights ready. She used a mix of candles and electric lights with mirrors to focus a powerful beam on the bench. It made it easier to see into the intricate workings of a device such as Jack's arm.

By the time she was done, there was a thump on the bench. She turned and saw it there.

It was beautiful. The most amazing thing she'd ever built. A system of pulleys, levers and pistons that could be directed by twitches of muscles on Jack's back, shoulders and pectorals.

It was so delicately primed that with patience and training, Jack could manipulate it as precisely as he did his real arm. It had been a frustrating couple of weeks for him to learn to use it, but once he had it had been delightful.

She knew full well that the touch of that metal hand on her skin was just as satisfactory as his flesh one. Different, but definitely as satisfactory.

That incredible night of passion however had turned out to be the sign Jack was looking for that he was as much a man as he had been before his arm had been blown off. When she'd woken the next morning, he'd been gone.

Kate shook the memories away and started to inspect the arm. She put on her monocular microscope and with the help of the bright light, could see deep into the delicate workings.

She could tell that Jack had told the truth—he had been taking good care of the arm. The top layers were beautifully free of dirt. But deeper it was another story and there was no way he'd be able to keep this clear. Dirt had clogged several of the wheels, and eventually jammed up the whole system.

"I'll need to take it apart and clean it," she said. "It looks as though some of the bearings may need to be reworked as well. I'll need it three days."

"Can it be done in two?"

"Not if you want it done properly." She turned the arm over to confirm her diagnosis. "It will cost you twenty pounds."

"Oh, come on, Katie." She heard the pout in his voice. "Surely we can come up with a better arrangement than that."

Time to make it clear, Kate thought, and she turned around. Only then did it occur to her that in order to remove his arm for her inspection, Jack would have to disrobe.

His musculature was perfection—doctors would study it if they could. His skin was tanned all over and Kate could guess at the hours he spent bare chested, washing or simply lying back and enjoying the bush.

Kate swallowed, her mouth suddenly dry. She wasn't going to go there again. No matter how he drew her.

"You will pay cash," Kate said. "You will leave here and you will return in three days with the money. I will have the arm ready for you. You will leave, and that will be that."

Jack frowned. Had he thought he would just walk in here and she'd welcome him with open arms?

Probably. She had every other time.

Stay firm, girl, she told herself. "If you want your arm back, you will leave and come back in three days with twenty pounds. I imagine that life in the bush would be pretty difficult for a one-armed man."

Jack shook his head. "You've become cruel, Katie."

"You made me that way, Jack Doolan."

He nodded. "Perhaps I did. Very well. Three days. Twenty pounds. Try not to dream of me, Katie." He winked and he was gone.

Kate leant against the bench. Damn him, he'd just guaranteed that she would, indeed, dream of him.

Jack stood on the street outside Kate's shop and wondered how that had gone so wrong.

He dreaded coming to see Kate because he knew he'd hurt her. Knew he'd be powerless to resist her, and yet equally powerless against the call of the bush.

City life wasn't for him. Bush life wasn't for her. And yet when they came together, the fire between them was undeniable.

Or it had been. What had changed?

Dear God—had Katie found a new man? A better man, who would stay in the city and take care of her like she deserved?

He headed down to the pub on the corner, to hear the latest gossip.

He sat at the bar and slapped a note on the wood. "Keep 'em coming until the money runs out."

The barman turned and sneered. "So, you're back, are you? Going to ruin Kate's life again?"

Bingo, Jack thought. Here's the reason Kate threw him out.

"Maybe I'm here to stay this time," Jack said. "After all, she is my wife."

"Yeah, right." The barman poured him a whisky. "You should just disappear and let Kate get on with her life."

"With you?"

The barman blushed. "If I'm lucky."

Ah, so not the actual man, but a someone who wanted to be. "Well, I'm not planning on going anywhere soon, so get the message out."

The barman muttered and disappeared and Jack sipped his whisky with a smile. Hopefully that would nip all the potential suitors in the bud.

He had a few more whiskies, and watched the sky outside darken. Finally, it was night and he knew Kate would be going to bed soon. She liked to be up with the birds and down with the sun. It was one of the things they had in common.

He wondered if she'd returned to sleeping in that horrid nightgown, or if she'd kept with the routine he'd taught her of sleeping naked.

"Nothing more soothing than the touch of skin on skin, Katie," he'd told her.

She hadn't believed him and truth be told, he'd given her reason not to believe him—every time he saw her body, he was hungry for her. But over time, they'd both come to enjoy quiet nights of comfort with each other.

Before the thought had fully formed, Jack was stumbling out of the pub and down to Katie's place. He sat down on her stoop—he was too drunk to avoid the traps at the moment. It took a few hours for him to sober up—he even had a snooze, leaning against her doorpost—but finally he felt he could do it.

The lock on the door was easy to pick, and once inside he danced his way across the floor. Silly woman hadn't changed the traps since he'd helped her set them. Jack thought that might mean that at some deep level, she wanted him to come to her, and only him.

Through the workshop. A different dance, but the same result. Then he was in the kitchen beyond. It was warm, embers glowing red in the fireplace. He took up the poker and stirred them around to ensure they'd stay hot, took off his shoes and left them by the fire to warm and then went over to the bedroom door.

He pushed it open slowly. Moonlight cascaded in the window and across Katie's sleeping form. Her blonde hair was roped together, the thick length lying across her pillow. He much preferred it out, and would ensure it was before this night was through.

The sheets were pulled up to her chest but not higher and so he could clearly see she had the hated nightgown on. Damn her. Still, that would be quickly rectified.

He undressed and climbed into the bed. Katie's body was warm, drawing him closer. He stopped, just shy of touching her, holding himself up and cursing that he didn't have his mechanical hand so he couldn't touch her. He watched her for a moment—the soft rise and fall of her chest, the tiny flare of her nostrils, the movement of her eyelashes as some dream played out behind them.

Then he leant forward and kissed her.

For a moment, her lips were unmoving, and then they shifted and he silently shouted with glee as she kissed him back. Knowing him even in her sleep.

Then she was gone, flying out of the bed. Jack overbalanced and fell on his face. By the time he recovered and was sitting up, Kate was standing on the other side of the room and he was staring at the end of a flintlock.

"I thought I made myself very clear," Kate said in a soft voice.

Jack put his hand up in a plea. "I love you, Katie."

"Not as much as you love the bush, and that is no longer enough for me. When you come to pick up your arm, I will give you the details of someone else who can fix it in future. You will leave and never see me again."

The flat certainty in her voice scared him. "Katie-"

"My name is Kate. Or Katherine. Not Katie. Now, leave my house and don't return until your arm is fixed."

Jack looked into his wife's eyes and realised it really was over. Finally, Katie had had enough of him.

"Very well." He got up, grabbed his clothes and went out into the kitchen, closing the bedroom door behind him. He dressed, put on his shoes and danced his way out of the shop.

Out on the street, he stopped and allowed himself the luxury of one tear, travelling slowly down his cheek.

He wiped it away. He was the wild colonial boy. There'd been a song written about him. If they knew of his exploits since, there would be many more.

He'd be fine. He'd get on with his life. He didn't need his wife.

Straightening his shoulders, he set off to find somewhere to drink until the pain was gone.

The next day, Jack Doolan decided to get to work. He was stuck in Sydney for three days—he should research what his next move out bush would be.

His first stop was a barber, where he was shaved and his hair cut. Next, a tailor, where he was able to get a cheap but reasonably well fitting suit. After that, a bootmaker for a pair of shiny new shoes.

Convinced he now looked the part of a respectable, albeit not wealthy man, he made his way to the bar of the Regent, one of the more exclusive hotels in Sydney.

The barman there was an old contact who had often proved useful. Jack handed over many pounds more than a glass of whisky would cost, took a sip of the amber fluid and smiled at the barman.

"Anyone interesting visiting?"

The barman nodded to a large woman in a turban sitting by the fire. "Mrs Williams over there is planning a trip to see her sister in Melbourne. She does not believe in steam, so will not be taking the train or a dirigible."

"I do admire a woman of principle," Jack murmured.

"And the Florences have just bought a station out past Dubbo and will be travelling there to set up a grand country home like in the old country. They'll be going by air but they've been very open about the location of their new home."

"How very traditional of them."

Jack took his whisky and went to sit behind Mrs Williams. The lady was discussing the details of her trip in great length to the woman she was with.

"My carriage is the most comfortable conveyance you can find," she was saying. "It is drawn by six black stallions, the finest horseflesh you can find. This journey will be a delight."

"Aren't you worried about bushrangers?" said her companion.

"I carry a gun," the stout lady said. "I am not afraid."

Probably never shot it, Jack thought. In a panicked state any shot would go wide, assuming she maintained enough control to draw it and didn't faint instead.

"And I will have four men travelling with me, each of them good shots."

That was more concerning news. It seemed that Mrs Williams might not be such a good target after all.

The thing Jack had learnt from his first iteration as a bushranger was to be smart about his targets and not get caught. The fact he hadn't been, and there was no warrant for his arrest, assured him he'd mastered the lesson.

He picked up his whisky glass to move over and sit near the Florences when a movement at the door caught his eye. He turned and his body stilled. Three policemen stood at the door, looking around the room.

Keep it casual, Doolan, he told himself. He always wore a kerchief over his face when he robbed—no one in town would know who he was. They were here for something else, not him.

Then one of the policemen focussed on him, pointed and then all three of them were looking right at him.

It was him they were after. He'd love to know how they knew him, but that was a mystery to ponder later. He looked around. The only exit was from behind the bar. Jack rushed over.

"Let me out this way, that's a good chap." Jack nodded at the door.

The barman shook his head. "Sorry, but the reward for you was worth more than what you pay."

Jack's heart sank. So it was his supposed ally who had dobbed him in.

The police officers started toward him. Jack thought about running but realised it was a foolish plan. They were going to catch him—there was no doubt about that. His only chance now was to bluff it out. Surely they couldn't prove anything?

"Good afternoon, gentlemen." He smiled at the police officers as they stopped in front of him. "Are you looking for me?"

"Jack Doolan, you are under arrest. Charged with bushranging."

"You're mistaken," Jack said. "But I'll come along, because I know you good gentlemen are just doing your job. All will be right in the end."

With a wink to his betrayer, Jack was escorted out of the hotel.

Kate was gently brushing dirt from one of the steel rods of Jack's arm when the pounding at the store door broke her concentration.

She put the piece down and arched her back, stretching it out. The arm had taken longer to pull apart and clean than she'd anticipated. She should charge Jack more, but she didn't want to get into another argument.

She went into the store and stopped two steps in, staring at the black-clad figures she could see through the glass. Why were the police here?

Shivering, she slowly walked forward and opened the door. "Good evening, officers. Please, come in." She stepped aside and welcomed them.

They came in and waited for her to close the door before speaking. "Katherine Doolan?"

"That is correct."

"Your husband is James Edward Doolan, better known as Jack Doolan?"

It didn't matter that she'd thrown him out, that she planned to move on with her life without him. Hearing Jack's name on the lips of the police had an icy hand crushing her heart. "Yes, he is. What is this about?"

"He's been arrested for bushranging. We need to search your home for ill-gotten gains."

Oh Jack, she thought. You stupid, foolish boy. "My husband and I are estranged and rarely see each other. I have nothing here of his."

"Nevertheless, you will allow us to search, Mrs Doolan, to prove your innocence."

She had no choice. Kate wrapped her arms around her waist and followed the two policemen around her home. They opened every drawer in the store, pulled every clockwork delicacy off its shelf and poked around behind it. They handled each item with a distinct lack of care and Kate cringed at the damage they might be doing.

Into her workroom. This took much longer to search. The police officers looked at the pile of parts on her bench.

"What is this?"

"An item I'm repairing for a client. A monkey. It plays the drum when you wind it." The words tumbled from her mouth. As the search continued, Kate wondered why, after everything, she was attempting to protect Jack. After all the pain he'd caused. After the wrong she didn't doubt he had done.

Because you love him, her conscience told her. *Jack was the only one apart from Papa to encourage your love of the mechanical. Jack was the one who believed. Jack was the one who supported you when you went into business.*

Jack is the only man to have found you so irresistible that he couldn't keep his hands from you. You. Not the money you now earn, the prestige and reputation you have built. You.

You love Jack Doolan and you always will, even though you cannot have him in your life.

It was only after the workshop had been turned upside down, her bedroom ransacked and even her flour upended and searched and the police officers stood at the door to her basement that Kate realised the real threat.

"What's down here?"

"Just storage," Kate said. "Nothing of import."

"We'll judge that."

They went downstairs and Kate followed, trembling. If they found the false bottom of her chest, not only would it destroy her plans but it would also be seen as proof of Jack's wickedness.

They went straight to the trunk and demanded it opened. Kate knelt down, unlocked it and then went through the process of opening it.

"That's a difficult chest to open," the police observed.

"It holds my most precious belongings." Kate finally lifted the lid. The police loomed over her shoulder. They reached down and started to pull things out of it, shaking the material then tossing it away.

Tears bloomed in Kate's eyes as her wedding dress was thrown onto the floor. If only Jack had stayed in the city with her, not returned to his bushranging ways.

The police looked into the now empty chest and Kate held her breath, waiting for them to realise the bottom was false.

Then they turned away and proceeded to search the rest of the basement. Kate slowly re-packed the trunk, this time putting the wedding dress on the top. She held it to her cheek and remembered the vows she'd made, to always love and honour Jack.

The police stomped back up the stairs and Kate followed them. In the store, they turned to face her again. "Do you know where your husband stashed the goods he stole from decent, respectable people?"

"No," Kate said. "My husband lives in the bush now. He rarely comes to Sydney and when he does, he never brings much money with him. Wherever he is keeping the outcome of his business, it's out there somewhere."

"Thank you, Mrs Doolan." They turned to leave.

"What happens to him now?"

One of the officers looked over his shoulder. "On Friday, he'll be facing Judge Griswold. On Saturday, he'll hang. Good day, Mrs Doolan."

Kate kept upright until she'd locked the door behind them and gone back into her workroom. Then she sank onto a chair.

Jack, arrested. Jack, dead.

The thought struck deep and her heart shattered, more viciously than it ever had done.

Lord knows she couldn't live with him any more, but she could bear the idea of his death even less.

Think, Kate, she told herself. *There has to be something you can do.*

One phrase leapt into her memory—*to be tried by Judge Griswold.*

A slow smile grew. The good judge would probably be devastated to know what his wife was doing with her spare time.

It hadn't been just any dirt that had ruined the internal workings of Lady Griswold's clockwork cockatoo. The insides had been coated with opium.

The bird had been a gift from the judge to his lady. He'd even escorted her to Kate's store to order and pay for the bird. He'd smiled so fondly at his pretty young wife, completely blind to her plans for her new toy.

It really did make a very good conveyance for the distribution of the drug.

So Kate could probably get the charges dropped, but what to do with him then? She sighed as she realised that it was going to take a great deal of her savings to get him out of New South Wales and safe.

She smiled again as sudden inspiration struck—she could get them *both* out of New South Wales.

She started to make plans.

On Saturday morning, Kate was admitted entrance to the Griswold mansion. Clasped in her hand was a copy of the morning's paper, the front page loudly declaring gleefully that Jack Doolan had been found guilty and was to hang this within hours.

Kate hated that she'd had to wait this long, but it had been important that the plan go smoothly. Reading the report this morning of how cockily Jack had faced his accusers, how even when found guilty he'd smiled and winked at Griswold, she'd found it hard to stomach her breakfast.

This had to work. She had to save him.

The door opened and she turned to face the Judge, but instead Lady Griswold came in. Shockingly, she was in just a nightgown and wrapper, her hair curled around her head.

"You can't tell him," the young woman hissed. "I'll destroy you."

"If my husband hangs, I will be destroyed," Kate said. "I have nothing to lose. Do you?"

The door opened again and the judge came in. He was a tall, big-boned, straight-backed man who perpetually looked down his nose at everyone. Except his wife, Kate had noted, and she saw it again now.

He frowned at Lady Griswold, but the hand he put on her shoulder was gentle. "Why are you here, my dove?"

"I wanted to see the wife of the notorious bushranger," Lady Griswold said. "I cannot believe we patronised her shop. We should endeavour never to do so again."

"If you must," Kate said. "I wish you joy in finding someone else to clean your bird."

Lady Griswold cast Kate a deathly scowl. The judge frowned. "Why did your bird need cleaning? You've only had it a few months?"

Kate lifted her chin and dared Lady Griswold to tell the truth.

"It must have been badly made."

"I have something for you, Lady Griswold." Kate reached into her reticule and pulled out a handkerchief, tied up with string. "I was unable to return this part to the bird as it was so dirty, and had to manufacture a new one. Perhaps your husband would like to see it and judge for himself?"

Lady Griswold went pale and Kate could see her waver on her feet before she leant against her husband.

"Lord Griswold," Kate said. "What would you do to protect your wife from the horrors of the world?"

The judge put his arm around Lady Griswold and frowned at Kate. "What sort of question is that?"

"I would do anything to save my husband," Kate said. She held the handkerchief up. "Even destroy your wife, if it came to that. Unless you release my husband into my care, I will be going to the newspapers to tell them Lady Griswold's secret."

The judge looked at Kate, then at his wife. He led Lady Griswold over to a chair and placed her gently upon it, kissing her forehead. Kate almost smiled—he truly did love her. This wasn't just a marriage of convenience.

Lady Griswold reached for him, but he pulled away. He approached Kate and snatched the handkerchief from her hand. He went to his desk, pulled out a knife and cut the string then unfolded the material. He stared at the white powder-coated cog for a long, long moment, then looked at his wife.

"Is this what I think it is?"

Lady Griswold stiffened and Kate did too, wondering what she would do.

"Let Jack Doolan go free," she said.

The judge shuddered and looked at Kate. "He robs people. Scares them. Destroys men's reputations. How can I let that evil loose on the people of New South Wales again?"

"You won't," Kate said. "I'm taking him to America. If he decides to return to his heinous ways, it will be their people at risk, not yours."

Lord Griswold wrapped up the cog again. "Jack Doolan doesn't deserve you as his wife, Mrs Doolan."

A ghost of a smile pulled at her lips. "On that we both agree, Lord Griswold. Yet when you love . . . "

He looked at his wife and nodded. He understood.

Kate stood in the gondola of the dirigible and watched Jack walk across the green grass of Hyde Park. Out in the fresh air, with the city around him, when by now his lifeless body should be hanging from the gallows.

While his step was jaunty, she noted him looking around him. Jack couldn't quite believe where he was, and anticipated it all being taken from him at the last moment.

He moved from her sight and she turned her attention to the door. Moments later he stepped into the gondola. His eyes riveted to hers and they stood in tableau, then he smiled.

There was a noise outside, and the weight of the dirigible suddenly shifted. The ropes were being disengaged, the craft preparing to take off. Jack went over to the window to watch them rise.

Not a word had he spoken and it irked Kate. "A thank you would be nice."

He spun. "You must allow me a moment or two to compose myself. Half an hour ago, I was facing the possibility of death."

"And now?"

Jack shook his head. "I don't understand. Three nights ago, you wanted to shoot me for climbing into your bed. Now, you're saving me?"

"I still want to shoot you for climbing into my bed unasked. In the future, you will only do so if I invite you. Understand?"

The smile exploded across his face and a thrill ran through her body. "Will I be invited?"

"It will take many days to travel to America. I'm sure you'll wear me down."

"America?"

"Judge Griswold wanted you out of New South Wales. I want to go to America, to study. There seemed no reason not to combine the two ideas."

Jack slumped onto a lounge. "What will I do in America?"

"A resourceful man like you will no doubt think of something. But note this—you don't get to leave me again. If you do, don't come back."

"Katie." He rushed forward and swept her into his arms. "Thank you, darling girl, thank you." He pulled her close and kissed her and this time, Kate kissed him back and decided she wasn't going to be pulling a gun on him for some time.

Kate sat and looked at the moonlight sparkling on the dark ocean below. Behind her, Jack snored gently. She wrapped her shawl tighter around her shoulders and acknowledged with a smile the blissful ache that filled her body.

In taking this journey, she'd acknowledged that she wouldn't be able to resist Jack. Once again, he would take her to bed and fill her heart and mind with carnal delight.

But she wasn't foolish enough to believe that what had happened would change the wild colonial boy. He might stay with her for a while when they reached California, but eventually the bush—or in this case, the west—would call for him.

So she'd let him have her body, but no more her heart. When he was gone, she'd have her career to fulfil her and the memories of this journey loving the wild colonial boy.

ESCAPEMENT

STEPHANIE GUNN

In the darkness, three things are constant:

The ticking of my clockwork Heart.

The twenty-two scars that encircle my right forearm.

The one hundred and four small, straight scars on my legs.

Each one of these scars, circle and line alike, was made by a Mother, her crescent knife cold as she made the practiced cut, her fingers colder as she rubbed ash into the new wound to ensure a keloid scar.

The scars on my arm mark the number of sun cycles I have survived. The scars on my legs, the moon cycles I have failed.

I sit here in the darkness, run my fingers over my arms, my legs, counting the scars that mark off my life. Listen to the ticking of my Heart.

I wait.

I was born with smooth planes of bone where my eyes should have been. I should have died, the way so many other babes born in the outer City die at birth. I did not. Even at a day old, the Mothers said, I appeared to see, my not-eyes following them as they moved around the room. Later, when I learned to walk, I never stumbled, even when they deliberately placed obstacles in my path.

I "see" the world as shadows. People are what I think of as light and colour. Each one is a unique shape, and in all, there are shadows within the light. In my sister, Eight, there is a shadow where her right leg should be, more shadows clustered within the cage of her ribs. In the seeing world, these shadows are a twisted leg and stunted lungs that make her wheeze when she walks.

If I could see myself, I know there would be shadows where my eyes should be. Perhaps there are more hidden inside where I cannot see, missing pieces that I do yet know.

We are all made of missing pieces, outside the Wall. None of us is whole.

All Sisters have a flat metal plate set flush against the skin between our breasts, anchored to the bone with screws. They are fixed there when we first bleed, our clockwork Hearts slotted onto the plate. From then on, the Heart will tick away every moment of our moon cycles.

Each morning, the Mothers make the rounds of the Dormitories, wind our Hearts with the heavy key they wear chained around their waist. There are ticking things beneath the Mothers' robes; I do not know their name or function.

The Mothers remind us, as they wind our Hearts, that if the clockwork winds down, our flesh hearts will fail.

The ticking of my Heart is so loud sometimes in the darkness of the Dormitory that often I forget that those gears and cogs don't actually drive the flow of blood around my body. That I have another heart at all.

I wore thirteen scars on my arm the first time the Fathers visited me.

Eight and I had begun our moon cycles at the same time, and we linked hands as we joined the Sisters moving towards the Moon House. She leaned heavily on me to compensate for her twisted leg, and by the time we entered the long hall, her breath came hard. We chose adjacent beds, lay down.

The only sounds I could hear were the ticking of our Hearts and the shuffling of the Mothers' soft-soled boots as they moved down the rows of beds, checking Hearts, checking flesh.

Some Sisters were proclaimed ripe, and given a key from the pouch at the Mother's waist. More were bade to leave the Moon House; some wept as they scuttled out, while others were silent.

I turned my head as a Mother reached Eight's bed. I looked towards the City. The Angel and the Towers were denser shadows in my internal darkness. It was a comfort to me, even then, the fact that I could always "see" the Angel and the Towers, no matter how great the distance or how many physical walls stood between us.

The ticking from beneath the Mother's robe grew louder as she finished with Eight, and moved to my bed. The sound grew louder again when she folded the skirt of my dress up to my waist. It was cold in the Moon House, and goose pimples rose in waves on my skin. The Mother's hands were like ice as she parted my thighs, slid her fingers inside me.

She kept her hand there a moment, the ticking beneath her robe growing louder still. I kept my not-eyes on the Angel and the Towers. And, as I lay there, the Mother's fingers pressing hard into me, I saw a light flaring high on one of the Towers, a light brighter than anything else I had ever seen in the darkness. I started, half sitting up. The Mother pushed me back down, muttering sounds that she probably thought were placating. She removed her fingers, folded my skirt back down.

I kept my eyes on that light, trying to assign a name to it, a colour. It flared brighter, and I felt something warm gathering deep inside of me.

The Mother pressed a key into my hand, and the light vanished; only the deep dark of the Tower there again.

I curled my fingers around the key. It was larger and heavier than the ones the Mothers used to wind our Hearts, the metal warming quickly against my skin.

Eight reached out to me, drawing my attention away from the Tower. She also had a key in her hand.

The Fathers came to us.

The one who was assigned to my bed was what I thought of as blue, shadows crowding deep in his belly. He was gentle enough, and there was little pain, a thing I was grateful for. Eight was not so lucky; her Father was rougher, and she made small, twisted sounds with every thrust.

After, we laid still until the Mothers bade us rise. We unhooked our Hearts from our chest plates, slotted them into the clocks on the wall. As one, we used the keys we had been given to wind the clocks. As one, we lay back down.

We Sisters spent three moon cycles in the Moon House, rising from our beds in the mornings only to use the latrines and wind our clocks. The Mothers brought us nutrient wafers. The bars had a strange, earthen taste that lingered in my mouth long after I had swallowed the last bite.

If, with three moon cycles, we did not bleed, we progressed to the Sun House.

As the clocks ticked, other Sisters bled, and left. Soon, only Eight and I remained.

The night before we were moved to the Sun House, Eight slipped out of her bed and into mine, pressed something flat into my hand.

"It's a photograph," she said. "I know you can't see it, Nine, not the way you see everything else." She took my fingers in hers, traced them on the cool, smooth paper." There is a man here. He's tall, with dark hair and eyes. Next to him is a woman. She's sitting up in bed, and she's dressed in white. Her hair is bright yellow, and she has something on her ears that glitters like water in the sun. She looks exhausted, but she's smiling. I've never seen someone with teeth so white. She's holding a baby in her arms, a beautiful, perfect thing wrapped up in a blue blanket. You can't see if all three are whole, but I think they must be. The baby, at least. Otherwise, why would she be smiling? The man is holding a tiny white thing. I don't know if it's food or a decoration, but on top of it is a flame."

"Flame? What is that?"

I heard her wave a hand through the air, as though searching for a description." When you burn something, like in the recycling centre, you can feel the heat?"

I nodded.

"There's light that goes with that. Bright, gold and red, with blue at the very bottom. Sometimes it burns your eyes, too, so you keep seeing the flame, even after you've looked away." Eight turned the paper over, guided my hands over the rougher side. I could feel lines and swirls impressed there." One of the workers told me what it was called, said that there were names written on the back."

"Names?"

"He said it's what people had, before the numbers." Eight traced her hand over the numbers embedded in the soft skin inside my left forearm. Mine are 120509, hers 120508, our nicknames arising from the last numbers. We are as close as Sisters can be." He also said that there was another word he recognised. 'Family'."

"Family?" I asked." What does that mean?"

"I'm not certain. When I went back to ask him, he was gone. Recycled, I suppose. He was old. Maybe family means happiness."

She let me hold the photograph a while longer before she fell asleep in my arms. She moved in her sleep, dreaming of the baby she would bear. I stared up at the shadow of the ceiling and thought of the strange words. Of *family*, of *flame*.

Of the light I had seen in the Tower. The brightest thing I had ever "seen".

From that moment on, I thought of it as the flame.

Our pains began on the same day, a fact that surprised neither Eight nor I.

The Mother who was tending us in the Sun House scuttled from bed to bed, bringing the scent of Eight's blood to me. We made no sound. This was not true pain; this was duty. This was how we served the City.

My child was born first. A daughter: her wailing loud in the Sun House. In my mind she was what I thought of as green, her colouring bright apart from slim shadows on the sides of her hands. When she curled her fingers around my thumb, I could feel the extra digit there, slender and wiry. I felt something warm spread behind my Heart. My daughter was as close to whole as anyone I had known. She would certainly be Chosen.

As Sisters, we were allowed only one chance to hold any viable children, to feed them with the rich birth milk. I held my daughter close, luxuriating in her warmth as she fed easily. I thought of the *photograph* that Eight had described, thought of that strange word, *family*.

I was so focused on my daughter that it took me long moments to realise that silence had fallen over the Sun House. I turned my head, saw the bundle of shadows that the Mother held. Eight's child was born twisted, dead.

That night, Eight burned the photograph. She never spoke of it again.

This is the world:

In the centre of everything, the Angel.

She stands in the centre of the inner City, watching over us all. Surrounding the Angel are the four Towers, the homes of the Chosen. They are the ones born whole and pure, the ones the outer City serves.

Around the inner City is the Wall. It is tall, broken only by four gates, one at each point of the compass. Outside the Wall, the outer City. Our buildings crowd close to the Wall. Many, I do not know the function of. I do not need to know. A Sister's life revolves around three only: the Dormitory, the Moon and Sun Houses.

Around the outer City, there is no wall. There is no need for one. Beyond us, there is only emptiness.

The Mothers describe the City as a machine, a great conglomeration of gears and cogs that circle around and around, everything centred on the Angel.

She watches over us, and she waits for the day when all of our sons and daughters will be born pure and whole, will be Chosen.

Eight told me once, before the first time we were visited by the Fathers, that the Angel was gold, the tall column she stands on black. In the morning light, Eight had said, the Angel gleams brighter than the sun. It was the only time that I had envied Eight's true sight.

The morning after my daughter's birth, I was roused early by a Mother. The Mother led me to the Wall, where together we waited for the gate to open. The baby mewled, pawed at my aching breasts. I wrapped her tighter, knowing that her hunger would not last long. In the Towers, she would be given food far superior to my thin milk.

The sound of grinding gears and cogs came from inside the Wall, and the gate rolled open. The air that moved over us was warm and scented with metal and oil, smothering the flesh and earth scent of the outer City. The Mother bent to bless the child, a ritual murmur, and then stood back to let me enter the inner City.

The tall shadows of the Towers rose before me as I approached the centre of the inner City. There were other buildings between them, low and long. I had never heard them spoken of. Knowing the Mother was watching me, I dared only a few quick glances at the buildings. No lights to be seen. No flame.

Then, as now, there is only a short span of time in which the gates were allowed to open, a cool sliver in between night and day. I hurried, knowing that I had to be back outside the Wall before the gate closed again. To be caught within was forbidden. The inner City was no place for the likes of me.

It *was* a place for my daughter. I approached the Angel, stepping around so I was on the opposite side to the gate I had entered. My daughter writhed, her arms working free again and reaching for my breasts.

"Reach out to the Angel," I whispered to her." Not to me."

I looked up at the Angel. To my not-eyes she was a shadow, a suggestion of outstretched wings. Something twisted behind my Heart, and I realised that I had been hoping for some miracle, that I would be able to truly see the Angel.

My daughter's wailing increased in volume when I laid her down at the base of the column. I held out my hand, and she grasped at my finger, drew it into her mouth and sucked. In my darkness, her fingers were pale green, but for the shadow of the extra sixth.

"They'll fix your hands," I said." The Mothers said it would be simple in the Towers. You will be Chosen."

The baby sucked harder, pulling half of my finger into her warm mouth. Around me, the inner City was silent and still.

I knelt down, pulled back a fold of the swaddling, laid my ear on my daughter's chest, listened the beating of her flesh heart.

A moment only I allowed myself, and then I left her there beneath the Angel. As I walked back to the gate I was aware of the ticking of my Heart beginning to slow, its winding overdue.

I left her behind, but ever after, I held the memory of her heart close. Regular and strong was its beat, a clock that would never need to be wound.

Twelve sun cycles passed.

When ripe, I would go to the Moon House and lie beneath a Father.

Most cycles, I conceived. But after that first time, I never progressed to the Sun House. Always, before three moon cycles, I bled.

In this time, Eight bore a half dozen babies. All were born early. All were born dead.

After the first time, we never held hands on the way to the Moon House again.

The Father shuddered as he spilled his seed in me. He kept his face turned away from my not-eyes as he lifted away.

When all of the Fathers had left, we lay still. Our Hearts fell into synchronisation with each other, then out again. There were only six of us this time, the smallest group of Sisters I had ever entered the Moon House with.

When the Mothers bade us, we rose, unhooked our Hearts and placed them in the clocks, wound them up. Mechanisms groaned as Hearts and clocks meshed and began to tick as one.

I pressed my fingers against the clock, feeling the vibrations of the mechanism moving through my skin. I had grown familiar with the Moon House clocks over the sun cycles. As my Heart ticks off my moon cycle, the larger clock ticks off a cycle of weeks. With each revolution of the clock's hands, one week passes, and one crescent-shaped marker emerges from the edge of the clock.

As always, without my Heart, I felt strange. Unanchored, unreal. The Mothers assure us that the Moon and Sun Houses can sustain us without our Hearts. So long as we stay within their walls, we are safe, and our flesh hearts will continue to beat.

The weeks passed. Each morning, we wound our clocks, used the latrines, consumed our nutrient wafers.

One by one, the other Sisters began to bleed. I smelled the copper of their blood, listened to them remove their Hearts from the clocks. The clocks, unwound, slowed and slowed, and finally stopped.

Finally, only I remained.

For the first time since my daughter, I progressed to the Sun House.

Only one bed in the Sun House creaked beneath the weight of a Sister. I chose the neighbouring bed, pressed my Heart into the clock above. The clocks were larger here, with two dials. The smaller one ticks away the weeks, the larger moves with the moon cycles. The crescents around the edge mark off the latter. As I wound the clock, a crescent clicked out, some arcane machinery inside recognising the revolutions made in the Moon House.

I lay back down, aware of the Sister in the other bed watching me.

"Nine," she said, her voice breathless from the baby crowding her lungs.

"Eight?"

She nodded, the shadows coiling in her skull shifting with the movement. It had been over a sun cycle since I had seen her up close, our cycles out of sync. In that time, shadow had eaten at the long bones of her arms and legs, curved like a cupped hand beneath her left breast.

I pulled my blanket over my legs, forced a smile." How long do you have?"

She touched the sheet stretched taut over her belly, skin moving against cotton with a ragged whisper." Only one moon cycle. The Mothers think that he could be whole. The first whole child born outside the City since the War." The shadows in her face twisted as she smiled." I think it's happening. We're all becoming Chosen."

"He? You think it's a boy?"

"A feeling. A mother's knowledge."

I thought of my own daughter, given to the Angel. She would be almost a woman now. If mothers had some esoteric sense of their children, then I should know where she was, what she was doing. When I searched my world for her, I saw nothing but darkness.

Turning over, I curled my legs up. I could see nothing within myself. I pressed my fingers to my stomach, the flesh softening now from the rich nutrient bars, and wondered what was growing there.

The day the second crescent appeared at the edge of my clock, Eight's pains began.

Mothers came and went. Day turned to night, and then day again. The black, clotted stench of old blood filled the room.

After the second night, they brought the knife.

There was no light, no colour to the thing sliced from Eight's womb. Just dense, fisted shadow.

The Mother who came the next morning told me that Eight had volunteered for recycling. The nutrient wafers she brought me tasted like blood, like bone.

A moon cycle later, I woke in the dead of night to find my sheets heavy with blood.

I stood, wrapped my blanket around me and did not bother to staunch the flow of blood. The floor of the Sun House had seen enough blood in its time, what would a few more drops matter?

On the threshold, I paused. Behind me, I heard a click as another crescent emerged from the clock above my bed. My Heart was still connected to the clock, the plate on my chest empty.

And then I saw it: the flame. High on the same Tower again, burning more brightly than I had remembered.

I stepped outside without conscious thought, focused only on the flame. My flesh heartbeat was erratic, but my heart was still beating. Without my clockwork Heart, I was still alive.

I watched the flame until a Mother found me kneeling on blood-soaked earth. She led me into the chapel, sponged the blood from my thighs. Sliced with her crescent knife, rubbed ash into the wound. Watched as I removed my Heart from the clock, returned it to my chest.

I had been lucky, the Mother said. Another few minutes outside without my Heart, and my flesh heart would have failed. Lucky I had stayed so close to the Sun House.

When I went outside again, the flame was gone. I rubbed at my bandaged thigh, knowing that there was little space left for more scars.

For two moon cycles, I waited. Twice, my own blood puddled useless and thin between my thighs. Then, finally, I was allowed to join the other ripe Sisters in the Moon House.

If I could have, I would have closed my eyes against both light and shadows. And if I had possessed true eyes, they would have flown open as the last Father entered the hall. For he shone with bright, perfect light, a flame walking in the shape of a man.

He burned so bright that he dimmed the other Fathers almost entirely. And I realised, as he walked down the beds, why it was that he was so bright.

He was whole.

He affected a limp, and I could tell by the shape of his light that he had one arm bound close to his body. Despite the binding, there were no shadows there, no missing pieces.

He paused at the foot of my bed, but a Mother came up, the ticking loud beneath her robe, and ushered him on to another Sister.

I wanted to push away the Father who came to me. Wanted to tell him to stop, even as his movements became more frantic, his seed spilling.

For the first time in my life, I willed my blood to come early.

I hurried along, shivering lightly in my thin robe. I worried my thumb against the newest scar on my thigh, worrying at the edges of it until the skin opened, began to bleed again.

All of the other Sisters and Mothers had been sleeping deeply when I had slipped out of the Dormitory. None of them had seen me go.

I didn't even know where I was going, not really. I just knew that I'd needed to get out of there.

Was I looking for the flaming man? I didn't know. I did know that I shouldn't have been surprised to find myself at the Wall. I leaned against the cool stone, listened to the machinery within click and groan. The gate nearby opened, warm air moving like breath against my skin.

And then I heard something else. Hidden beneath the sound of mechanics was the unmistakable sound of a weeping child.

"Hello?" I asked.

The weeping broke off abruptly.

"They will not speak back," a voice said from behind me.

I turned. Standing there was the flaming man. I stiffened, then fell quickly into a posture of obedience: head bowed, hands clasped." The Mothers sent me on an errand, Father," I lied.

"You're a Sister. You don't get sent anywhere but to the Moon and Sun Houses." He pronounced the words strangely, as though they fit ill in his mouth.

I groped for another lie." I . . . "

"It's okay. I'm not going to report you." His flames flickered, narrowed." You can see me somehow, can't you? Even though you don't have any eyes."

"I can hear well."

He laughed." What's your name?"

"Name?" The almost unfamiliar word brought with it a memory of Eight's photograph: ashes, now, as she was.

His light tightened, curled in upon itself." I forgot. They don't give you names, just numbers."

I looked up at him then. His arm was bound again, but he was still undoubtedly whole. And I knew, then, that he shouldn't be there either, that he was hiding something more than just his wholeness." There was someone who called me Nine. For the last number." I held out my arm, displaying my numbers.

"Other people wore numbers once," he said, his voice quiet." That ended, too." He cleared his throat." My name is Nataneal."

"Nataneal." I repeated the name slowly, its syllables like broken stone in my mouth." You don't have a number?"

He paused, then slid his bound arm free. He grasped my hand, pressed my fingers against the inside of his left arm. There were numbers there, but they were warm, not cool as mine were.

"They're false," I said." Who *are* you?"

"Who are *you*, Nine?" He slid his arm back into its binding." How do I know that you're not going to run back and report me?"

I pressed my hands together. My skin was warm from contact with his numbers.

"If you are going to report me, do it now," Nataneal said.

"Otherwise, I will be here again this time tomorrow."

In the Wall behind me, the gate machinery groaned, the gate sliding closed with a thud.

"If you come tomorrow, I'll tell you about the weeping child."

He left me alone there, his flame vanishing into the shadows hanging low over the outer City.

After a time, the child began to weep again.

That night, I dreamed of two heartbeats. They threaded together, falling into synchronisation, then moving in counterpoint, creating a strange and beautiful music.

The next morning, Nataneal was waiting for me at the Wall.

"You didn't report me," he said as I approached him.

"Is it that good?" I asked." Your deception? A limp and a bound arm?"

His flame swirled, moving into almost geometric shapes." No one looks closely. Out here, people barely look at each other at all. You're the only one who's looked at me directly. You saw me." He slid his arm out of its binding, straightened his spine." How did you know?"

I pulled my shawl tighter around my shoulders." You said you would tell me about the weeping child. Is it some trick of the machinery making that sound?"

"It is no trick."

We walked slowly along the Wall. The air grew warmer as we moved, and I knew that the gate was open.

Nataneal's light swirled for a moment, and then he turned to the Wall. I heard the grinding of stone against stone, then the sound of something heavy meeting the ground. Nataneal's hand pressed against mine. I felt the beat of his heart beneath his skin before he moved his fingers down to my wrist, lifted my hand towards the Wall.

I expected cold stone, and it took me a moment to realise that he was moving my hand further than it should have gone, that my hand was moving into the Wall itself. He kept his thumb pressed against my wrist for a moment, then his hand slid away.

"Be silent and still," he whispered." Wait."

My Heart ticked a dozen times, and then I felt something brush my fingers. I stiffened, thinking of the machinery, but realised quickly that what I touched wasn't cold metal, but warm and soft. Fingers, small and crusted, but alive. They curled around mine, probed into the cup of my palm, then fell away. The soft sound of weeping rose. I breathed in, tasted thick, fetid air.

"There's a child in there," I said." There's a child in the Wall."

Nataneal pulled my hand back. When I lifted my fingers, I smelled old blood, unwashed skin, darker things.

"A girl child," Nataneal said." Perhaps five or six sun cycles, small for her age."

"We have to let her out!" I grasped at the edge of the hole, my nails scratching at the mortar." Where is the door?"

"There is no door."

I ran my hands across the Wall, searching." There has to be! How else did she get in there?"

Nataneal withdrew a nutrient wafer from his pocket. By its scent, it was one of the richer ones from the Sun House. He handed it through the hole, then slid the stone back into place.

"They lower the child in through a small trap at the top of the Wall," he said, his voice flat. "It's done as soon as the child is old enough to understand the process of operating the gate. It's quite simple, just the pressing of a few levers, turning a wheel. Most are lowered in when they are three sun cycles or so. Once a week, someone comes to supply them with nutrient wafers, take away their wastes. When they remember, of course. Sometimes it takes weeks before someone notices that the gates haven't opened. The gates are not a priority for the City." He smoothed a hand over the loose stone." It took us many moon cycles to loosen this stone. It was the first one, back when the Walled children were just rumours."

"Children? There's more than one?"

"Two per gate, one at each side. Four gates, eight children. None of them last long, of course. Some go mad, scratch at their own throats and wrists until they bleed out. Some try to climb back up to the trap, not realising it cannot be opened from within. I heard of one who reached eight sun cycles before he grew too large for the space in the Wall and slowly suffocated. It doesn't matter to the City, of course. There's always new children, and it's a simple matter to reach in with long tools, slice the dead child into parts and draw them out one by one."

My flesh heart was thudding against the plate between my breasts, hard enough that I thought I should hear it. I didn't want to ask the question, knew that I had to. "Where do the children come from?"

"You and your Sisters breed them for the City. You leave them in the shadow of the Angel."

I bent over and retched. The thin bile that came up tasted like copper, like ash.

When I was done, I sank to my knees, pressed my forehead against the Wall. After a moment, Nataneal sat next to me, close enough that I could hear the thudding of his heart even over the ticking of my clockwork Heart.

"This is how the City runs," Nataneal said. "Once, before all this, they harnessed sparks in a different, forgotten fashion to run the machines, to illuminate, to pump water, to raise the gates. Now, Walled children control the gates, and belowground, children pump the bellows running the engines to move wastes along the pipes. There are steam engines on the Towers, but even there, children must climb to maintain them."

I looked up at the Towers, tried to gauge their height. Tried to imagine being that high. Vertigo clutched at me.

"There are no ropes, nothing to keep the children safe," Nataneal continued. "The children climb the cage holding the pipes and pumps. Many fall."

"I gave a child to the Angel," I said. "Twelve sun cycles ago. She was as close to whole as I have seen. They said that she would be Chosen, she would enter the Towers."

"They lied. No one has ever entered the Towers from outside."

I looked at his wholeness anew. "And has anyone come out?"

His light swirled, moved into that geometric pattern again. "I was one of the Chosen," he said. I smelled salt on the air. "They lie to us, too, Nine. They tell us that no one remains outside the Towers, that the world was blasted away by the War. They tell us that we are waiting until the world is safe enough for us to go outside again. They tell us nothing, except in the vaguest terms, and no one thinks to ask."

"Why are you telling me this?"

"Because you looked. Because you saw. Because we need you."

"We?"

"The revolution." He pressed his hand to mine briefly; I felt the fluttering of his pulse. "We should get back before anyone notices we're missing."

I pressed my hand against the Wall once more, let him lead me back.

This is the true world, as Nataneal told me:

The Angel stands in the centre of the inner City, the four Towers around her.The tall, black buildings are caged with brass, surrounded by pumps and pipes to bring water to those who live within, to remove wastes. Steam engines power these networks; larger engines at the base of each Tower provide power for everything else. All of these networks and engines are maintained by children who live in the low, grey Dormitories which squat between the Towers.

Over time, the children are affected by what Nataneal calls radiation. When they are too sick to work aboveground, they are sent below, to pump the bellows driving the pumps of the waste systems. The bellows are pumped around the clock, and once a child is sent belowground, they never see the sun again.

There are the Walled children, too, and probably others running systems that Nataneal didn't know about.

Within the radiation-shielded Towers, selective breeding maintains genetic purity. All are subjected to regular screening to ensure their own Chosen state.

All of the children of the Towers are educated, but none are told the truth.

Most do not question.But there are those who have, and they are working together inside to bring the truth to light, to free those born to slavery both within and without the Towers. Nataneal is one of the first to discover a way outside, but he will not be the last.

The Mother's fingers tore into me. I clenched against her, wanting to force her out.

She leaned over to check my Heart, her fingers still inside me, pushing harder. The ticking beneath her robes jarred and skipped. "There is no room for any more scars, Sister. This cycle will be your last."

She pulled her fingers out roughly, pressed a key into my hand. The metal was cold, and did not warm against my skin.

That night I lay awake in the Moon House, listening to the ticking of Hearts in the hall. I laid my fingers next to the plate set over my sternum, felt the beating of my flesh heart.

My fingers moved across the plate, found the empty socket where it intersected with my Heart. The Mothers told us that if we removed our Hearts outside the Moon or Sun Houses, we would die.

The Mothers said my daughter would be Chosen.

The Mothers said.

Nataneal was lied to. How much of what the Mothers said to us was a lie?

I slid my feet out of bed, the stone floor cold beneath my soles. The room smelled like sour sweat, like seed. There was a hint of a darker thing, too, a scent that put me in mind of the Walled child.

Death.

It was death that I smelled. Their death, and mine.

I pushed the door open, and, heartless, I stepped outside.

One step, two, and my own flesh heart continued to beat. Faster now, but steady, my blood pounding in my ears.

Three steps, four and I was running, *flying*, searching the houses and halls for Nataneal's flame.

In the end, he found me, his flame appearing from out of a small building leaning against the back of one of the men's halls.

His hands closed over my arms. "Nine, what is it? Are you well?" His fingers touched my empty Heart plate. "Did they . . . ?"

I shook my head. "They lied to us. They said that we'd die, but it does nothing. It doesn't keep us alive. It *controls* us." I paused. "How much else have they lied about?"

I saw his frown as a swirling in his flame. "You should come inside. It is safe in here."

He drew me into the building, and the world went away. I stumbled, and was glad for his hands on mine. Without that touch, I would have thought myself suspended in nothing. Even his flame was gone.

"You can see it, can't you?" he asked. "It's something like what they use to shield the Towers. It blocks most electromagnetic radiation, most sound as well."

He guided my hand to the wall. It felt smooth and slightly warm, like skin with no pores or hairs. I realised, too, that there was a steady ticking in the room. The sound of clockwork.

"It requires energy to pass through it constantly," he continued. "It's a simple engine, made by a member of the resistance."

"It's strange, not being able to see you," I said. I hesitated, then reached up, pressed my hand to his face, tracing the curve of his jaw and cheek. I encountered dampness; I touched my fingers to my lips and tasted salt. "The Mother said this cycle was my last chance. If I do not produce a child, I will be recycled."

"Recycled?"

I touched his face again, felt the shape of his frown. "They recycle our bodies when we are no longer useful to the City in any other way. And make us useful again, as much as they can." He was still frowning. "The nutrient wafers."

He swallowed hard. "And I always though the filtered water in the Towers was bad. Oh, Nine, what you have all lived."

His arms came around me then, pulling me close. I laid my cheek against his sternum, listened to his heartbeat, aware of my own synchronising with it.

"We have been doing testing, as much as we can out here," he said, his voice resonating within his chest. "Few, if any, of the Fathers possess fertile seed. There has been too much contamination, too much radiation." He swallowed again. "But I . . . "

I pulled back, just enough to be able to touch his face again. His eyes were closed, his lashes damp. "You have been kept shielded for most of your life," I said. "Your seed should be strong. If my fault in bearing lies with the Fathers . . . " I trailed off, unable to finish the thought.

"I wouldn't . . . I couldn't . . . " His eyes opened, and I knew he was looking directly at where my own eyes should be. "You have been forced enough."

It was my turn to swallow. "In the Towers, if people want to, how do they start?"

He smiled. "They kiss."

"Kiss? What is that?"

His smile widened, and I realised how young he was. At least a half dozen sun cycles less than me, probably more. "I'll show you."

And he did.

Afterwards, I knew that I carried a daughter.

I felt her flame within me, and though I could not see her, I knew also that she bore two shadows where her eyes should be. She would see the world as I did, my gift to her.

I was the only Sister moved to the Sun House. Inside, everything smelled like blood and death, and the rich nutrient wafers they brought reminded me of the Walled child. I pressed my fingers into my belly, thought of my daughters.

Nataneal was always nearby, his flame visible to me through the walls. I watched him talking to others, watched other bright flames join his, knew they were putting their plans into motion. And I began to hear words from outside the hall, repeated often, like a prayer: *When the Angel flies, we will all be free.*

When I could slip out in the early mornings, I met him at the Wall, brought nutrient wafers to the children.

One morning he met me with a bundle of cloth in his hand. He unfolded it, moved my hand to trace the shape of what lay there. Two small clockwork mechanisms, a meshwork of cogs and gears that vibrated at my touch.

Nataneal lifted one of the mechanisms and pressed it to my not-eye. The gears shivered, and I felt the teeth of cogs pressing into my skin, seeking purchase. Small points of pain flared, and for a moment, I saw Nataneal's face. He was beautiful, his eyes a bright, clear colour that I could not name.

The gears shivered again, and the mechanism fell away, leaving me in my darkness again.

Nataneal caught it neatly. "These are only a prototype. They can be modified."

I pressed my hand over his. The metal was warm between us. "I've seen all I need to. And you have beautiful eyes." I rose up on my toes to kiss him, then pressed our joined hands to my stomach. The clockwork eye shivered again. "I think our daughter will need them more, if she is to walk in two worlds."

"She will change everything." Nataneal pulled me close. "Things are moving quickly. Seeds are growing in the outer and inner Cities."

"'When the Angel flies, you will all be free'?" I asked. "I hear them chanting it outside the Sun House."

"We're painting it, too, anywhere we can. They remove the words, but we simply paint them again." He kissed the top of my head. "Before, things would have been so different. We would live together in a house, raise our children together. Sleep in the same bed every night. There would be no Mothers, no Towers. Just us."

"Maybe it can be that way again."

He was silent for a long time. "Maybe."

When my pains began, I was alone. It was night, and none of the Mothers would be due to enter the Sun House until morning. I thanked the Angel for that small mercy.

Beneath my mattress were the clockwork eyes. Their vibrations had comforted me through many sleepless nights, my daughter always turning in my womb, hands pressing out, reaching for them. I slid the eyes out now, cupped them in my palm.

I went to Nataneal's hidden place. He was awake, and waiting for me.

There, hidden from the City, our daughter was born.

She slipped into the world easily, and she did not cry. Nataneal slid the clockwork eyes into her empty eye pits. A sound like blinking, and then I heard the gears tighten.

I felt her smile, felt her clockwork eyes move from her mother to her father. And we were a family.

Nataneal produced a small curved knife. Not quite one of the Mothers' crescent knives, but not an ordinary knife, either. We cut her first arm scar ourselves, marking her birth.

Nataneal called her Lucia. He said that it meant "light".

We remained in the hidden place as long as we could, curled in each other's arms as Lucia fed and slept and fed. If we could have, we would have stayed there forever.But nothing remains forever. Even the Angel, Nataneal said, would fall to dust one day.

All I knew is that I wanted Lucia's life to be different to mine. I didn't want her to know the Moon and Sun Houses. I didn't want her to be Chosen. I wanted her to know a different world. One, that, perhaps, Nataneal's revolution could begin.

So when someone knocked at the outside of our shelter and summoned Nataneal, I was glad to let him go.

"The angel will fly," he said, kissing me, kissing Lucia. "The angel will fly, and we will all be free. Stay here.I will return."

It was an accident that undid us.

I'm not certain, even now, what it was that did it. Lucia's flailing hand as she fumbled for my breast, my own knee as I crouched to change her. But I know that the clockwork mechanism that sustained the warm skin that hid us from the City was broken. It ticked once, twice, sighed and was silent.

The light and shadow of the City flared into life in my inner vision. And for the first time, I "saw" my daughter. Brighter even than Nataneal, and flickering in an ever-changing spectrum of colours.

I held Lucia tight, unsure of what to do. There were other rebels hiding in the outer City, but I had no idea where they were. So I froze, and waited, and hoped that Nataneal would return.

It was the Mothers who came, the ticking beneath their robes filling the small space. Lucia began to cry.

They reached for us both, their hands like stone.

Even the Mothers, cruel as they were, could not bear to waste a living, almost whole human.

They gave me a choice. Lucia could have numbers set into her arm, could serve the City as I did. Or she could be given over to the Angel, a place found for her in the inner City.

I heard the things they did not say, and I chose the Angel. If they had given her numbers, they would have torn out her clockwork eyes, perhaps found some way to scar her inner sight, as well. No Father would ever want to look upon clockwork as they lay with her.

In the Angel's shadow, perhaps someone would take pity, let her keep her eyes.

And soon enough, the Angel was going to fly. And we would all be free and none of this would matter at all.

And so I entered the inner City again, passed through the gate opened by a Walled child. I called out softly as I passed, but there was no answer from within the Wall.

When I stepped into the square between the Towers and Dormitories, I stopped, my arms tightening around Lucia. For unlike last time, when the City had been still and dark, there was light and movement. A flash up in one of the Towers, bright as Nataneal's flame. And outside one of the Dormitories, a girl, her light shining green and blue and red. Almost whole, but for shadows wreathing her hands.

I smiled at her, allowing myself one moment only of thinking that she could be my older daughter. I wanted to go to her, see if the beating of her heart matched the one in my memory, but there was no time.

I crossed to the Angel, laid Lucia down in the shadow. Making certain that the Mother waiting at the gate could see me, I leant down, pressed my cheek to my daughter's chest, memorised her heartbeat.

They kept me alive afterwards. As punishment, perhaps, or as an example to others.

I was sent to haul water, to scrub floors, perform any menial task the Mothers could think of. I did whatever they said.

And I waited, the memories of three heartbeats dancing through my mind.

And so, sun cycles passed.

There were whispers, and occasionally I caught a glimpse of flame—of a whole person, a Chosen—flitting amongst the shadows of the outer City. I did not see Nataneal, but I heard his heartbeat always in my mind, and I knew that he lived. That he was working with the rebellion, seeking to free us all.

Then, one morning I awoke and saw his flame waiting at the Wall.

I slid from my bed, from the hall. No one stirred.

Nataneal's light was dull, eaten by shadows at the edges. When I wrapped my arms around him, I felt his bones pressing out against his skin.

I started to tell him about Lucia, but he pressed his fingers to my lips. "I know. It's the safest place for her. And I'm going to get her back." He kissed me quickly. "It's today, Nine. The Angel is going to fly today. We uncovered a cache of weapons, and we're going to use them to make her fly. And everyone will see, and they will know to rise up. And we will all be free, and we will be a family. You and me, and both of your daughters." He kissed me again, more gently this time. "Wait here, Nine. I will return."

I sat down, my back to the Wall. The cool brick warmed as the sun rose, then began to cool again.

I heard Nataneal's voice, amplified somehow: "When the Angel flies, we will all be free!"

The explosion, when it came, was quieter than I had expected it to be. Like something falling hard against soft sand, like the world inhaling. A moment later, a wave of heat prickled across my skin, and then, in the darkness behind my not-eyes, light flared. Pure white, it was brighter than anything I had ever seen, making even the flames of the Chosen seem dim. In the wake of the light came darkness, deep and thick and absolute.

I waited for my sense of the world to return, to be able to "see" the Wall, the Towers. There would be lights and colours, soon, too, as people saw the Angel fly and began to rise up.

Everything was black.

There were other sounds, short sharp barks that I could not identify. And then, only silence.

And so, I wait.

I run my fingers over the scars on my arms, on my legs, count them over and over. I listen to the ticking of my clockwork Heart.

The night passes, and it begins to slow, the silence between ticks expanding.

Everything stays black. Everything stays silent.

Nataneal will return soon, and he will bring my daughters, and we will be a family, and we will be free.

I just have to wait.

ABOUT THE CONTRIBUTORS

MARILAG ANGWAY likes reading and writing with a cup of tea or coffee and home-made treats. It's a good thing she keeps a regular supply of the aforementioned nearby. "Smuggler's Deal" is her second published steampunk tale in a world of amber-powered airships and floating cities. You can find her musings at storyandsomnomancy.wordpress.com though she does get carried away with geek-induced projects and is refusing responsibility for any reading, baking, or knitting cravings that ensue as a result of reading her blog.

CHERITH BALDRY was born in Lancaster, UK, and studied at the University of Manchester and St Anne's College, Oxford. After some years as a teacher, including at the University of Sierra Leone, Freetown, she became a full-time writer. She has a special interest in Arthurian romance and medieval literature, and has published novels and short fiction for adults, young adults and children. She is currently part of the Erin Hunter team writing the Warriors and Seekers series. Cherith has two grown-up sons and a granddaughter, and lives in Surrey in a household ruled by two cats. She enjoys music, especially early music, reading and travel.

GIO CLAIRVAL is an Italian-born writer and translator who has studied and lived most of her life in Paris and now commutes between Lake Como and the UK. Since she started writing short fiction four years ago, she has sold more than 20 stories to magazines such as *Weird Tales*, *Galaxy's Edge*, *Daily Science Fiction*, *Postscripts*, and several anthologies. You can find her at www.gioclairval.blogspot.com and on Twitter: @gioclair.

M. L. D. CURELAS lives in Calgary, Canada, with two humans and a varying number of guinea pigs. Raised on a diet of Victorian fiction and Stephen King, it's unsurprising that she now writes and edits fantasy and science fiction. Her most recent short fiction, a futuristic Weird West story, can be found in *Andromeda Spaceways Inflight Magazine*. She is also the owner of Tyche Books, a Canadian small-press which publishes science fiction and fantasy.

RAY DEAN was born and raised in Hawaii where she spent many a quiet hour reading and writing stories. Performing in theater and working backstage lead her into the delights of Living History, creating her own worlds through writing seemed the next logical step. Historical settings are her first love, but there is something heady about twisting the threads of time into little knots and creating new timelines to explore. There are endless possibilities that she is just beginning to explore.

STEPHANIE GUNN is a writer and one time (mad) scientist. She has had several short stories published, and has been Ditmar nominated and won two Tin Duck Awards for her reviewing. She is currently at work on a contemporary fantasy novel. She lives in Perth, Western Australia, with her husband, son and requisite fluffy cat.

RICHARD HARLAND is famous for his steampunk hat and steampunk guitar—check them out at www.richardharland.net. Before he published *Worldshaker*, the most steampunky things about him were his collection of thirty Victorian waistcoats and his (now sadly departed) mutton-chop sidewhiskers. *Worldshaker*, *Liberator* and *Song of the Slums* have been his international breakthrough novels, collecting overseas awards to add to his six Aurealises. In *Song of the Slums*, Verrol has a bad, dark past, Astor falls for him anyway, and they end up together in a world-conquering Victorian rock 'n roll band.

REBECCA HARWELL grew up in small-town Minnesota reading science fiction novels and comic books. She is currently studying creative writing and Japanese at Knox College with an eye on getting her master's degree in library science. Her debut novel *The Thunderbird Project* is available from Bedlam Press, an imprint of Necro Publications.

FAITH MUDGE is a Queensland writer with a passion for fantasy, folk tales and mythology from all over the world. Her stories feature in the anthologies *To Spin a Darker Stair, One Small Step, Dreaming of Djinn* and *The Year's Best Australian Fantasy & Horror 2012*. More of her work can be found on her blog at beyondthedreamline.wordpress.com.

NICOLE MURPHY is an author, editor and teacher. She is the author of more than two dozen short stories and five novels published, including the Dream of Asarlai trilogy. A new science fiction romance anthology, the Jorda Series, will be published later this year by Escape Publishing. Her most recent publication (under her nom de plume Elizabeth Dunk) is a collection of paranormal erotic novellas called *Release*, also published by Escape Publishing. She lives near Canberra and is madly in love with both her husband and their budgie, Freddie.

KATRINA NICHOLSON is an author/reviewer/screenwriter/library clerk from Sydney (Nova Scotia, not New South Wales). She has a degree in history, a diploma in writing for film and television, 11 published short stories, 2 produced short films, and several contest wins. You can read more of her work in the anthologies *Futuredaze, Tesseracts Fifteen, Future Embodied* and the Speculative Elements series or visit her online at www.katrinanicholson.com.

ANTHONY PANEGYRES is a Perth writer whose recent stories have been published in the Ticonderoga anthologies: *The Year's Best Australian Fantasy & Horror 2011* and *Dreaming of Djinn* as well as a number of premier literary journals including *Meanjin, Overland Literary Journal* (an Aurealis Award Finalist for Best Fantasy Short Story) and several other places. His latest story released, "Submerging" is in *Overland*.

AMANDA PILLAR is an awarding winning editor and speculative fiction author who lives in Victoria, Australia, with her partner and two children, Saxon and Lilith (Burmese cats). Amanda has had numerous short stories published and has co-edited the fiction anthologies *Voices, Grants Pass, The Phantom Queen Awakes,*

Scenes from the Second Storey, Ishtar and *Damnation and Dames*. Her first solo anthology was published by Ticonderoga Publications, titled *Bloodstones*. In her 'free time', she works as an archaeologist.

ANGELA REGA is a belly-dancing school librarian. Her work has appeared in publications including *The Year's Best Australian Fantasy and Horror*, Crossed Genres, Fablecroft, Belladonna Publishing and PS Publications. She drinks way too much coffee, often falls in love with poetry and can't imagine not writing. She lives with two very vocal cats and keeps a small website here: angierega.webs.com

CAROL RYLES began her professional life as a registered nurse, which took her to the Peoples' Republic of China working in occupational health and also teaching English to various colleges and schools. A graduate of Clarion West 2008, Carol has recently finished a PhD in creative writing at the University of WA focussing on Steampunk. Her short fiction has appeared in over a dozen small press publications and her website is at carolryles.net.

D C WHITE lives in Blackwood, South Australia, in his mountain stronghold where he variously writes, schemes, plots and attempts to take over the world. This does not usually end well. He is an avid cyclist but would like to point out none of his bikes have rockets or zeppelins. Yet.

978-0-9586856-6-5	Troy BY Simon Brown (tpb)
978-0-9586856-7-2	The Workers' Paradise EDS Farr & Evans (tpb)
978-0-9586856-8-9	Fantastic Wonder Stories ED Russell B. Farr (tpb)
978-0-9803531-0-5	Love in Vain BY Lewis Shiner (tpb)
978-0-9803531-2-9	Belong ED Russell B. Farr (tpb)
978-0-9803531-4-3	Ghost Seas BY Steven Utley (tpb)
978-0-9803531-6-7	Magic Dirt: the best of Sean Williams (tpb)
978-0-9803531-8-1	The Lady of Situations BY Stephen Dedman (tpb)
978-0-9806288-2-1	Basic Black BY Terry Dowling (tpb)
978-0-9806288-3-8	Make Believe BY Terry Dowling (tpb)
978-0-9806288-4-5	Scary Kisses ED Liz Grzyb (tpb)
978-0-9806288-6-9	Dead Sea Fruit BY Kaaron Warren (tpb)
978-0-9806288-8-3	The Girl With No Hands BY Angela Slatter (tpb)
978-0-9807813-1-1	Dead Red Heart ED Russell B. Farr (tpb)
978-0-9807813-2-8	More Scary Kisses ED Liz Grzyb (tpb)
978-0-9807813-4-2	Heliotrope BY Justina Robson (tpb)
978-0-9807813-7-3	Matilda Told Such Dreadful Lies BY Lucy Sussex (tpb)
978-1-921857-01-0	Bluegrass Symphony BY Lisa L. Hannett (tpb)
978-1-921857-06-5	The Hall of Lost Footsteps BY Sara Douglass (tpb)
978-1-921857-03-4	Damnation and Dames EDS Liz Grzyb & Amanda Pillar (tpb)
978-1-921857-08-9	Bread and Circuses BY Felicity Dowker (tpb)
978-1-921857-17-1	The 400-Million-Year Itch BY Steven Utley (tpb)
978-1-921857-24-9	Wild Chrome BY Greg Mellor (tpb)
978-1-921857-27-0	Bloodstones ED Amanda Pillar (tpb)
978-1-921857-30-0	Midnight and Moonshine BY Lisa L. Hannett & Angela Slatter (tpb)
978-1-921857-65-2	Mage Heart BY Jane Routley (tpb)
978-1-921857-66-9	Fire Angels BY Jane Routley (tpb)
978-1-921857-67-6	Aramaya BY Jane Routley (tpb)
978-1-921857-35-5	Dreaming of Djinn ED Liz Grzyb (tpb)
978-1-921857-38-6	Prickle Moon BY Juliet Marillier (tpb)
978-1-921857-43-0	The Bride Price BY Cat Sparks (tpb)
978-1-921857-46-1	The Year of Ancient Ghosts BY Kim Wilkins (tpb)
978-1-921857-33-1	Invisible Kingdoms BY Steven Utley (tpb)
978-1-921857-70-6	Havenstar BY Glenda Larke (tpb)
978-1-921857-59-1	Everything is a Graveyard BY Jason Fischer (tpb)
978-1-921857-53-9	Ambassador BY Patty Jansen (tpb)
978-1-921857-77-5	Death at the Blue Elephant BY Janeen Webb

TICONDEROGA PUBLICATIONS LIMITED HARDCOVER EDITIONS

TICONDEROGA PUBLICATIONS EBOOKS

THE YEAR'S BEST AUSTRALIAN FANTASY & HORROR SERIES
EDITED BY LIZ GRZYB & TALIE HELENE

WWW.TICONDEROGAPUBLICATIONS.COM

THANK YOU

The publisher would sincerely like to thank:

Elizabeth Grzyb, Marilag Angway, Cherith Baldry, Gio Clairval, M.L.D. Curelas, Ray Dean, Stephanie Gunn, Richard Harland, Rebecca Harwell, Faith Mudge, Nicole Murphy, Katrina Nicholson, Anthony Panegyres, Amanda Pillar, Angela Rega, Carol Ryles, D.C. White, Patty Jansen, Jonathan Strahan, Peter McNamara, Ellen Datlow, Grant Stone, Sean Williams, Simon Brown, Garth Nix, David Cake, Simon Oxwell, Grant Watson, Sue Manning, Steven Utley, Lewis Shiner, Lezli Robyn, Talie Helene, Isobelle Carmody, Stephen Dedman, Felicity Dowker, Terry Dowling, Jason Fischer, Dirk Flinthart, Lisa L. Hannett, Kathleen Jennings, Martin Livings, Penelope Love, Jason Nahrung, Angela Slatter, Anna Tambour, Kaaron Warren, Cat Sparks, Donna Maree Hanson, Robert Hood, Pete Kempshall, Karen Brooks, Jeremy G. Byrne, Kim Wilkins, Marianne de Pierres, Bill Congreve, Jack Dann, Janeen Webb, Lucy Sussex, the Mt Lawley Mafia, the Nedlands Yakuza, Shane Jiraiya Cummings, Angela Challis, Kate Williams, Andrew Williams, Kathryn Linge, Al Chan, Alisa and Tehani, Mel & Phil, Jennifer Sudbury, Paul Pryztula, Helen Grzyb, Hayley Lane, Georgina Walpole, Rushelle Lister, Nerida Fearnley-Gill, everyone we've missed . . .

. . . and you.

IN MEMORY OF
Eve Johnson (1945—2011)
Sara Douglass (1957—2011)
Steven Utley (1948—2013)

CPSIA information can be obtained at www.ICGtesting.com
Printed in the USA
BVOW05s2159021214

377646BV00001B/6/P

LIZ GRZYB was born in the middle of a thunderstorm in Perth, Western Australia. She is the editor of acclaimed paranormal romance anthologies *Scary Kisses* and *More Scary Kisses*, the Orientalist pantomime *Dreaming of Djinn*, the website Ticon4. com, co-editor of paranormal noir anthology *Damnation and Dames* and award-winning *The Year's Best Australian Fantasy and Horror* series.